First, a mad billionaire devised a reckless plan for vengeance against the world—and only rogue agent Blaine McCracken had the bravery and sheer bravado to save millions of innocent people from destruction in. . . .

THE OMEGA COMMAND

Then, a crazed villain set in motion an intricate scheme for world domination employing an extraordinary source of power. Blaine McCracken had to out-think and out-maneuver a madman in. . . .

THE ALPHA DECEPTION

Now, a frightening weapon is about to be unleashed against humanity. And something more important is also at stake: the life of Blaine McCracken's son. McCracken must achieve the impossible one more time in. . . .

THE GAMMA OPTION

THE GAMMA OPTION

Jon Land

FAWCETT GOLD MEDAL • NEW YORK

Library of Congress Catalog Number: 89-91412

ISBN 0-449-13399-0

Manufactured in the United States of America

First Edition: December 1989

DEDICATION

**For my parents again,
Because once was not enough**

ACKNOWLEDGEMENTS

In each successive book, the challenge to be accurate in all matters technical becomes greater. Thus, the list of those who provide assistance continues to grow. My apologies to any I have left out in the list that follows.

As always, I must start with a perfectly wondrous agent, Toni Mendez. It was Toni who taught me the importance of finding a great editor and I have been blessed with two: Ann Maurer, and especially Daniel Zitin whose creative genius makes my work better than it has a right to be. The entire Fawcett team headed by Leona Nevler continue to publish people as well as books and the support of that family at all levels is precious to me.

Special thanks on this one to—who else?—Dr. Mort Korn for his help with the extensive biological research and to Dr. Ken Ratzan for helping to turn a concept into a full-fledged idea.

John Signore and especially Emery Pineo continue to red pencil the most ludicrous of my assertions, while first draft reader Tony Shepperd blue pencils the rest.

Thanks to Mark Levine for a great tour of Boston, to Shlomo Giot for showing me an Israel I never dreamed of, to Alan Foster for a great day in London, and Jim Klein for finding Blaine McCracken a place to live in Portland!

Invaluable technical assistance was also rendered by David Schecter, Richard Levy, Jim Ramsey of McDonnell Douglas, and Shihan John Saviano in his usual capacity as choreographer for the many fight sequences.

A special thanks to Manijeh Taleghani and Bob Taleghani for

helping me construct the Iranian sequences and to Rob Lewis and the students of Reading School for their hospitality.

And finally my deepest thanks to the First National Company of *Les Miserables*, especially Mark Andrews and Lantz Landry (the best Gavroche of them all), for putting up with me for a dozen performances.

PROLOGUE

July 29, 1945: The Pacific Ocean

THE U.S.S. *INDIANAPOLIS* WAS SAILING TO HER DEATH.
Captain Charles Butler McVay III entered the cramped communications room and spoke to the ship's chief radioman only after making sure the door was sealed behind him.

"Anything, mister?"

"Negative, sir. No contact."

"Damn," McVay muttered, certain this time the ensign had caught the edge in his voice.

He had come down personally once more in the hope some word had come in—something, anything, pertaining to the status of what still remained in the *Indy*'s number three cargo hold. Three days before she had dropped the contents of cargo holds one and two on the island of Tinian. Ten days from San Francisco at top speed had got her there right on schedule, in spite of a stop at Pearl Harbor that had seen her take on numerous passengers with a keen interest in her journey.

All of them knew that contained within the *Indianapolis*'s storage holds one and two were the unassembled parts for two atomic bombs. None of them knew about the contents of storage hold number three.

But that was what we were supposed to drop at Tinian, McVay thought. He could accept the last minute switch from the primary plan to the backup formed by the atomic bombs. The rest he could not.

1

From Tinian, the *Indy* had been ordered to Leyte by way of Guam, the first stop surely to relieve him of the remainder of his cargo. But the touch saw the ship simply take on more supplies and set on her way again. So the unloading would take place on Leyte then. He at least expected an escort ship to be assigned for the voyage, yet none was offered, and under the circumstances McVay wanted no record of having requested one.

Doesn't anyone know what we're still carrying? he'd been tempted to ask at Guam.

They almost certainly didn't, though. And now, without an escort possessing sonar, the *Indianapolis* would have to depend on radar and visual contact to detect an enemy submarine.

The first day out of Guam the weather had cooperated brilliantly, but today brought a storm in the afternoon that didn't clear until nearly midnight. The storm left choppy seas and a clammy smell in the air that festered in the stifling humidity. With that in mind, the captain had allowed all ventilation ducts and most of the bulkheads to remain open throughout the ship. Otherwise the tropical climate would have made sleep impossible for his men.

One thing for certain, ships of the heavy cruiser class like the *Indianapolis* hadn't been built with comfort in mind. Commissioned in 1932, she was cumbersome to the eye but quick, with a top speed of thirty-two knots. The *Indy* had fought bravely as both sentinel and warrior, most recently as Admiral Spruance's flagship for the Fifth Fleet. That tour had ended when a Japanese kamikaze struck her off Okinawa in late March, and this latest mission had come up too fast to allow for a shakedown period following her repairs. McVay had done his best to make up for this with plenty of training exercises during her high speed run to Tinian, but the overflow of passengers always seemed to be getting in the way.

Damn them, the captain thought to himself with the sweat soaking through his uniform in the radio room, *damn them all. . . .*

McVay returned to the bridge uneasy and tense. His routing orders at Guam had stated simply to proceed to Leyte for a two week training mission with nothing whatsoever mentioned about the contents of cargo hold number three. Did the bastards expect him to sail the rest of the war with it on board his ship?

McVay chewed the thick air as he fought unsuccessfully to shove the question back in his mind. There was too much here that didn't make sense.

"Sir," came a desperate call from the radar operator immediately before him on the bridge, "I have incoming torpedoes!"

"Bearing!"

"Trying for a fix now, sir. . . . God, north by northwest. Heading right for us! Range one mile. Speed fifty knots!"

"Damn!" McVay barked. The low yield signature *Kaiten* subs the Japs were running called this area home. Why hadn't they given him an escort? "Right full rudder!" he ordered. "Engine room, we have incomings. I need evasive action. Get us the hell out of here!"

"Aye-aye, sir!" came the half-garbled reply.

The *Indianapolis*'s engines tried valiantly to provide the additional thrust required for the maneuver. But the extra armor plating that made her an effective warship sacrificed quickness and agility. She managed to turn, gaining only slight ground in the process against the onrushing torpedoes angling toward her.

"God help us," McVay muttered, and imagined in that instant he could see the promised steel death rise out of the ocean night like a giant shark ready to pounce.

Of the four torpedoes fired, only two hit the *Indianapolis*— both on her starboard side forward. A pair of violent explosions followed, and the cruiser's bottom and topsides vanished in a flash of brilliant orange that quickly gave way to black smoke. But the engines clung stubbornly to life, pushing the *Indianapolis* forward at top speed for an additional minute, in which she took on countless tons of water through the gaping holes in her hull.

Captain McVay's first thought was that they might be able to ride the damage out and stay afloat. But it was rapidly apparent from the ferocity of the flames and belching black smoke that

he was wrong. He knew his ship was doomed, knew it with a
steel heaviness that settled in his gut and climbed for his throat.
McVay shouted the order to abandon ship through the clog,
clinging desperately for balance against the ship's severe list to
starboard. His last order was for the radioman to send the ap-
propriate distress signal.

Of the twelve hundred men on board, the initial blasts and
fires had claimed one-third. The remaining eight hundred
made it over the side in time to see the *Indianapolis* roll onto
her side, and begin to drop bow first into the black depths
below.

Captain McVay coughed the water from his lungs, held over
the surface only by the life jacket he had pulled on at the last
instant. He had struck his head during the plunge downward,
and now a blurred darkness had become his world. The scent
of loosed diesel fuel filled his nostrils, and somewhere burned
the sight of the last of his ship's flaming carcass disappearing
beneath the sea.

Dazedly he felt himself being dragged toward a waiting circle
of entwined crewmen. With no time to launch the life rafts,
such a tactic formed their only hope of survival until a rescue
team arrived. McVay was conscious of his arms being raised to
the shoulders of others and his being supported in turn. Seawater
flooded his mouth, and he coughed fitfully again. His eyes teared
as he fought for breath, for life, against the raging waters heavy
with the smell of fear and death and—

McVay's eyes bulged at a dim sight revealed by the half
moon being abandoned by its covering clouds. An apparition
at first, but then a shape, slithered like a huge snake through
the water.

This can't be! . . . It can't be!

In that instant everything was clear to the captain. A new
coldness flooded him deeper than the sea's.

There! he thought to scream to the men around him. *Look
over there!*

But fresh floods of water flushed his nostrils and stung his
eyes anew. The clouds covered the sky once more in a dark

blanket that draped down to the water, the impossible shape lost as the sea raged against him and Captain Charles Butler McVay surrendered to oblivion.

PART ONE

Ghosts

Maine: Monday, May 1; two A.M.

CHAPTER 1

THE FIGURE SLID THROUGH THE NIGHT, THE LOW-LYING SEA mist making him seem more phantom than man as he approached the isolated townhouse. He had stolen a skiff and ridden it across the bay from the mainland. In order to avoid detection by possible security personnel, he had cut the engine and paddled the last stretch to McKinley Estates' private dock on Great Diamond Island.

It was not a place where he would have expected to find Blaine McCracken, but then it was difficult to tell what to expect from McCracken if truth was to be gained from experience. That McCracken was on the island was not in doubt; the problem was getting to him without being noticed. The townhouse was off by itself, in a grove at the head of a bank that looked out over the water. A single outside light shone down from the porch illuminating the front walk. The figure elected to make his approach from this point, using the light instead of tempting the darkness at the back of the townhouse.

Security systems became the problem now. McCracken would have several of them set to alert him to unwarranted approach. The figure eased forward, cloaked in the rolling mist. A waist-high brick wall surrounded the townhouse; an opening gave access to the front walk. The electric eyes built into the wall on either side of the walk appeared to be mere imperfections in the

brick, one high and one low to prevent leaping over or ducking
under to bypass the system.

Of course the walk itself might be wired, sensitive to weight
which would trigger an alarm. The freshly sodded grass inside
the wall would be watched over as well, probably by ultrasonic
waves. The figure understood the limits and constraints of such
systems. He knew there would be a single weakness to exploit,
a foot-wide strip on either side of the walk that acted as a buffer
between the two systems preventing overload and short-
circuiting.

The figure eased himself over the brick wall, and placed one
foot gingerly behind the other with barely a row of single grass
blades separating them from the walk. He proceeded to move
forward tightrope style toward the front door. He kept his arms
close to his sides, resisting the temptation to extend them for
balance. At last the porch was within reach. The figure held his
breath. He could tell by the way the boards were placed that the
porch and steps leading to it were wired. The most difficult task
of all thus lay before him: to get the door open and deactivate
the final alarm system while balanced precariously on the threshold.

The figure reached out and grasped the beam supporting the
overhang of the porch. Wasting no time, he vaulted up and over
the railing and projected himself forward through the air. He
rotated his body so his feet would reach the threshold an instant
before the rest of him hit the door. He managed to latch on to
the brass doorknob just as his feet touched down. With that in
his grasp to cushion him, the figure was able to absorb most of
the impact as his upper body thumped weakly against the door.

All the same he held his breath, half expecting an intrusion
alarm. When there was none he set to work immediately on the
locks, three of them, all strictly top of the line. But he had never
known a lock that couldn't be picked and had the knob ready to
turn in barely a minute. Now came the toughest part of all. Still
balanced precariously on the threshold, he had to crack the door
and disable the entry alarm at the same time. The alarm acti-
vating plunger would be placed low on the hinge side of the
door. Stretching to the maximum extent of his muscles, the

figure could just reach it with his left hand while holding on to the doorknob with his right.

First he removed a small square of putty from his pocket and reached down again with his left hand. The plunger would remain depressed until the door parted from it entirely. The figure started the door slowly inward, easing the putty into place a little at a time until it covered the whole of the plunger, holding it in its slot even without pressure from the door. Then the figure eased the door open the rest of way and slid inside with some of the sea mist trailing behind him.

A key pad before him with bright red light warned of the final security system, which would include a motion detector. The figure had the tools to bypass it, but he reached out first and pressed a sequence of four numbers with his index finger. The red light flashed green, and the figure allowed himself a smile.

Not like McCracken to be so foolish.

The moonlight through drawn glass curtains over a bay window that overlooked the water provided what little light he needed now. The stairs rose just to his right. The matter was finished so far as the figure was concerned, the rest a mere formality. McCracken's bedroom would face the ocean, and when he reached it all pretense of subtlety would be abandoned.

The figure crept onward, almost to the head of the stairs now, careful with each step, silent as the night that had delivered him here. He had barely reached the top and started to turn when the slightest motion froze him; no, not a motion so much as a shifting in the air, a breeze passing through an open window. The figure had just begun to slide on again when something cold and hard touched the back of his neck. A distinctive *click* sounded as hammer met pin.

"Bang," said McCracken.

"I've got to hand it to you, Henri," Blaine said when they were back downstairs. "You haven't lost a step in all these years."

Dejourner shrugged in the darkness. "Apparently, *mon ami*, I have lost something."

Blaine preceded him back down the stairs and hit a pair of

switches which activated recessed and track lighting throughout the first floor.

"Looks better with the lights on, old friend," he said and led Dejourner past the galley kitchen into a living area furnished in rich dark leathers. Oriental rugs in many shades lay on the polished hardwood floors. What might have been the dining alcove was dominated by custom-built cherry bookshelves packed with leatherbound books.

"I've taken to reading them," Blaine said, following Henri's gaping eyes.

"I must say, Blaine, that when my sources placed you in Portland, Maine, I was surprised and worried, but this—"

"Don't sell the city short. Riverfront redevelopment is a way of life around here. Take a look."

Another flip of a switch illuminated a deck with a clear view to the sea.

"Got a pair of bedrooms upstairs and a full gym in the basement. You know, I've got five apartments scattered around the country, but I seem to have settled here. Maybe it's because the long winter gives me an excuse to be isolated. Might try Canada next, who knows?"

"Then please excuse me for disturbing you."

"Solitude is fine, but the winter was long enough."

Blaine sat down in a leather chair that faced out to the deck. Henri Dejourner settled into the couch adjacent to him against the far wall. A brilliant landscape painting hung above it.

"I gotta tell you, Henri, no man could have negotiated my security systems better. It was a real treat watching you work again. The only one I can't figure is the alarm code. How'd you guess it?"

"Simple, *mon ami*. I pressed 1-9-5-0, the year of your birth. Since it's exactly twenty years after my own, it's easy to remember."

"Don't remind me. Turning forty wasn't exactly the happiest day of my life."

"And how do you think I felt turning sixty?"

McCracken couldn't say how Henri felt, but he looked marvelous. His still-full hair was the same shade of gray it had been when they had last met, and his frame, though small, remained lean and taut.

"And in spite of everything," the Frenchman said, "you were still lying in wait for me the whole time, laughing to yourself no doubt. You're still a magician, *mon ami.*"

"Johnny Wareagle's the magician, Henri. I rely on more traditional aids. Like a harbormaster named Abner who saw you make off with the skiff. He gave me a call."

"Ah, knows what to look for, does he?"

"He certainly does." After both of them had shared a smile, Blaine added, "You enjoyed yourself tonight, didn't you?"

Dejourner smiled fondly. "I miss the old days. When was it we met, Vietnam in '70 or '71?"

" 'Seventy on the crisscross. I was on my way in and you were on your way out. And it wasn't Nam, it was Cambodia."

"Forgive me."

"For that, of course. For tonight, I'm not so sure."

"Blaine?"

"Who were you testing tonight, Henri, you or me?"

"There would be no reason to test you, *mon ami.* I have kept tabs."

"Then you should have known that the last party that showed up on my doorstep unannounced went swimming."

"You gave him a life jacket, of course."

"Sure. I made sure his seatbelt was fastened before I made him drive his car into the bay. About a month ago I think it was. Figured he might be coming back for a second dunking. Abner keeps an eye out for me."

"You haven't changed, *mon ami.* That's good."

"The fact is I wouldn't have needed Abner a few years ago or these damn security systems either. I'm slipping. My last few missions haven't gone too well. I think I came here to hide out for the winter. Now I'll probably go somewhere else."

Dejourner waved him off. "You've never looked better."

"But I'm starting to have to work too hard at it. Gotta run faster and faster just to stay in the same place."

Dejourner was nodding. "As I recall, you spent five miserable years quite literally in the same place."

"No offense, Henri, but I learned to hate your country during those years."

"No offense taken."

"You made that time bearable. I was stuck sorting paperclips, but you saw fit to throw some real work my way. It's too bad our countries weren't enemies; we could have exchanged prisoners."

"With intelligence communities, enemies would be an accurate description. I was able to convince my superiors to let me use you only after persuading them it would make their American counterparts look bad. Such a rat race! You are lucky to be out of it."

"And you?"

"Still a rat, I'm afraid." Dejourner shrugged.

"Listen, I meant what I said about what you did for me back then, Henri," Blaine said. "I owe you. I don't forget my debts."

Dejourner grasped his meaning and waved his hands dramatically before him. "*Non, mon ami*. I have not come here to request one of your famous favors."

"Well, you sure as hell didn't fly across the ocean to play a game more fit for recruits many years younger than us."

"Please, Blaine, this is not easy for me. There is something I must tell you and I don't know how. I spent the flight over rehearsing a dozen speeches. None of them worked."

"Why don't you try number thirteen on me now?"

"It's not that simple. As many times as I rehearsed, I almost decided to just take the next flight home. I'm not sure I have any business being here. I'm not sure I have any business bringing you this news."

"We're friends, Henri. Friends always have business doing whatever they want."

Dejourner grimaced as if the words bottled up inside him were causing genuine pain. "You recall a British woman named Lauren Ericson? You met her—"

"In London thirteen years ago. Let's see, that would have made me twenty-seven: five years out of Nam and four operating in the same theater as you. Things were less complicated then."

"The woman, what do you remember of her?"

"A knockout. Thought she was a model at first but she turned out to be a doctor, studying to be an orthopedic surgeon, as I recall. I was working with the British rounding up Al-Fatah operatives. We were on speaking terms then.''

"Pre-McCrackenballs . . .''

"Yes. Lauren and I were an item for three months or so and then she broke it off. That's always the way it is for me.''

"Did she tell you why she broke it off?''

"She told me the same thing I've heard over and over again: I was a lot more fun to be with before she learned everything about me because she knew everything wasn't all and she didn't want to know it all. In a nutshell. My turn now, Henri. Where is this leading?''

"She died two months ago.''

Blaine wanted to feel grief but found it hard to muster any for someone he hadn't seen in thirteen years.

"You haven't come here to inform me I was mentioned in her will.''

"In a sense I have, *mon ami*. Lauren Ericson is survived by a son. He's yours.''

CHAPTER 2

THE NEWS HIT MCCRACKEN LIKE A HAMMER BLOW, KNOCK-
ing the breath hard out of him.

Dejourner had a memo pad out and was reading from it. "The boy's name is Matthew. He's three months past twelve and is enrolled in the third form at the Reading School in Reading, England. He is at present a boarder at the school after having lived the rest of his life in the village of Hambleden twenty-five minutes away."

"How did Lauren die?"

"Traffic accident."

"Does the boy . . ." .

"No, *mon ami*. He has no knowledge of you. Lauren told him his father deserted them."

"Then he does have some knowledge of me."

The Frenchman eyed him sternly. "Your shoulders are still broad, Blaine, but don't expect too much of them. She made the choice for reasons you understand as well as I. As near as I can figure, she broke off the relationship when she learned she was pregnant."

"Because she felt no father was better than—"

"One who could never be happy living a normal life . . ."

"A sane life, you mean."

"Call it what you will, but she knew it wasn't for you. A

16

child was the last thing you needed, and she understood that enough to do what she felt was right."

"There's more."

"There always is. The practical side—and Lauren was a practical woman. If you knew of the boy's existence, then so might your enemies. Once she elected to have the child, Lauren could not permit that. So the gesture probably was not aimed so much at you, as what you had given her."

"Given her?" Blaine rose from his chair, strode to the window, and stared out at the nearby waters as he spoke. "We ate lots of dinners, saw lots of shows, and had plenty of fun. I didn't mean to give her any more than I took."

"Apparently the child changed things."

Blaine swung around. "I think she mainly wanted a child, and there I was, ready and willing." He smiled ruefully at his reflection in the glass, observing the scar which ran through his left eyebrow and his eyes that were blacker than the night. "Hope the kid got her looks anyway."

"He did."

"You've *seen* him?"

"I . . . checked up on him at the school, made the proper arrangements for his boarding and the like."

Blaine closed the gap between them and watched the Frenchman's eyes waver. "Wait a minute, Henri. Suddenly I'm getting the feeling that your stake in this is deeper than you'd have me think."

Dejourner sighed deeply. His face looked flushed. "It is why I struggled so long and hard before coming to you, Blaine. Lauren was . . . my niece."

"Then you . . ."

Dejourner rose to face him, having to look up to meet his eyes. "You needed someone. So did she. Yes, I arranged it. And what it did for you at the time proved I was right. You were like a son to me, and I saw what that awful war had done to you. It stole from you your youth and set you on a path that denied honest sharing, compassion, love if you wish. I knew that path because I walked it myself." The Frenchman's expression grew somber. "I was almost fifty, single and alone, having known only love for my country, which as you often have told me can be a cold and callous partner. You had to see the other side. I had to show it to you.''

''When did you learn of the child?''

Dejourner looked away. ''I didn't know it was yours.''

''You suspected.''

''But I didn't know!'' Then, more softly, he added, ''I supposed I did not want to know. I did not learn the truth until a covenant in her will reached me with the entire story. Lauren had grown up an orphan. She did not want the same for her son.''

''Then she expected me to—''

''She expected you to be true to your own heart. She knew the kind of man you were, that you would do what was right and fair. I'm not sure, no, I *am* sure she had no desire for you to approach the boy. She merely wanted to insure his future would be watched over by someone she trusted.'' Henri's eyes reached out toward him. ''You must do what is right and fair for the boy, but you must also do the same for yourself.''

''A rather difficult combination to achieve under the circumstances.''

''Your heart will guide you, *mon ami*.''

''You don't really expect me to walk into the boy's life now, do you?''

''I expect you to do what is right. And whatever you choose, it will be right. I have done my part. I have stayed true to my conscience as well as Lauren's covenant.''

''And by so doing, you may be exposing the boy to the very things she wanted to avoid when she—and you—chose not to tell me he existed.''

Dejourner nodded. ''Now you can understand the predicament I have faced these past months. Sleep has not come easy, believe me. I thought of you, I thought of Lauren, but in the end I thought of the child, and that is what swayed me.'' The Frenchman reached out and grasped Blaine's forearm tenderly. ''He deserves to know you, *mon ami*, perhaps not as a father but at least as a man.'' Dejourner pulled away. ''I leave it to you.''

''How old are you, Johnny?'' McCracken asked the huge Indian. They sat facing each other in the log cabin Wareagle had built in the woods near Stickney Corner, Maine. The town was three hours from Portland, and Blaine had driven there the minute Dejourner had departed.

"Blainey?" Wareagle responded, turning so Blaine could see his tanned, leathery face that had remained unchanged for the nearly twenty years they'd known each other. They had served together in the same covert division in Vietnam, Johnny a lieutenant to Blaine's captain. If McCracken's exploits were legendary, then Wareagle's were the source of myth. He could charge into a minefield or weave through a firefight without fear, because death, he claimed, was something that stared you down before it took you. And your best chance to avoid it was to stare right back.

"I just got to thinking that with all the shit we've been through together, I don't even know how old you are."

Wareagle moved sideways to lift a boiling kettle from an open flame and poured the water into a pair of mugs that held his homemade tea. "As old as the last season and as young as the next."

"I mean in years, Indian."

"Blainey, a man's years vary like his thoughts. We are here from birth to the end of our chartered time, and what passes between is measured in whatever terms we choose."

"You're talking to a man who recently turned forty."

"A man who did not drive all the way up here to celebrate."

Wareagle finished stirring the cups and brought Blaine's over to him where he sat in the high wooden chair. McCracken felt himself swallowed by the size of the furnishings. Everything in the cabin, from the height of the ceilings to the furniture, had been built with Johnny's seven-foot proportions in mind. Blaine took the cup and sipped its steaming contents. He could taste the sweetness of the molasses and honey and felt somehow soothed.

"I got a belated birthday gift a few hours ago. Thirteen years belated."

Wareagle sat down opposite him and leaned back so his ponytail of coal black hair flopped over the chair's top. He said nothing.

"I've got a son, Johnny. He's twelve years old, his mother's dead, he's at a school over in England, and he doesn't even know I exist." Blaine's words came in a rush, as if hurrying the tale might make it easier to tell.

Wareagle just sat there across from him. Beyond the windows, dawn had come and gone, but the promise of the day was gray and overcast.

"I don't know what to do. I can't even think about it 'cause it scares me." Blaine forced a laugh. "Listen to this. Look at what we've been through, all we've done. After that, is this what it takes to scare me?"

"The unknown holds the most terrifying prospects for us all, Blainey."

"You know what I mean, Indian."

"As well as the problem facing you: either you go to England or you don't."

"Reduced to bare terms, that says it all."

"All life can be reduced to such terms, Blainey. We complicate our existences by creating additional choices that merely confuse our decisions. You speak of all we have accomplished and so often together. In those situations life stripped us of all choices and left us only with actions. We thrived because the thinking was spared us. We could heed the words of the spirits because nothing was in our heads to get in their way." Wareagle eased his chair a bit closer to McCracken's. "We faced physical complications with immediacy and relentlessness in the hellfire. That is what kept us alive. Moral complications must be treated the same."

"That doesn't answer my question."

"You didn't ask one."

"Then let me make it as uncomplicated as I can: do I walk into the boy's life or stay out of it?"

The Indian leaned back and sipped his tea. "What was I doing when you arrived?"

"Chopping wood outside."

"For when?"

"Winter."

"And now May is barely upon us. Preparing for what lies ahead is the essence of all life. Preparation holds the greatest opportunity for avoiding complications. But what if the seasons reversed themselves? What if winter began tomorrow? Then my pile of wood would be woefully inadequate. Would I freeze?''

''You'd find a way not to. You'd survive.''

''Even with the vital preparation unfinished?''

''The first cold wind would be your warning. Snow in May would give you a pretty good notion things were fucked up big time.''

''And what would I do?''

''Bring the wood inside, make sure it stayed dry, chop as much as you could, and stack it right here in the living room. Conserve whatever you had until you were sure you had enough.''

''And are emotions any different, Blainey? Must we not conserve and adapt them as well to the change of emotional seasons the spirits bring upon us without warning? We survived the hellfire because we expected whatever might come. Preparation helped, but keeping our minds open is what saved us. We responded to the moment, not the hour, and we never closed our eyes to what was before us in the hope it would go away. Ignoring the cold, Blainey, would not have made us warm. Yes, the wood must be chopped. We must never forgo preparation for any events, even those that frighten us with their suddenness. If we do not accept that suddenness, as we did in the hellfire, we die. There are many ways to die, Blainey.''

''And we've seen just about all of them, Indian.''

''Never all. Not even most.''

Blaine nodded. ''I think I get the idea.''

Wareagle sipped his tea. ''Travel well, my friend.''

CHAPTER 3

THE IVY-COLORED BRICK WALLS OF THE READING SCHOOL rose in the damp mist that had swept in across the countryside. Blaine drove through the front gate and down the tree-lined entry road that took him past a collection of playing fields, or "pitches" as they were called over here, en route to a central building adorned with steeples. He was still not entirely convinced he was doing the right thing, and each slow climb over a speed bump along the drive brought him that much closer to turning back.

He had flown TWA out of Boston Monday night and arrived at Heathrow early Tuesday morning. From there the M-4 brought him straight to the city of Reading, where he had made reservations at its largest hotel, the Ramada Inn. He was not expected at the school until two P.M., which gave him four hours to rest and recharge himself following his uneasy sleep in the first class section of the jet. He soaked in the bathtub, showered, and grabbed a sandwich in the simplest of the Ramada's restaurants, loitering the additional minutes away inattentively watching news on the television.

He crossed the Reading School's final speed bump at five minutes to two and asked a group of boys dressed in charcoal gray suits where he could find the residence of housemaster John Neville who was expecting him. The boys' answer came politely in unison and they pointed to the red brick house nearest at hand. Blaine parked his car and stepped outside. He felt the damp mist assault him instantly, reaching through his clothes and flesh for bones to chill. He noted a large bell tower perched atop the school's central building as he walked toward the housemaster's residence. He rang the buzzer and a chorus of heavy barks and snarls came from the inside before the chimes had even ceased.

"Come on now, back up!" he heard a thick voice order, and then the door was opening.

"Mr. Neville?"

"John. You must be McCracken. Henri told me to expect you to be right on time. Please, come in."

John Neville was as big and thick as his voice, a powerfully built man with bands of muscle swimming through forearms revealed beneath the sleeves of his rolled up rugby shirt. Blaine was impressed by the strength of his grip as they shook hands. Neville closed the door behind them and the dogs, huge German shepherds, growled their suspicion.

Neville tapped one on the snout. "Enough of that, Bodie. You and Doyle go play now."

"Bodie and Doyle?" Blaine asked.

Neville smiled warmly and the expression gave his face a youthful glow. His complexion was pitted, but there was color in his cheeks and life in his voice.

"I see you recall 'The Professionals.' "

"British detective series from years back. The dogs are named for the heroes. I spent considerable time over here years back."

"So Henri told me."

"What else did he tell you?"

"Just the barest details. You're good to do this, Blaine."

"I hope you're right."

"I've got tea ready in the living room."

They moved from the hall into a spacious den dominated by a fireplace layered with the remains of yesterday's fire. The radiators were old-fashioned, and to help break the chill a pair of space heaters had been strategically placed. The dogs followed them at every step, nuzzling against Neville for attention as soon as he sat down in the chair adjacent to the one he directed Blaine to. He fussed over Doyle, and Bodie growled from deep in his throat.

"Enough of that!" he scolded. "I won't tell you again."

Bodie lay down, whimpering softly.

John Neville handed a cup of tea across to McCracken from a tray. "Got something stronger to mix with that if you want."

"No, thanks. This will be fine."

Neville leaned back. A shock of dark hair slid over his forehead and he pushed it back. "You'll want to hear about the boy."

"About Matthew."

"Matt he likes to be called. Good student and a top athlete as well."

"Soccer?"

Neville shook his head and stroked Doyle's shoulders. "Rugby's the thing here. We're a relatively small school as far as enrollment goes, so we could never hope to compete effectively in either if we tried for both. Rugby's a tradition at Reading. There are lots of traditions. That bell tower you were admiring outside, seniors love to climb into it and carve their initials on the bell."

"Kids must really love this place."

"We do our best. Our situation's unique in that we're still actually a private school by definition. In addition to serving as housemaster for the boarders, I run the phys-ed and rugby programs." Neville hesitated. "Matt's in class now. I can get him, if you wish."

"No," Blaine said abruptly. "I mean, I don't want to disturb him. I don't want to . . . intrude."

"Do you see this as intruding?"

"I don't know what to see it as."

"Would have been much easier for you if you hadn't come. Not easier for him. He should know you."

"He doesn't even know I exist. You didn't say anything, did you?"

Neville shook his head. "Figured you'd want all that business left up to you. Your timing couldn't be better, though. There's a school holiday tomorrow. Perfect opportunity to get acquainted. First meeting ought to be the toughest. After rugby practice this afternoon'd be perfect, if you don't mind waiting."

"I don't mind," said McCracken.

* * *

John Neville had a class of second formers waiting for him in the gym and left McCracken to pass the time before a bay window in the dining room with Bodie on one side of him and Doyle on the other. He watched the boys of Reading School, all dressed neatly in their gray suits, and wondered which one of them was Matthew. Then with the coming of the three o'clock bell the students rapidly exchanged suits for rugby shirts and shorts in the school colors and trudged off to practice fields not far from the school. John Neville returned shortly thereafter with a mesh bag full of rugby balls in hand.

"We'll drive over," he told Blaine, loading the bag into the hatchback of the British version of a Ford Escort. Then, eyeing McCracken, he added, "You might not be dressed for the outdoors."

"I'll do fine."

In fact, he did anything but. After the drive, the walk across to the pitch where the third formers were practicing under the guidance of a small man with a mustache soaked his Italian loafers through to his socks. To make the proper impression at the school he had dressed well, in wear totally inappropriate for the damp outdoors. The cold was raw and unsettling, and the mist smelled like dank sweat. Neville had promised to come over and point Matt out as soon as he got his own practice started.

In the meantime Blaine was left again to his thoughts, again trying to distinguish which among the thirty boys performing warm-up exercises before him was Matt. He tried to narrow it down by recalling Lauren's looks and attempting to superimpose them over the faces of the boys. But it was all to no avail. Strange how he had spent his life in unfamiliar places and had always been able to distinguish between the friendlies and unfriendlies at a glance. Yet here he was now coming up short in pursuit of his own . . .

"Come on now!" the little man with the mustache was urging, as game practice commenced with a drill in which members of two sides circled around a ball trapped in their center. "Push it out now! That's it! And again! . . . And again!"

"Know the game at all, Blaine?" John Neville was asking, suddenly by his side.

"Bits and pieces."

"A game made for children, this is. They can take the rough-and-tumble. Take a hard hit and bounce right back. The older one gets, the—"

"Thank you."

"For what?"

"The small talk to help me relax. It isn't necessary."

Neville simply nodded and let his own thoughts stray briefly. "Playing on the right across the field. Striped shirt muddied in the front."

And with his heart crashing against his ribs, Blaine found the boy just as a teammate gave him a perfect pass on the run and Matthew Ericson streaked down the far sideline like a champion thoroughbred. A deft stutter step stranded one opponent in his tracks, and a fake pass to the side left him with a clear path to the goal line.

The boy ran with graceful, loping strides, propelled by a high leg kick that tossed mud behind him off his soggy cleats. With token pursuit closing at the last, he slid to touch the ball to the ground in the end zone to insure the points. Then he rose to the shoulder slaps and praise of his teammates and mustachioed coach. He walked back toward the center line just as gracefully as he had sped in for the score, front thigh muscles rippling with definition. His hair was straight and longish, curled at the ends now from the dampness. His eyes were brown and radiant and he carried himself with a smoothness and confidence that seemed entirely natural.

"Want me to call him over?" Neville offered.

"No, please. Let him be."

"Him or you?"

"What?"

Neville smiled. "After practice then?"

"Yes. Much better."

"With you to be introduced as . . ."

"A friend of his mother's. A good friend."

"And tomorrow's holiday?"

"We'll do something. If he wants."

"You're underestimating him, Blaine. Not only will he want

to, it won't take him long to figure out what's going on. You'd be wise to prepare for that."

"I'll try."

"I was a friend of your mother," he told the boy before John Neville had a chance to as they shook hands after practice. "A good friend."

The boy's grip was sweaty but firm. Blaine was surprised when he smiled. "Really? Did you know her from America?"

"Accent give me away?"

Another smile. "Would she have mentioned you, sir?"

"Call me Blaine, please. No, I don't think she would have."

In the next instant neither knew what to say, and John Neville stepped in.

"Matt, Mr. McCrack—er, Blaine—is going to be in the country for a bit and would like very much to spend some time with you. I suggested tomorrow's school holiday as a possibility."

"If you don't have any plans," Blaine added, wanting the boy to have a way out, or maybe himself.

"I'd like that very much, sir."

"Blaine."

"He was thinking an outing to London might be smart," Neville proposed.

"Oh yes! Smashing!" The boy beamed. "It's been ages since I've been there."

"Done, then," Neville concluded.

But it isn't done, Blaine reckoned, *not by a longshot. Do I tell him, and if so when? Damn you, Henri, for dropping all this in my lap. . . .*

Later, thrashing his thoughts about, Blaine drove from the school through Henley on Thames to the small Norman village of Hambleden where Lauren Ericson had lived and been buried. The village was quiet to the point of seeming deserted, and Blaine found himself easing the car door shut to avoid an echo. The moist air had the same sweaty feel as it had back in Reading. Here, though, it was laced with the warm scent of wood smoke coming from chimneys on houses that might have been fashioned out of the same light reddish brick. It was difficult to date the structures since even the newer ones had been built to blend in with and maintain the village's rustic appeal. There were graves in the churchyard dating back to the eleventh century but only a few dug in the last few years, and their tombstones hadn't been aged as the buildings had.

Lauren's was a simple affair wedged in a small family plot her ancestors had obtained four centuries before. Dying, Blaine supposed, should be like coming home, and perhaps this was as close to that ideal as possible. He knelt by the grave wanting to feel something other than the confusion and uncertainty racing through him.

In recent weeks he had for some reason been reminiscing about his own parents, and all this served to only intensify his confused feelings. How unglamorous the story was. His parents had married late and had him, their only child, later. His father was an insurance salesman who made his living on the road and died in a Milwaukee hotel room of a heart attack at the age of sixty when Blaine was in high school. His mother had held up through it bravely and built a decent life for herself that ended after a painful struggle with cancer while Blaine was in Vietnam following an aborted attempt at college. She'd been dead for six months before he learned of it, due to the incommunicado status of men who were assigned to clandestine duty such as his. In those same six months and the six that came before he had not been allowed to send a single letter. Strange how when word came about her death he wondered more than anything what he might have said if he had been permitted.

Even with everything else considered, that was the only time he really hated the war, for not allowing him the dignity of rushing to his mother's deathbed or at least attending her funeral. And though he tried, he was unable to remember what mission he'd been on at the moment of her passing.

Blaine supposed the advanced ages of his parents had helped make him independent almost from the cradle. He had always gone his own way, never with the crowd, and spent many of his early years resenting his parents for being so much older than those of his friends. In later years he loved them even more for it. At the very least they were there. At the most, they had somehow helped mold him into the man he had become.

He thought of all the high school sporting events his father had been unable to attend and how guilty he felt for preferring this to having the old man standing out among the other parents, looking more like grandfather than father. He thought of Matthew streaking down the sidelines to bring Reading School the rugby championship . . . with no parent to cheer him on, no face to pick out amidst the crowd. And if it wasn't McCracken's face, then whose would it be? Besides Henri Dejourner there was no one. Blaine had never turned his back on an obligation before, and this was no time to start. The boy was strong and brave and beautiful, but time might work as his enemy under the circumstances. He hadn't gone through a Christmas alone yet, or a birthday. Blaine knew all about that and it was never easy.

"I wish I could cry for you, Lauren," he said over the grave. "I'm sorry we shared so little time. But I won't abandon what we produced. You have my word on that."

CHAPTER 4

"**Y**OU MET MY MOTHER IN ENGLAND, THEN?" MATT ASKED as they took the fast train toward London from Reading the next morning.

McCracken nodded. "I was over here for an extended time, almost a year."

"On business?"

"Sort of."

The boy hesitated before speaking again. "Did it have anything to do with you being a soldier?"

The question took Blaine by surprise and his face showed it. "What makes you ask that?"

"The way you move. The way you look at people. I've studied a lot about soldiers."

"Yes," Blaine told him. "I was in the army."

"Were you in a war?"

Another nod. "Vietnam."

The boy looked genuinely proud. "Really? As what, sir? Please, do tell me!"

"Only if you promise to call me Blaine. The story gets a little complicated."

"I'll understand. I'll try anyway."

Blaine didn't want to lie, but he couldn't tell the truth yet either, at least not the whole truth. "I was trained as a Green Beret."

Matt's mouth dropped. "The Special Forces!"

"We weren't called that yet, but yes."

"They predated our Special Air Service. They were the first specially trained commandos in the western alliance since World War II."

"I was fortunate enough to miss that one," Blaine said.

Matt flashed a smile that quickly melted back into a questioning stare. "You said it was complicated."

"Well, yes."

"You started to tell me."

What the hell, Blaine figured. "How are you at keeping a secret?"

"Good. Very good."

"Okay. Vietnam was a funny war because lots of people were running different parts of it. The army had its hands tied and that pretty much explains why we got pounded like we did. But an authorized faction of the army got together with the CIA and decided to run part of the war its own way. I was part of what they called the Phoenix Project. We did most of our work behind enemy lines and we never issued reports. Make sense?"

"Wow," Matt said. "But what did you—"

Blaine cut him off. "That's for another day, Matt, later." Then, sensing the boy's disappointment, he added, "I've still got some friends in the SAS by the way. Like to come out and see them train sometime?"

"It's top secret, sir. No visitors allowed."

"You've got connections, kid."

"Could we, si—, Blaine? Could we really?"

"Just name the time."

"I'd like that. I really would." His face turned quizzical again. "But what exactly did you do while you were in London?"

"When we get to the city, I'll show you."

They came to Parliament Square in the middle of the day. Blaine had never intended to give the boy such a detailed glimpse into his history, much less such an infamous occurrence. But, damn it, he was caught up in it all, the boy's adulation and interest serving to open up areas of discussion he had kept closed for years. And didn't Matt have a right to know, if anyone did?

"What's so important about Churchill's statue?" he wondered as they drew up close to it.

"Bet you didn't know they had to rebuild a section."

"I didn't. Is it important?"

"Not really. Except for the reason."

"Reason?"

They moved closer.

"Notice the slight discoloration in the great coat right after it breaks beneath his stomach?"

"I guess so. Why?"

"They repaired it after I shot off a rather important anatomical area."

The boy's eyes bulged, then glared at him disbelievingly. "You're making it up."

"You don't really believe that."

"Okay, why did you do it then?"

Blaine eased his arm tenderly around the boy's shoulder. "Another story for another day, kid."

They spent hours at Madame Tussaud's Wax Museum. Not surprisingly, Matt was most fascinated by the military exhibits. Blaine found himself enjoying the time just as much. After all, besides rejection his greatest fear in starting this relationship twelve years late was that he would have nothing in common with the boy. Well, he couldn't have asked for much more than this and dared to wonder whether such interests could be hereditary.

They climbed to the whispering pews of St. Paul's Cathedral and lunched at a traditional London pub in the business district called Smithfield's. From there they took the underground to Pall Mall where Matt spent ten minutes expounding to Mc-Cracken, and a half-dozen others who had gathered, on the rigorous combat training endured by the red-clad, black-capped horsemen who ceremonially patrol the gates.

"Do you think I should join the army?" Matt asked as they strolled away.

"That depends on a lot of things you're too young to consider now."

"Not really," Matthew responded maturely. "Seventh formers at Reading can sign up either with the RAF or the infantry on Friday afternoons to cover their community service. That's not very far off at all.''

"No, it isn't."

"So, should I sign up or not?"

Blaine tried to show how happy he was at being consulted. "It sounds like you've already made up your mind. If it's important to you, absolutely."

"Was it important to you?"

"To enlist, you mean? Well, there was this thing called the draft and my number was about to come up anyway and college was a bore, so I joined. That way I got my choice of service."

"And you chose Green Beret . . ."

Blaine hedged. "Well, actually it was chosen for me a few months into training."

"You didn't tell me that."

"Got to save some stuff for later."

"And what about what you did in the Phoenix Project?"

"Also later."

Matt hesitated. "You haven't told me much about what you're doing now." And before McCracken could answer, the boy did it for him, a smile flashing through the words. "I know—later."

It was well past dark by the time Blaine got the boy back to Reading School and watched him disappear through a door.

"Thought it was you," John Neville said as he approached McCracken with Bodie and Doyle restrained on leashes. They fought to greet McCracken as well. "I've just been out walking my dogs."

"Sorry I'm so late."

"I didn't give you a curfew. It went well. I can tell that much."

"It went great. It scares me it went so great."

"Why should it scare you?"

Blaine turned fast enough to draw a slight growl from Doyle. Neville spoke again before he had a chance to.

"It didn't go great enough for you to tell him who you were, did it?"

"I didn't want to spoil the day."

"Do you think it would have?"

"Maybe."

"For you or for him?" Neville eyed him suspiciously. "You're hedging, mate. Something's holding you back."

They started walking toward the playing pitches which fronted the school. With the wind gone, it felt warmer than it had the previous afternoon.

"How much did Henri Dejourner tell you about me?" Blaine asked.

"Very little, I'm afraid."

"Then let me fill in a few of the holes. The boy's mother kept his existence secret from me for a reason. Back then I was involved in governmental matters that required an expert hand. Things haven't changed all that much since."

Neville was nodding. "I'd expected as much. Or close to it. It's your eyes. I've known men like you before."

Blaine shook his head. "You've never known a man like me, John. It's not possible, believe me. Right now I'm trying to sort out emotions that I've never felt before. Today was special for me in a way I can't describe, and it's tempting to see it as a sign of a new phase in my life. But the trouble is I've got lots of enemies. What I'm trying to say is that makes Matt vulnerable if I decide to enter his life on a full-time basis. No, change that. He's *already* vulnerable and has been since Henri Dejourner paid you a visit. Whatever I decide to do—"

Neville stroked Bodie's head as he interrupted. "He's in good hands."

"You've got to watch over him, John. You've got to be extra careful."

"Consider it done."

Blaine couldn't sleep. His thoughts kept hammering away at him and there seemed no way to soften them.

He was worried. He was scared.

The fragility of life was nothing new to him. He had seen firsthand how quickly it could be snuffed out and had considered his own passing often enough to be unfazed by it. There was no sense worrying over that moment, because when it came even he would be powerless to prevent it. Yet now life's fragility took on deeper meaning. The very focus of his existence was in turmoil. What did he owe the boy? And what did he owe himself? He was forty years old and had celebrated that milestone with a disheartening realization. The events he had found himself a part of lately were all random, unconnected, unlike his Vietnam service and after.

And after . . .

And after . . .

The phone on the nighttable rang, jarring him, and Blaine felt for it in the darkness.

"Yes?"

"Would this be Mr. Blaine McCracken?"

"It would."

"This is Chief Inspector Alvin Willie of the Reading Police, sir. There's been some trouble at the Reading School. You'd better get down here."

CHAPTER 5

CHIEF INSPECTOR ALVIN WILLIE WAS A PORTLY MAN WITH A huge bald head and no neck to speak of. He was dressed in civilian clothes and his shirt was only half tucked into his trousers. He showed McCracken the splinters where the front door of housemaster John Neville's residence had been kicked in.

"Rather amateurish, I'd say," the chief said.

"No," Blaine told him, still in a daze. "He'd want to attract attention. He'd want to draw John down here."

"Sounds foolish."

"Anything but. Where's the body?"

"This way," Chief Willie said, and started forward through the hall.

They first came upon the partially covered corpses of Bodie and Doyle. Blood had pooled beneath their open mouths and Blaine could tell from the angle of their heads that the poor animals' necks had been snapped. Inside the den a uniformed officer was ready to cover Neville's body with a sheet when a glance from Willie stopped him. The corpse's head and shoulders were propped up against a wall. The face was frozen in twisted pain, the neck bent at an impossible curve, obviously having been snapped as well. But there was something strange about the positioning. Neville hadn't died there; he had been dragged over and propped up, as if to be made a witness to something after death.

Blaine shuddered at the strength required to finish the muscular Neville *and* his two dogs. Someone was making a point, someone who enjoyed his work. And the point could only have been aimed at him. But what had gone on in this room after the housemaster had been killed?

"It happened between ninety minutes and two hours ago," Chief Willie explained. He was sweating profusely, the perspiration soaking through his clothes and shining off his exposed dome. "As near as we can tell, whoever was responsible entered through the residence, and after . . . doing all this, made his way to the area of the boys' rooms upstairs."

"Was there a delay between the time the killer finished here and went upstairs?"

Alvin Willie looked surprised by Blaine's conclusion. "We think so, yes, judging by the interval between the time the dogs stopped barking and . . ."

"And what?"

"The Ericson boy's roommate was knocked unconscious prior to the boy being taken."

"How did you know to call me?"

"It was in the boy's file. A note pinned to it in what we believe is Neville's writing."

"Damn. He never should have written anything down . . ."

"Excuse me?"

"Nothing."

"If there's anything I should know that could help me in all this . . ."

"I would tell you, Chief. Believe me, there isn't. This isn't your problem anymore," Blaine added, regretting it immediately.

"You're damn well wrong about that. There's a man dead here and a boy's missing you're linked to. I need some answers. First off, what is your connection to the kidnapped boy?"

But McCracken's mind had wandered to the moments leading to Neville's death. He would have charged down the stairs with the dogs ahead of him, perhaps a weapon in hand. He would have known instantly what was happening and with the dogs should have made a decent fight of it. That worried Blaine more than anything else. Two dogs meant two killers, he saw that now. They could have entered in any number of ways but they chose one that guaranteed a confrontation. And after Neville was dead, what then?

"You hear me?" Alvin Willie was asking as Blaine brushed by him to proceed along with the scenario in his mind.

There was something anomalous here. A man like Neville would have called the police first.

"He didn't call you, did he?" Blaine asked suddenly.

"I got a question on the table for you first, mister!"

"The lines were cut from the outside, weren't they?"

Willie's huge jowls puckered. "How in the hell did you know that?"

"They wanted to take him alone."

"They? Who's they?"

"Two people did this, Chief Inspector. If your lab men are worth anything, they'll confirm it."

McCracken started for the staircase, but Willie cut him off.

"What's your connection with the missing boy, Mr. Mc-Cracken?"

"You read his file."

"I read a note attached to his file. Didn't say much at all. Just your name, the time you were arriving yesterday, and the hotel where you were staying."

"That's it, then."

Alvin Willie was losing his patience. "I got a dead house-master who was a damn good bloke and a kidnapped—"

Willie stopped with the approach of another uniformed officer down the stairs.

"I've got the boy's statement, sir."

"What boy?" McCracken demanded.

Willie barely acknowledged him. "That's none of your business."

McCracken edged himself up close to the fat man, pushing down the urge to jack him against the wall. "You wanna know how wrong you are, Chief? You want the answer to your questions? Fine. The kidnapped boy's my son, and he got taken almost surely because of me. I saw him for the first time yesterday and the details of that don't matter. All I can tell you is that all this is almost surely meant as a warning for me. Somebody's showing off. Somebody wants me to know how ruthless they are. They probably want something from me in return for the boy. But don't bother trying to run a make on me because every U.S. agency with three letters will tell you to get fucked. Am I making myself clear?''

Alvin Willie managed a nod. He could not recall a time when he'd been more intimidated by a single man. There was strength behind this one, incredible strength, but it was his resolve that did the trick more than anything.

''You'll want to read the statement, then.''

''I'll want to see the boy who gave it.''

''I wasn't supposed to be awake, sir,'' the boy whose name was Gilbert told him. ''I wasn't supposed to be by the window.''

''I understand,'' Blaine said. ''This is just between us.''

''But the police, I gave them that statement.''

''Did you tell them everything?''

''I think I did.''

''But you're not sure.''

''I keep remembering . . . stuff. It probably doesn't matter.''

''It probably does. You know Matthew Ericson, don't you?''

The boy nodded enthusiastically. ''Yes, sir! We're mates.''

''Then you'll want to help him, which means you've got to help me.''

Gilbert shrugged. ''I have trouble sleeping sometimes. Sitting by the window helps. See, I've got asthma so I can't have a roommate since I make a lot of noise when I'm asleep. On bad nights, I'm afraid to fall asleep and that's why I stay up. Going to the window makes me tired again.''

''Did it tonight?''

''It started to. But then I heard . . .''

''Heard what?'' Blaine eased himself closer and made sure his tone was soft. ''Please, there's nothing to be scared of now.''

''I heard Mr. Neville's dogs barking. They do it a lot at night but this was . . . different. I'm not sure how.''

''It doesn't matter. What next?''

"Well, there was noise, like something breaking and then lots of sounds before everything got quiet again. And there was a scream, just one, and the dogs whimpering. I was scared. I jumped back into bed but I was shaking so hard I started to wheeze. I went back to the window after a few minutes and that's when I saw them."

"Saw who?"

"Two figures."

"Big men or small?"

The boy looked in the window's direction. "The policeman didn't believe me, either. He tried to make me change what I said, what I saw."

"Change what?"

"They weren't men, sir. They were women."

"But I'm not a hundred percent sure," Gilbert added almost immediately. "I mean it was so dark and everything."

"You know what you saw, though."

A reluctant nod.

"The women, were they small or big?"

"One was tall."

"How tall?"

"I don't know. Very, I guess."

"As tall as me?" Blaine asked, rising to his full height.

"At least. Taller I think. She was the one carrying something over her shoulder."

Matthew, Blaine thought as he fought to assimilate the boy's story. A pair of *women*? That possibility juxtaposed against the scene downstairs didn't hold. To think that two women could have so effortlessly slain Neville and his dogs . . . Whoever they were, the killers had performed from the start with deadly professionalism, each move undertaken to obtain a desired reaction to which they were prepared to respond. Neville had played right into their hands. It was all a show.

All for Blaine's benefit.

They liked to kill, that much was certain. Professionals could have made off with the boy with no fuss at all, but obviously that wasn't enough for them. If revenge was the point, however, he would have found the boy's body along with Neville's. The

choice of kidnapping instead meant someone wanted something
to hold over his head, and the display of violence downstairs
was meant as a demonstration that they were willing to go to
any lengths to . . .

To *what*?

McCracken found Alvin Willie waiting for him at the bottom of the stairs. "Look, Mr. McCracken, I don't know who
or what you are, and I don't really want to. But I do know
that Reading is my town and the people hurt here are my
people and—"

"Except one, Chief," Blaine interrupted, "except one."

He had to think it out rationally. There was logic in each move
the female killers had made, except the propping up of Neville's
body. What he had to do was backtrack, learn who they were
and who had hired them by first learning how they had learned
about Matthew.

There was only one answer: Henri Dejourner. Henri was the
only other man who knew of Blaine's connection to the boy.
Somewhere, somehow, Dejourner's security had been penetrated. That was the place he would start but he had to act fast.
Whatever the kidnappers wanted from him, they would be making it known soon. McCracken had to grab the offensive before
that time came.

Never one to travel unprepared, Blaine had flown overseas
with a custom-designed Uzi coated with detector jamming Teflon. He pulled it from its taped position beneath the bed, made
sure it was ready, and then dialed Henri's private contact number.

The phone rang and kept ringing, unanswered.

Impossible! It was manned always, if not by Henri himself
then by an underling he trusted. Could whatever was going on
here extend somehow into France as well? He had to find out.
A moment later another number was dialed and once again he
was listening to the ring.

"Hello?" responded a sleepy voice.

"Ah, Daniels, it's been too long."

"Who is th—No, it couldn't be. . . ."

"I need your all-powerful agency to run something down for me."

"Now? Do you know what time it—"

"Now. Am I making myself clear, Daniels? Or would you prefer that I—"

"Just tell me what you need."

"I can't reach Dejourner. No answer."

"Give me half an hour. I'll call you back."

"Sorry, Daniels. I may need you but I still don't trust you. I'll call you back. Twenty minutes."

"You're an ass, McCracken."

"The Frenchman's line has been disconnected," Daniels reported twenty minutes later. "He was killed this afternoon."

Blaine's stomach sank. "How?"

"Neck snapped. By hand, they tell me. Three bodyguards bought it in similar fashion, except one took longer to die. Made it to the hospital where he claimed a couple of women did it all. Women! Do you believe it?"

"Yes."

"Wait a minute, McCracken. If you're up to something that the Company should be informed of—"

"You'll be the first to know, Daniels, and that's a promise."

Blaine hung up. Things were coming together and the picture wasn't pleasant. Matthew's kidnappers had killed Henri Dejourner as well as John Neville. Very professional. Very brutal. Because they wanted something from him. So be it. McCracken would play along as long as necessary, make them think the upper hand was theirs until he got the boy back. He felt the old familiar rage building up inside him, swelling to what scientists called critical mass. If they harmed the boy in any way, he would kill them all.

His eyes strayed to the phone, knowing what was coming next even before the ring jarred him. He thrust the receiver to his ear with his heart pounding.

"I trust the bad news about Mr. Dejourner has reached you, Mr. McCracken," a voice said.

"The boy . . ."

"We have him," the voice said. "He is safe. He is comfortable."

"And I'm supposed to believe that?"

"It's the truth."

"What do I have to do to get him back?"

"Not on the phone, Mr. McCracken."

"I know your voice. I'm sure of it, I know your voice."

"I know your room. I can come up straightaway."

"The temptation to kill you might prove too much."

"I don't think so. After all, you do want to see your son again, don't you?"

The knock on the door came less than three minutes later.

"Come in," Blaine called out. He was seated in a chair against the wall farthest from the door. "It's open."

The door opened, brushing over the carpet. A dark-skinned, bearded figure entered. McCracken made sure he could see the Uzi.

The man closed the door behind him and stopped. "You don't need that."

"I know. I just wanted you to know how it feels, having your back up against the wall. And it relaxes me to know I can splatter the organ of my choice if the spirit moves me."

The figured swallowed hard, still in the shadows cast by the single lamp. "Don't forget your son, which is what this is all about."

"Oh, I wasn't talking about killing you. A simple maiming would suffice once you've told me what you've come to say. Whatever it is you won't hurt the boy no matter what I do to you because you need me to deliver. You're a worm, nothing more."

The figure stepped further into the light, and Blaine blinked several times to make sure he had the face right. It was Mohammed Fett, an Arab power broker who fluctuated back and forth between the moderate forces of the PLO and the various radical cells populating the Mideast.

"Robes are more fitting for you than Giorgio Armani, Fett."

"Ah, but when in Rome . . ."

"Your geography's off. This is Reading, England, where one Matthew Ericson resided until a few hours ago."

Fett came slightly more forward, slowly, making sure his hands were in plain view. "It was necessary because we need you. Desperately."

"You couldn't think of a better way to ask for my help?"

"We tried. You rebuked all our advances. Surely you remember. The channels, the contacts—we tried. We even sent a representative directly to you. You treated him rather rudely."

Blaine did remember all too well. An Arab force had sought him out just over a month before and he had refused even to speak to them. He had mentioned to Henri Dejourner how the last agent they sent to his island condominium had ended up in the bay.

"You do remember! I can tell! You are going to work for us, Mr. McCracken. You won't like it but you have no choice, just as we have no choice."

"Someone holding something over your head too, Fett?"

"Millions of Arab lives . . . if it matters to you."

"Not nearly as much as Matthew Ericson's does."

"Listen to me," Fett responded, voice tense. "Israel is going to strike at us. There is going to be a war, and this time they are going to be the ones to start it."

"You expect me to believe that?"

"I expect you to stop it for your son's sake, and for the sake of the world."

"Spare me. Please."

"Listen to me, McCracken. You and I have fought before on different sides. But there are forces at work this time that bode ill for me and for you as well."

"And were these the forces responsible for the deaths of John Neville and Henri Dejourner?"

"The people retained exceeded their mandate."

"They did a hell of a lot more than that. You should have seen the housemaster's residence, Fett. Whoever killed him enjoyed it and they wanted me to know that. What did they want him to see after he was dead?"

"I—"

"You might be bringing me one message, but those women were delivering a different one."

"My point exactly. Their role in this has ended. You have only me to deal with now."

"My lucky day . . ."

"There will be far more deaths on your head if you do not act, if *we* do not act."

"Against Israel?"

"Against a militant force *within* Israel. This force is in possession of a weapon of incredible scope. If utilized, it will destroy the Arab world as it is known today."

"And I'm supposed to stop it from being utilized, is that it?"

"Exactly."

Blaine felt himself starting to fume again. "Know something, Fett? I could torture the boy's location out of you now."

"That would be useless because I don't know it. Steps were taken to guard against just what you are threatening."

"Fine. Now explain why me? What makes me so important to you?"

Fett shrugged. "It was not my idea. I warned them against angering you. I told them what you were capable of. She overruled me."

"She?"

"You've heard of Evira no doubt."

"Have I ever. She's an Arab agent operating within Israel, certainly the most wanted terrorist in the entire country."

"Not a terrorist, McCracken! Not even a militant!"

"Call her whatever you want. She chose me?"

"She *insisted* on you. There have been leaks, deep ones, within our organization. Evira fears her own identity has been compromised. An outsider seemed the only hope, and you were the only choice she presented."

Blaine eased off. "So you're saying Israel has this weapon and I'm supposed to prevent it from being used."

Fett nodded. "In return for the life of your son, yes. But it becomes even more complicated. The government of Israel is not to blame here, but a cell operating within the country. With the government's blessing or not, it is difficult to tell. The Israelis are masters of misdirection. But the weapon exists and the cell intends to use it; there's no misreading that.''

"Can you tell me more about this cell?''

Fett shook his head. "I only know what I've been allowed to. The rest of what you need to hear will come from one closer to Evira.''

"Another messenger, Fett?''

"Only this time the journey will be yours, McCracken. To Tel Aviv. I have your ticket with me.''

PART TWO

Critical Mass

Jaffa: Thursday, May 4; two P.M.

CHAPTER 6

MCCRACKEN'S THOUGHTS SWIRLED AS THE 747 DIPPED INTO its descent for Ben-Gurion Airport. Fett had handed him a ticket on an El Al jet that left for Israel just after dawn. When he at last closed the door behind the Arab, Blaine had never felt more helpless or alone. Ever since learning of Matthew's kidnapping, he'd been filled with a cold dread, exactly the kind of feeling that Lauren had wished to spare him by never mentioning his son's existence. To say nothing of sparing the boy the terrors that had now befallen him.

He wondered how it was possible to develop such strong feelings of love and devotion for Matthew after knowing him for barely two days. The feelings were foreign to Blaine, terrifying in their implications. He forced himself to focus on the task at hand. All he had was a cryptic instruction from Fett on where to meet Evira's contact:

Go to the Jaffa Flea Market. Present yourself in the gift shop featuring leather handbags over its door on the market's last corner.

Once there, McCracken would be filled in on further details that Fett himself wasn't privy to. With the leaks to consider, Evira was taking no chances. Similarly, Blaine was forbidden to contact anyone else for help. Under those circumstances, useless were his allies in intelligence and the vast cache of favors owed him by friendly forces within Israel, forces he was now

ironically pitted against. He knew these men well. If they caught
him working for the other side, they would kill him without
hesitation.

He'd spent five hard months in Israel in 1973, but they'd been
worthwhile ones. It was his first action after being pulled out of
Nam, and it reassured him that his skills were still required now
that the Phoenix Project was history. One well kept secret about
the Yom Kippur War was that Israel knew it was coming, just
as she had in '68. But this time Nixon and the Americans absolutely forbade her to make the first move on threats of a total
cut-off. Let the Arabs fire the first shots and Nixon promised to
back Israel with everything he had.

"Everything" turned out to be five hundred Special Forces
troops fresh from the Phoenix Project under the command of
Blaine McCracken. They were spirited into the country hours
before the war started and worked the magic they had refined
so well in Vietnam. The terrain was different, but that was all.
Infiltration behind enemy lines was still the key. Lines of communication were disrupted, so that contradictory and downright
ludicrous orders reached the Arab fighters at the front. Direct
intelligence gathered by McCracken and his men paved the road
the Israelis could have taken straight to Cairo and Damascus if
Nixon hadn't intervened again. As for direct engagements in
battle, each of Blaine's men was worth a hundred untrained
Arabs, and the kill ratio was not far from that. His troops were
sharp, seasoned, and unwilling to accept defeat again. Winning
was a nice feeling and a number of them, including McCracken
and Johnny Wareagle, stayed on afterward to savor it while
educating Israeli paratroopers in the lessons of the Phoenix
Project.

After landing in Tel Aviv, Blaine negotiated customs easily,
stowed his single suitcase temporarily in an airport locker, and
pushed his way through the throngs of travelers for the taxi stand
outside Ben Guiron. The driver left him to his thoughts in the
cab's backseat and pulled into traffic headed for Tel Aviv.

The Mossad, the Israeli intelligence service, maintains regular shifts at Ben Gurion Airport. Often disguised as fidgety
travelers, or fliers seated near their suitcases in apparent con-

sternation over a delay, even garbed as sanitation personnel, they wait and watch day and night for the entry of suspicious persons. Although possible routes of enemy penetration into Israel are many and diverse, it remains surprising how many potential enemies make their entry right at Ben Gurion.

The Mossad agent who spotted the casually dressed bearded man making his way from immigration to baggage claim was on duty behind a monetary exchange counter. As soon as the bearded man had gone, he moved to a phone directly behind his desk and dialed his control.

"Are we expecting anything from the Americans?" he queried after standard codes were exchanged.

"CIA?"

"Independent more likely. Possibly by invitation."

"I'll run the checks. Someone grab your eye?"

"Yes. An old friend of ours just flew in. . . ."

McCracken had the driver take him into Jaffa and deposit him at the Ottoman Clock Tower in Haganah Square. With the bustling modern skyscrapers of Tel Aviv looming above, the old city of Jaffa maintained a tight, imponderable hold on the past, thanks to the outdoor flea market filled with salesmen pitching their wares from stands on the sidewalk, moving carts, or open-front shops. The peddlers and shopkeepers strain their voices to have their boasts of bargains heard and heeded. The quality of merchandise is generally low, but the spirit of the merchants who battle for street space and customers is keen.

From the clock tower, Blaine headed down Yefet Street and swung left on to Oley Tsiyon toward the center of the market. Less than a block later his nose was assaulted by the sharp aroma of freshly caught fish being showcased on hooks or ice at the market across the street. The entrance to the flea market just beyond was signalled by arrays of Oriental rugs draped over car hoods and roofs. As more merchants appeared, the market's borders continued to expand, filling up every available foot of sidewalk and storefront and forcing would-be buyers into the streets to compete for space with vehicular traffic.

The shop Fett had sent him to was of the permanent variety: a building, not a pushcart. Blaine took his time getting there,

wanting to become familiar with his surroundings. In addition
to the rugs piled everywhere, used clothing seemed a hot item
along with cheap, flashy pieces of jewelry. McCracken was most
intrigued, though, by the miniature warehouse-like buildings
selling ancient appliances. The incredibly high duties placed on
such merchandise by the Israeli government turned convenience
items like modern refrigerators and televisions into luxuries here.
These items were recycled over and over again to meet the demand for them, in spite of the fact that many looked antiquated
to the point of decay.

The buildings housing them were no different. Jaffa was a
city mired in its historical past, the ancient structures virtually
untouched by redevelopment or renewal. Torn and tattered awn-
ings flapped in the faint breeze. Windows peeked out from behind shutters more broken than whole. The buildings were
constructed mostly of stone, smoked gray or black through the
years. These aged structures had a dusty, heated scent that Mc-
Cracken found repellent.

A man easing a battered refrigerator from the back of his
truck forced Blaine to veer off the sidewalk onto the street.
Traffic was snarled, and all movements had been reduced to
maddening stops and starts, accompanied by a regular chorus
of horns. He passed an old man whose wares were laid out on
a blanket in what should have been the right-hand lane. The old
man was munching on a pita sandwich and barking to passersby
amidst mouthfuls.

The street and sidewalks grew more cluttered by the moment,
although more people seemed to be looking than buying. Mc-
Cracken eased by an Arab merchant operating from behind a
pushcart and slid between a pair of cars frozen in traffic. A
young man on a bicycle nearly collided with him, and Blaine
was forced up against a boy pulling a pair of used jeans on over
his gym shorts to check the fit while the salesman spit on in
Hebrew about the potential bargain.

The knickknack shop Fett had directed him to was located on
a corner at the southern edge of the market. Blaine dodged a
bunch of leather handbags dangling over the entrance and
stepped inside, delighted to be out of the sun. The smell of

leather replaced that of age in his nose. Blaine felt immediately better.

A young woman approached him in search of a sale.

"I believe you're holding something for me," he told her, and produced the Egyptian bill Fett had given him back in Reading as the signal.

"Right this way," the young woman said.

They moved to a door in the rear of the shop. She opened it for him and smiled. Blaine accepted the invitation and entered. There, seated behind a single desk in the cramped quarters, was an old crone, her gray hair tied up in a bun and her stooped frame draped in a baggy black dress.

"Close the door!" she ordered. After McCracken had done so, she said, "Sit! Now!"

There was only one chair available, that being right in front of the desk she was squeezed behind. All light in the room came through a single uncovered window, and it was more than enough for Blaine to size up the crone. He noticed that only one eye was regarding him. The other was shut and almost encased by layers of sun-wrinkled flesh. Her hands were not visible, and Blaine wondered if they might be holding a weapon on him even now.

"You know why you here?" the hag wanted to know after he was seated.

"Not really."

"You know!" she raged. "You had the bill!"

"Oh, I know what I'm doing here all right. But I'm not clear on why I'm not talking to Evira herself."

"Evira wants it this way."

"Do you know where they're holding my son?"

"I not speak of—"

"But Evira does, doesn't she?"

"I know only what she tells me, what she wants me to know. I here to explain as best I can. I know what Fett told you."

"Then we both know he told me nothing."

"He told you what he knew. Evira don't trust him. Evira trust no one but you. You only man who can stop weapon from being used."

"*What* weapon?"

"What you know of Yosef Rasin?" she asked him instead of answering.

"Fanatic from the Meir Kahane school, only a hundred times more fanatical. Hates all Arabs and encourages turmoil in the occupied zones. On one occasion he publicly demanded forced birth control for all Arabs living in Israel. I think castration was the word he used. Even so, his fanaticism has found a following. With half the government willing to concede a Palestinian state on the West Bank, there are plenty in this country who are starting to take his side because they've got nowhere else to go."

"What is 'his side'?"

"That Israel—and the world—would be better off if no Arab was left alive."

The hag looked at him with her one good eye. "Fett told you of weapon that can wipe out the whole Arab world?"

"Yes."

"Rasin has it."

And out of the madness of the past sixteen hours, Blaine saw sense starting to form. No wonder the Arabs were desperate. If they even suspected Rasin possessed such a weapon, they'd pull out all the stops.

"Wait a minute," Blaine said, following his own thoughts. "Why don't you just kill him? You wouldn't need me for that."

A sudden breeze flapped the curtain and blew through the half-open window. Straying strands of the crone's gray hair blew across her face. "Can't. Rasin gone. Disappeared underground with his weapon. Trail there but need you to follow it."

"Why can't Evira follow it herself?"

"I not know."

"I think you do. And I think we're gonna sit here until you tell me."

"Your son be no closer to safety as long as we do."

Blaine's anger flared. The deep scar that ran down his forehead through his left eyebrow turned milk white against the red flush of his face. His beard bristled. He leaned menacingly across the table.

"You know something, old woman? I believe that you don't know a thing about the boy. But I know Evira does since she set this whole thing up. So here's how we're going to play it: you contact her and set up a meeting between us or the deal's off. I won't lift a finger for you and your people, and I don't think Evira would be pleased with that after all she went through to recruit me."

"No," the hag acknowledged, "Evira wouldn't."

Blaine watched her as her left hand probed to the dead tissue around her left eye. The skin peeled back in her hand and took a hefty measure of the wrinkles on her cheek with it. The left hand continued to peel and tear while the right stripped off the gray wig to reveal a bun of dark black hair. She stared across the desk at Blaine with both eyes now, as the age of her face lay in strips on the table before them.

"Nice to meet you, Mr. McCracken," said Evira.

"Come in, Colonel Ben-Neser!"

From his position in a shabby apartment, overlooking the market from above a furniture store, Yuri Ben-Neser lifted the walkie-talkie to his lips. "Have you got her, Ari?"

"Yes," Ari told him. "Far edge of the market on the corner. Leather handbags hanging outside the entrance."

Ben-Neser moved to the window. "I can see it! I can see it!" he said thankfully, propping the walkie-talkie upon his shoulder so he could use his single arm to mop his brow. He'd lost the other in the Yom Kippur War of '73.

Ben-Neser had spent the last two years searching for the elusive Evira. He had heard all the stories, all the legends. Some said she had killed every agent who got even remotely close. Others claimed she had not once taken up arms within the state of Israel, that she was in fact an Israeli citizen. Another legend claimed she directed each and every terrorist attack that took place within the country. Ben-Neser preferred to accept the most secure intelligence on her, which had it that she was committed to organizing Israel's Arabs into a force that could someday take over the country from the inside. Even this conservative analysis stated that she had agents placed in every sphere of Israeli life, including the cabinet itself. For this reason, cabinet meetings of late had been held in absolute secrecy. Ben-Neser himself favored neither the views of Kahane, nor the far more radical position of Rasin. But the notion of a legion of Arabs and those loyal to them spying on the state from within was terrifying. It certainly justified for him the risk he was taking by conducting this unauthorized mission.

"She's meeting with someone, sir," Ari was saying.

Ben-Neser felt the phantom pain of his missing arm as he always did when he was nervous. If anything went wrong, the ramification would be catastrophic. He had to bring this off without a hitch.

"Recognize him?" he asked Ari.

"Big. Rugged with a beard. Looks American."

American? Ben-Neser wondered to himself. The last thing he needed here was just that sort of complication.

"Do we move in?" Ari asked.

"No," Ben-Neser said from his position by the window of the apartment, choking down the urge to rub the arm that was no longer there. "Where are you?"

"Shop featuring plumbing fixtures diagonally across the street from Evira."

"Hold your position. I'm coming down."

McCracken continued to gaze across the table at the woman whose age had shrunk by upwards of forty years. She returned his gawking stare with an admiring one of her own while she continued to pick at the stray patches of theatrical makeup stuck on her flesh.

"I'm sorry this was necessary," she said.

"And just what are you referring to, the disguise or the taking of my son?"

"Both, I guess. The boy's fine. Better than fine. He's safe."

"Safe from whom?"

"My enemies are now your enemies."

"Arab?"

"As well as Israeli. What we're facing here doesn't discriminate. You'll find we have extraordinarily few allies, perhaps just each other."

"Then how about you deliver Matthew back to Reading School to prove your good faith?"

She looked at him almost sadly. "I can't do that. You know I can't."

"Look, lady, the hag I was talking to a few minutes ago and Fett built a pretty good case. If this bit about Rasin and his weapon are true, then I'm on your side already."

"Like you were on the side of the French, of the British, even the Americans?" she shot back at him. "I know you better than you think. The side you start out on may not be the side you end up on, depending on the dictates of your conscience. You think I don't approve of those traits?" she added, more softly, voice laced with admiration. "They are precisely what persuaded me that you were the only one left for me to work with now that my own network has been compromised."

"Then you also know my word is my bond. Let the boy go. I'll work with you."

"I can't. I made promises, gave assurances. Can't you see that?"

"What I see every time I close my eyes is what a pair of killers did to John Neville."

"I don't condone the actions of butchers."

"But you used them, didn't you? Cut the bullshit, lady. If you're so fond of the way I operate, you must have figured out you're already working in a bigger ballgame."

She looked hurt. What little light reached her face told Blaine she was thirty at most and probably younger. Her features were more European than Arabic. She had skin that was soft and smooth, and high cheekbones that complemented an angular chin and large round eyes. Her complexion looked more tanned than naturally bronze.

"Let's get to the point, Evira," Blaine resumed. "Let's get to Rasin. How'd you find out about the existence of this super-weapon?"

"I've had agents planted within his group for sometime."

"Arabs?"

"Seventeen percent of Israel's citizens are Arabs, but they're Israelis first. This is their nation, too. And as their numbers have grown they have been accepted as part of the nation." She paused. "By most of the nation anyway. Rasin has seized upon the reality of their growing influence, along with the possible formation of a Palestinian state on the West Bank, and used them to spread his message of hate. His cause has fostered a dangerous, militant faction. He has become enamored of the power it has provided him. Fanaticism is a powerful voice, Blaine McCracken, one the Arabs of Israel find impossible to silence. He seeks to propel himself into power by creating a climate of fear fanatics thrive in. He has his hardcore followers, along with those afraid to oppose him.''

She leaned farther across the table. "Some months ago, he began holding meetings in secret. Representatives of his movement in Haifa, Jerusalem, Tel Aviv, and the settlements were all briefed on his discovery of a means to eliminate the Arab problem forever, to destroy the entire Arab world. An agent I planted within Rasin's camp was present at those briefings. He reported to me what he had heard. That was the last we heard from him. That was just about a month ago, near the time Rasin himself disappeared. He hasn't been seen since. That's what made me try to contact you."

"Destroy the Arab world," Blaine repeated. "Your contact's words or Rasin's?"

"Rasin's expoundings were bolder, yet vague. Perhaps obliterate would be a better word than destroy. Rasin didn't state it that way, but what else could we be facing?"

"How did he state it?"

"In shadows and riddles. The Arab peoples both nearest and farthest would be put down in a way that would make it impossible for them to ever rise up again."

"And yet here we have Israel sitting square in the center of all these Arab peoples. How can this weapon Rasin claims he has destroy one without the other?"

"His briefings were quite clear about this result. 'An oasis in the middle of the desert of destruction' were his exact words."

"Then we must be talking about some kind of selective destruction. What he seems to be talking about is a weapon that can't possibly exist."

"Only within the parameters our reason permits us to consider."

"Your reason, Evira, and your fight. I've read the files on you, and if there's any truth to them at all, then I've got to figure you're just as able to track Rasin down as I am."

She shrugged. "Perhaps. We'll never know for sure because I have my own target to pursue: Amir Hassani."

"An Ar—"

"Go ahead. Finish. You were about to say 'Arab,' weren't you?" She didn't let him answer. "Yes, I am an Arab, Mr. Blaine McCracken, but my birth place was annexed, which makes me an Israeli, too. My loyalty may be divided, but on both counts Hassani is as much my enemy as Rasin. He is against everything I stand for."

"And just what is that?"

"Peace. Does that surprise you?"

"Coming from a woman who kidnaps children to further her ends, frankly it does."

"Not just my ends, Mr. Blaine McCracken, the *world's* ends. What do you know of Hassani?"

"No more than anyone else, I suppose. He's a real enigma, installed as military strongman of a beaten and impoverished Iran in a coup after the war was finally settled with Iraq and Khomeini passed on to the nuthouse in the sky. He came back from exile, à la Khomeini, and promised to return national pride and prosperity to a country sorely lacking in both."

"And has he?"

"In the past six months things have gotten steadily worse. He woos the wealthy and powerful like the Shah did while giving limitless power to the Revolutionary Guard like Khomeini."

"And caught in the middle are the Iranian masses who mean nothing to him. But you left out one thing. Hassani has used his position to rally other militant Arab leaders, and he has convinced them that with the Iran-Iraq war no longer serving as a distraction, they can turn all their attention toward a common enemy."

"Israel," Blaine surmised.

"Of course. Hassani has brought together a collection of madmen who want nothing more than to see Israel destroyed and collectively are in possession of the means to assure it happens."

"Then we're facing two madmen, each of which is poised to destroy the world of the other."

"And they'll succeed unless we are successful in stopping them."

"Stop or kill?"

"One and the same."

Blaine shook his head mockingly. "This really isn't your game, is it? Why don't you just come out and say what you mean: you plan to kill Hassani while I kill Rasin."

Evira's eyes were cold. "Whatever is necessary."

"How did you learn so much about Hassani? You work in Israel, not Iran."

She just looked at him, and might have been about to speak when Blaine suddenly answered his own question.

"Unless . . . unless you found out about Hassani's plans through the agents you planted with Rasin. Of course!"

"You see what I mean now."

"What I see is an Israeli fanatic with a weapon he intends to use because of what a militant Iranian is planning. In Rasin's mind, what he's doing is self-defense, a preventive strike."

"But it cuts both ways," Evira explained. "Part of the reason why Hassani has been able at last to unite the various militant factions of the Arab world is the symbol Rasin and his rising popularity presents. His following is no longer limited or hidden away. It is thriving in Israel and it is powerful. Can you imagine the kind of concessions he'll demand, and the price Israel will be forced to pay, once he and his party capture enough seats in parliament for Rasin to become kingmaker? Hassani and the other madmen cannot wait to find out. They feel Israel must be destroyed before the tide becomes too strong to turn. . . ."

"Which, accordingly, provides Rasin with the perfect rationale to utilize his superweapon. My God, it's almost as if the Hassani and the others had played right into his hands."

"In any case he has the weapon and the justification to unleash it." Her eyes became pleading. "I couldn't trust anyone else, don't you see? Hassani's people have penetrated my organization, and Rasin's people are onto me. You were my only hope. Tell me you wouldn't have done the same thing if our positions were reversed!"

"I wouldn't. There's a code that must not have made it to

your part of the world yet. We don't involve family. We never involve family.''

"Our way of life is facing destruction. Israel's, too. I hate the militants as much as you do. I'm going to kill Hassani. I want him stopped as much as I want Rasin stopped. This is our only chance to beat down what both of them represent forever.''

"Only to do so you have to employ their methods, so you become no better than they are.'' Blaine paused and looked at her with eyes of ice. "Tell me how civilized you are, but first tell me what will happen if I get up from this table and walk away.''

Evira hesitated only slightly. "Your son will die.''

CHAPTER 7

COLONEL BEN-NESER STOOD NERVOUSLY IN THE OPEN WARE-house across from the gift shop. Shielded by porcelain fixtures, he gazed across the street, clenching and unclenching his remaining hand into a fist. Evira was barely thirty yards away from him. A quick dash across the street and he could take her himself. Screw the complications and get it over with.

Still, the American Evira was meeting with provided an unexpected complication. Bad enough the colonel should be about to initiate a wholly unsanctioned operation. But if an American, innocent or otherwise, should perish as a result the political fallout might be sufficient to cost Ben-Neser his career.

What little remained of it, that is. He had been born to be a soldier, not a bureaucrat. He came from a tradition of warriors and had proved himself worthy of that legacy as an infantryman in the Six-Day War of '67. Six years later the Yom Kippur engagement had seen him perform heroically in a leadership capacity until his tenure was ended prematurely. He was rounding up strays when a boy lunged out and tossed a grenade. While the attention of his men remained fixed on the escaping boy, Ben-Neser had focused on the grenade. Calculating instantly that the only hope his squad had of survival lay in his tossing it away from them, he had managed to lift and start to hurl the grenade when it detonated. The colonel's men were saved, but his arm was reduced to sinews sprouting from the shoulder joint.

The rehabilitation period had been long, and Ben-Neser resisted the use of prostheses and learned to live with a single arm. The best therapy was determination, and he focused all he had into becoming the best marksman in Israel. He learned how to steady the rifle with a single arm and could reload as quickly as any man with two. A decade's assignments had culminated in a single mistake—a civilian lunging in front of a bullet meant for a much wanted terrorist—and he was reassigned to Mossad as a field control officer, an overseer of other people's work. With each report, he found himself contemplating not how the operation had been done, but how he would have done it himself. The frustration mounted.

It spilled over when the first hard reports on Evira began to cross his desk. He maneuvered to get himself appointed as head of the team gathering intelligence on her and then became obsessed with putting an end to her shadowy and elusive movements within Israel. In these past two years he had considered nothing else, and when at last a report linked her to a booth in the Jaffa Market, Ben-Neser elected to hold on to the memo and deal with it himself. The commandos with him knew no better. He was their control, after all, and they saw no reason to doubt this sudden change in plans.

"Come in, Colonel," a voice squawked over his walkie-talkie.

"I read you, Ari."

"All men are in position. Ready to move on your signal."

Ben-Neser reviewed for himself the final deployments he had decided on once Evira's position was confirmed. Besides himself and Ari, he had a detachment of six commandos at his disposal. Of these, two had been placed upon the flat roof of the long angular building that housed Ben-Neser's location along with a dozen other sidewalk shops. One had been stationed around the corner from the target shop on the chance Evira might manage to flee in that direction. The remaining three were all planted among the locals: one seated before a blanket crammed with cheap watches, a second in apron selling food from a heated pushcart, and a third looking like an eager patron who had yet to purchase a thing.

The phantom pain scratched at Ben-Neser again. Had he already passed the point of no return, or was there still time to abort? No matter the results here today, he knew the ramifications so far as his future was concerned. But he was approaching the end of his run anyway and desperately wanted to take something with him, something beyond the anonymity of the kills he had made over the decade he had served as a marksman.

Ben-Neser turned his walkie-talkie to the channel that connected him with his commandos. "We move on my signal. Get ready. No shooting unless absolutely necessary. Clear? I want her taken alive. That's the first priority." He gazed across the street one last time. With the itch of a no-longer-existent arm driving him to shudders, Ben-Neser spoke again. "Thirty seconds, people. On my mark . . ."

"You don't have a choice and neither do I," Evira was saying.

McCracken glared at her from across the table. "Do you really expect to be able to reach Hassani? You're talking about a man who is almost never seen and about whom virtually nothing is known."

"Some is known. Enough. The underground movement in Tehran is small but well focused. They will help me."

"Killing him will almost certainly mean your own death."

She returned his emotionless stare. "Would you not do the same thing if in my position?"

"I'm still not quite clear on what that position is."

"I'm an Arab and so is Hassani. Is that it?"

"Not at all."

"It is in enough ways, Blaine McCracken, and you know it. Yes, I am an Arab, and no one wants to see a Palestinian homeland more than me. I've worked most of my life toward that end." Her voice thickened. "When the soldiers came and— Well, that doesn't matter now. Hassani speaks to my people in a language of death and violence. He preaches, lives it. Accept that dogma and even with a homeland there can never be peace. Palestinians must get what they deserve, but men like Hassani will never give it to us. To them, we're just tools for them to use for their own ends."

"Except there's also Yosef Rasin," McCracken told her. "Hassani can kill your dream from one side, Rasin from the other. A pair of fanatics from opposite directions aiming toward the same goal.''

"You will find him. You will stop him.''

Blaine almost laughed. "You overestimate me.''

"No,'' Evira retorted immediately. "I have followed your career, studied it. You are driven by ideals and nothing stops you when they are at stake. I . . . emulate that. I have since the beginning. I obtained all your files. I've read everything Israeli and Egyptian intelligence has to say about you.''

"Lies and exaggerations mostly.''

"For the sake of your son, let's hope not.''

When his count had reached five, Colonel Ben-Neser saw a pair of jeeps crowded with Israeli soldiers pull over to the side of Oley Tsiyon where the flea market splintered to the left down an alley.

"Hold your positions!'' he ordered his men. Since this mission was not logged, the area had not been sealed. The army had no idea what was going on. "Ari, come in,'' he barked into his walkie-talkie.

"I read you, sir.''

"Do you see them?''

"Routine patrol.''

"It wasn't scheduled, damn it! I checked the logs.''

"They're here, Commander. Our only choice is to abort.''

"No! We can't. We'll lose Evira if we do, maybe forever!''

"What then?''

Ben-Neser watched the soldiers climbing from their jeeps and stretching leisurely as they adjusted their automatic rifles to be within easy reach if needed.

"Approach them,'' the colonel ordered Ari. "Approach them and identify yourself. Do it quietly. Don't let anyone else realize what is going on. Tell them to get the fuck out.''

"They're soldiers. They might question.''

"Not Mossad, they won't question Mossad.'' Ben-Neser swung his binoculars quickly back toward the the gift shop. "Go to them, Ari. Do as I say.''

Seconds later, Ari's shape appeared from a centrally placed jewelry shop. He made his way down the crowded sidewalk in the direction of the soldiers who had only just begun to move away from their jeeps. He approached the officer wearing the beret of the team leader. Ari was all smiles, like a tourist might be, his shirt untucked, his walk loose-limbed. Ben-Neser could see they were a yard apart, Ari identifying himself and the officer seeming to heed him. A hand raised by the bereted leader into the air held up the progress of his team into the square.

That's it, damn it, that's it!

The bereted officer started to turn. Ben-Neser had actually relaxed, when the officer swung round and leveled into a combat stance with rifle angling straight for Ari. The brief reports sounded like hammers striking nails and Ari's body was tossed backward, blood spouting from the punctures in his chest.

"My God," was all Ben-Neser could mutter. In his hand he felt the sweat-soaked plastic of his walkie-talkie. Somewhere in his mind he recorded the sight of the men who could not have been soldiers at all fanning out through the crowded square that was suddenly bursting with panic. In that instant he forgot totally about Evira, thought only of Ari, a friend and soldier, who lay dead because of him and his damned obsession.

The walkie-talkie was at his lips now. He heard himself speaking into it, forming the words in the last instant before they emerged.

"They're not soldiers! Take them!" he ordered.

"Shots!" Blaine shouted, lunging from his chair.

"Wait!" Evira responded, hand feeling for one of the pistols in a drawer that had been open through the course of their conversation. "Take this."

She was by his side when they re-entered the store, pressing a gun into his hand. Panicked bystanders rushed by outside, colliding with displays that had been set up on the sidewalk. Blaine and Evira stayed pinned behind the doorway and peered out. Beyond, all was chaos. A small group of gunmen dressed as merchants were firing upon two jeeploads of uniformed soldiers. The soldiers' bullets cut indiscriminate lines through the crowd, their fire slowed only when sniper bullets rained on them from the roof of the building across the street.

"Yours?" Blaine asked.

"No! I don't know who they are! I swear it! Let's get out of here!"

Pistols in hand they ducked out the doorway to be swept away by the crowd rushing from the area.

Colonel Ben-Neser wasn't thinking anymore, simply watching and reacting. He had drawn his pistol and rushed from the cover of the warehouse onto the sidewalk. He had seen at least three of the enemy's number fall to the fire of his riflemen on the roof. But the fake soldiers had retreated behind the cover of their jeeps and were concentrating their fire upward in an incessant hail. After Ari, he had watched his aproned commando fall to a second barrage that commenced as soon as Ben-Neser had given the order to move in. He felt himself struck each time a bullet found one of his men. This was his fault, damn it, *his* fault!

Above him, one of the marksmen found a clear bead on another of the soldiers, but the others honed savagely in on his position and blasted away. The man was pitched backward while the second marksman seized what he thought would be the advantage and showed himself long enough to aim. But the soldiers' fire never let up. Bullets punched into the second man and sent his body headlong from the roof on to the street a dozen yards in front of Ben-Neser.

"Bastards," he moaned.

The surge of the crowd reached him then and Ben-Neser was tossed about like a puppet in their midst. A hard smack to his arm tore the pistol from his grip and he lowered himself to feel for it amidst the sea of thrashing feet.

The drop was what saved his life.

The fake soldiers had turned to spray the crowd. The butchers! Of course, with the marksmen neutralized the only shots aimed their way were coming from figures disguised within the crowd. So they had taken the most obvious, and most barbaric, action. They must have come to protect Evira, he theorized with a guilty chill. And he had handed his team to them on a silver platter by having Ari approach.

Bodies toppled over him while more of the panicked crowd struggled to flee. Two of his remaining men posted in the square,

meanwhile, saw the direction the fake soldiers' firings were taking. To save whatever lives they could, they broke off from the
crowd and rushed into the center of the square to draw the bullets to themselves.

Ben-Neser saw this just as he recovered his pistol and pushed
himself on his elbows over a pair of fallen tourists, both near
death. He fired a full clip in the time it took the imposters to cut
down these two men and a third who had circled in from around
the corner, leaving him as the last.

"You fuckers!" Ben-Neser screamed as he lurched to his feet
with a fresh clip snapped home. He was charging now, charging
through the remnants of the crowd with pistol burning in his
hand.

He felt the hot gush of pain to his armless shoulder, and for
that instant he was back in the West Bank the day he had lost
the limb. The phantom itching was replaced by the same fiery
agony he had felt when the grenade blew into him, and once
again he was melting into nothingness, this time with nothing
to pull him out.

Evira and Blaine's original aim had been to swing left outside
the shop and rush away amidst the chaos. But their turn had
brought them almost face-to-face with a pistol-wielding man
shoving his way toward them.

"Mossad!" Evira screamed, and instantly they swung around
to head toward the center of the chaos that had overrun the
market.

The flow of panic was moving in all directions and they let
themselves be swept up in it. The street was cluttered with wares
abandoned by peddlers to the fate of the crowd, some of whom
still managed to stoop to retrieve attractive items on their way.
Maneuverability was cut further by the dozens of cars immobi-
lized on the street. Windows and windshields had been punctured by bullets and most of the drivers huddled beneath their
dashboards for dear life.

When the soldiers turned their fire suddenly and inexplicably
into the crowd, Blaine and Evira dove to the sidewalk together.

"What the hell is this?" Blaine raged, grasping the Beretta
Evira had provided.

"They're not soldiers!"

"Obviously. But who then? *Who?*"

"I don't know! I don't know!"

Bullets continued to cascade above them while behind them the Mossad man they'd fled from was rushing the gunmen head on, pistol clacking futilely. He was blown backward at the same time a screech rang out from across the street.

"You fuckers!"

A one-armed man was charging straight for the remaining trio of soldiers. He had managed six shots before a bullet toppled him. The fall separated him from his gun, and somehow he had the composure to crawl for it as the uniformed figures spun from their positions of cover to finish him off.

"Come on!" Evira urged, tugging on McCracken's arm. "We can get out of here now!"

"Not yet," was all Blaine said as he pulled away and crawled stealthily toward the street.

Colonel Yuri Ben-Neser knew he was dead. It came to him in slow motion as the trio of uniformed shapes swarmed his way with rifles angled down. He wouldn't close his eyes, wouldn't let them linger over the kill or enjoy it. The pistol was just out of his grasp and he shoved himself toward it, pain exploding in his shoulder with each push over the stones.

His fingers had just struck the pistol's sweat-soaked butt when his eyes caught the blur of a shape rising directly before him and just to one side of the uniformed figures.

He's not one of mine, was Ben-Neser's only thought, as the man steadied his pistol and opened fire on the trio of fake soldiers. They tried to return it, but the man was in motion by then; twisting, diving, rolling, all the time shooting.

His bullets seemed to jolt the fake soldiers all at once, almost simultaneously. He kept firing until they crumpled over, not more than a shot or two having missed the mark.

Ben-Neser thought surely he was dreaming, or perhaps a guardian angel had been sent down to save him. No man could shoot like that. Yet it was a man who leaned over him and touched his pulse.

"You'll be all right," came a voice attached to the shape, and Ben-Neser passed out before he had the chance to say how very much he doubted that.

CHAPTER 8

THE ROOM EVIRA LED THEM TO WAS LOCATED IN A BLOCK OF apartment units close enough to the flea market to hear the constant blare of sirens arriving on the scene. The room was sparsely furnished with a pair of stained fabric chairs and a single day bed. There was a refrigerator, a stove, a small kitchen table, and a sink. The bathroom facilities in the building were limited to two per floor, one for each gender.

Evira locked the door behind them.

"We have little time," she began. "I am due to leave shortly. For Tehran. For Hassani."

Evira sat down in the chair closest to the window. Blaine took the stained, rust-colored one across from her. At one time, he supposed, the fabric had probably matched, but now one chair was sun-bleached while the other retained a measure of its original color.

"If Mossad's on to you, lady," he told her, "you'll be lucky to see the outside of this country again."

She shrugged. "It's not Mossad I'm worried about as much as Rasin. Those fake soldiers must have been sent by him. His penetration of my organization extends even deeper than I thought."

"What are you talking about?"

"He found me through you."

"Then you've got a double-edged problem: Mossad and Rasin. That makes them my problem, too."

"Yes, but the chaos in the square will take time to sort out. That will give us the hours we need."

"You maybe, but what about me? If that one-armed man didn't recognize me on sight, it won't take him long to pull my face out of an Identikit. I'm in lots of files over here. You've read most of them, remember?"

"I'll tell you what you need to know. You'll have to move fast."

"Sorry, lady, it's not that simple. See, this wasn't part of the deal. The Israelis catch me and my son is fucked. . . ."

"You'll be out of the country before they start to look."

"You didn't let me finish. You just admitted that the penetration of your network goes deeper than you think. How deep? All the way down to Fett, you think? You did say they found you through me. Think about it. What if Fett was working for Rasin? What if he set this whole thing up just to flush you out for the man himself?"

She looked at him, didn't protest.

"Then it would be Rasin holding my son's life, not you."

She thought quickly. "Fett still has the boy. I know where. I'll make arrangements. He'll be safe. I promise."

"And that's supposed to mean something to me? If you don't have the kid, I've got no reason to do business with you."

"Except you know that even if you're right I'm the only one who can help you get him back. I've learned to trust no one, just as you have. Fett doesn't know I've kept tabs on his movements. I can get the boy away from him. You *must* believe that."

"I do believe you'll try, but that's not worth much with that pair of murderous women running around, possibly working for Rasin. So here's how we're going to play it. I'm gonna send a message to an old friend of mine back in the States, briefing him on what's gone down. If anything happens to me, and the boy doesn't end up back in Reading, he'll come after you, *all* of you. That's a fate I wouldn't wish on my worst enemy, but I'd wish it on the kidnappers of children."

"He's that good?"

"Lady, he makes me look like a green recruit."

She nodded, forming fresh thoughts even then. "Would he have risked everything to save the one-armed man just as you did?"

"Would've used less bullets to get it done, too."

"It was a stupid move, you know. You could have been killed. What of your son then?"

"Frankly, it didn't cross my mind. There was a man out there who was about to get butchered. In the context of the moment, that was all that mattered."

"I've heard that about you," she commented reflectively. "But to see it, to see you . . ."

"Save the praise. It's what I am, what I do. Hell, you're the one who had to have me working on this with you. You know my philosophy. Saving an individual life is as important to me as saving a million."

"I know that. What I don't know is why."

Blaine started to smile, then stopped. "Matt asked a lot of the same questions yesterday. I didn't tell him the whole truth about what his daddy did in the war. I gave him the standard Phoenix Project story and conveniently left out the fact that plenty of the people we killed didn't deserve to die. Just innocent victims who happened to be in the wrong place when our bombs went off or our assassination squads hit. What did we care? Our philosophy was win at any cost, and if the whole war had been fought that way we might have won it. I got caught up in it but I wasn't there all that long, and when I came out I swore I'd never take another innocent life again." Blaine's eyes became cold. "Which is why I'll work with you but you'll never get my respect. You broke a cardinal rule when you nabbed the boy, you broke the *only* rule."

She leaned forward abruptly in her chair. "Would you like to hear about point of view, Mr. Blaine McCracken, about perspective? Before the '73 war I lived in one of the finest houses in the West Bank. My father was a businessman and local leader. We had nothing against the Israelis. We co-existed peacefully without incident. Even when the war came, we did not take sides. My brothers rotated constant shifts to bring the Israeli soldiers nearest us additional water and fruit.

"But when victory came, more soldiers, or maybe they were

the same ones my brothers had brought food to, came to our house with an order from the government to seize our property. We were thrust out into the streets, first to a tent in what had become the occupied zone. From the tent we could look out and see the grand house where we had tried to live in harmony with our neighbors.''

''So you hate the Israelis for what they did. Is that what your crusade has been all about?''

''At first, I suppose, it was. I left my family at eighteen and went into Lebanon, to one of the terrorist training camps. I was filled not so much with hate as a desperate desire to act, against what I did not know. I guess my original aim was violence, but that changed. You see my father was still a politician, a diplomat. He still had Israeli contacts and he did his best in those early years to negotiate on behalf of the vast displaced peoples. Factions resulted. The militants saw him as a collaborator. He was beaten almost to death and forced to flee. And you know what the worst of it was? It was my brothers who turned him in. . . .''

McCracken scowled in disgust.

''You assumed I hate the Israelis, Blaine McCracken. Perhaps I do. But I hate the Palestinians for the same reason. These past years of bloodshed in the occupied zones have only reinforced my hatred of the entire system, along with the response of others to it. Guns are not the answer; that much has been shown already. Peace can be achieved only from the inside out, organizing the Arab voice within Israel into an assertive, powerful one in a way that makes Jewish citizens understand and accept us without resenting us. The radicals accuse me of choosing means that will take too long to achieve anything. But the violence has raged for two thousand years and where has that gotten us?

''I have the skills of a terrorist, yes, but I vowed never to use them except in defense of my own life, for otherwise I would be reduced to the level I hated the most.''

''But something changed your mind. You've decided to go after Hassani with those very skills you denounced.''

She looked at him more closely. ''I had no choice in any of the actions I authorized. We made overtures toward you a month ago. When you resisted out contacts, I turned to Fett, who discovered the existence of your son through an informant in Dejourner's network."

"Fine. So let me get to work so the boy can be returned. Where do I start my search for Rasin?"

Evira leaned back again and the sunlight caught her dark, vibrant features. She looked suddenly young to him, even innocent, long hair framing a face that in that moment might have been a schoolgirl's.

"There is a man named Moshe Traymir," she told him, "a soldier who was part of the Lebanon refugee camp massacres. He was stripped of rank and court-martialed in disgrace, but he became one of Rasin's bodyguards. My people saw them leaving the country by plane on several occasions. If anyone knows where Rasin can be found, it is Traymir."

"Where can I find him?"

"He's taken a most fitting job. He is an animal keeper at the Safari Park in Ramat Gan."

Colonel Yuri Ben-Neser walked slowly down the Tayelet on his way to Atarim Square. His left shoulder was bandaged and wrapped, and to his dismay the phantom itching intensified with the coming of this fresh wound. It was only ten hours earlier that his planned taking of Evira had ended in disaster. Ben-Neser had responded as the soldier in him dictated. From the hospital, he had reported everything, confessed everything, through proper channels. Disgrace was certain now, perhaps even imprisonment. Yet that prospect did not weigh as heavily on the colonel as the fate of his team did. Six had died in the square and a seventh was not expected to live through the night.

Atarim Square contains a cluster of open-air cafes, restaurants, and snack bars, each featuring a different menu, design, and atmosphere. Lying between the Carlton and Mariah hotels just above the shores of the Mediterranean, it is normally reached by way of the HaYarkon Street. But Ben-Neser came by way of the Tayelet's long stretch of asphalt promenade because the sounds of the sea just below calmed him. Compared to its vastness and power, he was nothing, and what had happened in Jaffa today was also nothing.

Mossad, of course, thought otherwise. The founder of Mos-

sad had been named Isser, and since then all of his successors
had taken the same name. Unlike their counterparts in other
intelligence services, heads of Mossad took a direct interest and
involvement in the affairs of their organization. It was not a
political or bureaucratic appointment. They were all field men
first and brought that perspective to the job. Ben-Neser hoped
that would work for him. That was his only hope.

He found Isser waiting for him just as planned, in Atarim
Square beneath the blue-canopied table in the largest of cafes.
It was not isolated, but the tables immediately around it were
unoccupied. Isser was sipping what could have been either a
weak drink or club soda. As he approached, Ben-Neser felt his
heart quicken and breath become short.

Isser was a short, barrel-chested man with menacing blue
eyes. His hair was strangely thick on the sides but thinning on
top. His bulging forearms rested atop the table, a manila folder
pinned beneath one. He did not acknowledge Ben-Neser's approach until the one-armed man was right before him.

"Sit down, Yuri."

Ben-Neser did so stiffly. Every speech he had rehearsed fluttered out of his mind, and he simply gulped down some air.

"You are probably wondering why I asked to meet with you
personally."

Ben-Neser gulped more air.

"There will be no inquiry on this, Yuri, no formal hearing.
It must remain between just you and me. Is that clear?"

Ben-Neser nodded. He felt a small hope rising in him.

"I have read the report on this afternoon's affair. I will not
dwell on what you have done. You understand the impropriety
of your actions, as well as the ramifications. But there are other
matters involved here that are more pressing now."

Ben-Neser eyed the head of Mossad as he slid an eight-by-ten
photograph from the manila folder that had been beneath his
forearm.

"Is this the man who saved your life, the one your men had
spotted with Evira previous to that?"

Ben-Neser focused in the dim light on the half-smiling
bearded face and recognized it instantly.

"Yes, but how did you—"

"This man was identified entering the country earlier today on an El Al jet out of London. He is a former American operative who in years past worked extremely closely with us on a number of affairs."

"Former?"

"Details unimportant at this time. His name is at the bottom of the photograph."

Ben-Neser scanned down and read it aloud. "Blaine Mc-Cracken . . ."

"You sound as if you know him, Yuri."

"I thought I recognized him. Yes, I should have remembered immediately. I worked with him in '73. I was attached to his unit for a stretch of the Yom Kippur War."

"Yes," Isser droned ironically, "he is a hero to our country in every sense of the word."

"Then what was he doing in the company of the most wanted Arab operative at large in Israel?"

"Interesting question."

"You didn't dwell on his past. Is it possible that he's turned?"

"You worked with him, Yuri. What do you think?"

"I worked with him, Isser. I don't know him. I remember him being single-minded, ruthless, accustomed to getting what he wants. If he was meeting with Evira, he had his reasons."

"An obvious conclusion," Isser commented, easing his drink to the side. The limes in the glass were starting to sink past the melting ice toward the bottom. "Expand on it."

"I . . . can't. There's too much I don't know."

"Let me help you, then. What were your conclusions about the 'soldiers' your men encountered in the square."

"Imposters there to protect Evira, perhaps dispatched when our presence was betrayed."

"They were all Israelis, Yuri," Isser said flatly. "All dismissed or suspended for some breech of discipline, outcasts perhaps, but Israelis nonetheless."

"What? This is madness! Israelis killing Israelis? It makes no sense."

"Let us take it a step further. If they did belong to Evira, why would Blaine McCracken, the man she was meeting with, risk his life to save you during the battle?"

"But if they weren't Evira's, then who were they?"

"That is the crux of our quandary, Colonel."

"My God, they must have been sent by someone else to take care of Evira in a much cruder way than we had planned. But who, Isser, who?"

"Someone with access to such men, Yuri. Someone in our own government. A shadow army, a shadow movement, who for some reason made it their business to go after Evira. We cannot afford to have this possibility spread any farther than it has already." Isser's voice hardened as the bands of muscle through his forearms seemed to throb. "That makes you a liability to us, a liability we cannot permit anyone else to gain access to before we have sorted this out. I am forced to reassign you, Colonel, out of necessity as much as punishment. . . ."

And as Isser continued Ben-Neser found himself wishing Blaine McCracken hadn't bothered to save him in the first place.

Thursday night had given way to the early hours of Friday morning when Moshe Traymir came on duty at the Safari Park and Zoological Center in the Ramat Gan sector of Tel Aviv. His apartment was only a few blocks from the zoo and, as on most nights, he was slightly drunk when he arrived. Drinking was how he coped with his disgrace in the wake of the Beirut massacres. Traymir sat through the token trials and seethed. Not that he wasn't guilty; he was. But he and the others were scapegoats, and there wasn't anything they could do or say about it. Traymir had kept his mouth shut and been spared imprisonment as a result. This alternative seemed only the slightly better of two evils, until he was approached and recruited by a man with need of services Traymir was well versed in providing.

As usual, his steps toward the front entrance of the park were lumbering and labored. It was strange for a man who hated animals to be working at Tel Aviv's Zoological Center, but the hours suited him well. The hard muscle of his soldier days had been replaced by fat over his large, big-boned frame. His heavy beard was grubby and untrimmed. He seldom bathed. Traymir cared about none of this. He cared only about doing whatever was necessary to rid Israel of the Arabs who were destroying her.

Traymir whistled softly to himself as he started his rounds. The Zoological Center was unique for the many hundreds of animals in dozens of species which roamed free about the grounds, forming territories and respecting those of others. Traymir hated them all because all of them appeared to hate him. Many of the animals had got used to the other guards, even formed a kinship with them. But they refused to so much as approach Traymir. Most of the animals were sleeping now, but the long-necked ostriches were still prowling about and he could see a number of zebras munching on the grass under the moon as he passed them. He could never tell whether the rhinos and hippos were sleeping or not, big stupid beasts that they were. Traymir had once tossed stones at a rhino to see how many had to hit it before the beast would bother to move.

He belched and continued drunkenly to follow the sweeping road that cut through the first half of the safari park en route to the more traditional zoo. Despite his drunkenness, he began to sense that something was amiss. It wasn't so much what he saw, as what he didn't see. Not a single other guard was making his rounds. They should have been easily visible under the full moon. Strange. In spite himself, he grasped for his walkie-talkie.

"Yo, anybody home?"

Silence.

"This is Traymir. Anyone read me?"

Static.

He was beginning to wonder what was up when one of the security-handler four-door jeeps caught his eye. One of its back doors was partially open. He approached warily.

"Hello?" he called. "Anybody there?"

Traymir had just reached down for the open door's handle when the sound of footsteps rushing at him forced a turn. His eyes had time only to regard a heavy hand surging forward. There was a burst of pain to his chest and then a numbing over his head as he slumped. He was never sure if he lost total consciousness or not, only that the assailant had shoved him into the backseat. Next he felt a splash and something thick and warm oozed over him, almost making him gag. Through the daze, he heard himself moan. Next he felt the jeep moving and struggled to lift himself from semiconsciousness, but his head ached and his breaths hurt him.

Inside of a minute later, he had come alert enough to realize the huge steel gate mechanically sliding open before them belonged to the high-fenced home of the lions.

"Hey," Traymir muttered.

But by then the driver had already passed through. The first gate started its slide back across and as soon as it locked home a second gate before them opened. The double gate system assured against the possibility of the lions wandering off when someone drove into their territory. Suddenly Traymir felt scared. The thick ooze coated his clothes and face. He wiped it away and his fingers came away smeared with something that felt and smelled like blood.

"Hey!" Louder.

The driver passed through the second gate and Traymir heard it clang closed behind them. Since the jeep was sometimes used to transport animals, a steel grating separated the front seat from the back, and the door locks were controlled from the front as well.

"Who are you? What do you want?" he demanded, trying to sound brave.

"I think I'd better do the asking, Traymir," the driver answered, and slid the Jeep to a halt. "It's your own time we're wasting. I'm here about Yosef Rasin. I want to know where I can find him."

Traymir stiffened as bravely as he could manage. As of yet he could see none of the lions, but in the darkness shapes stirred and he thought he heard a soft, rumbling growl.

"You are from the government. I should have known. Go ahead, shoot me. I won't talk."

McCracken didn't show him a gun. "Sorry to disappoint you, Traymir. It really would be easier for you if you told me where I could find Rasin."

The lions appeared out of nowhere, a half dozen at first with at least that many stalking behind them. They circled the jeep as if it were an animal they had chosen for a kill. Traymir's eyes darted fearfully from them back at the stone-faced bearded man in the front seat.

"What did you—"

"Toss on you? Deer's blood, Traymir. I'm told the scent of it drives lions crazy. Really whets their appetite."

Blaine eased his hand to the power window switch and slid the rear right window down ever so slightly. Immediately the lions' growls turned to roars. Their faces twisted angrily and a pair of females rose to stick their forepaws toward the cracked window.

"You've got a well stocked infirmary here, Traymir. I found your supply of deer's blood there after I incapacitated your five fellow guards. Feel like talking yet?"

Traymir shrunk away. He bit his lip.

McCracken slid the window down further to allow one of the lionness's paws to push all the way through.

"No!" Traymir begged, shoulders pressed against the opposite door and window now.

"Funny thing," Blaine went on. "Nobody's fed them yet tonight. They're not in the best of moods. Hate to see what they would do to a man who tasted like a deer."

"Please, anything! Just ask!" Traymir crimped down in his seat, maneuvering himself as far from the open window as possible.

"You work for Rasin. Yes or no?"

"Yes! Since my court-martial."

"Your role?"

"Bodyguard and nothing more. When he traveled mostly."

"Traveled where?"

Traymir hesitated.

McCracken slid down the window enough for a second lionness to stick both her paws through, steady herself with one, and swipe inside the cab with the other, snarling as she did. Meanwhile, a male leaped atop the roof and clawed at the other window with alternating paws. Traymir reeled into the center of his seat, besieged from both sides now.

"Japan!" Traymir screeched at last. "But that was a year ago. . . ."

"Why did he go there?"

"To meet with a man known as the Bujin!" Traymir screamed

over the roaring of the lions, arms tucked against himself to make as small a target as possible.

Bujin was Japanese for *warrior*, and Blaine had heard of the man before. A profiteer, information broker, and arms dealer. A dabbler in many things who had become one of the most pursued men in all of Japan. The Bujin was wanted by government and police authorities along with forces within the Japanese mafia, whom he had apparently dishonored at some point.

"What did Rasin seek the Bujin out for?"

"I don't know. I swear it. They met in private. I merely drove Rasin there and waited with a team of others outside."

"Where did they meet?"

And when Traymir hesitated again, the driver's side rear window was lowered enough to match the one on the passenger side. The female lions were tearing at the remaining glass on the right with both claws and teeth, while the male on the roof was working on the left. Traymir heard both panes crack and watched them being stripped away piece by piece.

"Drive out! Please!"

"Talk!"

"Outside Tokyo!" Traymir screamed at him. "A building in the woods. Well guarded. We never saw the guards but they were there."

"The address!"

Traymir provided it.

"What else?"

One of the lionnesses had managed to wedge her upper torso inside the cab. Traymir lurched away from her flailing claws and felt those of the male on the other side graze his shoulder.

"Nothing more!"

"What else?"

"*Nothing!* Do you think I wouldn't tell you? Please get me out of here!"

Satisfied, Blaine put the jeep into drive and eased it forward slowly enough to allow the lions to extract themselves from the cab. The females scratched at the fender, charging along with him as he slid away, and the male jumped from the roof with a thud. They followed for a time but had given up the chase by the time the jeep reached the double-gated exit route three hundred yards beyond.

"You really have a way with animals, Traymir," Blaine said to the shrivelled hunk cowering in the backseat.

CHAPTER 9

THE BUS HEADING FOR SOUTH TEHRAN HAD BEEN PACKED ALL the way from the airport. Evira had boarded early enough to gain a cherished window seat two-thirds of the way back. The old man who had grabbed the seat next to her had drifted quickly off to sleep and been snoring for most of the journey.

Naziabad had once been a factory district that had now evolved into a slum for Tehran's poor and forgotten. The outcasts in a city that had become outcast itself, first during the war with Iraq, and now even more so as Iran paid the price for a war that had drained the economy dry. Buildings crumbled and were looted. Few windows remained whole and few families remained in their own homes. Men lived alone or in small groups, sleeping in doorways. The air smelled of crumbling brick and dust, but even this was welcome after the stifling bus ride from just outside Mehrabad Airport where Evira had landed only two hours before.

For her, travel within the Arab countries was not a problem. Over the years she had built up a string of identities and passports which listed her as a citizen of each, thus permitting effortless passage between them. After parting with McCracken, she had made her way to Cairo and boarded an Iran Air jet bound for Tehran early Friday morning.

Evira was breathing hard when the bus came to its last stop in Naziabad. She did not fancy herself a killer but nonetheless was fully committed to assassinating General Amir Hassani. Joined together at last against Israel, the militants he had rallied around him represented a force that could destabilize the entire region beyond repair.

Hassani himself was an enigma. A Revolutionary Guardsman who rose to general in the last months of the war, he vanished during the cease-fire and was not heard from through much of the peace talks. He reappeared only after Khomeini's death when the Revolutionary Guard summoned him from exile following the failed attempts by several of the Ayahtolla's successors to re-unify the country. His stated commitment to rebuild Iran started not surprisingly with the military at the sacrifice of the lower classes. Beyond the military, he wooed the rich and powerful and attempted to solidify his own power by appealing to the mullahs as well.

But Hassani's ambitions stretched far beyond Iran. His goal was the unification of Arab radicals all over the Mideast for the ultimate destruction of Israel. And in spite of this he was still only the second most dangerous man in the world. McCracken would stop the first while Evira put an end to Hassani's reign. She hated herself for what she had done to force McCracken to help her, yet even now could see no other alternative.

Her thoughts rekindled memories of her own family. Since setting forth on the life she saw as her destiny, she had not once seen her brothers. The one in his twenties had become a guerrilla fighter in Lebanon. Of the two still in their teens, one had been killed by Israeli soldiers during the uprisings in the occupied zone. Of the other, she knew nothing. Often she had been tempted to venture into the West Bank and seek out the remnants of her family, but with so heavy a presence of soldiers, the risks were too great. If the Israelis had managed to pin down her background, all her family members would be under constant watch on the chance she would someday show her face in the area. So she stayed on the move and took up residence under their very noses, mixing with their people, wishing that they would see that they were more alike than different, as she did.

Help for her in Tehran would come from the growing Iranian underground, made up of the thousands who had become fed up with Khomeini even before the close of the war. But Hassani presented them with an even clearer symbol to rally against. His policies had forced thousands upon thousands into a life in the streets, made beggars by the priorities the general had set for the country. Unorganized, the disenchanted lingered in the murkiness of fear and discontent beneath the shadow of Hassani's murderous and power-crazed Revolutionary Guardsmen.

Evira had been able to place an agent within one of the burgeoning underground cells and contact had been initiated on several occasions. They had agreed to help her get close to Hassani and offered to aid her in any way they could. Evira relayed the message that a weapon would be required. As for an escape route, well, she was not unrealistic in appraising the likelihood of this for herself.

Though it was midday, the streets of Tehran's Naziabad district were virtually deserted. Where shops, restaurants, and stores had once been there were boarded-up windows and chained doors. Sidewalk vendors had disappeared. In the streets there were not even any Revolutionary Guardsmen to be seen, only urchins and beggars foraging among the trash cans and fighting one another for scraps of food. All the same, Evira kept her head down to avoid being noticed. She had changed into the garb of a poor Iranian woman at the airport, but close inspection of her features or even the meager belongings she toted in a small satchel could reveal the ruse.

The building she was heading for was a plastics factory that had only in the past six months been closed down by Hassani. Its size and location made it the perfect place for this particular cell to hold meetings. She ducked down a bordering side street and climbed a steep set of steps to a hidden entrance. As promised, the lock on the door was not fastened all the way and needed only to be yanked on to give way. Evira threw back the hasp and shoved her shoulder against the heavy door. It creaked open and she entered, expecting to be met almost immediately by a member of the cell.

But there was no one. She pushed on warily. In months past this floor had contained offices; the factory itself was contained in the basement. The corridor had already turned dusty and decrepit. Tattered bedrolls lay here and there as testament to the homeless who had never returned to claim them.

Up ahead, a slightly open door grabbed her eye. Still, she heard and saw no one. Something was wrong. If the cell members were present, surely they would have already announced themselves.

Just outside the door, a flood of cold fear coursed through her. The door squeaked slowly open before her and Evira entered a room dominated by a long wood conference table surrounded by high-backed leather chairs. The next thing she saw was that the chairs were all occupied . . . by corpses, sitting there with the last bit of life frozen on their faces, many covered with blood.

Evira knew this was the cell that had been waiting to help her. But they hadn't only been killed, their bodies had been *arranged* for effect.

For her.

Evira sensed what was coming next even before she heard the rumble of boots. What saved her was desperation and the good fortune to see an old Mauser pistol still holstered around the waist of one of the seated corpses. She lunged and grasped it in the same motion. It was in her hand even as she dove down and to the side. Her eyes caught a pair of doors bursting open at opposite sides of the room to allow a quartet of Hassani's Revolutionary Guards to charge in with automatic rifles already blasting.

Fortunately, their fire was aimed high toward a figure they had every reason to believe would be standing. The bullets sizzled through the air, ricocheting off wood and walls and striking the already dead figures around the conference table.

Evira's dive had given her the table for cover and she immediately shoved herself beneath it. The legs and thighs of the guardsmen were visible, worthy targets even if not likely to be fatal, and she fired the ancient Mauser at one figure and then the next. The guards collapsed before they could right their fire. Keeping low, Evira darted out from beneath the table and aimed her pistol at their writhing frames. Only a pair remained conscious, and these she killed quickly on her way toward the same door through which she had entered the room.

She bolted into the corridor and pulled the heavy door closed behind her. She pressed her shoulders tight against the wall and felt a shard of wood explode just over her right shoulder. Another Revolutionary Guardsman was charging from the end of the corridor opposite the door she had used to enter the building. She swung toward that door only to see it crash open and two more guards push through into the corridor. Both routes of exit were cut off for her.

Evira fired a pair of bullets in each direction, leaving her with a single shell in the Mauser and no spare clip. The three onrushing guardsmen pinned themselves against the walls nearest them, which allowed her to charge across the corridor for another door that had caught her eye.

She saw it was locked and fired her final bullet into the latch. It gave enough for her forward charge to shatter it. The guardsmen picked up the chase again, firing a stream of bullets in her direction.

Evira found herself on a stairway bathed in coal black darkness broken only by the scant light provided by the open door behind her. She plunged down the steps blindly, hands feeling about the wall to keep her bearings. The bottom of the stairs came up fast and she nearly tripped over herself. Her stumble took her against an extension of the same wall and her head banged up against something metallic. Stunned, she maintained the presence of mind to realize it was a control box and quickly had it open.

Above her, the three guards were following in her wake. Her only chance was to distract them, and the control box held the means. Evira pried it open and slid the switches on the right side into the *on* position, and then did the same with the switches on the left. Immediately the overhead fluorescent lights struggled to catch and a whining whirl signalled that the processing machines were coming back to life. The whine gave way to an almost deafening screech. Everywhere on the floor before her huge machines performed their tasks with no materials to process, screeching as if to protest that fact. The resulting chaos was hers to take the best advantage of as she could. She rushed from the junction station to the largest machine she could find, intending to keep using it and the others for cover until she could find an alternate route out.

A bullet chimed above her head as she neared the huge machine that pressed unfinished plastic into the desired width. It was a gear-driven monstrosity with a tread that led to a pair of huge, narrowly spaced rubber rollers running in tandem toward each other to allow the plastic to slide through. Beyond this was a rolling machine that accepted the plastic sheeting and twisted it up into rolls ready for shipping. The other machines were almost as loud but not nearly as impressive, nor were they large enough to use for concealment.

The three guards fanned out, cutting off possible angles of escape. The strategy, she realized, meant she now had a single man to deal with three times instead of three men. Her new advantage was further helped by the noise that buried all possible communication among her pursuers. Evira couldn't reach any of the possible exit routes yet, but with all the guards eliminated by the skills she would now be able to utilize, she would have her choice of doors.

Having crawled to the back edge of the rolling machine, Evira reached up for a rounded wooden shaft. Closer inspection revealed that it had a hook at the top for hoisting the rolled plastic up for stacking. The edge was not only sharpened, but also could be manipulated by a mechanism connected to it at the handle, much like a pincer apparatus. Apply pressure to a simple hand grip and the pincer-like hook snapped closed around the roll of plastic. Evira drew the instrument to her and edged on.

Ten feet away a Revolutionary Guardsman moved slowly forward in the aisle on the other side of the huge machines. If she was fortunate, he would not think to lean over and glance beneath the apparatus where he would certainly see her. Evira eased into a turn to start back toward the rolling machine again. She moved parallel to the guard, matching his pace as they approached each other. Her timing would have to be perfect. She had the pincer apparatus, yes, but the guard had something much more comforting—a machine gun. She must both disable him and get his gun.

Evira brought the pincer rod up close to her just as the guard reached the other side of the churning rolling machine. The moving tread slid in and between the powerful rollers, which ground in protest as rubber squeezed against rubber. Evira stayed low until the guard had just moved beyond her in the other aisle. Then she sprang.

The guard picked out her shape at the last instant, too late to stop her from jabbing the pincers against his throat and working the apparatus at the bottom of the shaft to perfection. The powerful tongs, sharp enough to grip tough plastic, dug part way into the flesh on the sides of his throat. His scream almost rose above the awful din of the machines, and he dropped his rifle as his hands flailed upward toward his punctured neck.

Before the guard knew what was happening, Evira jerked down on the pincers, and he found himself on the moving tread, only feet from the rollers. With the man's head almost to the rollers, Evira leaned over to grab his rifle. She grasped the welcome steel only to find it attached to his shoulder by a strap. She tried to gain the leverage required to pull it free, but the motion exposed her to one of his fellows who had been attracted by the commotion.

His bullets grazed Evira's side. Her own scream was lost in the final one gurgling from the guardsman as the bones of his face and neck were crushed in the rolling mechanism, jamming it. Evira wasn't sure how bad her wound was, but it wasn't bad enough to stop her from realizing she needed a weapon desperately.

Some thick shards of plastic lay on the floor beneath her, and she wedged them in her belt before lunging for the dead guardsman's rifle, which was resting outside of the rolling machine. One of the remaining guardsmen was spewing fire from atop the pressing machine ten feet before her. The dead man's gun was jammed in the pressing apparatus, but Evira was able to twist the barrel around and locate the trigger. A bullet grazed her collarbone, and she wailed in agony but managed to fire blindly forward. The guard's hands clutched for his midsection and he keeled over to the floor.

Evira ducked low and slammed her shoulders against the rolling machine. There was no time to celebrate, not with the final guard still about. She started to edge forward, the pain in her side and collarbone rocking her, making her pay for every step.

The final guard materialized off her right flank. She registered that his leg was bloody and realized her single spray had wounded him. He fired a burst at her, but she had already lunged down and to the side, thinking she could perhaps reach the stairs ahead of him. But she stumbled over a crate and fell to even more pain and shock. The guardsman charged with his rifle aimed dead at her.

Evira remembered the thin shards of plastic she had wedged in her belt. Without thinking further, she drew one out and hurled it as he skidded to a halt to steady his aim. A scream curdled her ears and she saw that he was groping desperately for the shard of plastic that had lodged in his left eye.

Seizing the advantage, Evira regained her feet and rushed into him with a force that spun both of them around against the front of the pressing machine. The man forgot his pain long enough to grasp her at the shoulders and slam her backward against the steel. Her insides shook as he bent her over the tread. She saw the shard of plastic yanked from his dead eye was still in his hand. He swiped at her and narrowly missed her throat when Evira twisted. He swiped again and she deflected the blow with her functioning arm, sending further agony through her wounded side and collarbone.

The force of his momentum bent her further over the tread. Her feet lost touch with the floor, and the man's eyes glistened as he pursued the most obvious strategy available to him. All he had to do was keep her going, and the pressing machine would swallow her up. He shoved harder and Evira felt her back and shoulders begin their slide to a bloody end.

Evira managed to grasp the safety rails that rose slightly over the tread and stop her progress. But by then the guard was standing over her, straddling the apparatus with a foot poised on each of the rails. He yanked a pistol from his belt and snarled, his own back less than a foot from the monstrous rollers that pressed plastic into programmed widths and sent it spewing out the other side.

Evira could see the trigger starting to give when a piece of corrugated piping from the ceiling directly above him gave way and smashed him hard in the chest. The angle of the blow forced him backward. He recovered his bearings, but not before the ever-churning rollers caught him by the holster and began to reel him in. The pistol jumped from his hands as his arms flailed to grasp something to pull him out, but there was nothing to find. His screams overwhelmed the factory's sounds and Evira thought she heard bones crunching as the rest of his frame vanished into the mechanism.

All command of her senses and motor functions was lost as Evira sank dazedly to the floor. All she would remember later was the impossible sight of a small shape climbing down from the rafters, from the same area as the corrugated pipe that had miraculously smashed into the final guardsman. And then the shape was hovering over her, passing in and out of her blurred vision.

A boy! It was a boy!

"Don't worry," came his voice as he struggled for a grip on her. "I'll get you out of here before more of them come."

CHAPTER 10

"ARE YOU SURE THIS IS THE PLACE?"

McCracken bolted upright abruptly at the driver's question. He realized he must have been dozing the last stretch of the way from the airport and gazed at the computerized meter which listed the fee due in both yen and dollars in bright LED figures.

"Planning to retire early?" Blaine asked in English.

"This the place?" the driver responded, anxious to be gone.

Blaine gazed out the open window through the postdawn light, not sure of the answer himself. The address was thirty miles outside Tokyo in the Japanese countryside. A dirt road had taken them the final stretch of the way and at its end stood a bridge rising over a small rushing brook. They were in a placid forest, full of blooming flowers and trees, the only evidence of man being the perfect landscaping and a dark-stained wood building across the bridge. It was constructed against a sloping hillside, accessible only by a set of steep stone steps and rimmed everywhere by plush, full trees that swayed faintly in the breeze. Blaine looked back toward the driver, wondering in that instant whether Traymir had misled him, whether—

His thoughts veered suddenly. Just as suddenly, his hand swept for the door latch.

"This will do fine," he told the driver, and fumbled amidst his wad of cash for the amount rung up on the meter.

He stepped away from the car and the driver backed fast down

93

the dirt road. *Bujin* did mean warrior and the man who had taken that name was obviously taking it to heart. The building before him, Blaine realized, was a martial arts training hall, or *dojo*. He knew it by feeling more than sight, and he felt immediately at home.

He had come to Japan after his tour in Israel was over with Vietnam still weighing heavily on his mind. The Cong had taught him much about what Johnny Wareagle still referred to as the hellfire, not the least of which was how inadequately prepared American soldiers were to go up against Oriental prowess and philosophy. It had been that lack of understanding, McCracken felt, that had cost the U.S. the war and plenty of men their lives. The true warrior learns from his enemies, and he came to Japan to sample a number of arts. Eventually he settled on a school of Dai-Ito Ryu Ju-Jitsu that included study of the wooden sword in addition to traditional self-defense forms. His *sensei* was named Yamagita Hiroshi, a descendant of a long line of actual samurai and top instructor for the Japanese police and military. Blaine trained day and night, working his mind as hard as his body, until he began to grasp what had made his foe in Vietnam so difficult. His goal was to make himself proficient in such skills, but what he learned, finally, was just how much he would never know. He had stayed in touch with Hiroshi for years afterward until the master fell into disfavor with the Japanese government and disappeared.

Blaine approached the wooden bridge slowly, making sure his hands were always in plain view. He stole one last glance at the cab before it passed out of sight, and turned back to find a dark figure facing him from the center of the bridge. The figure was dressed in the black robe and *hakama* traditional to the samurai warrior. Angled across his left hip was the handle of a razor-sharp long sword or *katana*, its black scabbard comfortably wedged through the belt tied within his robes. His right hand rested on the sword's equally black handle.

There was a soft shuffling behind him and Blaine swung around to find another samurai, hands within easy reach of the sword stretching across his left hip. Before Blaine could move or speak, another two swordsmen closed in on him from either side. Facing modern day samurai presented him with a situation

even he would never be able to talk himself out of under the
circumstances. He was trespassing, an uninvited guest on another's land, and that marked a violation of the sacred code of
honor. His best chance of survival was to do precisely as he was
instructed.

The samurai on the bridge beckoned him on and McCracken
started forward with the other swordsmen maintaining a sword's
distance away. The bridge creaked as he moved across it with
the lead samurai waiting on the other side ready to lead him up
the stone steps. A single sliding door stood at the top, and the
lead samurai opened it to reveal a small foyer with yet another
set of doors just ahead, this time of the paper variety called *shoji*.
His escort parted these doors gracefully as well, glad to see
McCracken had knelt to remove his shoes. Bowing slightly, he
bade Blaine to enter. Blaine returned the gesture and passed
through, feeling more than hearing the *shoji* doors close behind
him.

He found himself in a large room with a ceiling full of regularly placed skylights arranged three to a row. Through them
the sight was breathtaking, the sky seeming a reach away from
the trees scratching at the glass. But Blaine was concerned more
with a figure kneeling before a wall highlighted by a hand-etched
scroll bearing the Japanese calligraphy for *Bujin*. Within easy
reach by the figure's side rested a *katana* in its scabbard.

The kneeling figure seemed to read his thoughts and turned
an open hand behind him. McCracken followed the gesture toward another *katana* that had been placed in the corner of the
straw *tatami* mat diagonally across from the kneeling figure's
position. Grasping the unspoken instruction, Blaine slid across
the *tatami* and bowed toward *kamiza*, the seat of honor his host
was facing. Then he eased himself on his knees toward the second sword. Honor was everything here. To disgrace himself in
any way was to assure his own death. He had not been searched
outside, partly because the samurai would have sensed he was
weaponless and partly because his honor was not to be violated
either. If he dared reach now for a weapon other than the long
sword by his side, he'd be dead before he touched it. He had to
play along in the hope the Bujin would at least give him a chance
to explain himself under interrogation.

If that was not to be the case, the noble thing for the Bujin to do under the circumstances would be to offer Blaine a sword to fight with in combat against him. The Bujin would realize merely from the way Blaine moved that he had had some training. But since that training was pitifully inadequate next to that of such a master, Blaine would need to rely on subterfuge to survive. One opening and one quick lunge would be all it would take and likely all he could hope to get.

At last the Bujin's body began to turn. Blaine tensed, thinking of his sword and how fast he could grab and draw it if it came to that.

But the Bujin was smiling. Then he was chuckling, soon laughing.

"You are too ugly a man to kill before breakfast, *Fudo-san*," the black robed figure said as he slid himself forward across the *tatami* until the sun blazed on his face.

It was Yamagita Hiroshi.

"You're the Bujin!" Blaine exclaimed in surprise.

"Yes, *Fudo-san*," Hiroshi returned in perfect English. "Strange our paths should cross this way."

"Even stranger since no one's heard from you in over a decade now."

"No one's heard from Hiroshi because Hiroshi ceased to exist."

"Care to tell me why?"

"In time, *Fudo-san*, in time. For now your appearance tells me you need sake and a warm bed. You should have felt it was I as soon as you saw me. Fatigue can do that to a man."

Hiroshi rose and McCracken joined him on foot. The two men met in the center of the mat and shook hands warmly. The *sensei* regarded his former pupil with a knowing grin.

"You are still *Fudo-san*, as stubborn and unwilling to change as ever. And you have become stronger in the years since our parting. I can feel that strength."

"I'm forty now, *sensei*. What you feel are my bones calcifying."

Hiroshi laughed again. "Dangle a bit of yarn before an old sleeping cat and see how fast he remembers his lessons."

"Do you know why I've come?" McCracken asked him.

"I have my suspicions. Let us discuss matters over that sake I promised you. Come."

They walked side by side through another set of *shoji* doors. McCracken recalled that the original *dojo* where he had trained with Hiroshi had looked much the same, simple and plain, the way a training hall was meant to. Even then Hiroshi's school had been closed to the public and only pull from officials within the Japanese government won Blaine an interview. Much to his surprise, Hiroshi could recount Blaine's exploits in Vietnam more clearly than he remembered them himself.

"There is a great warrior God in Japanese folklore," the master had told him that day. "He was named Fudo and he carried a sword in one hand and a rope in the other, the tools he used to first subdue evil and then bind it. He would only use his sword to kill when another's had shed blood already and was about to again. He stood up for the weak and innocent and was feared by all who carried blackness in their hearts. I will call you *Fudo-san* because you are such a man. I will agree to teach you because you are such a man."

McCracken's views on his life and work jibed almost perfectly with the creed of the samurai, and Hiroshi sensed that Blaine was destined for life as a *ronin*, or masterless samurai. He would be a protector and lone avenger much as the god Fudo had been himself.

But the significance of *"Fudo-san"* extended to a more subtle level. The word *fudo* can also mean *immovable*, and this too was a quality Hiroshi sensed in McCracken from the start. He was not a man prone to change easily, nor would he ever be. The times would pass and McCracken would pass with them, though on his own terms.

They moved down a small narrow corridor into a smaller room lined with more formal *tatami* mats. Blaine's nostrils caught the faintly medicinal smell of warming sake and saw the ceramic flasks sitting within a pot of steaming water suspended above an open flame. Hiroshi knelt before them and poured out a pair of cups, handing the first to McCracken.

"We will drink to old times, *Fudo-san.*"

"And speak of newer ones, Hiroshi. Why did you disappear? What happened? Why did you—"

"Become the Bujin?" Hiroshi completed for him. "The answer is rather long and complicated, tedious, too."

"I'm not going anywhere."

"Tradition, *Fudo-san*, is the curse of our people. It binds us to the past in a way we do not always understand but must accept because it makes us what we are." He paused long enough to take a healthy sip of his sake. "There was a man, a bully, who made it his business to take money from working people in exchange for not hurting them, their families, or their businesses. The man was backed by a gang, and the few times police were summoned there was no one but the complainant to back up the story, and the complainant conveniently vanished or changed his mind soon after. Such is not unusual in Japan. It wasn't my business . . . until this man, this bully, staked a claim in the village where I had been raised. The elders came to me. I had no choice but to intercede.

"I tried to reason with the man. I went alone, with honor. He laughed in my face, chastised my old ways, and had his men show their guns. He told me I would die if I ever showed my face to him again. He dishonored me, *Fudo-san*. He left me with no choice, if I had ever really had one. I waited for him one morning in the rice paddy he walked through to reach his office. He walked without fear, for who would dare touch him?" Hiroshi paused again but did not sip any sake. "I touched him. I drew him down into the mud and held him under until he passed out. Then I left him there to drown in the muck like the sewer rat that he was."

"No one saw you?"

"It didn't matter. I was bound by the oath I had sworn as an officer in the service of Japan to report my crime. There was an uproar when I did, a public outcry in which some supported my actions and some condemned them. The dead man's friends vowed vengeance. The government was helpless to support me. I had placed them in an impossible position. So I made the rest easy for all concerned. I disappeared. I became someone else."

"A *ronin*, masterless in your own right. Hiring yourself out."

"To gain money to support the kind of people the man I killed had bullied. It was my way of making up for the disgrace I had committed to maintain honor. Such a dichotomy, so difficult to resolve. I chose a means of escape by which I could live with myself. I began training warriors as they were trained in days lost. Four of them escorted you into my *dojo*."

"Oh yeah. Tough hombres."

"To be sure, *Fudo-san*. They and dozens of others have trained as men were trained in a time long past. They live and work here in the *dojo* as *uchideshi*. Their life is their training."

"And is your life to be their *sensei* or to be the Bujin, Hiroshi?"

"It is to be both, and it is their lot to serve me in both respects. A man does what he must to survive and find meaning in his life. Our paths are not much different. I seek to be of service to those who have been turned away at more traditional stations."

"With one crucial distinction, *sensei*: I don't keep time with men like Yosef Rasin—a recent client of yours."

Hiroshi noticed Blaine hadn't touched his sake and didn't press him about it. He nodded. "Just as I thought. I had my suspicions about Rasin from the beginning, but he was most convincing and offered to pay handsomely for a small service on my part."

"Let me be the judge of how small."

"He needed a salvage operation conducted. He wanted me to arrange and front it for him so there would be no traces leading back to him or to Israel."

"And did you agree?"

"No. The risk of exposure would have been too great and it was not something I dabbled in ordinarily. I merely pointed him in the direction of a salvage specialist and reluctantly agreed to act as go-between."

"What was it that he wanted to salvage?"

"I never desired to find out. It was big, though. The kind of equipment he required was proof of this."

"And was the salvage completed successfully?"

Hiroshi went back to his sake.

"Sensei?"

"I . . . don't know. There was an accident. The salvage vessel exploded at sea. There were no survivors."

"An accident . . . "

"I had no reason to suspect anything else."

"But your feelings told you otherwise. Rasin had the men killed and all evidence of his operation eliminated after he had what he came for."

Hiroshi nodded very slowly. "He dishonored me, *Fudo-san*. He betrayed my trust. When he killed those men, I was a party to it. Someday I will have the chance to repay him for that. Meanwhile, I have vowed never to meet with someone again who comes without references."

"But you let me through."

Hiroshi smiled. "I saw it was you before giving my men their orders. I wanted to see how you would react to my little game."

"And were you pleased? We're talking teacher to student again, *sensei*."

Hiroshi's gaze was noncommittal. "You have the feeling of a great volcano when it is ready to erupt after years of inactivity."

"Physically?"

"More mentally, perhaps even spiritually. You have been away from your training for too long. You think instead of feel. Each thought is a risk for the time it takes to complete it."

"But risk is part of life, and you took one when you agreed to work with Rasin. You risked your honor, Hiroshi. You risked all the good you have tried to do in a single move."

"What do you mean?"

"What if I told you I'm here because Rasin's got a weapon capable of wiping out the entire Arab world while leaving Israel unscathed? What if I told you all indications point to the fact that that's what your salvage team pulled out of the sea for him?"

Hiroshi refilled his own sake cup emotionlessly. "And just who is it the *ronin* McCracken has chosen to work for on this pursuit?"

"Not chosen, been forced. I haven't told you everything. There's a boy I recently learned was my son. The Arabs have him."

"My God . . ."

"I haven't got a choice, Hiroshi, any more than you had one when that animal began terrorizing your village. The moderate Arabs want me to stop Rasin and his weapon, while they work toward stopping a mad Iranian from uniting the militant forces against Israel."

"So complicated."

"Less so if we can learn what the salvage team pulled out of the sea before Rasin killed them."

Hiroshi sipped at his sake as McCracken swirled the cooling contents of his cup.

"I know the coordinates of the salvage. That is all."

"Then give them to me, *sensei*, and I'll be on my way and out of yours."

Hiroshi shook his head. "No, there must be something more I can do. Please let me help. You spoke of your son. I have an army of warriors I can dispatch to—"

"No, *sensei*. This is one I've got to go alone. Believe me, I have to."

Hiroshi regarded him sternly. "There is a saying in zen, *Fudo-san*, that a man who tries to shoulder the weight of the world will be crushed by his burden before he can lift it."

"It's not the entire world this time, *sensei*. It's just my little part of it."

CHAPTER 11

Evira's MIND FLIRTED WITH CONSCIOUSNESS, LANGUISHING between dreams and reality. She felt the sting of cold liquid at her lips, felt her head being lifted.

"You've got to drink this," a voice told her. "The doctor said so."

Her eyes had been open but now she found herself able to see. By her side, half-behind her as he eased her head up from the pillow, was a young boy. His age was shrouded in the blurriness of her vision, but eleven or twelve years old seemed a fair estimate. His auburn hair hung shaggily over his forehead and ears, dangling to his shoulders. His eyes of the same color shone wide and bright, trusting in a way that only a child's can be. His clothes were formed of mere rags; a man's shirt too big for him and pinned at the back; a pair of pants that might have been burlap sacks, somehow cut and sewn in the shape of trousers. Evira glimpsed splotches of dirt coating his face and turned her eyes back to the water he had placed before her lips. The hand holding the cup was black with grime that turned the water sooty when it rolled over his flesh.

"Where . . . am I?" Evira managed.

"Safe."

She felt the last of the drops of water sliding down the corners of her mouth. She was too weak to wipe them. "Who are you?"

"Kourosh," the boy responded.

Slowly memories began to unfold in her mind, forming themselves in sequence. She remembered resigning herself to death with the last of the Revolutionary Guards standing over her in the plastics factory. She remembered a pipe crashing into him and her savior dropping down from the rafters. She remembered her savior's face—the boy Kourosh's face. From there everything became hazy. A man who smelled like alcohol had asked her questions Evira lacked the strength to answer. There had been fresh pain to her wounds and now, as she rested on what seemed to be an ancient mattress placed atop squeezed-together crates, she could feel the well wrapped bandages binding her torn tissue. Beyond that there were only recollections of the boy coming with water, always around her.

Kourosh had backed slightly away and sat himself atop a crate of his own that sagged in the center from his meager weight. His build was surprisingly sturdy, considering the obvious effects of malnutrition. Evira noted most of the color on his face came from the permanently painted grime. He seemed comfortable in his vigil as she glanced over at him.

"My wounds, how bad are they?"

"The doctor said if you could speak within two days, you'd live. It's been barely one."

"I'm remembering now. The doctor, he was a young man, very young."

Kourosh smiled fully. He had a complete set of teeth, though the front ones were yellowed.

"Oh, he's not really a doctor. We just call him that since he was studying to be one when he was a student."

"We?"

"The people," Kourosh told her.

"You're with the underground," Evira said.

"And proud of it."

She tried to stir, fresh thoughts racing through her. "Who else knows I'm here?"

"No one. Just the doctor and he won't talk." Kourosh thrust a thumb back at himself. "He owes me."

At last Evira gazed about her. They were in a single room which featured a partially boarded-up window not far from her perch. The room had only the assorted crates and a single battered chair for furniture. A large collection of American comic books was gathered on the floor with several selections pinned to the wall as a kind of wallpaper.

"You brought me here? By yourself?"

"We're not that far from the factory. Just a few blocks."

"You live here."

"I live here," the boy said, and lowered his face. Then it brightened. "It's my home, better than lots have got, too."

"You were in the factory when the soldiers came."

Kourosh nodded.

"You saw what happened before I arrived?"

Another nod, then a sigh. "They sent me on an errand. I always come and go through the basement because there's less chance of being seen. I had just come back when I heard the shooting. I could tell they weren't our guns. I know the sounds."

"But you didn't run. You stayed."

"Because I knew you were coming. I wanted to warn you, but I had to hide when more of the soldiers came. I hid in the basement, in the rafters."

"Lucky for me . . ."

Kourosh smiled at her, and in that moment Evira saw him as the boy he should have been but in this world was not allowed to be. He was a creature of a society that no longer knew or understood youth and so refused to permit it.

"You should rest," he told her.

"I've rested enough."

"You must get your strength back."

"Can you bring the others to me?"

Kourosh shrugged his small and weary shoulders. "There are no others."

"But the underground . . ."

"The ones I know—rounded up, gone, or dead back at the factory."

"The doctor?"

"I looked for him this morning. He's gone too."

Damn, Evira thought, *I'm alone here. . . .*

"I know why you came," Kourosh said suddenly. "You came to kill the animal Hassani and the underground was going to help you."

Evira forced herself part way up through the pain.

"You don't need them," the boy continued. "I can help you. I know the city and I know where you can find him."

"Where?"

"He's moved into the royal palace that the Shah built in Niavarin. I can get you in there. I've got a way. When you're ready."

She found her shoulders slumping back to the tattered mattress in spite of her efforts to keep them upright. "That might be quite awhile."

"You're strong. I saw what you did in the factory basement. A few more days, that's all."

"With you taking care of me, I don't doubt it."

"I know how to change your bandages. The doctor, he showed me. I already changed them once while you were asleep."

"Well," she said, "if we're going to be partners I'd better know more about you than your name."

Evira forgot her pain while she listened to his story. Kourosh was an orphan, as she suspected. He had been born nearly twelve years before. There had been little good about his life at the start and things got rapidly worse. The war with Iraq took his father by conscription and returned him in a box. With no means of support, his mother placed seven-year-old Kourosh in a school supported by the Revolutionary Council, and it was from there just over two years later that he too was conscripted into the army.

With soldiers falling to Iraq at a frightening clip, the decision was made to utilize children on the front lines. Initially they were given some training and armed. But as armaments began to grow scarce, they were simply sent with clubs and sticks into Iraqi strongholds or used to clear mine fields. Each life lost by a boy meant one kept by a man who could thus continue fighting for the true Islamic destiny. The Revolutionary Council needed no further justifications because no one was pressing for any.

Kourosh was meant to die in one of the attack waves. They trimmed his hair short and dressed him like a soldier. Then he and the others were packed into trucks and transported west on a rain-swept day. Several of the trucks ran off the muddy roads and the boys were sent off to sit amongst the trees while the still-functional trucks were used to drag the others back on to the road. There were soldiers watching them, of course, but they couldn't watch everybody. When the children were herded over to help push one of the trucks from a ditch, Kourosh escaped into the woods with several other boys.

For a time it was a great adventure. The boys were older than he and they let him tag along until they reached Tehran, where they were determined to become criminals and rob women of their money and groceries. Kourosh couldn't accept that. Each woman they accosted reminded him of his mother, vague as she was in his memory, and he strayed from the others and eventually went out on his own. It had been years since he had been home, but he remembered his address and returned to it.

His mother wasn't there. No one knew where she was.

Kourosh returned to the streets, and the streets became his only parents. He stole what he had to in order to eat. He found the empty room to which he later brought Evira and moved in. From spaces between the boards over his window he could see the plastics factory and thus observe who came and went there. Many a night he heard the faint rush of footsteps heading toward it and came to recognize the regulars who frequented the building. He judged they were counterrevolutionaries drawn from frustrated students, the heroes of the poor, and wished he were old enough to join them. In his imagination they became his friends and companions, the only ones he had.

One night, he noticed that a guard was lingering around the plastics building. When the guardsman departed, Kourosh didn't hesitate at all. He rushed from his room across the street and through the door he had seen entered so many times. Inside he found the students in a large conference room. At first they regarded his rantings as a playful nuisance, but Kourosh got enough of their attention to convince them a raid was coming. All underground movements learn to move quickly and cover their tracks, and by the time the raid occurred less than an hour later all evidence of their presence had been erased. As a result, the boy became a fixture in their midst, asking nothing in return, though a few of the students kept him as clean as they could, kept him well fed, and endeavored to teach him English, using the comic books, he explained, as tools.

"You really think you can get me into the palace when Hassani is there?" she asked him when he was finished.

"I told you I could, didn't I?"

"Then why don't you tell me how. Let's start with a map."

The four old men sat at the shaded table in the backyard of the spacious home in the city of Hertzelia, the posh suburb a half hour outside of Tel Aviv. The two directly across from one another were huddled in deep concentration over a checkerboard with nearly the same number of black pieces remaining as red. The paler of the two, a gaunt man with three days stubble upon his cheeks, jumped a black with his red.

"King me!" he demanded triumphantly.

His slightly older opponent, a short pudgy man with only the remnants of his hair, humphed in response and slammed a captured red back into the game.

"Damn you, Abraham. You play *meshuge*."

"Go ahead, damn me, Isaac. Damn me all you want. This time I'm winning."

"The two of you should be ashamed of yourselves, whining on the sabbath," chastised a man with a glass eye that refused to look in the same direction as his real one. "I've got winners." He shifted uncomfortably in his chair.

"What you've got is hemorrhoids, Saul," Isaac told him.

"Yes, from sitting in the same place too long watching the two of you."

The fourth man's reaction to all this was to blow his monstrous nose into a handkerchief.

"Do you have to do that in front of all of us, Joshua?" Abraham wanted to know.

"What, then? I should take a walk in the woods every time I have to blow?"

"No," Saul said, "you'd scare away all the birds."

Now it was Joshua who humphed. In point of fact, none of the men were going by the names given them at birth. They had gone by so many different names in their lifetimes, what difference did another make, especially if it was by their own choosing? The four men had taken the names of four kings and warriors. The names fit well with the project they had undertaken.

It was Isaac's move again and he huddled close enough to the board pieces to lick them before making it. To the four old men, life was very much like a game of checkers. Forget chess with all its complications. Life was most easily endured when reduced to its simplest elements. They had learned that credo forty years before and had continued to practice it ever since.

Joshua considered blowing his nose again, then thought better of it.

"Still no further word from Tehran?" he asked.

"You were expecting maybe a miracle?" Saul answered.

"We shouldn't have needed a miracle. It was all planned. That woman, what was her name again?"

"Evira."

"She should have died in Tehran. We were assured there wouldn't be a problem. What went wrong?"

"How should I know?" asked Isaac, who was growing increasingly impatient with Abraham's refusal to move. His hand kept sneaking out only to jump back before committing himself. "We made sure word of her coming was leaked to the Revolutionary Guard, but the soldiers dispatched were killed, all of them, and she disappeared. End of story."

Abraham laughed humorlessly and at last made his move. "Not if she is still at large."

"Go ahead," Isaac blared. "You're going to repeat the same thing you said this morning. 'Why don't we find her and finish the job?' She's gone, that's why. Someone helped her and that someone is still helping her."

"Not one of ours."

"Surely not. Perhaps one of nobody's. It has been known to happen."

"Not in Tehran it hasn't."

"The point," Saul said, "is that she is probably on the run and thus no longer poses a threat to our plans."

"Don't underestimate her," Isaac urged, watching Abraham contemplate a counter to his latest move. "We know what she went to Tehran to accomplish and we also know we cannot allow her to be successful."

"She has little time left."

"She has enough."

"How many days is it now?" Joshua asked of himself, tucking his hanky into his fist in order to count fingers. "Depends on whether you count today or not. . . ."

"*Putz,*" Saul muttered. "You can't remember May fourteenth, Independence Day, after how hard we fought to win it?"

"Eight days," Joshua said finally. "Counting today."

"*Putz.*"

And on the game board Abraham had pounced on Isaac's apparently ill-conceived move by lodging a double jump and seizing one of his opponent's kings. "Sometimes, old friend, you make a simple game more complicated than it was meant to be."

Isaac followed up with no delay at all, triple jumping Abraham and leaving him with a single doomed piece on the board. "Sometimes you make it too simple."

Yosef Rasin stood on the terrace that overlooked the orange orchards of the kibbutz where he had lived as a child. To him the smells carried on the stiff breeze were more than those of citrus; they were the smells of Israel, the nation he had dedicated his life to. Rasin ran a hand through his blowing curls, noticeably thinner than they once were. He was no longer a young man. Where before dreams seemed to have forever to come true, now even tomorrow seemed too much to wait for.

Not tomorrow anyway. But soon, ever so soon. . . .

Rasin gripped the railing tight with both hands. His grip felt weak. The paunch of his belly felt larger. The Israeli sun seemed daily to sap more of his strength. In this respect his fate was that of his nation. Pleading. Desperate. Running out of time. Interesting how they had aged along parallel lines.

And yet he stood here a prisoner of his own conscience, thanks to the plan he had undertaken. He had come to the kibbutz in the fertile lands en route to the Negev when his enemies began to search for him. These were high stakes they were playing for, and Rasin could afford no chances. The people of his kibbutz thought him a hero. Hiding him was a privilege. They would reveal no information about him and the isolated nature of their kibbutz made it the perfect hiding place. It had not become commercial as so many others had. There was no hotel, outside business, nor any wish for tourist trade. The people here kept to themselves and did not advertise their existence with signs on the highway. Rasin's flesh crawled at the thought of the commercialism that had beset others.

He took another deep breath. The scents were of many things but mostly they were of home. He gazed out at the orange trees lined in rows beneath him. In his mind they became a vast crowd of people cheering and praising him. He could see them clearly, arms thrusting up and down, chanting his name. Rasin could feel the euphoria. He touched his unshaven face and was glad the people below were not close enough to see how unkempt he was. Involuntarily, he raised his hands from the railing into the air, a gesture for the people to silence themselves. They obliged instantly to heed the command of their hero.

"My friends," he called out to them, "a great day is upon us, a *holy* day, for is this not the first time in our long, oppressed history that we have been truly independent from the hate and ugliness that has surrounded us always?"

"YES!"

"And is this not the first time we, the people of Israel, stand together as one and look to our borders without fear? When we can walk the streets, any street, and not worry for our lives or the lives of our children, either now or in the future?"

"YES!"

The applause and cheering became tumultuous. Rasin could feel his ears ringing. He found himself having to scream over it into his imaginary microphone.

"The Arab peoples have been vanquished at last! The Arab peoples have been reduced to the significance of the grains of sand that populate their deserts! Their entire way of life has been reduced to a desert. Was this my choice? Was this something that came easy to me?"

Silence now, hushed and thick.

"No, I tell you, no! I have not committed the deed I have done with a light heart. But I accept the responsibility for it. I accept it as I accept the charge of leadership for this great country I love and cherish. Let us not look to the past for what we have been forced to bury. Let us look to the future for what we can now build in peace."

The applause thundered over his final words and Rasin raised his hands in triumph, eyes watering, the fulfillment of his greatest dream—

"Yosef . . ."

—before him.

"Yosef, I'm sorry to bother you."

The voice from behind him broke Rasin's trance. Before him the oranges were oranges again. His hands dug back into the railing. He was disappointed.

"You know I don't like to be disturbed when I'm thinking, Daniel."

"There are matters that must be addressed, sir. They require your immediate attention."

Rasin swung abruptly around. "It is Israel that requires my attention, Daniel. Nothing more. Nothing less."

"This is what we must speak about, Yosef. Threats. Complications."

Rasin's eyes narrowed into slits of repressed rage. When he spoke Daniel noted his voice was hoarse again.

"You have my attention."

At first Rasin had tried peacefully to prove his points to the Israeli public, to work within the system to affect the changes he felt were so desperately needed. His militant stands began with the signing of the Camp David accords. Giving back the Sinai was a tragic error, not for strategic reasons so much as for the precedent it set. Once the givebacks began, they never stopped. A Palestinian state was closer than ever to existence on the West Bank that belonged to Israel and only to Israel. Did the present leadership think the Arab rabble would be appeased with that? Did they think it would bring peace? Rasin knew it wouldn't. For him the issue was a simple one: either the Arab world would survive or Israel would. And he had been blessed with the means to ensure the latter. No, not blessed—chosen. And if not by God, then by whom? Everything had been too neat and clean to be anything but predestined. The weapon was his to employ when and how he saw fit.

The breeze blew his hair and Rasin squinted his eyes into the sun. To the casual observer, he might have looked like a school-teacher or mundane public official. His face was nothing if not simple, forgettable, and Rasin was glad for that. There was strength in simplicity, and he used it to distill the essence of truth.

The Arab peoples of the Mideast had to be shown the error of their ways. Plain. Simple. Period. He had the means, though it would not be the ends that provided the justification. That came from the past, from the proven brutality of a culture that had been at war since the dawn of its existence. The barbarians of the modern world, full of inbred hate and a death wish. The names they went by—Al-Fatah, Black September, PLO, PLF, the Islamic Jihad—were all fronts formed in an attempt to legitimize their existence. But Rasin saw through the fronts; the issue in his mind was simple. The Arabs hated the Israelis and would destroy them if given the opportunity. The only way to stop them was to find the opportunity first.

And now to use it.

"We have completed our interrogation of the traitor Traymir."

"And?"

"Your fears have been confirmed. He sent McCracken to Japan, to the Bujin."

"And what have you done?"

"About Traymir?"

"No, about McCracken."

"The Bujin spirited him away before we could act."

"That is hardly a surprise."

"His next destination is equally obvious. He could do us irreparable harm if he finds . . ."

"Finds what, Daniel? No trace was left, no evidence. That was made sure of."

"This is McCracken we are talking about, not an ordinary man. He has skills and resources that defy our comprehension."

Rasin came forward and calmly tapped Daniel on both shoulders. "Perhaps you forget, my friend, the circumstances of his employ this time. He has no friends, no government resources behind him, and the life of his son is at stake."

"He has brought down operations single-handedly before. Several times."

"Then we will deal with him at our convenience. If your information is correct, it should be relatively simple. Relax."

But Daniel tensed and pulled away.

"Speak your mind, my friend," Rasin bade him.

"When we learned of his involvement, we should have killed him immediately. I warned you of the consequences of failure."

Rasin nodded. Daniel was right, of course. The problems had begun with the discovery that Evira had planted an agent high within their midst, an agent who they could only assume had passed on Rasin's possession of the superweapon before his capture. When word of the woman's desperate interest in McCracken surfaced, Rasin took the most logical step available to him: Help Evira play out her cards through Fett, let her retain McCracken's services so his own people might be led to her in the process. Everything would have gone as planned if not for the presence of the one-armed man and his team who had come after Evira in Jaffa. Even allowing for McCracken's prowess, the unexpected had hurt more than anything.

"Your point is well taken," Rasin conceded. "Now tell me about the woman."

"She has vanished."

"That is the best you can do?"

"She is no longer in the country." Then, eyeing Rasin closely, he continued, "That could be enough. If she even suspects the truth, if that suspicion takes her to—"

"Enough! She could not possibly suspect the truth, no one could. Do you hear me, Daniel? No one! Every detail of this operation has been thought out to the letter. All we are facing are minor inconveniences. Look at me, Daniel. Look at me!"

Rasin grasped the younger man at the shoulders and held him there tight. "Do you think I like living in this self-imposed exile? Do you know why I speak to the orange groves? Not out of madness, Daniel, but frustration. It pains me so much to be isolated and alone when I am so needed. But that is going to change soon and nothing, *no one!*, is going to stop it! We are barely a week from the culmination of my operation. I will be a hero. Israel will be mine, to cherish and lead as I was born to.''

Rasin steadied himself, released his grip, and backed slightly off.

"Independence Day, Daniel. May fourteenth. Next Sunday. One week from tomorrow."

Daniel's response was one word:

"McCracken."

"We know where he is going. We will finish him there."

"And if we fail?"

Rasin squinted his acknowledgement. "Then perhaps the time has come again to use Evira's plan against her." His eyes were cold now, showing no hesitation. "Contact the women. Tell them to go to where McCracken's son is being held. Tell them to kill the boy."

PART THREE

The *Indianapolis*

Guam: Monday, May 8; eleven A.M.

CHAPTER 12

"**Y**o!" McCracken heard as a hand jostled him at the shoulder. "Hope you don't mind me waking you up."

"You interrupted a good dream," he told the woman who was standing over him with her hands on her hips.

"I am ever so sorry. But I thought you might want to join me on deck now that we've reached your goddamn coordinates."

"Aye-aye, sir," Blaine returned, but Patty Hunsecker was already through the cabin door.

Blaine threw his legs over the edge of the cot and stretched. They had been at sea for nearly twenty hours now and few of them had been easy. The Pacific was in a mean mood, seas choppy and rough. The only brief calm had come in the first few hours after setting out from Guam. If McCracken had his bearings correct, they were now somewhere around the halfway point between Guam and the island of Leyte with nothing around them but sky and water.

Thirty-six hours earlier on Saturday, Hiroshi had arranged for a private jet to fly Blaine to Guam's Tamuning Airport. The country's strong Pacific military presence included a complete naval air station which very likely contained the equipment he required. Unfortunately, though, under the circumstances he could not approach any legitimate authority for help. Not only had Evira forbidden him to do so, but now Mossad was on his trail and Mossad's ears were everywhere.

117

Again Hiroshi provided the answer. The waters around Guam, including the nearby Marianas, contained a hotbed of research projects, and all those in the area for such purposes had to register with the naval station. Hiroshi's check found several teams with the necessary equipment, but only one he could pin an immediate location to: a young woman named Patty Hunsecker, who was studying ecological balance in the Marianas Trench. Her boat was docked for the time being so she could assemble data to meet a grant deadline.

He had found her in a small bar overlooking Apra Harbor, where her boat was moored a hundred yards away. She was attractive but didn't look as though she had done much about it lately. There were papers strewn all over her corner table, and a half-drunk mug of beer stood out amid the clutter.

"Excuse me," Blaine said to her when he reached the table.

"No."

"What?"

"I said no. You're not excused. Go away. Whatever it is, I'm too busy."

"You think I'm trying to pick you up?"

She looked him up and down and cast a disapproving scowl. "Mister, you wouldn't have a chance even if I did have the time."

"It's your ship I'm after, Miss Hunsecker."

"Wait a minute, how did you know my name?"

"Mine's McCracken, if it matters."

"It doesn't."

Blaine was going to sit down, then thought better of it and answered her question. "Naval records," he said, which was mostly the truth.

She threw her pen down hard on the table where the scraps of paper swallowed it. "What's this got to do with my ship?"

"I'd like to charter it."

Patty Hunsecker smirked. "Yeah? Well, just take your rods and reels and head down two bars."

"What I'm after is stuck on the ocean floor and isn't likely to bite at any bait, Miss Hunksitter,—"

"That's *Hunsecker*."

"—and I don't need a captain who knows where to find marlin. I need a boat with high tech salvage gear, strictly state of the art.''

"Sorry," Patty snapped back, feeling about the paper for her pen, "I'm not for hire.''

This time Blaine did slide into the booth opposite her.

"I didn't ask you to sit down.''

"And I'm afraid I wasn't asking to use your boat. You see, any ship operating in these waters does so with the permission of the United States Navy. In other words they own your ass.''

"Nobody owns my ass, mister!''

"Miss Hunsecker," Blaine responded immediately, "I could go to the navy right now and have your boat impounded indefinitely. I'm trying to do this the easy way.''

"You talk like a *federale*.''

"Of sorts.''

"How long?" she sighed.

"Two days, three at most.''

"At which point my grant becomes history. Look, it might not mean much to you, but the whole future of the world is tied up in the secrets of the ocean.''

"Absolutely," McCracken told her, "but not for the reasons you think.''

And now, as he pulled on his sneakers to join her on deck, Blaine reflected on how well he had come to know her in a single day. She might have come on a little strong, but Patty Hunsecker wasn't a bad person, and not an unattractive one either. Her blond hair was cut short and worn in a shaggy style that required little care and could survive the harshness of constant exposure to salt air and water. The sun had become so much a friend to her that she wore her tan naturally and without worry. They had sat on deck in the dark hours of Sunday night, as her boat, the *Runaway*, glided through the currents on autopilot.

"Interesting name," McCracken had said.

"More than interesting—accurate. Describes my life.''

"In Bel Air?''

"The little time I spent there. I was always off at schools, and when I came home my parents weren't there. Always loved the sea, though. My grandmother died, and as soon as I turned twenty-one I used the trust fund she had left me to buy this ship, outfit it, and run away. Learned what I had to in college. My parents thought I was studying acting.''

"They must have had good reason to if you fooled them for four years.''

"I left after three,'' Patty Hunsecker corrected. "Knew what I had to by then. The rest I could learn out here. Kind of on-the-job training.''

"With all that money, why bother about the grant?''

"Legitimacy, proof that someone cares about what you're trying to do. Otherwise I'd just be the young dreamer my parents figured I was when I sailed off.''

"Motored,'' Blaine said.

"Excuse me for saying so, mister, but it doesn't seem much different for you.''

"We're all running away from something, Patty, and I've got an Indian friend who'll tell you it's always ourselves. We create our own little worlds of illusions, and once they're gone, all we're left with is reality. That can be pretty tough to take.''

"But in the end we're the only ones who can figure it out for ourselves, right? I think that's what I like most about making a home for myself here on the *Runaway*.''

"Except you're still running, still deluding yourself. It might be the Pacific Ocean, but when you're out here and can't see anyone else it's *your* ocean, which puts us right back where we started. Believe me, I know where you're coming from. You're out here to save the water. For a long time I was out to save the world.''

"Not this time?''

"It might come to that, yeah, but all I give a damn about is one twelve-year-old boy who deserves more than the short end of the stick he got stuck with at birth. It's time he saw it in all its length.''

Patty Hunsecker eyed him quizzically but didn't press. Mc-Cracken had taken his leave soon after and drifted off into an uneasy sleep that ended only when she had awakened him minutes before. Yawning as he stepped up into the morning sun, he noticed Patty had settled herself before one of the many gadgets on the deck of the *Runaway*.

"This might be your lucky day, McCracken," she said without looking up at him.

"Planning to ask me out?"

"Even better." Her eyes rose slowly. "My readings indicate that your coordinates are located smack dab on a large swell in the surface of the sea."

"Is that good?"

"Well, since the pressure in regular depths in these parts is sufficient to turn any ship into a tin can, it is if you were hoping to find something reasonably intact."

"Then it's a ship that's down there?"

"Magnetometer readings indicated a large steel mass almost directly beneath our present position."

"And can you find it?"

"With a little help from a friend, absolutely."

"Excuse me?"

"RUSS."

"Who?"

"Not who, what. RUSS, R-U-S-S. Stands for Robotic Underwater Systems Sight. Step right this way and I'll introduce you."

McCracken followed Patty to the stern to a mechanism tightly wrapped in a custom-fit tarpaulin. She undid the zippers and ties, and he helped her strip the covering off to reveal a white squat object as long as he was tall, looking like a miniature submarine or an overweight torpedo.

"Meet RUSS."

"The pleasure's all mine."

RUSS was mostly white with some red splashed on and came complete with a miniature conning tower like the kind found on manned submarines. Its front nose was composed of specially sealed glass, and Blaine didn't have to be told to know that a camera behind it broadcast everything it saw back to the *Runaway*. It was sitting on some sort of motorized hydraulic mechanism obviously constructed to ease the process of lowering it to and raising it back from the water.

"RUSS weighs in at well over a thousand pounds," Patty explained, reading his mind.

"Lotta weight for a little guy."

"There has to be, considering the kind of pressure he's subjected to in depths like the Marianas. It has something to do with weight displacement and pressure per cubic inch. RUSS's hull is so dense, he can resist the pressure up to virtually any depth. And he's powered by a special fuel cell that allows for extended journeys in the depths without having to recharge."

"So we lower him into the water . . ."

"And I drive him robotically from up here and hope he finds whatever it is you're looking for."

Patty dropped the *Runaway*'s anchor and, with McCracken looking on, activated the hydraulic mechanism which slowly eased the submersible toward the gunwale and then lowered it into the sea. The flip of a final switch released RUSS into the water and he sank slowly, almost gratefully, like a fish tossed back after being snared.

The last of his miniature conning tower was still visible when McCracken watched Patty grasp a portable instrument panel complete with four multi-directional levers surrounding a center joystick.

"This is how I drive him," she explained.

"Looks simple."

"Because it is. Fully transistorized and, of course, waterproof."

Patty eased the joystick forward and Blaine could see RUSS level out just beneath the surface. A light touch on one of the four levers and it began its descent straight down into the deep blue of the water. Fortunately RUSS possessed cameras aiming both straight above and straight below to insure it never missed anything.

"It'll be between twenty and twenty-five minutes before he reaches the swell in the ocean floor we're over. Here, let me show you the rest of the setup."

They moved toward a canopied section of the deck nearest the cabin, and Patty took a chair behind what looked to be a combination computer monitor and television screen. Closer inspection revealed it to be both; the screen was atop the monitor and joined to it by a host of wires running like spaghetti through the rear panels. Patty began typing commands into the keyboard before her and instantly the screens jumped to life.

"I drive RUSS but it's the computer that talks to him."

"What do you mean?"

"Well, this kind of exploration has reached new heights—perhaps I should say depths—technologically. Can you see the picture forming on the television screen?"

McCracken leaned forward until the glare was minimized. "Looks like a big swimming pool."

"The biggest. We're seeing exactly what RUSS sees as he drops further and further down. Assume he finds . . . whatever it is you're looking for."

"I don't know what I'm looking for."

"Assume he finds it anyway. Not only do we get pictures, but thanks to the computer we get measurements, structural analyses, even infrared dating to get a general idea how old the find is. We can also use the computer to have RUSS focus his camera in close on anything we choose. That usually comes in especially handy when . . ."

Patty Hunsecker continued to expound on the various capabilities and virtues of the RUSS system. RUSS and other submersibles like it were no doubt on the verge of opening up whole new, never-before-seen worlds and lowering the risk to human life substantially in the process. After she was finished, they spent the next few minutes watching the screen that pictured exactly what RUSS saw as he sank into the depths.

"I notice the picture isn't getting any darker even though he's sinking lower and lower."

"Very good," Patty complimented. "I might make a scientist out of you yet. That's something I neglected to explain. RUSS's seeing eye automatically adjusts the light exposure to give us a consistent look. Any darker and we wouldn't be able to see a thing. Too much light and the contrast would make accurate identification difficult."

"Where is he?"

Patty punched a few keys on her terminal. Figures danced about the screen almost instantly.

"I'm getting confused readings. Too many echoes, too many—"

She stopped when a beeping sound started up. Blaine was unable to pin down exactly which of the machines it was coming from.

"What is it?"

"His vertical sensors, elaborate sonar actually, have locked on to something."

"What?"

"School of fish probably. . . ."

The beeping sound became more rapid. Patty checked the figures running wildly across her monitor.

"Well, it's no school of fish, and it seems to be centered almost directly on the underwater rise he's coming down on. Looks like we're about to find what you dragged me out here for, McCracken."

Blaine's head was almost against hers as they gazed at the television screen. His heart picked up its pace. Something dread and cold grabbed him from within, telling him he didn't really want to know what RUSS was about to find. The beeping became maddening and Patty turned a switch to lower the decibel level. When it became constant, she flipped another of the levers on the transistorized board on her left and brought RUSS to a dead stop in the water.

"Christ, he must be right over it! Your coordinates were right on the mark."

"You were expecting any different?"

"I didn't know what to expect, but I'll tell you this much: for an object to remain totally anchored on the bottom, it's got to carry a lot of bulk and weight."

Patty flipped a few buttons and the picture sharpened in view. There was a shape barely discernible in the darkness. Patty gave it as much brightness as she could, and Blaine immediately made out a huge ship's tower, something from a heavy cruiser or battleship maybe. His first thought was that he was at the wrong coordinates. Otherwise they had come all this way just to find another relic from World War II.

Patty used the joystick to maneuver RUSS closer to and over the vessel that was still gaining shape.

"What is it?" she asked Blaine.

"Some sort of warship," McCracken confirmed to himself.

"Heavy cruiser class, I think. Had their heyday in World War II and haven't seen much of the seas since. Time passed them by."

"Well, it looks pretty much intact. Wait, spoke too soon. Take a look at this," Patty said, and slowed RUSS over the starboard side forward beneath a huge gun turret. She maneuvered the joystick to drop RUSS low and back him away from the ship's hull to provide a more complete view of what they had uncovered through the front-mounted camera.

"Christ, what the hell did that?"

McCracken saw the jagged holes in the ship's starboard hull but didn't reply. He felt a growing realization of what they had found here but pushed it back, terrified of the consequences it might imply.

"Wake up, McCracken! I asked you what the hell did that?"

"Torpedoes," he said finally. "You can tell by the angle of entry and blast radius. Those babies carried a rather precise signature."

"This ship was sunk in World War II?"

McCracken's response was to move closer to the monitor screen. "Take RUSS forward to her bow. Let's see if we can read her name."

She turned back toward him before maneuvering the joystick. "You know what this ship is, don't you?"

"I don't know anything. Not yet."

She shrugged him off and started to work the red, ball-topped handle to bring RUSS forward along the length of the dead cruiser.

"My God, could any bodies still be inside?"

"Judging by the position of the holes that sunk her, I'd say the great majority of those on board got off alive."

"To be rescued?"

"Maybe."

"You're not telling me everything you know!"

"I don't want to distract you from your driving."

RUSS had almost reached the boat's front section. They could see she was wedged in the silt of the upward slope of a rise in the ocean floor. She was keeling over to starboard and seemed on the verge of tumbling over onto the submersible that had invaded her world of death.

"She's remarkably well preserved," McCracken noted.

"You find lots of weird stuff in the Marianas, and everyone's got a different interpretation for it. Hold on, I think we've got something. . . ."

Patty slowed RUSS to a stop and McCracken was certain he could make out a sequence of letters on the screen before him. There was some sort of pattern; though the paint had been lost years before, the stenciled border was still intact. Patty brought the submersible backward and held it in place over the boldest letters left.

U S, then a blank space followed by a splotch of shapes that were unreadable.

"I'm going to infrared," Patty told him, and flipped another switch. "Now let's add magnification and see what we come up with. . . . There we go. That does it. . . . What the hell? . . ."

McCracken saw the letters and felt the same kind of cold dread those on the ship must have felt forty-five years ago when she was hit. His breath tasted drier than salt. Up until the last he had hoped his initial suspicions were wrong. But the corpse ship's name running across the screen eliminated any chance of that:

USS *Indianapolis*

CHAPTER 13

"I KNOW THAT NAME," PATTY WAS SAYING. "I KNOW IT from somewhere . . ."

"The *Indianapolis* was the ship that delivered the atom bombs that were used on Hiroshima and Nagasaki. It dropped them at Tinian, then stopped briefly at Guam en route to Leyte, where it was sunk by a Japanese submarine."

"Of course! Those holes we found farther back on starboard. It fits! It fits!" She sounded genuinely excited. "We're looking at one of the great finds in salvage history."

"Except we can't legitimately claim it," Blaine told her. "Because someone else got here first."

"Slide RUSS back along the hull to around the midpoint," Blaine told her.

"Why?"

"Because I thought I noticed something on the screen before when he moved by. His camera wasn't angled right for proper viewing, so it was only a glimpse."

"Whatever you say . . ."

Patty maneuvered RUSS so he was actually gliding sideways, which slowed him because of the increased resistance, but provided an excellent view of the long stretch of hull in the process.

"There!" McCracken said suddenly. "Stop!"

Patty pulled the small joystick toward her and the submersible's eye locked on a large hole a third of the way down the exposed reaches of the *Indianapolis*'s hull.

"Doesn't look like a torpedo did that," she commented. "It's a perfect circle."

"More likely cutting tools."

She went to magnification again and the screen filled with a close-up of the hole. "On the money, McCracken. The edges are sliced evenly. Somebody made an entrance for themselves into that ship right here, and not too long ago either." She looked up at him as he continued to lean over her shoulder. "The salvage team that preceded us here?"

"That would be my guess. But it seems a little deep for divers."

"They could have ridden down in a manned submersible and emerged into the water only after the hole was made. You should see what some of the big salvage boys carry for equipment. High tech to the max. Strictly state of the art."

"Bring RUSS up."

"But he could fit through that hole. They left us a doorway inside that ship to see what they might have made off with. Don't you want to—"

"Bring him up. We've got to get out of here."

She sensed nervousness in his voice and went to work on the transistorized console immediately. An instant later RUSS had begun his rise and the *Indianapolis* had disappeared from view, returned to the isolation it had lived in for over forty-five years.

"You spoke of a weapon the salvage team came here to recover," Patty said. "What you're telling me is that this is the ship they pulled it off of."

"At least tried to."

"They were successful, all right, and if you let me send RUSS inside, I can—"

"Just keep bringing him up."

"You're scared. I can hear it in your voice. But what does this have to do with the weapon you're searching for now? You said it yourself. The *Indianapolis* dropped its cargo off at Tinian. Her storage holds were empty when she was sunk."

"Maybe. Maybe not."

"What do you mean?"

"I don't know. All I know is that we're not going to find out here in the middle of the—"

"Go on. Finish what you were saying."

But McCracken wasn't listening to her. His ears had detected a faint hum approaching in the distance.

"Get on your radio and call the naval station."

"What?"

"Signal a Mayday! Give them our position!" Blaine commanded, because by then the hum had given way to a louder whirl, and his eyes picked up a dim speck on the open skyline— the shape of a plane slowly gaining size and substance as it soared toward them.

"Jesus Christ," Patty Hunsecker muttered, already heading for the radio inside the cabin.

Blaine followed her inside. The plane was now only seconds away.

"What have you got for weapons on board this tub?"

"Saving the oceans is a pacifistic mission."

"I was afraid of that. . . ."

"Some spear guns, a flare pistol. That's about it, I'm afraid." Patty searched the band for the proper sending frequency with the mike pressed to her lips. "Guam Station, this is *Runaway*. This is a Mayday call. Repeat, this is a Mayday call. Our position is . . ."

The rest of her message was drowned out by the screech of the aircraft zooming over them and the explosion of water as a grenade dropped from it exploded just behind the *Runaway*'s stern.

"They're trying to kill us!" Patty shrieked in the midst of her repeat message to Guam Station. In the small portal window before them, they saw the twin-engined plane bank for another pass.

"Very observant. Just keep sending . . . after you hand me those spear guns."

Patty Hunsecker didn't bother to protest, just rushed to a supply closet at the foot of the cabin stairs and yanked out a trio of state-of-the-art spear guns. They were plenty dangerous if wielded properly, but were meant to be used underwater and thus limited for this purpose.

"Runaway, *we read you*," a voice squawked over the radio. *"This is Guam Station, please come in. I say again, please come in. Over. . . ."*

The attacking plane swirled in from the bow, and the portal exploded into flying shards of glass behind the bullets rupturing it. McCracken flung himself on Patty, discarding the spear guns long enough to tackle her to the floor. Above them the radio smoked and fizzled.

"Damn," she moaned.

"Did you give them our coordinates?"

"Yes, but that doesn't mean they heard anything."

Blaine's ears picked up the quickening of the plane's engine as it came at them yet again, over the stern this time. Staying low, he pulled the spear guns toward him and was moving toward the cabin door when the next explosion rocked him. The *Runaway* shook like a ship struck by a great wave, then listed sharply to starboard. He slid toward the steps to the deck and just managed to avoid the ruined radio as it came flying down from its perch. He tried to grab hold of Patty, but she slipped away from him. He saw her head ram hard into the wall. She slumped over and Blaine propped her up against the bulkhead nearest the door to keep her safe from the water that would be rushing in momentarily.

McCracken was moving for the deck, spear guns in hand, when the plane swooped down again. The next blast took them on the stern, and the dread smell of smoke and loose oil flooded his nostrils. He knocked the cabin door open with his shoulders, and thick, black smoke flooded down into the cabin. The stern of the *Runaway* was taking on water, and the rearmost section of gunwale was even with the sea. All of RUSS's hydraulic lift was now under the surface.

The plane was coming in again, from the side this time, and Blaine got his first clear look at what he was facing. It was a twin-engined job all right, a red and white Cessna 310, something any fool could rent at any flying outlet. An expanded fuel capacity and a stopover at the nearest island to fill it would have made this attack mission logistically simple. Though it was only a regular plane, the grenades and gunfire were coming from an open side window that was much too small to bother considering as a target.

But what else did he have?

The plane whirled closer, and Blaine grabbed one of the spear guns and rose to a kneeling position amidst the noxious smoke, which grew even blacker. He wanted to make sure the gunman saw him, so he would have the pilot drop even farther, which would make it easier for Blaine's intended shot to find the mark.

The bullets pierced the gunwale and Blaine held his ground as shards of wood sprayed around him. He waited until the plane's call letters were close enough to read before taking final aim with the spear gun. He never felt himself pull the spear gun's trigger, and he knew he had done so only when the mechanism kicked briefly. The spent spear was still hurtling upward when the plane flew past with barely thirty feet separating it from the sea. But the spear missed the open window and clanged harmlessly against the Cessna's frame.

Blaine watched helplessly as the plane banked round for another run. Seconds later it plunged for the *Runaway* again, machine gunner clacking off a burst that effectively pinned Blaine when he started to move to another area of the deck. A misthrown grenade exploded in the water and showered him. A few seconds were now his and he seized them, knowing what he had to do.

It was imperative to knock out the pilot, instead of trying for the gunman. He could never manage the task with a spear alone, though, especially fired at so difficult an angle. He needed something more, but where to find it? He pushed himself through the deepening pool in the stern and reached into the wood-strewn muck. His hand closed on a long, thick shard that had wedged in the remnants of the deck, a piece of RUSS's titanium hydraulic mechanism. He held his breath and went under to achieve the purchase he needed to pull it free.

When he came back up with the shard in hand, the Cessna was diving directly for him again. The grenade was right on target this time, blowing out the top of the cabin and sending the top section collapsing inward along with the canopy housing Patty's equipment. He smelled ruined wood and found himself clawing through water as the *Runaway* began to drop farther and faster beneath the surface. He passed the engine opening and could smell the hot stench of an oil fire struggling to burn under the floods of seawater pouring through the hatch.

Blaine reached his two remaining spear guns as the plane flew well beyond him and banked around for another attack run. He wrenched free the steel line from one of the spear guns and used it to fasten the six-inch shard of titanium steel from RUSS's lift onto the point of the second spear.

Work, damn you! Work!

As the Cessna came in fast, the gunman misjudged Blaine's position and his bullets plunged into the sea. Again the plane soared and its engine sputtered as the pilot brought it around again too steeply. Blaine made sure the steel shard was wedged tight to the spear as the Cessna came straight for him. This time he rose to meet it. No calculation of the physics was involved in the shot he was about to attempt, just a reliance on the feeling of when and at what angle he should pull the trigger.

The plane's attack run brought it directly into the sun. The pilot would have to squint, at least some portion of his vision obscured by the blinding light off the Pacific. It was the final edge Blaine needed.

McCracken rose to a full standing position, the water now stretching all the way up to his thighs and rising farther by the second. He wanted this to appear to be a futile last stand. He wanted them to think he was resigned to death so they would descend all the way to finish him.

He imagined he could feel the heat of bullets singeing the air around him; it was impossible to tell how close the last few came before he brought the spear gun to his shoulder. The plane roared at him and he imagined he could see the pilot's eyes, not squinting but bulging, and suddenly in surprise. The weapon was just fifty feet away when Blaine pulled the trigger.

The spear jetted out and seemed to wobble briefly under the extra weight of the attached steel shard before straightening out on line with the windshield. McCracken saw the spear ram home when the plane was just twenty feet over him. He did not see the windshield disintegrate on impact or the splinters of glass spray into the pilot's face, which drove his hands upward from the stick. What he did see was the Cessna list and drop suddenly, falling as if knocked off the edge of a table. It struck the hard surface of the water and broke apart on impact without flames or smoke, its fuselage continuing to skim the surface as if on water skis, shredding pieces of itself along the way.

Blaine had that moment to enjoy his triumph and no more, for the *Runaway* was relinquishing its last grasp on life. By the time he got back to Patty the water was up to his stomach and was lapping at her chest in what remained of the cabin. Her pulse was still strong and he pulled her to him with an arm cupped lifesaving-style beneath her throat. Then he eased the two of them out the doorway and away from the sinking ship.

He swam only slightly, reluctant even then to abandon the vehicle that was their only hope to survive the fury of the sea. The life jackets were under ten feet of water in the cabin, and to make a try for them would mean leaving Patty alone. He knew that if Patty's Mayday message had gotten through, even under the best of conditions it would be many hours before the rescue party dispatched from Guam could find and save them. Much too long in any event for him to maintain his hold on Patty and save himself. But it would be much, much longer if her broadcast of their coordinates didn't get through at all. A wide-scale search would be required and that could take days. The sight of something white bobbing in the sea before him caught Blaine's eye. His first thought was *Shark!* but his next was something else entirely. Holding tight to Patty, he paddled for the object.

At last he was close enough to reach out and grasp RUSS's transistorized control panel. Bracing it against Patty, he fiddled with the joystick, then eased it toward him. He clung to hope, with nothing else to hold on to.

A slight churning in the water made him swing to the right. RUSS's miniature conning tower crested through the surface and its automatic bilge pumps sent water through its vents. RUSS had the look of a small but majestic whale rising proudly from the sea. Still using the joystick, McCracken brought RUSS up close enough to pet it affectionately and then lay the unconscious Patty over its cylindrical bulk before he flung himself upon it. He ended up straddling the submersible as if it were a horse. Feeling it bob slightly beneath him, he made sure Patty was safe, maneuvered the joystick to head RUSS forward, and slammed the submersible's sides with make-believe spurs.

"Hiyo, Silver! Away!"

CHAPTER 14

AMIR HASSANI STOOD IN THE CENTER OF THE PLUSH LIBRARY deep within the fortified confines of the former Shah's royal palace in the Niavarin district of northeast Tehran. A huge section of the room was dominated by bookshelves housing the royal library of first editions in all languages. There were four long shelves holding books of every conceivable color binding, in addition to the neatly layered stacks from floor to ceiling on the three walls enclosing the shelves.

But as his feet padded across the luscious deep red floral carpet, Hassani was aware of the books only from the scent of leather that filled his nostrils as he addressed his audience. The representatives of the various groups that had united behind him sat in seven high-back chairs upholstered in a red velvet that matched perfectly the red of the rug. At present they sat collectively aghast and dumbfounded by his report pertaining to the first stage of the plan that would ultimately see them seize power throughout the Mideast.

"The key to the success we are about to achieve," he said, nearing the end of his presentation, "has been and will continue to be the level of secrecy I have employed in the operation that will set us on our way. There have been no leaks in security. We are poised on the brink of something awesome. It is within our grasp, and if we maintain the resolve to reach out for it, soon the state of Israel will cease to exist."

The library hall was enormous, and the result was a back-ground echo that would have unnerved his audience had they possessed the inclination to notice. Of the seven, three had come in military uniforms, three in traditional Arab robes, and one in an expensive western-style suit. They came from Syria, Libya, Jordan, Iraq, and Saudi Arabia. For himself, as always, Hassani had chosen a general's uniform from the Revolutionary Guard he was still proud to be a part of. He wore it boldly, defiantly, as if refusing to acknowledge a war had ever been lost or, more likely, to illustrate the point that a more important war was about to be won.

"You speak of the destruction of Israel," the Iraqi delegate said, "yet you continue to avoid the specifics. My concern is that we are being attentive here to the same kind of mindless rhetoric that preceded your unsuccessful campaign against my nation."

Hassani did his very best to smile at the man he had been at war with just a few years before. His cap was tilted so low over his forehead that it shadowed his face all the way down to his beard. His eyes were narrow and seldom met those of the person he was addressing. He never allowed anyone a close look at him, as if any glimpse might strip away part of his aura. He was a specter who had never been interviewed by the Western press, which condemned him for being elusive and enigmatic, and for making a travesty of Iran's post-war economic recovery.

But his smile was that of a man who saw what others failed even to look at. He had been one of the nation's military leaders, a great favorite, during the war with Iraq. His militance had forced him to flee when the final, humbling terms of peace were agreed upon. He returned, however, during the military coup that followed Khomeini's death and the failure of any of his successors to be installed as president of Iran with a promise to restore pride and hope.

"And is it not a great blessing," he continued, only half looking at the delegate from Iraq, "that the strife between our nations is at last over so we can contend with our true enemy? No one supported the end of our war more than I, not because I wished to accept defeat, but because a greater victory, a victory with the word of Allah behind it, was on the horizon. Your final roles in this victory need not be made known until the last day is upon us.''

"But I have people to organize," the Syrian delegate protested. "You promised us Israel would be ours to take in a vast sweep across lands that are rightfully ours."

"Rightfully the Palestinians, you mean," exclaimed the representative from the PLO. "Who, may I remind you, are supplying the largest complement of manpower to this invasion."

"Now just wait a—"

"Gentlemen," Hassani interrupted, raising his voice only slightly and turning his face rapidly from one man to the other, "listen to yourselves. You make the lot of the Jew easy by bickering with each other. Israel is not our greatest enemy; we are our own greatest enemy, and that in the past has prevented the miracle we have now accomplished by uniting our forces together. It also accounts for my reasons in continuing to hold back the final elements of our plan."

"Are you saying you don't trust us?" asked the delegate from Saudi Arabia, the single one dressed in a western suit.

"Of course I'm not. But for this operation to be successful I said from the beginning that I required *your* trust, your single-minded devotion to a cause that will only just be beginning when we overrun Israel. If one of you disagreed with the substance of my plan, you could leave here and destroy it. My holding it back is simply insurance against the exercise of such poor judgment. I would be foolish not to heed the lessons of the past. You will know what you need when you need to know it."

"Hah!" the Libyan delegate laughed, rising to his feet and looking cramped in the medal-layered khaki uniform that was too tight on him. "We sit here and listen to a man who has already lost one war. I say to you, General, that you have accomplished your task by bringing us together and uniting us behind the common goal of Israel's destruction. Now let us do it our way. Am I right?" he asked of the Iraqi delegate, searching for support.

"No," the darker man said, "you are not." The Iraqi's eyes turned to Hassani who had stood rigid and silent through the Libyan's tirade. "General Hassani did not lose the war. No man could have done more when faced against the might of Iraq."

"Listen," the Libyan responded, "I am not arguing intentions, only procedure. Comrades, together we have at our disposal millions of troops who can enter Israel from all sides and avoid the mistakes of '67 and '73. We can have them prepared within two weeks and leave words behind."

"You would have them die for their cause?" Hassani asked.

"Of course I would! Any Arab would!"

"To die in pursuit of a dream instead of seeing that dream come to fruition? I think not. Our peoples need no more martyrs. I am not advocating denying Arabs the chance to fight for what they so richly deserve. But let them fight for certain victory instead of almost certain death at the hands of the cursed Jewish state."

"Certain death to the Israelis as well," the PLO delegate added.

"And they will use their bombs to obliterate all of us in a last desperate attack. What have we gained? Nothing, gentlemen, nothing at all. Overrunning Israel isn't an end, it's a means for all of you to come to power in your individual countries and unite the Mideast as it has never been united before. We have been mistaken in the past to be so narrow and shortsighted in our goals."

"You continue to ignore the obvious," the Saudi protested. "Israel may never have faced as strong an enemy as we are, but neither have we faced as strong an Israel. Nuclear weapons aside, her conventional arsenal, including jet fighters, is terrifying."

"Granted, Mr. Ambassador. And to combat that force we now have in our possession a weapon that will render Israel helpless."

"Why have we not been told of this weapon before?"

"There was no reason. Just as there is no reason to be any more specific today."

"When then?" the Syrian asked.

"At our next meeting; Sunday, May fourteenth," the general returned. "Israeli Independence Day. Three days before our invasion begins."

On a street set back from the square in front of the royal palace, a van with traditional Islamic markings was parked. Such

vans were a fixture in the streets of Tehran, though most couldn't
have said what they were, other than some version of public
works.

In the back of this particular van sat a pair of men working
amidst the most sophisticated recording equipment available in
the world. Months before, the Mossad had managed to plant
bugs throughout the royal palace, a new kind of bug with a built-
in jamming device that made finding it by any kind of electronic
sweep impossible.

In spite of all this, extraordinarily few dividends had been
paid, as General Hassani spent little time speaking of anything
they could truly make use of. The men in the van had not seen
the delegates enter, so the meeting itself came as a complete
shock. The man wearing headphones had started scribbling notes
as was his routine, but quickly his hand began shaking too much
to keep it up.

The bastards were going to destroy Israel!

The man wearing the headphones knew all the procedures
and precautions. He knew he should have continued to listen
patiently, even with the meeting winding down. But time had
become the crucial factor in his mind, hours the issue now instead of days.

"Get us out of here!" he ordered the agent working the recording meters and levels.

"What?"

"Get behind the wheel and drive!"

"But we're supposed to—"

"I don't care! Do you hear me? I don't care! Get me to the
relay point. Get me there fast."

Evira was regaining her strength. Monday had marked her
third morning in the small room, and each had seen her awaken
able to do more. She was exercising regularly on the dusty floor
now, working flexibility back into her wounded side and neck.

Kourosh had been there with her breakfast each morning when
she awoke, some bakery goods stolen from the first batch placed
out in a store window six blocks away. Two mornings back he
had also managed to find coffee, but it had cooled by the time
he brought it up to her. She found herself following his flight

through the cracks in the boards over the window, amazed at
how he took to the streets as if he owned them. He bounded
gracefully about with each gutter and sidewalk crack stored in
his memory, long hair flapping about to the whims of the wind.

Kourosh had made a world for himself in the streets, but all
the same he had become as dependent on her as she had on him.
She knew he had failed to answer all her questions at once out
of fear he might return from one of his jaunts to find her gone,
no longer in need of him. Evira would have told him not to
worry, except she knew it wouldn't have changed anything. Trust
was something that did not exist in the boy's life. So their strange
relationship was based on needs that were different for each but
for the present were strong enough to keep them together.

She watched from the window now in expectation of his
bouncy return down the street. Thus far he had provided her
with several hastily drawn maps of the royal palace. Different
sections were sketched on individual sheets of gray cardboard,
drawn elaborately and exaggerated the way drawings in his comic
books were. To see the whole of the palace and the sprawling
grounds enclosing it, Evira needed only to arrange the cardboard sheets together like a puzzle. It was a huge white stone
and marble structure built by the Shah less than twenty years
before, surrounded by an outer retaining wall stretching fifteen
feet high. Within the grounds, besides the palace there was a
school, a guards' barracks, and an older palace that had been
transformed into office space with the construction of the newer
one. The main entrance was inside the front wall, accessible
only by a drive that circled round a hilly garden to prevent the
gates from being rammed. There was a servants' entrance located near the school on the northern side and a guards' entrance
near the barracks on the south.

The inside of the complex had been constructed with cele-
brations in mind. The front door opened onto a huge two-story
ballroom, complete with skylights. A service entrance on the
northern side opened onto the kitchen, with the formal dining
room situated between this and the ballroom. The sleeping quarters on the second floor had been divided into separate wings
for children and adults, the children's bedrooms facing the east
while the adults' faced the south.

Nothing in the drawings gave her a notion as to how the palace might be penetrated. For this she would have to rely again on Kourosh, as she would for finding a time when the general was inside.

No longer requiring as much sleep to heal herself during these long hours, Evira found herself bored. She picked up one of Kourosh's comic books and skimmed through it, amazed at how the same things appealed to children of all cultures. She had finished one and closed it when something caught her eye: a stamp of the bookstore where it had been purchased—Steimatzky, the largest chain in Israel. Strange. The anomaly seemed small, but Evira had learned long before that nothing was small. She inspected his horde of comics and found the same was true for all of them. It was no fluke. Every issue had been purchased at the Steimatzky chain.

Kourosh bounded into the room while she was still inspecting the comics, and she looked up at him embarrassed, as if she had violated his privacy.

"Superman's my favorite," he told her, and she noticed he had a tightly wrapped package beneath his arm. "I got a surprise for you."

"A good one, I hope."

"Wait until you see it!" He placed it atop a pair of crates and started to undo the string.

"Kourosh," Evira called to him. "Who was it who taught you how to speak English?"

He turned to her and raised his eyebrows. "The students, like I told you."

"Were they the same students who gave you the comic books?"

"Yes. Does it matter?"

"No. It's just that, well, I know English, too. I can pick up where they left off."

He turned excitedly from his chore of unwrapping her surprise. "Could you really?"

"It would be my pleasure. It's the least I can do for you after all you've done for me."

He looked suddenly sad. "I miss them."

"Miss who?"

"The students."

"The ones who were killed back at the plastics factory?"

"No, the ones who gave me the comic books, who taught me English. They haven't been around in a while."

"Say something in English for me," Evira requested, even more intrigued.

Kourosh's expression turned suddenly playful. "What do you want to hear?" he said in better English than she would have thought possible.

"Anything."

The first few lines he spoke were enough to confirm what she suspected but could make no sense of. She was good with languages. Learning them, recognizing tone and intonation, came naturally for her. Which was why she was sure that Kourosh had learned his English from Israelis!

"How many students?" she broke in suddenly.

"Oh, plenty. All haters of injustice and poverty."

"And you didn't meet them until . . ."

"I don't know. Six months ago, maybe nine. I met them through the others in the plastics factory."

"But you don't see them anymore."

"I go but they are no longer there. They used to meet in a building not far from here, but it's deserted now. It looks like no one was ever there."

Evira was barely hearing him. A classic stratagem was being employed. The insurgent cells in Teheran had been infiltrated by Israelis.

What have I stumbled upon here? Israelis posing as students in Tehran?

A large group that had settled in the area and then departed, possibly leaving some of their number in place.

"Do you want to see your surprise?" Kourosh was asking.

She nodded, and he went back to tearing the brown bag apart until he could gently lift the contents from inside and hold them out for her to see.

"What do you think?"

She looked at him speechless, for her means of access to the royal palace and Hassani were before her.

Kourosh was holding the uniform of a palace servant.

* * *

The two women approached the heavy front door of the stone house in Falmouth, England, unconcerned about being seen. Clearly the house was too isolated for neighbors to be a problem, and if someone had unexpectedly been in the vicinity one of them would have felt their presence earlier.

The smaller of the two led the way, the larger one bringing up the rear with the graceful menace of a jungle cat. She was exceedingly tall for a woman, six inches over six feet not counting the boots she was never without. She moved soundlessly, except for the slight creaking of her skin-tight leather pants and matching waist-length jacket. Her hair was cut close and sharply edged in punk style, with wisps jutting in every direction. The smaller woman had a tomboy haircut but was dressed like a schoolgirl in plaid skirt and green sweater. Her persistent smile seemed as false as the larger one's ever-present scowl looked natural.

The door opened just as the two women began ascending the steps.

"What are you two doing here?" It was the puzzled voice of the Arab power broker Mohammed Fett.

"We have come for the boy," the smaller one said.

"Ah, Tilly," Fett said, "you are too late. He was moved to the other location two days ago."

"Other location," the taller one echoed.

"On whose orders?" Tilly asked.

"Rasin's, of course."

Tilly turned behind her to the large figure in black leather. "Lace, did you hear what he said?"

"Regrettable," Lace said. She stepped forward until she was next to Tilly.

"What's wrong?" Fett asked.

"Rasin sent us to kill the boy," Lace told him.

"*What?*" the flabbergasted Fett exclaimed, and then he realized what had happened. "Evira! It must have been Evira's doing. Of course! She must have— But I know where he was taken. I can send you there."

Lace shook her head. "He won't be there any longer."

"You shouldn't have been so careless," Tilly added immediately.

"It's all right," Fett assured them, stepping out onto the porch. "I'll alert my people. The boy will be found, I assure you."

"Yes," Lace said as her hands darted up from her hips and closed on Fett's head. "He will."

With that she lifted Fett effortlessly off the stone until his head was even with hers and his toes were dangling. He was still trying to speak when she twisted his head violently to the right. There was a snap, and his whole body spasmed. Lace pressed him close against her then to feel his final breath against her face as it fled from his dangling body. He was suddenly quite cold.

"Fool," she said, and tossed him aside. She felt very hot. "Tilly," she called.

The smaller woman opened the door and passed through ahead of Lace, who dragged Fett's body behind her. She placed him in a chair and arranged him so he could watch what transpired with his dead eyes. There were only two things Lace enjoyed doing, and it was nice when they could be done in sequence, for that heightened the pleasure of both. She kissed the corpse once on the lips and turned to find Tilly already on the floor with her skirt and panties torn off and fingers stroking her vagina.

"It was beautiful, Lace," she said to her friend, who was pulling off her leather jacket. "Beautiful."

"Like you, Tilly. Like you."

And then Lace was on top of her. Their mouths met in a hot passion as Lace's hand replaced Tilly's over her clitoris. The smaller woman's fingers raked through the stubbly blond hair of her partner, as the dead eyes of Fett looked on.

"Beautiful," they said almost in unison.

CHAPTER 15

MCCRACKEN AND PATTY HUNSECKER SPENT SIX MISERABLE hours atop RUSS before the navy search planes out of Guam finally spotted them late Monday afternoon. Blaine greeted their universal drop-wing signal that they'd sighted him with no small degree of relief; he had feared days more would pass before they found him. He also knew that Patty could not go much longer without medical attention. When she failed to come to during their first hours at sea, Blaine feared she had slipped into a coma.

Dusk was fast approaching when a jet-powered helicopter, adorned with navy colors, hovered over them and lowered a line. McCracken sent Patty up ahead of him and found her already being worked on by paramedics when he joined her inside the cabin.

"Guam," he told the pilot with a healthy smirk. "And step on it."

Patty Hunsecker regained consciousness in the early hours of Tuesday morning after being hospitalized at the naval base. Blaine was at her side when she awoke, glad for the opportunity to talk before he had to leave the island.

"Managed to save RUSS, though," he said, after doing his best to apologize for what he had cost her. "Crew on the chopper wasn't exactly overjoyed."

"I'm sure you didn't give them much choice."

"I was a perfect gentleman about it. Merely threatened to break their fingers one by one."

"How'd you explain to the Navy what happened?"

"Some double-talk about an explosion. It'll hold long enough for me to sneak off the island."

"Probably help if I backed you up."

"The thought had crossed my mind."

"Just tell me what you told them."

When he was finished, Blaine's tone turned apologetic. "When all this is over I'll make sure the government picks up the tab to re-outfit you."

"How do you plan on managing that?" she asked, skeptically.

"Let's just say they owe me lots of favors. In the meantime, why don't you rest up at Bel Air? Get reacquainted with your family. They really are concerned."

"You spoke with them?"

"In your condition I thought next of kin should be advised."

"You're a bastard, McCracken."

"Go home, Patty."

"Stop running, you mean."

He took her hand. "I have to go."

"But you waited until I regained consciousness."

"It was the proper thing to do."

"And if it had taken another day?"

Blaine shrugged.

"You're a strange man, McCracken."

"I do my best."

The Mossad chief, Isser, conferred with the prime minister of Israel at least once a day and often more frequently than that. Seldom, though, did they meet in person because of the security problems posed by Isser's secret identity. The head of Mossad needed anonymity to perform his duties and never compromised that if it was at all possible.

Today it wasn't. Isser had requested an in-person meeting and the prime minister was wise enough not to ask why. They met in the older man's private study in his home. He had feigned illness earlier in the day to establish the ruse, and Isser was waiting for him when he stepped through the door, white hair flung wildly across his scalp and still wearing his bathrobe. The sickness might have been a ruse, but Isser felt saddened by how stooped his shoulders had become, how frail and old he looked.

"You'd better sit down," the Mossad chief advised.

"I'm not really sick, remember? This is just a costume for the benefit of anyone who might be sneaking a peek."

"That doesn't mean you won't be sick after I'm finished."

The prime minister settled himself in a leather chair and Isser placed a cassette tape player on the table closest to him. He pushed the *play* button and spoke as he waited for the voices from Tehran to replace his. "This reached me from our team covering Hassani just hours ago. It speaks for itself."

As if on cue, the voice of General Amir Hassani came on. He greeted the delegates seated around him, and Isser fast-forwarded to the spot where the discussion got interesting. The prime minister sat transfixed through it all, mouth dropping at the intent of the words. Near the end of General Hassani's final speech, Isser switched it off.

"The 'delegates' were never named but I recognize their voices. I know them, don't I, Isser?"

"Seven of our nation's greatest enemies."

"And they have come together to plan our destruction."

Isser nodded. "Hassani has turned their fanaticism into ambition. Ambition makes a much more potent foe."

The prime minister rose from his chair and paced nervously to the window, then started back. "My God, could this truly be?"

"You heard the tape, sir. We have no choice but to believe it can."

"A mass invasion preceded by the employment of this . . . weapon. What weapon, Isser?"

"My men have no idea. You heard the tape. This was apparently the first mention even the delegates had heard of it." Isser hesitated as if to catch his thoughts. "Hassani's movements since he came to power have been strange. He disappears for days on end, weeks sometimes. We can only assume now that those disappearances are directly related to his unification of the militant Arab world and this mysterious superweapon he refers to.''

"A collection of madmen!"

"Poised along our very borders."

"Any conventional attack we can put down, but obviously General Hassani has something more in store for us."

"Most certainly," Isser agreed. "And you are correct in limiting our problem to the general himself."

The prime minister returned to his chair and sank into it, appearing to have been swallowed. "Go on."

"The tape says their next meeting will be held on our Independence Day. Accordingly, I suggest we activate Operation Firestorm ahead of schedule."

"The old bastards would never go for it."

"Then we won't give them a choice. We agreed to underwrite their bizarre plan on the condition that final control was left in our hands. I suggest we exercise it."

"Easier said than done. The old men have planned everything to the minute. And you forget, my friend, that part of what attracted us to Operation Firestorm was the fact that traditional lines of communication were bypassed. The old men's soldiers are divided into individual insurgent cells that will not connect with each other until the hour of Firestorm is upon us. Before that time, reaching them all to move up the timetable is not feasible."

Isser wasn't ready to give in yet. "I'll pay Isaac another visit in Hertzelia. Maybe we can work something out."

"You seem to get on quite well with the old war horse." The prime minister chuckled, making fun of himself at the same time since he was not far from being a contemporary of Isaac's.

Isser nodded. "I met with them last two days ago. Apparently their people alerted them to the next step Evira took after Ben-Neser's failed attempt to take her in Jaffa Square."

"Which was?"

"She went to Tehran to assassinate Hassani."

"And the old men stopped her, no doubt. My God, they don't

miss anything when it comes to their mission. If they had left Evira alone, maybe Hassani wouldn't have been around to chair that meeting we just heard. Ironic, isn't it?''

"They stopped her, sir, but they didn't kill her. She remains at large, although stripped of her contacts and probably on the run.''

The prime minister laughed again, only this time there was no trace of amusement. "Hah! Perhaps we should help her. Whatever threat we are facing begins and ends with Hassani. Eliminate him and . . . Achhhhh, what am I saying? We must look for other options anywhere we can find them.''

"One might be closer than we think.''

The prime minister leaned forward. "What are you talking about?''

"Back to Jaffa Square again. You read my report?''

"Yes. Of course.''

"My correspondence with U.S. intelligence has convinced me the American agent McCracken was operating on his own when he met with Evira. The picture remains vague, but the trail that led him here indicates he was somehow co-erced.''

"By Evira? For what possible reason?'

"We don't know. What we do know is that McCracken went to Japan from here and then to Guam.''

"Guam?''

"The specific destinations are unimportant. What is important is that he is obviously on the trail of something that Evira put him onto. And something is obviously stopping him from seeking outside help, at least openly.''

"What is your point?''

"Evira wanted McCracken for this job and only McCracken. And whatever she has set him after must have something to do with what took her to Tehran to kill Hassani.''

"You're jumping from one assumption to another, Isser.''

"The key is those ex-soldiers that fired on the crowd in Jaffa. Assume they were there to kill Evira, perhaps McCracken as well. Then Evira reappears in Tehran intending to kill Hassani. The connection is obvious.''

"Not to me.'' The old man sighed.

"Evira needed McCracken, and the reason must somehow be connected to her plan to assassinate Hassani. My hope is that if we can find out what McCracken is pursuing, the shadows of Hassani's plan will gain substance. So McCracken pursues the answers . . ."

"While we pursue McCracken," completed the prime minister. "I remember him and his men from the Yom Kippur War in '73. Good luck finding him, Isser."

"We have the Americans' cooperation."

"With McCracken, that may work against us."

Yosef Rasin listened to Daniel's report with growing impatience. Distance had already blurred a connection further disrupted by scrambling and rerouting.

"The boy was gone by the time the women arrived, you say," Rasin commented when Daniel was finished, apparently more interested in that than in the failure to kill McCracken in the Pacific.

"It was Evira's work. We have confirmed that much."

"Interesting she would care enough about the boy to go to such trouble."

"We have misjudged her before. Several times. Word is she is still at large in Tehran. Do you hear me? Tehran!"

"I hear you, Daniel. There is no reason to shout."

"What if she knows the truth? What if she understands the true substance of our plan? What if she has figured out the—"

"She understands nothing! You are giving her credit for reaching conclusions she could not possibly have reached."

"But she is still out there, still dangerous."

"She is *not* the problem, Daniel. McCracken is the problem." Rasin paused. "We can assume he found what he was looking for, of course."

"Yes."

"Then his next move is obvious. We must anticipate his questions, and where the answers to those questions will take him. Yes. Yes . . ."

"And then what?"

"Send our two women to America. We will leave his elimination to them this time. No mistakes that way, Daniel," Rasin told him. "No mistakes at all."

CHAPTER 16

"**M**ORNING, HANK," MCCRACKEN SAID TO THE FIGURE seated on the steps of the Lincoln Memorial. And when Belgrade started to rise, Blaine signaled him back down. "No need for formality among friends. Besides, don't want the contents of those file folders under your leg to blow away now, do we?"

"Jesus H., MacNuts," Belgrade responded in his lazy South Carolina drawl. "You better be right about how important this is."

"How many terrorists have I brought in for you, old buddy? This wipes the slate clean."

"All the same, if they hang my ass in a sling, I'd like to think it was worth it."

"Sling ain't been made big enough to cover your ass, Hank."

McCracken had reached Washington Tuesday evening and found himself with no desire to do anything but take a long shower. After the shower he ordered up a meal from room service and then felt he was ready to get Hank Belgrade out of bed. The call to his old friend, who now liaised between the departments of State and Defense and handled the dirty linen of both, had not taken very long. Belgrade hadn't put up an argument but Blaine could tell from his voice that he was baffled by the information requested.

When Blaine finally did drift off to sleep, he dreamed of

Matthew, of the first time he had seen the boy charging down the sideline of the rugby pitch. The pride warmed him in the dream, overcoming the raw cold of that damp day. But then the dream turned sour and he stood on the sideline looking for Matthew and not being able to find him among the other boys. And then John Neville was by his side with his head twisted all around and blood leaking from the sides of his mouth and not seeming to know he was dead.

Leave me alone, Blaine wanted to tell the corpse in the dream. *It wasn't my fault!*

And even then he wasn't sure what he was referring to, or which of the characters in the dream he was addressing. At last he woke up to a sky still dark, sweating despite the low temperature of the air-conditioned room and tangled tightly in his bedsheet. He took another shower, a cold one this time, and sat by the window looking out on the stillness of the Washington night.

He slid off to sleep again in the chair, where he was warmed by the sun as it began to stream through the window. He was awakened finally by his eight A.M. wake-up call. He showered and had barely dried himself when room service arrived with the breakfast he had preordered the night before. A fresh set of clothes was the next order of business, and Saks was more than happy to oblige.

At ten A.M. sharp a taxi deposited him at the Vietnam memorial, and he was drawn to the black granite display. The men who had died with him weren't even listed here because they had been part of something so secret that its existence, and thus their passing, remained unacknowledged. How meaningless their deaths seemed in view of that. Blaine passed the notes squeezed into the cracks and the flowers left at the foot of the wall. He stole one last glance backward at the dark stone as he made his way toward the Lincoln Memorial where Hank Belgrade was waiting.

"Okay, MacNuts," Belgrade said, making sure the file folders were safely stowed beneath one of his plump thighs as Blaine sat down next to him, "I got the dope you asked for. But I ain't about to budge this leg until I know what in hell accounts for your sudden interest in the long dead *Indianapolis*."

"As they say, the reports of her death were somewhat exaggerated."

"Son, you may have made me a hero plenty often in these parts, but I tend to be in a bitch of a mood when someone disturbs my beauty sleep with one riddle and then greets me in the morning with another."

"Then I'll come right to the point. The *Indianapolis* is enjoying a second life."

Belgrade's eyes widened. "You mean someone's found her?"

"Absolutely."

"You talk like someone who's—"

"Seen her? You bet that unslung ass of your, Hank. Not up close and personal, but on a sharp screen to be sure."

"Where's all this leading?"

"Long story. Since I know you're tired, I'll stick to the most crucial elements. Does the name Yosef Rasin mean anything to you?"

"Sure. Israeli militant who'd like to see every Arab in the world blown to hell."

"He got to the *Indianapolis* ahead of me and pulled something out of its hull."

"That's crazy! Do you know what you're saying?"

"I know what I saw. Neat hole had been sliced right out of her side to allow divers to pass through. They didn't go in to raid the storage lockers, that's a safe bet."

"So what did they go in for?"

"I was hoping you could tell me."

"Sorry."

"Then how about a weapon that can wipe out all the Arab nations while leaving Israel totally intact?"

"You're serious about this, aren't you?" Belgrade asked, trying for a laugh that wouldn't come.

"I'd hate to say deadly so under the circumstances."

"If it was on board the *Indianapolis*, that means it was ours."

"Yup."

"Then what you're saying is that she was carrying something else besides the atomic bombs."

"That's right."

Belgrade looked genuinely scared by the prospects. "Okay. What exactly are you looking for?"

"If the *Indianapolis* was carrying something else, I wouldn't expect the crew or even the captain to know. But someone had to do the loading, someone had to notice something."

"She was loaded in San Francisco," Belgrade said.

"But she stopped at Pearl Harbor en route to Tinian. The additional baggage could have been put on board there."

Belgrade shook his head. "Nope. I've been over the logs. She stopped at Pearl only long enough to pick up the observers who were the original nuke groupies. We were about to make history, in case you've forgotten."

"My guess is another kind of history was under consideration as well."

"Our mystery superweapon, of course."

"There you go."

"Only the files, memos, and reports I just accessed make no mention of any, Blaine. It's all here, just like you requested, but I can save you the bother of poring over it all by saying that even the most classified upper echelon memos say nothing about another weapon on board the *Indianapolis*."

"Then they buried it, Hank. They were better at burying things in those days."

"Not this good. They couldn't have hidden the existence of the kind of weapon you're talking about."

"Unless they had their reasons."

"And either way what you're telling me is that this Rasin character has dug up what they tried to bury."

"Like the fabled Phoenix, Hank. You and I know all about that bird from previous experience."

"Let me give it to you in a nutshell, then," Belgrade offered. "Of the original team of crew members who loaded the *Indianapolis* before she set out for Tinian, only one is still alive. Bos'n's mate by the name of Bart Joyce who currently runs a restaurant up in Boston."

"Anything else I should know about him?"

"Other than his address, that's all I've got."

McCracken looked at him closely. "Maybe on him it is.

But I can tell from your reactions to what I've said that you dug out plenty more in your travels last night. Care to enlighten me?''

Belgrade hedged. "It's all here. In the files."

"How about just the highlights?"

Belgrade sighed and gazed quickly over his shoulder as if expecting someone to be there. "MacNuts, you opened up a can of worms with this thing big enough to fish the whole damn Mississippi. Follow me close now, 'cause I ain't tellin' this story twice. The *Indianapolis* dropped her bombs at Tinian and proceeded as planned to Guam. Then she got routed without explanation—or escort—to Leyte."

"You mean they sent her out there with their secret weapon still aboard?"

"*Your* secret weapon, not theirs. Anyway she was sunk just before midnight and the captain responded by sending a distress signal. The SOS was picked up within five minutes at Tolosa and was taken to the commander personally."

"He turn a deaf ear, did he?"

"And a blind eye. Ordered no reply to be made or response team sent. Told the yeoman to notify him and only him if any further messages were received."

"He sent no help to a ship sinking in the middle of the Pacific?"

"Not a single vessel. Don't ask me to explain that or how it was covered up at the naval board of inquiry."

"Wow . . ."

"It gets worse. It's a pretty safe bet that if the *Indianapolis*'s distress signal reached Tolosa, it reached plenty of other places as well, but no one acted, *no one*."

"But Tolosa's the only one we can be sure of."

"Yes and no."

"What do you mean?"

"That by the time the board of inquiry was held, the base commander was dead and the radio log at Tolosa destroyed. Everything else was hearsay."

"How convenient . . ."

"I'll leave the editorializing to you, MacNuts. Plenty of balls to bust here, for sure, and more to come. A day later a pilot flying four hundred miles out of Manila came upon pieces of the wreckage that had been adrift. . . ."

"Don't tell me, let me guess. His report was dismissed as well."

"On the money, MacNuts, but remember to forget where you heard it."

"None of this is classified anymore, though."

"Sure. Except you'd have to know where to look, and there aren't many people who do. In fact, you can count 'em on one hand."

"How was it the surviving crew members of the *Indianapolis* ever got rescued?"

"A young pilot flying a Ventura caught sight of them on routine patrol and called for a rescue effort without going through channels."

"Bold young man."

"He was praised for it, but it's my guess he had the boys in Washington seething. Only three hundred of the twelve hundred crew members survived, but a day or two more would have claimed them as well."

"Seems to me, Hank, that our government was determined to make sure no trace of the *Indianapolis* ever made it back, crew included. That Japanese sub that sank her did Uncle Sam and Harry Truman a whopping big favor."

"That's a ludicrous proposition. No one even thought to consider it."

"Until now," McCracken told him.

To Evira the fresh air and sunlight had never felt more welcome on her face. After four days of being confined to Kourosh's small room, she at last felt well enough to venture outside. Kourosh had learned that the general was hosting a gala dinner party for the highest ranking Iranian officials in his continued attempt to reunify the country. The dinner was scheduled for tomorrow, which meant Evira had only today to acclimate herself to the setting and prepare a plan. With the maid's uniform the boy had stolen from a laundry, she could get inside through the servants' entrance and blend with others on duty. She would have to go in weaponless, though, because a thorough search of anyone entering the palace grounds seemed a certainty. But finding a weapon did not concern her as much as the chance that one of the supervisors might realize she didn't belong. She would have to hope the hectic pace of such a huge event would be sufficient cover.

That morning Kourosh had supplied her with heavy, drab clothes, including the typical shawl and veil of an impoverished Iranian woman. Many such women lingered outside the walls of Hassani's palace these days. It caused more trouble to shoo the people away, so the Revolutionary Guardsmen let them stay most of the time.

The hardest task before them was getting there. The Niavarin district was three hours from Naziabad under present conditions. Kourosh led her on a long walk to the nearest bus stop, where her heart sank at the sight of the dozens in line ahead of them.

"Make believe you're blind," he instructed her.

"Blind?"

"Do it! Hurry! Before we're noticed!"

Evira did her best. The boy pretended to be her son, and because of her handicap even the poor of Tehran let them go to the front of the line. Furthermore, once on board the jam-packed bus, they were given seats. Four more bus changes followed with long walks in between. Finding herself utterly exhausted, Evira could do nothing but rely on already depleted reserves of energy; she began to fear she would not have the strength to complete her mission.

Secretly she was hoping she and Kourosh would run into one of the "students" who had taught the boy English and given him those comic books. In the back of her mind the anomalous presence of significant numbers of Israelis in the city continued to nag at her. Who were they? What were they there for? Her sources in Mossad knew of no operation, and she was unable to imagine what a small complement of Israelis could accomplish anyway.

"Here we are," Kourosh told her. "You can look up now. Nobody's watching."

Evira turned her eyes slowly upward toward the main entrance of the royal palace. From this far away, the fifteen-foot security wall obscured much of the white-stone structure. But the distance could not hide the fact that Kourosh's drawings had not done justice to the scope of the complex. Her heart sank at the huge amount of territory, gardens and greenery, that lay between the wall and the palace itself. Already she was rethinking her plans. Making use of the servant's uniform remained critical, but clearly she needed a new scheme to gain access.

What would Blaine McCracken do?

Take matters one step at a time, to begin with. He would think only as far ahead as the next corner. Alternatives always presented themselves. The key was to keep the mind open enough to seize the proper one.

"You said there were tunnels running beneath the palace," she said to Kourosh. "What if you found me an entrance to them? Could I get into the palace that way?"

The boy shrugged. "If you didn't get lost. The chances you would are too great. And even if you succeeded—"

"Here now," a husky voice said from behind them, "what have we here?"

Evira went back into her blind woman act and grasped Kourosh's shoulder.

"This blind hag your mother, young one?" a second man asked, this one bearded and smelly, bigger than the first.

"Lucky to be blind, too, she is, so she can't see how ugly you are," Kourosh responded.

The first one laughed and then the bigger one joined in.

"You've got lots of spunk, don't you, young one? Need some discipline, though, you do." He winked to his fellow. "And then we'll see about your mother."

His hand lashed out at Kourosh, knuckles whipping toward the boy's cheek. At the last, the very last, Evira moved her fingers from Kourosh's shoulder and grabbed the hand in midair. She twisted the captured wrist violently and the bone cracked in an instant, drawing a howl of agony from the big man. The smaller one lunged at her and Evira countered with a foot that lodged squarely and expertly in his groin, doubling him over.

"You shouldn't have made her mad," Kourosh yelled after them, already leading his blind mother down the street again.

CHAPTER 17

BART JOYCE'S ESTABLISHMENT, THE CITYSIDE DELI AND Restaurant, was located in the Quincy Market–Faneuil Hall complex of outdoor shops on Boston's south side. The cab left McCracken off on Congress Street and he stepped out into an unseasonably warm May day. The area was packed with people, and Blaine noticed several milling about behind him near the monster truck *Godzilla*, which was displayed on a brick island to advertise the upcoming car show at the Boston Garden.

McCracken tempted fate with a daring dash in front of speeding vehicles and approached the statue of Samuel Adams that eternally greeted visitors at the entrance to the complex. It seemed to him that Adams's granite eyes were leering at *Godzilla* across the street, as if resenting the monster truck for infringing on his territory. Blaine tapped the statue's base tenderly to reassure it before heading for the cobblestone walk that would take him to the Cityside.

Faneuil Hall had become a model for other developments like it all across the country, combining strong historic elements with modern shopping convenience. The colonial buildings, restored to their original beauty, housed a variety of shops ranging from food and clothing to electronics and tourist knickknacks. Though Faneuil Hall is the title normally attributed to the entire complex, it actually makes up only a single large building just beyond Congress Street. Blaine passed it as he moved into the more expansive Quincy Market, formed by three parallel buildings separated by twin three-hundred–yard cobblestone walkways, each about thirty yards wide.

People moved in all directions around him, strolling, window shopping, emerging from stores with bags in hand, or relaxing on benches eating cookies or ice cream. Blaine continued to ease by them until a sign finally alerted him to the Cityside Deli and Restaurant over to his left in the center building. A large canopy stretched over a host of outdoor tables that looked across at the stores forming the South Market. Even at this midafternoon hour few vacancies could be found, and waitresses shuffled agilely in the aisles balancing trays of drinks and sandwiches.

McCracken moved up to the cash register and waited for a couple to pay their check before leaning over toward the hostess behind the counter.

"Is Bart Joyce around?"

"I think he's in the office. Who should I say is here?"

"He won't know me. Tell him it's a personal matter and that it's important."

The hostess agreeably picked up a telephone, hit two numbers, and spoke briefly into the receiver.

"He'll be right up," she said, looking back at McCracken.

It was two minutes later when Blaine heard a voice at his side say, "Hi, I'm Bart Joyce. What can I do for you?"

Joyce might have traveled the world as a twenty-two-year-old bos'n's mate, but today he was all Boston. His pronunciation of "Bart" sounded more like "Baaaaaht," and he looked the part as well—big and stocky with a belly draped over his belt and the start of a seasonal New England tan showing on his bald dome and oversized jowls.

Blaine showed him the ID Hank Belgrade had furnished him to make such encounters simpler. "Can we talk somewhere, Mr. Joyce?"

Joyce inspected the ID and stiffened suspiciously. "There's a table open over there by the chain."

"Somewhere more private would be my choice."

"This'll do."

Blaine followed Bart Joyce to the table squeezed between

other patrons on one side and strollers down the South Market on the other.

"You got no business with me anymore," Joyce snapped harshly when they were seated.

"Something changed."

"Oh yeah? What's that?"

"Why don't you tell me about loading the *Indianapolis* in San Francisco prior to her departure for Tinian."

Bart Joyce squeezed his features into a mean stare. "Wait a minute, what's this all about?"

"It's about exactly what I just asked you."

He shook his head. "You're no spook, least not in the traditional sense, but even if you were, you wouldn't give two shits about something I did over forty years ago."

"So what am I?"

"Some reporter or something digging for yet another story on the late, great *Indianapolis*. I eat assholes like you for breakfast. I'm gonna do you a favor and let you leave now on your own."

Joyce might have been about to stand up. Instead of waiting to find out, McCracken jammed a hand across the table and pinned his forearm in place. What surprised Joyce more than the move itself was the fact that his arm was already starting to go numb from the pressure the man was giving it.

"Now why don't you stay awhile? See, you were on the right track before. I am a spook, just not in the traditional sense."

"What sense, then?"

"I work for myself. I normally only take on assignments I believe in. This time it was different. This time I was forced into helping some people I don't particularly like, which tends to put me in a very bad mood." Blaine's eyes narrowed like a Doberman ready to attack and he gave Joyce just a little extra pressure on the arm. "You wanna know something, Mr. Joyce? You can kill a man in under two seconds with your hands if you know the right ways, and there are plenty of them. I could reach across the table, prove it to you, and be gone from here without anyone raising an eyebrow from their chicken soup. That's not what I have in mind, though. I just want you to understand that

I'm plenty pissed off already. People talking tough when I want to talk serious piss me off even more. But what gets me the most pissed off of all is innocent people dying for no reason, which is just what's going to happen unless you and I have a heart-to-heart right now.''

Joyce threw the arm that was still his up in a gesture of conciliation. ''Look, buddy, I got a past I'd rather forget and I get kind of ornery when strangers make me remember. Let's start over fresh, okay?''

''Let's start with the *Indianapolis*,'' Blaine said, and let go of his arm.

Joyce shook the limb to bring the circulation back. ''What do you want to know?''

''You were on the loading crew, correct?''

''Absolutely. Never been more fucking frightened in my whole life. I mean that was a hell of a thing we were loading, right? Fucking atomic bombs. Nobody knew what they were back then. Be like fucking death rays are now. We didn't load the bombs themselves; lots of people think we did but we didn't. All it was were the unassembled parts, most of them crated up real tight.'' Joyce leaned a little forward, defenses lowering. ''Now look, I know you're probably here because somewhere along the line somebody told you there were more than two bombs on board the *Indy*. But trust me, there weren't. And even if there were, they're buried with her.''

''Somebody found her.''

Joyce's face seemed to droop. ''What?''

''Why the concern? Why worry if two bombs were all you loaded? History can certainly account for both of them.''

''Don't play games with me, okay, mister? Lay it out plain and simple.''

''Fair enough. I know something else was loaded onto the *Indianapolis* besides those unassembled atomic bombs. I know because whatever it was was salvaged from the wreck about a year ago.''

''My God . . .''

''Plain and simple, here's the story. There's a madman in Israel named Rasin who's got it in for all Arabs; good, bad, doesn't matter a damn to him. He's going to kill them all without harming a hair on his country's chinny chin chin with that other weapon you loaded onto the *Indianapolis*.''

''I didn't load it!'' Joyce blared loud enough to draw attention from nearby tables. ''Hey, you want to go somewhere more private?''

''This is doing just fine. Keep talking.''

''I helped load the bombs, I'll admit that, but that's all I loaded. The bunch of us felt like part of history, so it was only right we go out and celebrate 'fore we set out the next morning. Night falls and five of us get lucky and find broads. War freaks these women turn out to be. Figured we could be sure of an easy fuck if we took them to see the ship carrying *the* atomic bombs.''

''Word treason mean anything to you then?''

''Mister, only word in my vocab that night was horny. What was the harm in it anyway? The women were too smashed to remember a damn thing besides me slamming 'em hot and heavy.''

''Get back to the ship.''

''Yeah, that's just what we did. Middle of the night, we brought them to the dock. The *Indy* wasn't due to set off until dawn. Trouble was, the dock was swarming with people, lots of whom I didn't recognize and a few others I didn't want to.''

''Why?''

''Get to that later. Anyway, what I saw was a bunch of guys loading something else on board the ship.''

''Loading what?''

''Cannisters. One at a time. Real careful they were.''

''Describe these cannisters.''

''I don't know, 'bout the size of scuba tanks I guess. All silver-gray and smooth, marked with some kind of symbol.''

''What kind of symbol?''

''Looked like a funny kind of *v*. Yeah, I think it was the Greek letter gamma.''

''Get back to those people you preferred not to recognize. . . .''

''Hey, I had good reason. One of them walked with canes in both hands. Even drunk, that's something you can't forget. He looked like he was supervising everything, but I've never seen a more miserable face in my life. I didn't see it again until a couple years later, and I don't mean on no baseball card, either.''

''Go on.''

''His picture was on the front page of the paper. Story was about Nazis, infamous Nazis still at large.''

''Who did the story say he was?'' Blaine asked after a long pause.

''A scientist. Went by the name of Bechman. Don't know anything else about him, 'sides the obvious. We musta needed him for something real big, and whatever it was I figure got placed on the *Indy* next to the bombs.''

''So you kept your mouth shut.''

''Damn straight. I was plenty scared, too. Here it was we all thought we'd loaded the most dangerous weapon man had ever come up with only to come back at night to see something else being loaded in secret. Shit, at least we knew what the A-bombs were supposed to do. Had no idea what the shit in those cannisters was capable of, and none of us were about to let on we had any idea they were on board. I was the only one knew about the cannisters who made it out of the water alive and I still never told, even after . . .''

''After what, Bart?''

''I've said enough.''

''Not nearly.''

The man's oversized jowls puckered with fear. He leaned farther over the table and lowered his voice.

''You gotta understand nobody would've ever believed me. I had no proof.''

''Go on.''

''Thing was, in the water we got ourselves all linked together in tight circles. Could fall asleep and not drift off that way. We kept regular watch for the sharks. I was right next to the captain himself, dragged him into our circle with my own two hands. A few minutes later the moon pops out and his eyes go all kind of funny. We were facing the same direction so I could see the

same thing he did: a conning tower, Mr. Spook, from a submarine.''

"The *Indianapolis* was sunk by a sub."

"Sure. Only this one was one of ours."

CHAPTER 18

"DO I HAVE TO SPELL IT OUT FOR YOU?" BART JOYCE WAS saying, the floodgates fully open now with his secret released at last. "Fucking American sub sunk our ship. Coulda been an accident, except she surfaced and still left us there. They wanted the lot of us dead, Mr. Spook, and they did everything they could to make sure that was the only way we'd be found. Our *own* sub, damn it, our *own government* . . ."

Joyce's voice tailed off and Blaine's mind raced ahead. He was stunned but somehow not surprised. Joyce had supplied the missing piece to his puzzle, and out of the madness came the sense. The *Indianapolis* had indeed sailed from San Francisco with something other than A-bombs: cannisters only a select few knew about, marked by the Greek letter gamma. Obviously the intention was to unload them at Tinian in addition to, perhaps instead of, the bombs. But equally obvious was the fact that something had happened en route that required a change in strategy. The cannisters had never been unloaded and the *Indianapolis* had been sunk to conceal their existence.

But why?

The key was Bechman. Joyce remembered him as a Nazi scientist, and it was common knowledge the Nazis were advanced far beyond the allies from a weapons standpoint. The end of the war, in fact, became a battle between the Russians and Americans to gain their services. But with Bechman the

Americans must have had reason to jump the gun, and that reason could only have been the gamma cannisters. Whatever they were, their very existence had called for all traces of the *Indianapolis* and her final mission to be buried forever.

"I never told anyone," Bart Joyce was saying, "I never—"

Joyce's head snapped backward suddenly, and a red circle appeared in the center of his forehead. He toppled over as if someone had yanked the chair out from under him. Blaine's dive took him to the ground ahead of Joyce's corpse, and ahead of the next burst which shattered the empty glasses on the table top. Blaine brought the table down over him to use for cover while those patrons nearest him scattered screaming. Traveling on a regular flight from Washington with no luggage had made bringing a gun along impossible without attracting undue attention to himself. He had never felt more helpless.

The automatic fire continued to dig chasms out of the table, causing pandemonium through the restaurant and in the cobblestone walkway beyond it. Whoever the shooter was, he was good. He knew enough to keep his concentration on his target through everything. His mistake had been not going for McCracken first.

The bullets ceased thudding into the wood over him, and Blaine stayed low at the feet of the panicked crowd that was rushing everywhere at once. Find the origin of the shots and he would find the shooter. The pyramid-shaped roof of the South Market thirty yards across the cobblestones was the only possible location. Blaine climbed to his feet and scanned the roofline but found no sign of anyone perched there.

The gunman would be on his way down then, to attempt an escape or perhaps another try at Blaine. McCracken's eyes swept across the scene at store level and encountered the shape of a small man emerging rather calmly from one of the shops. A second glance told him it was a woman wearing a boyish haircut, tight jeans, and a leather jacket. She seemed unfazed by the panic swarming around her.

Blaine picked up his pace through the crowd, intending to cut the woman off. Sirens were already screaming as she walked briskly toward the Congress Street side of the marketplace. She never so much as gazed back, so Blaine had no chance to meet her eyes as he fought his way through the surging crowd.

So intent was his focus on this woman that he almost missed the second. His first glimpse was of a figure in black rising out of nowhere and the crowd suddenly spreading before her twenty-five yards from the street. He saw the machine pistol next and dove headlong behind a steel divider as the *rat-tat-tat* split the air. The bullets clanged and ricocheted wildly. Glass from a nearby flower shop shattered and sprayed the air. The panicked crowd charged everywhere in search of escape. McCracken ran low to the ground as he tried to close the gap between himself and the shooter.

A pair of police cars spun to a halt on Congress Street, and the officers lunged out with guns drawn.

"Stop! Police!"

McCracken heard that command just before the woman turned and emptied the rest of her clip in their direction. One of the cops was blown backward instantly, while the other managed a single shot before his chest was shredded. McCracken was back on his feet now, slithering forward behind what meager cover he could find. The taller woman tossed the machine pistol aside as another police car screeched to a halt before her. The officers had barely started to jump out when the smaller of the women yanked a nine-millimeter automatic from inside her leather jacket. She lunged forward, firing repeatedly, even after the policemen had fallen. She stopped only when she drew even with her much larger companion.

The big one turned and Blaine fixed his stare on her. She was decked out in black leather and had blond stubble for hair. She was huge, maybe a couple inches under seven feet if you included her boots.

McCracken thought of the killers of John Neville and Henri Dejourner and went cold.

These two! It had to be!

They must have read his expression, because before Blaine could get near them, the huge one with spiked hair led the other toward the closest abandoned police car and lunged inside. These women had orchestrated this entire murderous episode, and had earlier killed a pair of men he liked. What's more, they had

kidnapped Matthew and might thus be his only chance of finding the boy if Evira had failed to recover him from Rasin's
clutches.

The women in the police car headed into traffic on Congress
Street, bearing onto North Street even as McCracken stood there.
He began to sprint futilely in their direction. A vehicle was what
he needed, and the perfect one for the job loomed directly before
him.

Godzilla bucked and thumped like a horse restrained for too
long. A driver who'd been about to ease it onto a nearby carrier
had abandoned the monster truck with the gunshots and left the
door open. A deft leap brought Blaine into the cab and he
slammed the door behind him. The cockpit looked not much
different from an ordinary pickup truck, except for a series of
additional gauges mounted upon the dashboard. What was new
to him was the notion of driving from a vantage point over a
dozen feet off the ground.

McCracken shoved *Godzilla* into reverse, and the monster
truck's long-idling engine greeted the move with a huge thrust
backward that threw him toward the dashboard. After fastening
the shoulder harness, Blaine spun the wheel for North Street,
intending to veer directly across Congress in pursuit of the police car comandeered by the two women. He shifted into drive
and gave the monster truck some gas.

Godzilla shot forward as a pair of police cars from opposite
directions spun into screeching skids that brought them hood to
hood directly before him. Blaine was in no mood or position to
change his course at that point. The murderous women already
had a headstart on him. Blaine simply kept the champion car
crusher going toward the pair of police cars.

He felt only a brief jolt as the crusher's Alaskan tundra tires
rolled upward onto the hoods, one tire for each. Then Blaine
felt a settling and heard the sound of twisting, collapsing metal.
Godzilla's progress never stopped. Its back tires finished the job
its front ones had started before the stunned police could even
draw their guns. He managed a glance in the rearview mirror
and saw the police cars compressed into neat rectangles in the
center of Congress Street as he steamed down North Street.

Faneuil Hall was on his right and the modern Bostonian Hotel on his left as he started his pursuit of the murderous women. Where there was no room in the pulled-over traffic to maneuver, Blaine created it. Fenders, doors, even entire front or rear ends were destroyed as a result. McCracken for his part barely felt a single impact, and only occasional glances in *Godzilla*'s rearview mirror revealed the carnage left in his wake.

He turned right onto Surface Road beneath the Route 93 overpass and was caught instantly in a hopeless snarl of traffic. Frustration had just started to set in when he noticed a single police car in the midst of it, the only squad car that was heading away from the chaos instead of toward it.

The women! It had to be!

He had them now. No reason to rush or be too bold. Just lay back and make his move once traffic started going again.

Who was he kidding? He was behind the wheel of a towering monster the women had certainly noticed by now. They would know it was him. They would know because they were professionals.

As he formed that very thought, traffic started flowing again and the police car veered instantly right onto Central Street at the very rear of the marketplace.

"Come on!" Blaine urged the traffic before him, losing his patience at the last second and forcing a pair of cars into a wild spin when he cut between them to continue his pursuit.

He caught a glimpse of the squad car as it grazed the rear of a delivery van that had backed up blindly. The driver had just lunged out, arms raised, when *Godzilla* slammed his van sideways from its path. The vehicle rocked as if weightless and McCracken continued on his way after the women, who had turned onto Milk Street from Central.

Milk Street was strangely free of traffic, but India Street adjacent to it was jammed. The women had at last activated their siren to clear their path, which was much too narrow for *Godzilla* to manage without endangering the lives of dozens of motorists by crushing their vehicles. That left him with only one option.

Blaine spun *Godzilla* to the right and drove the tires on its driver's side up onto the row of cars parked bumper to bumper along the street, while his passenger-side tires balanced precariously on the sidewalk. Parking meters toppled like twigs before him. Water sprayed from a ruined fire hydrant, and McCracken reached for the windshield wiper switch. He kept the fleeing police car in sight as best he could as it passed back beneath the Route 93 overpass en route to Surface Road once more.

A ramp leading onto the expressway was dead ahead. The women were heading toward it now, knowing full well there was no way he could catch them on the open road. No way at all. Blaine did the best he could to give chase, honking his horn to keep Surface Road passable and alert unsuspecting drivers to what was coming.

It seemed futile. The squad car was gone up the ramp by the time McCracken pushed *Godzilla* through a red light after it. Expressway pace would provide the women the advantage they needed, with the monster truck's size and poor visibility certain to cause chain collisions that would create a hopeless snarl. Still Blaine gave it gas and reached the head of the ramp. Frustration simmered within him, and he was about to pound the windshield when the greatest sight ever greeted his eyes:

Traffic, enough to keep the squad car from getting up speed. Already the women were opting for an immediate exit ramp labeled "South Station." Blaine felt recharged. *Godzilla* filled out the width of an entire lane, but that was plenty enough to keep him on the trail. Cars before him blindly tried for lane changes left and right, and the monster truck claimed their vacated spots and rolled on to take whatever else it wanted. He motored onto the exit ramp with the squad car dead ahead, heading toward an area of heavy construction with a right down Summer Street.

Godzilla followed its quarry from Summer onto High Street by way of a short cut across Bay Bank Plaza which sent pedestrians scurrying. To keep close on High Street, Blaine mashed parked cars where space demanded. Whatever time was lost in the effort was made up by the constant weaves the squad car was forced to make to avoid cars. They came at last to Bedford Street and crashed through a sawhorse without seeing the telltale sign:

CLOSED FOR CONSTRUCTION

Construction on a water main had shut down Bedford Street from end to end, but the squad car had already committed. The street was totally torn up; it was an obstacle course of deep holes, sawhorses, and open ditches.

The women's car took an awful beating, but *Godzilla* negotiated the conditions easily. McCracken felt himself being jolted upward in his seat time and time again, but he was gaining, damn it, he was gaining!

Just a car-length away, he saw the huge blonde lean out the passenger window and fire pistols with both hands. *Godzilla's* windshield exploded and Blaine ducked low to avoid the spray of glass. The next series of shots clanged off the crusher's grill and Blaine knew the blonde was now aiming for the tires or the radiator. But the tires were solid all the way through and the radiator reenforced with extra layers of steel.

Feeling confident, Blaine rose just enough to see over the dashboard and jammed *Godzilla's* accelerator all the way to the floor. The crusher's engine roared as it shot forward with a burst of speed that brought its monstrous tires within a yard of the police car. Then an unmarked ditch off to the right caught one of *Godzilla's* tires. Blaine felt the sudden drop with a jolt. He gunned the engine but the monster truck was caught at a difficult angle even for the 640-cubic-inch engine to power out of. As the squad car struggled down the rest of Bedford Street, Blaine rocked *Godzilla* between forward and reverse. At last the monster truck jumped free. Blaine gunned the engine and roared the final stretch down Bedford Street to where it ended directly before Lafayette Place. He had either a left or right to take now, and he was certain the women had turned right.

Soon after swinging onto Chauncy Street, he saw the tail of their squad car screech into another right. McCracken sped past traffic, which pulled over in front of him, and followed the women down Summer Street. The traffic was heavy, but by blowing his horn to alert drivers to his presence he succeeded in having enough cars pull over to keep his path cleared.

When he passed between South Station and the Federal Reserve Building, traffic suddenly thinned. He had the squad car

dead in his sights. Only a hundred yards separated them, but
the women were speeding away from the field, seizing the open
stretch down Summer Street for their final escape.

McCracken was fighting with *Godzilla* for more speed when
ahead he saw an eighteen-wheel tractor trailer backing slowly
across the width of Summer Street. It was obviously having
trouble negotiating a delivery slot in a building on his side of
the road. The squad car came to a halt behind the eighteen
wheeler, trapped once and for all.

Seeing his chance, Blaine darted into the empty lanes of op-
posing traffic and sped forward. He sideswiped one car and then
squeezed between two others. Suddenly the police car was directly before him. He gave *Godzilla* all the gas it would take and
felt it shoot forward as though eager for the task ahead.

The monster truck mounted the squad car, and trunk, roof,
then hood gave way like plastic. A series of pops followed as
jagged metal pressed into the tires and flattened them. The police car sunk even lower. *Godzilla* continued to roll forward.

At last the crusher touched pavement again and Blaine threw
Godzilla into neutral and jumped down. He reached the driver's
door, ready and eager to deal with the women inside.

A frightened Boston police officer with his face bleeding from
a host of cuts gazed up at him in abject terror. And all Mc-
Cracken could do was melt innocently away, wondering where
exactly it had been that he'd lost the women.

CHAPTER 19

"**Y**OU DON'T MIND ME SAYING, MR. M., YOU LOOK, AYAH, like fucking hell."

McCracken almost asked the harbormaster, with his sun-wrinkled flesh, sunken eyes, and liver-spotted hands, who was he to judge? But instead he just shrugged and settled farther back on the bench to wait for the ferry to take him across the bay to Great Diamond Island.

"Been a slow night, has it, Abner?"

"Was till near about two hours ago. Someone at the Estates must be having a party I'd say, ayah."

Blaine forced his shoulders upright at that. "Lots of people make the trip over?"

"Near 'bout a dozen, ten anyway," the harbormaster replied. His faced angled in its typical quizzical expression. "Funny thing now that I think about it, they were all men. Three cars, three or four to a car."

"Shit," McCracken said, standing up.

"Huh?"

"How long ago, Abner?"

"Couple hours, like I said."

"How long exactly?"

The harbormaster scratched at a wrinkled, sunken eye with a finger blackened with dirt. "Five runs back. Say two-and-a-half hours." His eyes bulged suddenly. "Hold on. You're gettin' that

176

look you had when you made that man drive his car into the bay. Took me a half day to dredge it out. Don't make me do that with three cars, not three cars, please!''

"Don't worry, Abner, I'm not in the mood."

Blaine's mind was working fast. After abandoning *Godzilla*, he had stolen a car from the Boston Aquarium parking lot and driven straight through to Maine. He arrived at the harbor two hours past sunset, which would have given the women plenty of time to have arranged for a team to be waiting at his island condominium. They would have expected him to head back home under the circumstances. The only anomaly was that they hadn't left any of their number here at the harbor. Then again, if they tried for him here and missed, he was gone. If they went for him on the island, their chances would be better and his opportunity for escape far worse. Should have been more careful with Abner, though, maybe sent the cars over one or two at a time to avoid suspicion. They'd learn their lesson when he didn't show up.

"Still got that double-barrel twelve gauge, Abner?" he asked the harbormaster.

"Mr. M., you promised you wouldn't—"

"I'm not gonna use it on them, Abner. I just need a little insurance. Like to borrow it, if I could."

The old man eased himself behind the counter and drew the iron relic out. "Take care of it now. It belonged to my daddy."

"Which makes it older than you."

"Ayah. Considerably."

"Terrific."

Abner handed it over. "Tip you gave me last Christmas more 'an entitles you to the favor, but if you're in trouble, Mr. M., seems a mite better to sit here awhile and think it out, I'd say."

"No can do, Abner," Blaine said, already making his way for the door.

"Got someplace you gotta be?"

"Just going to visit a friend."

McCracken made sure to announce his presence on Johnny Wareagle's land by breaking selected trip wires in a pattern that could only be purposeful. The last thing he wanted to chance after coming this far was an arrow from one of Johnny's many bows.

"How unnecessary, Blainey," Wareagle said after McCracken stepped through a door that had already been opened for him.

"Good evening to you, too, Indian. Suppose you were expecting me."

"For several days now. The disruption of your manitou is brighter than a beacon. I could feel you drawing closer and closer, almost since the very time we parted ten days ago."

"I've seen plenty of the world," Blaine told him, "some of which hasn't been seen by anyone for over forty-five years."

Wareagle looked at him more closely.

"It's a long story, Indian. And right now I've got to tell the last part of it to someone else. Let's take a ride."

McCracken filled Johnny in on everything that had occurred over the past ten days, from the details of Matthew's kidnapping to his travels to Japan by way of Israel and then, literally, into the Pacific Ocean. The Indian had been concerned by the cryptic message received the week before with instructions of what to do in the event of Blaine's death. He claimed he paid it little heed since he knew McCracken would be returning.

"I guess what it comes down to, Indian," Blaine said at the end, "is that the world has never mattered less to me. It's just one life I'm out to save this time, and if I can't get the boy out of this alive, then stopping Rasin won't mean shit."

"But you would try anyway, even if not for the boy."

"A couple of years ago for sure. Today I don't know. What all this has shown me is whatever I've felt I've been lacking these last few months is purely a state of mind."

"Everything is a state of mind, Blainey, and that state of mind affects our state of being as well. When there is harmony between them, we are content with our lives. When one is out of balance, we search blindly for that which can be found only inside ourselves."

"Should I take that to heart?"

"The boy became the stitching which rejoined your two states together. That is what has changed in you these past months, but even I did not realize it clearly until now.''

Blaine felt himself nodding. "It was like an emptiness. I felt it go away that day I spent with him in London, and even when those women kidnapped him the emptiness didn't return.''

"Because in either case the boy supplied you with purpose. Through all our years in the hellfire and beyond, purpose is what maintained harmony in the triangle of your mind, body, and spirit. The betrayals—and your acceptance of them—stole that purpose away and cast you on your own, where you had to create your own purpose. Sometimes the justifications came up short. You became an orphan of your own lost emotions. But then you saw yourself in the boy and that changed everything.''

"He's mine, Johnny. In this whole crazy life I've led he's all I've got that's really mine.''

Wareagle looked at him from the driver's seat of the Jeep slicing through the night. "No, Blainey, he is but another object to pursue in striving to find meaning and purpose in your life. You said so yourself. Think of the original hellfire that first brought us together. We were not concerned with victory as much as continuation. One mission mattered most in that it set the stage for another. They called it the Phoenix Project after a bird who rose from its own ashes, in the hope that our war effort could do the same. But as we strove toward this end, our own spirits were being reduced to ashes.''

"So what are you telling me, to stop reaching, to stop striving?''

"I am telling you nothing, Blainey, except that if it hadn't been the boy, it would have been something else. That is neither good nor bad, just what is necessary for your existence. That is what you must understand.''

"Let's make a phone call," McCracken said as a gas station appeared before them.

Hank Belgrade was less than happy to hear from him.

"My phone may be tapped," the State and Defense Department liaison told him. "Keep talking at your own risk.''

"Now that's no way to greet an old friend, Hank.''

"Look who's talking. When we met in Washington, you could have told me you'd been flagged."

"Flagged? Again? What color this time?"

"You mean you didn't know? Christ . . . The code is blue."

"Well, that's something to be thankful for. I'm used to red."

"Wait a minute, you really didn't know about this?"

"First I've heard of it. Who's after me?"

"Can't tell for sure but I'm proceeding on the notion that they know about our meeting and are just playing it cool in the hope that we do lunch in the near future."

"Only if you're buying."

"They don't know about the material I furnished you on the *Indianapolis*. That's something anyway."

"Do they know about Boston, Hank?"

"What about Boston?"

"I met with Bart Joyce, who had a chance to be most enlightening before a pair of ladies eliminated his need for a government pension."

"What in hell are you talking about?"

"Watch "Headline News" at the top of the hour to hear all about it."

Belgrade hesitated. "You didn't call me to discuss my viewing habits."

"Nope. See, there's another favor I need. . . ."

"You gonna put my kids through college if they boot me out of government service?"

"By the time they find out they'll be patting me on the back again and you, too."

"What is it this time?"

"An extension of our original discussion. Something else was indeed loaded on board the *Indianapolis*, cannisters marked with the Greek letter gamma. Bart Joyce saw them being loaded. A rather interesting gent was supervising the work who happened to be an ex-Nazi scientist named Bechman."

"Wait a minute, MacNuts, you're talking way out of my league now. Ex-Nazis working for our government? Why don't you call your friends at the Gap?"

"I don't have their number handy. Besides, I don't feel like breaking anyone new into this story. Somebody's after me, remember?''

"But you don't know who or why."

"Well, I've got a couple ideas. . . ."

"You want me to find out what happened to Bechman?"

"At least what he may have been working on in our behalf during those last days of the war."

"This stuff may be buried too deep for me to dig up."

"I've got faith in your ability to shovel."

"Yeah, well, you never were much of a judge of character." Belgrade paused. "I know you're on the trail of something big here, MacNuts, and that's good enough for me. But it would make my life a little easier if you gave me some reason to share your concern."

"No sweat, Hank. See, it goes like this. If what Joyce said is true, then I've got to figure we loaded this gamma secret weapon with the full intention of using it on the Japanese either in addition to or instead of the A-bombs. Only something stopped us. And something led to a decision to sink the *Indianapolis* and cut our losses."

"*What?*"

"Joyce saw the sub that did it. The story about the Japs being responsible was a cover. It explains why no escort was ordered, why the distress signal was ignored, why everything possible was done to make sure the survivors weren't rescued."

"Holy shit . . ."

"Now Yosef Rasin is in possession of the superweapon we sunk the *Indianapolis* to keep secret, and I've got to ask myself what happens if he doesn't know what stopped us from using it when we had the chance. That clear enough for ya, Hank?"

"Crystal. Now get off the phone so I can make some calls."

"Stay away from the window," the man advised, reaching for the boy's shoulder.

"Why?" Matthew demanded as he twisted from the man's grasp.

The man pulled away as if his hand had been burned. After removing Matthew from Fett's charge, he and the two others assigned to the boy had expected a response on his part of fear, obedience, submissiveness. What they had gotten was obstinance and rebelliousness.

"It's safer," the man said. "That's all."

"From who?"

"People who want to hurt you."

"I don't have to look out the window to see *them*," the boy shot back. He continued to gaze stubbornly outward.

"We're not your enemy."

"That's what the man you took me from said."

"He was lying."

"And you're not?"

The man reached across him and yanked down the shade.

"Why don't you just let me go?" the boy asked matter-of-factly.

"It's for your own good."

"The other man said that too."

"This time it's the truth."

Matthew tilted his head back toward the covered window. "He'll find me, you know."

The man smiled, glad at last his reassurance might mean something. "I promise you he won't. You don't have to be scared."

"Not the Arab," the boy snapped disparagingly. "Blaine McCracken. When he finds out what you've done, he'll find me. I wouldn't want to be in your shoes when he gets here."

The man looked at him dumbfounded. He had not had much experience with children, and if this was any indication of what they were like, he had no desire to have any experience with them again. He watched the boy swing arrogantly back to the window, and with a quick flick of his hand the shade spun from the glass again.

"He'll be coming," Matthew assured. "And it won't be long now either."

"You cheated! I take my eye off the board for one second and you make an extra move!"

"Putz," Abraham snapped back at Joshua, waving an arm before his face.

"You took three of my men with one jump from a spot you shouldn't have been in."

"You forgot I moved there move before last. You forgot and you want to blame me because you're going soft in the brains."

"Putz," Joshua snarled this time.

Sitting in the shade outside the house in Hertzelia, not far from where the two old men were playing checkers, Isaac and Isser caught pieces of the argument.

"Are they always like this?" the head of Mossad wanted to know.

"You want them—we—should change after all these years? We're soldiers, Isser, and nothing frustrates soldiers more than age." He cocked an eye back toward the deck. "They fight with each other mostly to remember. Believe me, I'm no better, and someday neither will you be."

"Will there be a 'someday' for me, Isaac, for my children?"

"There has been one these past forty-five years and there always will be. We were there at the start, don't forget. We've seen it all."

"You mean you *had* seen it all. You haven't seen Hassani."

"I've seen others like him. Plenty."

"So you're not worried."

"Worried? Of course I'm worried. I was worried in '48 and '67 and in '73 too. And I'm worried today after what you've told me. But you learn after awhile that if God wasn't resigned to taking care of us, we wouldn't have survived this long."

"God might need some help this time. I've laid out the scenario of what we may be facing. I want you to consider moving up the timetable for Operation Firestorm."

Isaac just looked at him, wisps of his stray white hair blowing in the breeze.

"You don't seem surprised by my request."

"I didn't think you came here to discuss history."

"Can you do it?"

"You knew the answer to that even before you came, Isser. You know the logistics. Our people are too spread out, they're not in contact with each other. We all agreed it was the safest setup on the chance that one of the cells was penetrated. No trail, remember?"

"Unfortunately, yes."

"For a year now we have planned everything toward a single day. Thousands of people are involved, *hundreds* of thousands. Firestorm can't be moved up. Not by a week, not by a day, not even by an hour. All was finalized when we received those Comanches from the Americans."

"Apaches, Isaac. They're called Apaches."

"Whatever they are called, I can do nothing to move up the timetable."

"Even if it means Hassani's forces beat us to the punch?"

Before Isaac could respond, red and black game pieces flew wildly off the deck, followed by the checkerboard itself as Saul fought to position himself between Abraham and Joshua.

"You can't plan for everything," the old man told the chief of Mossad, "but you do the best you can." A grimace stretched across his face as his eyes found the ruined checkerboard halfway between their chairs and the deck. "The problem is sometimes no matter what you do, nobody wins."

It was past midnight when Blaine called Hank Belgrade at a second number, as arranged at the end of their last conversation.

"I found your Nazi for you, MacNuts," Belgrade said.

"He's alive?"

"Yes and no."

"I don't like the sound of that, Hank."

"Wait until you hear the details. Dr. Hans Bechman was the charter member of something called the Paperclip Club. Ring any bells?"

"Nazis who we wanted to salvage from the war were identified by a paperclip attached to their files. Right?"

"On the money. Except Bechman came over so early he didn't even have a file. I haven't got a clue as to what he was working on for us in 1945, but as near as I can make it out, his specialty for the Reich was genetic engineering."

"Gene splicing, recombinant DNA, and the like?"

"Yup. Man was way ahead of his time. Fortunately, Hitler didn't think much of his work when compared to the nerve gases those Nazis were creating, so his project never really found an audience. It if had . . ."

"You still haven't told me if he's alive or not."

"Yes, he's alive, or at least what I've been able to dig up indicates he is. Over eighty now and who knows in what condition, but alive. Trouble is you can't get to him."

"Try me," Blaine said.

"Look, MacNuts, this is out of even your league."

"Just tell me where to go, Hank."

"It's not that simple. Men like Bechman aren't allowed to retire to beachfront property in Florida for obvious reasons. Government takes care of them a different way and my balls are on the line for merely mentioning this to you."

"You haven't mentioned anything yet."

Hank Belgrade took a deep breath. "Senior citizens who fall into the know-too-much category require special care. Think about it, MacNuts, all those deep dark secrets stored in a mind going soft. Our enemies could have a field day picking those minds apart."

"So no gin rummy in South Beach. What, then?"

"Permanent residence at a very secret retirement community known only as the O.K. Corral."

"And don't tell me when I get there I'm supposed to ask for Wyatt Earp."

"Not quite. The official in charge of the community calls himself Doc Holliday."

PART FOUR

The O.K. Corral

Tehran: Thursday, May 11; eight P.M.

CHAPTER 20

"**I**'D BETTER LEAVE YOU HERE," KOUROSH TOLD EVIRA, AND she felt reluctant at this point to go on without him, having become so dependent on the boy these past few days.

She pulled at the wretched clothes draped over the royal palace's maid's uniform. "I'm ready."

"No, you're not," the urchin insisted dramatically. "How can you kill the animal Hassani without a weapon? I told you you should have let me try to get one for you."

"I'll be searched before being allowed into the palace. If they find a weapon, everything we've accomplished will go for naught."

"But you will kill him."

"I'll kill him."

"I'll be waiting for you when you come out."

Kourosh reached out to touch her briefly before he bounded off, looking back once before turning the first corner. Evira was left with only the tiniest hope she could make good on her promise. To start with, her wounds, though somewhat healed, still pained her and would undoubtedly slow down her motions. Beyond that, there was the reality of the style of mission she was about to undertake in the fortress before her. This kind of work had never been her specialty as it had been McCracken's. Killing was something she loathed. Through the entire course of her exploits, she had killed only in self-defense. She tried to tell

herself that tonight was no different, but the convincing came
with difficulty.

Evira stripped off her rags to reveal the uniform beneath and
emerged from the shadows of the square in front of the royal
palace. Her heart thudded with the awareness that the next few
moments were the most crucial of all. If her plan failed to provide access to the grounds, nothing else mattered. She slid between a pair of sedans arriving with guests and bypassed the
main gate in favor of the private side street that led to the servant's entrance near the school. She stayed close enough to the
huge wall to avoid detection, and if approached would have to
go into her charade earlier than she planned.

Any route of entry she chose would face her with Revolutionary Guardsmen who were not about to let her pass through without proper identification unless she *appeared* as though she
belonged. This illusion would be created with the help of her
servant's uniform.

Taking a heavy breath, she veered from the shadow of the
security wall toward the Revolutionary Guardsmen who stood
at attention before the blocked-off side street delivery vehicles
had been using throughout the afternoon.

"That van you just let pass through," she called to them from
several yards away, quickening her step and fixing a look of
anxiety on her face, "was it the baker? Tell me if you've seen
the baker."

The lead guard swung toward her with a start. "Who are you
to ask?"

"I am the server in charge of the dessert table and there will
be hell to pay if he does not arrive with the rest of his wares
soon."

"Where is your badge?" he demanded, noticing her empty
lapel.

"I took it off so it wouldn't fall into the punch. Be most
embarrassing, wouldn't you say? Now what of the baker?"

"He wasn't in the van."

"Damn! There will be hell to pay for this, hell I say!" She
came closer to the guard. "You will summon me as soon as his
goods arrive. You will call the kitchen and ask for Manijeh.
Yes?"

The guard stiffened. "I will send him through as I have sent the others through. I am nobody's messenger."

"As you wish. But if anyone asks me . . ."

She began to ease by him and past the wary guards who eyed her still, though more amused by the tirade than suspicious.

"Be gone with you!" the lead guard shouted. "Be gone and let me do my job!"

At that instant another delivery vehicle caught his attention long enough to keep her safe from further scrutiny while she moved along the wall. She made her way straight to an entrance two hundred yards down, near a building she recognized from Kourosh's drawings as the school. The guards here accepted her ruse even more easily, with one insisting on escorting her back to the kitchen in keeping with procedure.

He guided her to the servants' entrance, which led directly into the kitchen. She recalled the dining room sat between this and the majestic, two-story ballroom.

Passing into the kitchen, the last thing she wanted to do was attract attention, so she simply fell into the long chain of servants picking up trays of glasses and hors d'oeuvres. The door they took out of the kitchen bypassed the dining room altogether and led down through a vestibule into the ballroom. At this point she had no conception of what the next stage of her plan would be and willed herself to stay calm so her thoughts might flow freely.

Just like McCracken would do.

Evira held tight to her tray of hors d'oeuvres and entered the ballroom. She couldn't help but be impressed once she entered. Even Kourosh's exaggerated drawings had not done it justice. It was huge and sprawling, nearly sixty yards square, with a hand-sewn Kerman pattern rug covering much of that. The serving tables were placed upon the rug. A number of crystal chandeliers of various sizes dangled from the two-story-high ceiling, which, given the perfect weather conditions, might be opened later to let the stars shine in. Enormous bouquets of flowers and countless potted plants added to the beauty of the room. Furthermore, the ballroom had been constructed in such a way that the mezzanine balcony swept down along one wall

so that a truly grand entrance could be made down the spi-
raling staircase.

Fortunately, though, as far as she could tell General Hassani
had yet to make his entrance. Of course. The meal for such an
affair would be served late to allow him to make the most fash-
ionable appearance possible and to allow his powerful guests
ample time to mingle among themselves prior to this. After all,
once he arrived all attention would be centered on him.

Evira's mind began to work.

She placed the tray of hot hors d'oeuvres on a table and picked
up a tray of empty champagne glasses. Iran might have angrily
denounced all ties with the West, but the serving procedures
here were entirely western. A throwback to the days of the Shah
and a testament to Hassani's all-out efforts to win the support of
the wealthy and powerful.

Returning to the kitchen area, Evira was given a fresh tray of
filled glasses in return for her tray of empty ones. She was careful to balance the tray on one hand as the other servants were
doing, so as to have a hand free to serve with. She had trouble
with the process at the outset, and a vision of her tray's contents
tumbling to the rug and drawing the attention of everyone in the
room made her even more nervous. But her champagne was
much in demand and her load was quickly lightened, allowing
her to roam easily about. Her thoughts again turned to the next
phase of her strategy.

Since he had yet to make his appearance, Hassani must still
be upstairs, either relaxing or dressing. He would be under
guard, yes, but would hardly be expecting an attack now and
was probably the most accessible to her he would be all evening.

If she could find him.

If she could find a weapon. *I should have listened to Kourosh,*
she thought. *As it turned out, I wasn't searched at all. . . .*

Her eyes turned to focus on the women. They were to a person
elegantly dressed in lavish, western-style gowns. She watched
them eagerly, not sure yet what she expected to see that might
help her.

The answer came to Evira as she was straightening the arrangements of fruit on a table filled with a seemingly endless
variety. A number of women disappeared into an alcove off the

wall farthest from the kitchen only to return quickly to the ball-room. Evira suspected that what she would find there was the ladies' room, and with that observation began at last to formulate the plan that would get her to Hassani.

Carrying her nearly empty tray, she eased closer to the alcove, pretending to offer champagne to the ladies as they emerged. When there was a lull in the flow of traffic, Evira ducked into the alcove. As expected, there before her was a heavy wood door leading into a ladies' room, unoccupied at present unless she badly missed her guess. She propped the tray up against the wall, eased her hand over the knob, turned it, and pushed the door inward. She entered, prepared to pretend she was there to tidy up if approached.

The bathroom was indeed deserted. It, too, was lavish and smelled strongly of lavender. Evira entered one of the stalls and locked the door behind her. There was a crack sufficient for her to peer through, and she agonized through the comings and goings of several small groups of women, knowing she could only execute her plan if one entered alone. At last her patience was rewarded by the sight of a single beautiful woman entering the room. As the woman's hand pushed open the door to the stall two down from hers, Evira sprang outward and grasped her by the neck. She quickly located the carotid arteries and squeezed off the blood flow to the woman's brain. Then she dragged her into the stall on the chance that another guest was about to enter.

The woman was unconscious within twenty seconds. Evira's next task was to get her victim inside what must have been the supply closet located just to the right of the bathroom's entrance. Evira's heart was thudding madly as she slid out of the stall and moved quickly for it. She held the woman's unconscious frame in one arm, while the other reached to grasp the closet door's knob.

It wouldn't turn. *Locked, damn it, locked!*

Immediately Evira's ears probed for the inevitable clip-clapping of high heels against the hardwood floors where the carpeting ended outside the main door. At most she judged she had another minute, with the chance of considerably less than that. She eased the woman down and grabbed in her pocket for the pair of safety pins Kourosh had gotten for her.

Evira felt sweat starting to form on her brow as she knelt to work one of the pins into the lock. She jerked it too hard and it bent. She withdrew it with care and fingered her second one. Working more carefully, she inserted it into the lock and began to feel for the tumblers. She closed her eyes to better picture its insides and at last felt it give. The knob twisted in her hand and the door opened inward.

She pulled the unconscious woman into the supply closet and managed to get the door closed just before a new group of women entered the bathroom. Evira didn't make a move or a sound, was careful to keep a hand close to her victim's mouth just in case she stirred unexpectedly. When this latest group of women had gone, she found the closet's light switch and went to work on her prisoner.

The woman was just about her size, a blessing indeed. After quickly removing her gown, stockings, and formal shoes, Evira went to work stripping away parts of her undergarments to bind and gag her. As further insurance, she tied the woman's bound hands and feet to a storage rack well away from the door itself. Confident her captive was secure, Evira removed the maid's uniform and struggled into the gown, adjusting it as best she could. The stockings were a perfect fit, but the high-heeled shoes presented a problem. Evira grimaced as she squeezed them over her feet. It had been years since she had worn such shoes, and these were at least one size too small.

Evira worked through the sounds of women coming and going in the bathroom, no longer able to afford the luxury of patience. Hassani was sure to make his entrance soon. When the bathroom was next deserted she slipped out of the supply closet and made straight for the mirror. Everything considered, she didn't look at all bad except for her hair, which simply didn't match the part she was trying to play. She picked at it as best she could and hoped she could pass a cursory scrutiny when she returned to the ballroom.

The door to the bathroom opened and Evira turned with a start. A pair of women entered but gave her only passing notice. Avoiding their eyes, she slid out the door.

She could tell already the too-tight heels were going to be a real problem if fast motions were required of her. But she would have to put up with them for now. Returning to the ballroom was unthinkable. She could be recognized by another of the servants or, worse, the gown she had donned might be recognized and her entire plan thrown into shambles.

What she needed was to make use of the nearest route upstairs. The problem was the only stairs Kourosh's drawings had included necessitated her risking an approach through the ballroom, and those would be too heavily guarded in any event. She moved out of the alcove and turned left instead of making the right that would have taken her back into the ballroom.

Her heart pounded excitedly at the sight of another door. She opened it and breathed easier when she saw a staircase climbing upward for the second floor and the royal chambers where Hassani must still be. It was secluded and would give her room to maneuver even if it were guarded. She realized she was wearing a good disguise, because even the guardsmen would approach her with respect and reverence, not wanting to risk the penalties of insulting an honored guest. That would give her the time she needed to deal with them.

She began her ascent of the staircase, starting to consider now the problem of finding a weapon, when she noticed the shape of the single guardsman on duty on the landing. Suddenly the last pieces of her plan were in place, and Evira approached the guard with a wide, disarming smile. Just as she drew close to him, her right hand shot out in a half fist. In the dim light he never saw the blow coming, and it rammed unimpeded into his Adam's apple, crushing it. The guard pitched to his knees gasping, still with the sense to claw for his weapon. Evira jammed it to the rug with her foot as she leaned far enough over to smash him across the face with the back of her forearm. The guard fluttered into unconsciousness. Death would come soon, and not wanting to risk letting his corpse be found, Evira dragged him into a darkened alcove on the second floor.

A weapon was hers for the choosing now, and she rejected the rifle in favor of the Soviet-made nine-millimeter Greysa pistol. It was bulky and poorly weighted, but it could be concealed in the back of her gown.

Knowing from Kourosh's drawing exactly where the royal
quarters were located, she cut across the corridor to the head of
the wall. Evira trembled with the realization that her target was
only a single turn away. She reached the wall and peered around
it. Before her, three-quarters of the way down the hall, a pair of
armed guards stood vigilantly outside the massive door leading
into the royal chambers. Evira eyed the men carefully from her
position. They were both armed with automatic rifles, obviously
formidable and just as obviously guarding the general himself.

Evira's heart leaped with expectation. The fact that she had
come this far and was so close to the completion of her task,
made her almost forget that not only did she have to overcome
the guards, but that she must do so without attracting the attention of Hassani within the chambers. The slightest misjudgment
or mistake on her part and he would trigger an alarm that would
summon the whole of the palace's security force to this very
spot.

Accordingly, her next thought was simply to wait for the general to emerge and to shoot him as he headed for the main
staircase. But that plan was fraught with risk, a shot from anything but point blank range with the Greysa not being totally
reliable. Moreover, the guards might spot her and prevent her
from taking action. No, she had to spring on Hassani where he
felt the safest. Wasting no further time, Evira steadied herself
and headed around the corner.

She did not bother trying to disguise her presence from the
guards; there was no sense in that. Instead she lurched drunkenly down the hallway, wavering from side to side.

"My general," she called flippantly. "Where is my general?
I have come as you told me. . . ."

She walked straight toward the two guards.

"He sent for me," she announced to them, tottering on her
high heels.

The two guards gazed at each other but neither moved or
spoke.

"Tell him I'm here, please," she requested, as if assuming
they knew who she was and had been given notification of her
expected arrival. "You'd best hurry. The guests downstairs are
growing impatient."

The next moment was one of doubt, and Evira seized it. The Greysa pistol was in her hand before either guard could notice the motion; not to fire, since that would have given her away to the target within. Instead Evira rammed the heavy pistol's butt into the bridge of the closest guard's nose. The man had barely even slumped when she whipped around and struck the second guard across the face with the barrel, opening a nasty gash. He was stunned, but still able to start for his rifle when Evira grasped his head in her free hand. She pinned it long enough to pound his skull twice with the Greysa. She felt him go limp.

Sensing movement, Evira swung back toward the first guard. His face was a sea of blood as he struggled to bring his rifle up, and his mouth was starting to form a warning to the man inside the room. Before any sound could emerge, Evira drove the point of her heel straight into the soft flesh of his throat. The guard was jolted backward, eyes bulging, when she cracked the pistol with all her might into his temple. His body kicked once and then spasmed over on the floor.

Concerned over the sounds of the commotion, Evira hesitated not at all. She steadied the Greysa pistol in one hand as she reached for the door knob with the other.

CHAPTER 21

THE KNOB WOULDN'T TURN, THE DOOR LOCKED FROM THE inside. Not surprising by any means, but still something she had failed to consider. In her mind she had seen herself plunging straight inside and shooting Hassani on sight, emptying her clip into him. She would have to think of something else now.

The door, like the wall around it, was made of rich, ancient wood. It would be impossible to kick or shoulder through without alerting Hassani to the impending attack. Certainly she could not wait for him to emerge on his own. Evira thought fast. She wiped the sweat from her palm, re-gripped the Greysa, and knocked lightly on the door.

"Message for you, General," she said, lowering her voice to disguise it as a man's.

She waited, heard nothing. A dread fear filled her that she had walked into a trap, that either the chambers beyond the heavy door were empty or a host of Revolutionary Guardsmen lay in wait behind it. Still she knocked again.

"General?"

She heard the footsteps first, then an impatient voice from within.

"Coming." The sounds of locks being turned now. "There better be good reason for this interruption. I was just ready to—"

Evira watched the double doors being pulled back.

"—come down. Now what is—"

She didn't hesitate. All she saw was a glimpse of Hassani's face and the bold black-green uniform beneath it. The Greysa came up, and before she knew what she was doing, it was erupting in her hand. The first bullet took the general in the face, obliterating his features. The next pounded his chest as he reeled helplessly backward. Evira pumped a third into his head and a final one dead on line with his heart. She stood over him with the gun still smoking in her hand and knew he was dead, felt the warmth of satisfaction surge through her. In that instant, her life meant nothing, but only that instant, for in the next her ears caught the sounds of guards alerted by the Greysa's resounding reports.

Her cold resolve had blotted out just how loud the explosions had been. A regiment of guards was already en route in her direction. Evira bolted for the door, still clinging to the Greysa although clearly it could be of little use. Escape was the thing now, the warm rush caused by her successful execution of Hassani cooling under its consideration. Shouts and screams from all levels of the palace echoed through her ears as she passed back into the corridor.

She swung left outside the master chambers instead of right, hoping for a private stairway on this side of the corridor as well. Sure enough there it was, a virtual twin of the one she had ascended to reach Hassani in the first place. Evira bolted toward it and got there just in time to hear the flood of footsteps pouring up it. She had the instant she needed to duck behind the door and keep herself pinned there after it flew open to allow a dozen guardsmen to rush by for the general's chambers. She planned her next move for the moment they had all passed inside, planned it perfectly, and plunged around the door and onto the steps without being seen.

In seconds more, guards would be posted at all levels, the presence of a killer obvious. For now, though, the steps were hers. She descended fast after pulling off her high heels to quicken her pace. She almost discarded them, then realized their presence would alert the guards that it was a woman they were after. So she held on to the shoes, at least until an opportune time for disposal came about. If she encountered no further guards en route, there was a chance, just a chance, she could find a way out of this. But how? Hiding in the labyrinth of the palace's design was a possibility. Yet with the building certain to be sealed and an all-out search conducted, that seemed to be only delaying the inevitable. What she needed was a way out of this building.

First off, there was the blood splattered over the front of her gown to consider. She had to get back to the supply closet in the bathroom and redon her maid's uniform. Her only chance of survival under the circumstances seemed to lie in getting out of the palace in much the same way she had gotten in. If she were spotted by anyone as she was now she was finished.

She followed this set of steps as far as they went, to a basement area, she guessed, which ran directly beneath the first level. She passed through a doorway into a musty damp space built as a vast play area for the royal children. The sole light came from the meager rays shed from the area of the stairway, and with this well behind her, Evira embraced the darkness. She knew it would hinder pursuit, and she flirted with the notion of hiding down here until a better strategy availed itself. If only she had committed to memory the underground escape tunnel Kourosh had alluded to. If only . . .

Evira slid on through the darkness as quickly as she could, having to feel her way now. At last a light shining dimly from beneath a door grabbed her attention and she passed inside to find a storage room lined with various food supplies and assorted kitchen necessities. A pungent smell she recognized from her initial entry into the kitchen found her nose and she realized this storeroom must have been located directly beneath the kitchen. She was on the wrong side of the palace to reclaim her servant's uniform, and there was no way she could make it back unseen to the bathroom from this vantage point anyway. It was also possible the woman she had gagged and bound had been found by now so the Revolutionary Guardsmen knew just what to look for.

What then?

Make use of what you have, would be the advice of Blaine McCracken. And what she had was the kitchen directly above her.

The stairs upward led into the vestibule that permitted access to the dining room as well as the kitchen and ballroom. She chose to enter the dining room straightaway in the hope of finding a single servant to overcome. But the room was deserted, the first course of *dolmas*, or grape leaves, and cheese portioned out at the individual settings. That left her with only the kitchen as an alternative, and she eased toward the swinging doors that led directly into it from the dining room. She eased one open enough to see chefs arguing with guardsmen over the fate of the meal being prepared. As near as she could tell, the kitchen's orders were to proceed with the preparations.

That was crazy! The anomaly made no sense. A festive meal with the bullet-ravaged corpse of the nation's leader upstairs? What was going on?

Evira turned her attention back to escaping. She moved through the door, careful to still its swinging, and concealed herself between parallel stacks of pots and pans, eyeing the kitchen before her. The stoves were of the gas variety, many of them cluttered with simmering food which emanated sharp, pungent odors. The smoke rising formed her next strategy.

Though the gas stoves were safe, open flames could mean extreme danger if the proper conditions were created. Evira eased herself a little forward. On a shelf just before her rested two glass jugs full of cooking oil and a box of wooden matches.

She emerged from her hiding place for the brief moment it took to jump up and grab one of the jugs of cooking oil and the matches from the shelf, all in the same motion. The jug was heavier than expected, and nearly toppled from her grasp as she brought it down with her next to the nearest stove, all its burners busy with pots.

She twisted the top of the jug off and eased it over until the thick oil began to ooze out. She poured it under and around the hot stove and then slid back away from the stove with a trail of the oil left before her. Watching its thick shine begin to widen, she struck a single match and tossed it slightly ahead.

The flames caught instantly and spread in a fast, straight line toward the pool of oil collected under the stove. There was a *poof!* followed by an expulsion of black smoke as the burners caught fire and flames reached out from the stove. Pots spewed their boiling contents about in all directions and the flames engulfed the white frame of the stove, spreading in bursts to the ones on either side of it.

One of the kitchen workers pulled the fire alarm and old-fashioned bells chimed through the palace. A pair of chefs came forward with fire extinguishers in hand but were blown back when flames spurted outward. The sprinkler system was activated by then, but another explosion rocketed more flames into another section of the kitchen and quickly the fire spread beyond the ability of the sprinklers to contain it. The bells continued to sound and Evira saw the kitchen workers rushing toward the nearest emergency exit. But the Revolutionary Guard had closed them off with the killer still at large, which forced the throng to head for the ballroom instead.

In the darkness and smoke Evira stalked toward a servant whose coughs had slowed her down. Evira grabbed her from behind, and before she could scream for help Evira had knocked her out and dragged her unconscious form into the shadows.

Evira struggled to remove the uniform from the woman, then removed her own gown. She donned the uniform in its place and moved into the vestibule that led into the ballroom.

She entered it among a host of coughing kitchen personnel who were collectively struggling for breath or wiping grime from their faces. Around her all was bedlam. The Revolutionary Guards had closed off all exits in a concerted attempt to keep those present inside until order was restored. No one was allowed to leave. But in the next moment there was a huge gas explosion in the kitchen that shook the palace walls. A secondary explosion immediately afterward was punctuated by thick black smoke filling the first floor.

Pandemonium ensued. Instantly all the main doors were jammed with desperate shapes fleeing into the night, guests mixing with servants as they passed out of the palace onto the sprawling grounds. To the commoners gathered in the streets beyond the royal palace, it made for entertaining viewing indeed, the sight of all those in charred formal dress reduced to a desperate mass. A few of the commoners cheered. Others jeered. There were few guardsmen about to silence them.

The main gates had to be opened to allow the fire apparatus

to pass into the complex, and it was through these in the confusion that Evira managed to slide off unseen into the night.

A pair of men dressed as commoners viewed the fire raging
from within the palace with as much confusion as delight.

"What do you think?" the bearded one asked of the other,
who was clean shaven. In times like this they always resorted to
Hebrew, keeping their voices soft.

"It's not us," the clean shaven one replied. "It couldn't be."

"Unless there's something the old men didn't tell us. Unless
this was a part of the operation we were not made privy to."

"Relax. It's just coincidence. Nothing more."

But the bearded one continued to watch as the black smoke
billowed from the windows ruptured by the blasts or by firemen.

"I'm just worried Firestorm may have started without us."

"How could it, my friend? After all, we and the others *are*
Firestorm."

"Three days?" the bearded one asked.

"Three days," the other acknowledged.

Kourosh was waiting for Evira in the small room that had
become her home and refuge. He grabbed her arms when she
entered, bouncing buoyantly about.

"I saw the flames from around the corner. I ran when I heard
the sirens coming. I knew it was you! I knew it!"

"I got lucky," Evira said, tussling his hair.

"Did you do it? Did you kill him?"

The hate in his voice disturbed her, but she nodded.

"How? Gun? Knife? The fire?"

His morbid curiosity should have revolted her but didn't. She
had come to understand that he had grown up knowing no different. Besides, he had a right to know.

"Gun," was all she said.

"Are they chasing you? Might they come here?"

"I don't think so."

He gripped her arms tighter, the perpetual grime on his cheeks
seeming darker than ever. "I know other places we can hide.
They'll never find us. You'll see!"

Evira shook her head. "Don't worry. There's an escape route. You need only get me to the airport tomorrow."

"Escape route?"

"Yes."

"For . . . you?"

She nodded. "And you, my young friend. You saved my life. I could never leave this country without you."

The boy threw himself into her arms and Evira hugged him tight, never remembering a time when an embrace felt more special.

Evira approached the Iran Air ticket counter at six o'clock the next morning. Since many of the international flights originating in Tehran departed even before this, she would have preferred to have come earlier. But the contact who would get her on her way with tickets on the first available flight out of the country didn't come on duty until six. Evira got in line at her station and resigned herself to waiting. Strangely, none of the newspapers or the state television station had said anything about Hassani's assassination. There was mention of the fire and a statement supposedly from the general was read. She wondered how and when the news of his death would be announced and why it was being concealed.

Evira never considered for a second leaving Kourosh in Tehran. She realized there would be a problem since the original escape plan was for one, not two, and Kourosh had no passport in any event. Still she remained adamant. He would come with her or she would stay until she could come up with a way to get him out as well. She clung to the hope her contact would be able to resolve the problem in a matter of minutes.

At last her turn came and she stepped up to the counter. The woman smiled at her perfunctorily and Evira handed her over a passport. The clerk reached under the counter and came up with an envelope.

"Cairo," she said simply. "Gate fifteen."

"Complications," Evira returned. "I'll need two."

The clerk's expression changed a bit. "It will take time."

"I have it."

"A passport?"

"My problem. Just get me another ticket."

The woman disappeared through a door behind the long service counter and Evira had settled herself to waiting patiently when she heard a commotion behind her. Turning, she saw a half-dozen Revolutionary Guardsmen making their way through the terminal in her general direction. Evira turned back, heart leaping in her chest. But such appearances were not uncommon. She needed only to remain calm. The clerk would take care of her.

"Cairo is much too hot this time of year, I'm afraid," came a voice from almost directly behind her, a voice she recognized but realized couldn't be. "Yes, Evira, I'm talking to you."

She turned at that and froze. There, standing slightly ahead of six Revolutionary Guardsmen, with bystanders clustering about, was General Amir Hassani, alive and in the flesh. Another pair of soldiers closed in on her from either side, rifles at the ready.

You're dead! Evira wanted to scream at Hassani but her eyes locked on the boy who stood transfixed in rage behind the soldiers.

"Run!" she screamed at him. "Run!"

And to distract the soldiers she made a feeble lunge toward Hassani, Evira feeling the rifle blow to the back of her head only briefly before oblivion welcomed her.

CHAPTER 22

"**W**ELL, INDIAN, FOR BETTER OR FOR WORSE, HERE WE are," McCracken said, easing their car off to the shoulder.

Wareagle nodded in the direction of a sign ahead which stated its message with crystal clarity.

WARNING!
AIR FORCE GUNNERY
RANGE AREA
ROAD ENDS 1 MILE AHEAD

Hank Belgrade had explained it all to Blaine on the phone the previous evening, how the gunnery range which ran between Arizona's Sierra Estrella and Maricopa Mountains was an elaborate hoax meant to disguise the existence of the O.K. Corral. Belgrade couldn't be much more specific in his directions than to say the retirement community for aging government personnel was situated between Phoenix and Casa Grande, before Route 85 reached the southern part of the state.

After obtaining that information, Blaine and Johnny had driven to Boston's Logan Airport and taken the next flight out bound for Phoenix. There were two stopovers and a long delay en route. The Thursday morning dawn was breaking by the time they finally landed.

"What now, Blainey?" Wareagle wondered, with the letters of the warning sign before them seeming to slide in the sun.

"We drive on like we're not supposed to and see what we find. It's tough country. Can't be the first time somebody strayed off the road and got themselves stuck."

"You plan to drive straight up to their front door?"

"That's the idea for now, Indian. Just make sure those spirits of yours fasten their seatbelts."

"They've been quiet today, Blainey."

"Too busy watching us maybe."

"Too busy laughing more likely."

The area they were crossing was basically desert, and Blaine was forced to turn the rental car's air conditioning off when the temperature needle flirted dangerously with the high zone. They opened all four windows in the sedan, which proved a blessing when they were perhaps five miles in.

"I hear something, Blainey," Wareagle said suddenly.

"Not me."

"Coming from the west, a little more than a mile off."

"What is it, a chopper?"

Wareagle tilted his head from the window as if the air might tell him. "Hughes Thunderhawk, overhauled from its time in the hellfire."

"Kind of like us, eh, Indian?"

"It's closing, Blainey."

"I figured they'd spot us before long. Must have sensors laid through the ground. Or maybe it's just a routine patrol."

"Too fast for routine."

"Then what do you say we meet them on our own terms?"

McCracken had the sedan pulled over, the hood popped and his head beneath it, when his ears finally picked up what Johnny Wareagle's had well ahead of him. The steady *wop-wop-wop* sifted through the wind at an ever-increasing volume until the dust started to kick up around him announcing the chopper's arrival. Blaine gazed upward and feigned absolute shock over the black chopper's appearance. He began to wave his arms frantically to signal it, as a motorist in grave trouble would have.

In his mind he could hear the pilot issuing a report back to the command center of the O.K. Corral, perhaps speaking to base leader Doc Holliday himself. A car had wandered into their territory and overheated. No sense making a big fuss. Just send some help fast or call the nearest Triple A. Wareagle had stayed hunched in the backseat the whole time the chopper was overhead. That way the report would mention only one man present, which was what they had to think if Blaine's plan was going to work.

"You have entered an air force gunnery range area and are in extreme danger," came the obligatory call over the chopper's PA system. *"Please leave with your vehicle immediately. Repeat, please leave with your vehicle immediately."*

McCracken threw up his arms helplessly once more and then pointed in frustration at the engine. He made sure they could see him shrug. He saw the pilot's hand signal before the chopper swung round and headed back to the west and the O.K. Corral.

"How long you figure it'll be before they can get help to us, Indian?" he asked when Wareagle had emerged from the backseat.

"My guess would be ten minutes, maybe fifteen. We're close, Blainey."

"Spirits tell you anything specific about the Corral we'll soon be heading for?"

"A prison, Blainey, where the souls of the past loiter in the present without regard for the future."

"So what else is new?"

As Wareagle had predicted, the jeep came kicking dust down the single unpaved road inside of fifteen minutes later. Blaine made a show of stepping away from his still-open hood and waving his arms again as is if to attract the driver. The jeep was marked in the colors and symbols of the air force, but the two men inside were dressed in civilian clothes.

"Am I glad to see you!" he shouted out when they pulled their jeep up not far from him.

They stepped down wordlessly, facial features obscured by the dark-tinted goggles each wore to keep the desert dust from their eyes while riding in the open jeep.

"What's the problem?" one of them asked.

"Bastard overheated. Should've known not to trust a rental in these parts."

One of the men pulled off his goggles to reveal a pair of expressionless eyes. He nodded to the other who headed back to the jeep.

"I really appreciate your help," Blaine said. "Hey, you boys air force, or what?"

The man said nothing, just stood there.

"Well, thank the boys in the chopper for me, too."

At the jeep, the second man had just reached into the back for a water jug when Johnny Wareagle rose from behind it and latched a hand over his wrist so he wouldn't foolishly try for a weapon. Meanwhile, McCracken more crudely rammed a fist into the stomach of the man nearest him. The man doubled over and Blaine followed the blow up by slamming him hard under the chin. His head snapped back in whiplash and he passed out instantly. Blaine turned to see Wareagle approaching with a slight grin etched over his leathery face and the man he'd downed hoisted effortlessly over his shoulder.

"You must learn to be subtle, Blainey."

"You know what they say about an old dog, Indian."

"Perhaps. But the teeth remain sharp and dangerous still."

"So long as he doesn't try and change his bite."

They drove the rental car a short way off the single dirt road and camouflaged it as best they could with brush. By the time they climbed into the purloined jeep, its previous two occupants had been bound, gagged, and stored in the sedan's back and front seats. Blaine had left the windows partway down to make sure they'd have air. He drove the jeep with Johnny Wareagle in the seat next to him. They had donned the large tinted goggles worn by the other men both to shut out the spray of desert dust and to mask their features. Since the men from the O.K. Corral were dressed in civilian clothes, they didn't feel their own garb would be a problem.

"Rover One, this is Holliday," a voice squawked over a mobile radio beneath the dash when they were six minutes into their drive west. "You boys plan on making a report anytime soon?"

Blaine made sure to hold the mike well away from his lips when he responded. "Assistance rendered. On our way in."

"No reason to be so formal about it. See ya for lunch, boys," Holliday said, and signed off.

The tall steel fence came into view a bit under ten minutes later, just before they swung up the last of a rise that descended quickly into a valley at the foot of Arizona's Maricopa Mountains.

"I don't see a checkpoint," Blaine noted. "No guards to concern ourselves with."

"Electronic surveillance," Wareagle put forth. "Cameras mounted on or near the fence. The gate will be opened from a monitoring station if we're permitted to pass through."

As they drew closer to the fence, more signs alerting them to the presence of an air force gunnery range were visible, plastered all over the steel link.

"Wish I could," Blaine said out loud in response to the boldest sign of them all, one ordering all newcomers to TURN BACK NOW!

They reached the gate and could do nothing but wait. When it did not slide open immediately, McCracken inspected it from the driver's seat to see if he could ram the jeep right through and up the last of the rise. Probably could have, but it was a bad idea. If they couldn't gain legitimate access to the O.K. Corral, the thing to do would be to circle round from the side on foot and make their entry at night. But the gate slid sideways at last and Blaine drove through it after a glance at Wareagle. He continued the uphill climb and saw in the rearview mirror that the gate had closed behind them.

"Once we get there, we'll still have to find Bechman," he said.

"The spirits would not have let us come this far if that was not their intention," Johnny told him.

"Let's hope so."

The early afternoon sun beat down on them and Blaine felt his flesh seeming to wilt. The dry desert heat had his mouth tasting like dust, and he was about to reach back for one of the jeep's water jugs when the rise suddenly leveled off to reveal the valley beneath them. Blaine's eyes bulged behind his goggles.

"Jesus Christ, is that a mirage, Indian, or am I crazy?"

"It is indeed an illusion, Blainey, but not meant for us."

In the valley before them, a perfect town had been built with unpainted wood. The only tall structure was a church steeple on the outskirts, and Blaine distinguished freshly sodded parks and even a bubbling stream around which the entire secret retirement community had been constructed.

"Certainly has all the comforts of home," Blaine commented, and he started the jeep downward.

As they drew closer they could see that virtually all the structures were one-story in design, and all were equipped with wheelchair ramps as well as steps for easy entry. Everything had been built in consideration of the O.K. Corral's residents, many of them old or infirm.

He slowed the jeep briefly at a sign posted off the road where it turned to pavement, a sign painted far less professionally than the previous ones and bearing a wholly different message:

WELCOME
TO THE O.K. CORRAL!

"Guess we should take them up on the offer, Indian."

"Why not?" Wareagle shrugged.

And McCracken headed the jeep on into the makeshift town. They kept their goggles on, ready now to abandon the jeep at the first opportunity. Everywhere they looked were indications of time gone wrong. The place was laid out like an old-style western town. Each of the small shops had its own hand-carved or painted sign above its doorway, which furthered the illusion still more. There was an ice cream shop and even a small movie house featuring posters of coming attractions and a marquee boldly advertising the latest bill. They drove the jeep past a parklike setting lined with canopied tables around the pond. Many of the tables were occupied by figures snoozing, staring, or reading a book or newspaper.

"Think they got their own printing press, too?" Blaine wondered.

"Why not?" Johnny Wareagle responded. "They've fabricated their own reality here. They want time to seem frozen, unchanged. The residents will have no means of noting the passage of days that way. They lose touch with what they were before coming here, who they were."

"Turned docile and quiet, behavior modification taken to a new level. Jesus Christ, Indian, when you think of all the secrets stowed within the minds in residence here. . . ." He slid the jeep on, taking in the sights passed on the way. "Think the library has a preferred reading list?" Blaine asked as they edged past it.

"Of more concern to us now, Blainey, is whether or not the sheriff's office over there has cells."

"Whoops."

Blaine swung the jeep beyond the sheriff's office and made a left turn, coming to a halt before a bakery featuring the smell of fresh-baked breads and cookies floating through its open doors.

"All the comforts of home, eh, Indian?" Blaine repeated.

"A lie, Blainey, meant to disguise the truths of the past, to bury these truths from the world they were perpetrated on."

"A graveyard for secrets, in other words."

"And a resting place for the souls of men before they are ready to join the spirits."

They climbed from the jeep and headed for cover. Suddenly an old man with a shock of gray hair stormed out the door of the bakery waving his arms and yelling at them.

"How do you expect my customers to get in with your damn machine blocking the door?"

"Huh?"

The man wiped his hands on his stained apron. Blaine thought he looked vaguely familiar.

"Rush starts soon. Get your machine out of the way. Scat now! Scat! Damn law-and-order people never cared a damn for the needs of anyone else. Always taking, always taking. Jesus . . ."

The old man disappeared back inside the bakery shaking his head.

"We'd do best to move the jeep, Blainey."

But Blaine's mind was elsewhere. "I know that man," he

said slowly. "I know I've seen him before. . . . Shit, his name's Kirkland. He was Allen Dulles's number one operations man with the old CIA under Kennedy and Johnson. What the hell is this place?"

"Just what we expected it to be."

They had returned to the jeep now and were backing it into another slot before the bookstore, since it looked closed today.

"They must have given the residents jobs," McCracken surmised.

"And thus a purpose, aimed at making them forget what their purpose was before they arrived. Their very existences have been redefined."

"Drugs?"

"For a time, probably. But these men have outlived their eras. With nothing to go back to, they would welcome the new way of looking at themselves."

"Like us, Indian?"

"I don't think they have beds ready for us yet."

"But think about it. In a manner of speaking, we've outlived our eras too. Yet instead of coming to a place like this to play checkers and fish, we redefined our lives on our own terms. Not much different than these folks when you look at it that way."

They were only a few steps away from the jeep when a loud voice rang out from just behind them.

" 'Bout time you boys got back. The Doc was startin' to worry up a storm, I tell ya."

McCracken, closer than Johnny was to the speaker, turned slowly to find a tobacco-chomping icy-eyed man dressed like a western gunman, albeit without the six-gun. Blaine shrugged and cut the distance between them routinely. The man's eyes fell on Wareagle.

"Hey, wait a minute, you're not—"

He had started to go for his walkie-talkie when Blaine was upon him, his grasp harsh and painful. The man looked at him and spat tobacco on the neatly paved road.

"Who the fuck are you?" he demanded.

"Ike Clanton, and that there's my little brother Billy. And unless you're Wyatt Earp, I'd say you're in a heap of trouble."

The man spat again. "This some kind of joke?"

"Oh, yeah. The joke's called the O.K. Corral, and the punch line's got to do with some half-assed cowboys running herd on a bunch of old men."

Blaine started to ease himself and his captive down the road with Wareagle on the deputy's other side.

"This is a U.S. government installation, mister. I don't know who or what you are, but you're in a heap more trouble than you know and it's getting worse by the second."

They reached the bookstore, and a quick shoulder from Wareagle had the locked door swinging open. The trio passed inside and Blaine immediately passed the guard to the huge Indian. Wareagle responded in turn by grasping the man around the neck in a death lock that shut off virtually all his air.

"I haven't had a good day," Blaine told the man who was straining up on the tips of his toes to lessen the pressure being applied to his throat. "In fact, I've had a pretty lousy week, lousy enough to not care much at all if the Indian has to break your neck. 'Less, of course, you tell us what we've come to find out."

The icy-eyed man struggled for air and a stream of chalky brown tobacco juice dropped onto his white cowboy shirt.

"You'll never get away with this."

"Interesting cliche. Shame to waste it. We're looking for a man named Hans Bechman. Used to be a German scientist until he signed up with this nuthouse."

Wareagle allowed the guard some welcome breath. "No names, not real ones anyway. They never tell us any real names."

"This one would be in a wheelchair," Blaine explained further, recalling Bart Joyce's description of the man he had seen directing the loading of cannisters onto the *Indianapolis*.

"Lots of people here in wheelchairs, mister."

"This one would have come in one. Heavy German accent, too. Know the man?"

"No."

"You're lying. I can tell by your eyes. Look, friend, there's a new sheriff in town and he's about to snap your neck. Last chance. Know him or not?"

Wareagle increased the pressure and lifted the guard off the floor.

"Yes! Yes!"

Again Johnny let up on the pressure and eased him part of the way back down.

"Lives in number forty-nine," the captive deputy said. "Almost never comes out. Keeps all to himself."

"Very good."

"Not really. You're wasting your time if you expect to get something out of him. Man's lost more marbles than a ten-year-old can sink in a hole. Doesn't even know who he is most of the time."

"Guess we'll have to jog his memory," McCracken said.

He nodded to Wareagle, who increased his pressure on the deputy's neck enough to put him to sleep.

"Think we should tie him up, Indian?"

"Not unless we plan on being here past the coming of the moon, Blainey."

The residence numbered forty-nine was located in the northern sector of the O.K. Corral, set off the path of stores and shops and away from the clutter of old folks loitering the day away in the shade. This and the others clustered around it had the look of hand-built cabins or cottages, the old-west motif still dominant. McCracken noted that although there seemed to be no rules to that effect, most of the residents kept to themselves. He and Wareagle saw scarcely any socializing as they circled about. It seemed the residents still stubbornly clung to the secrets that had brought them there for the last of their days. It was as if holding firm at all costs to those secrets was the only way to maintain even a limited grasp of the past, which fluttered like dust in the wind of their memory. There was hardly a sound in the air, other than the occasional jeep patrolling or the church bells clanging every quarter hour.

Blaine made sure no one was about before he and Wareagle approached the door marked with a forty-nine. They had no idea what to expect inside and could only hope Hans Bechman had enough command of his faculties to provide the final piece of the puzzle that began in 1945 on board the *Indianapolis*.

Wareagle remained in the shadows while McCracken eased up to the door and knocked. When no sound or response came from within, he knocked again louder.

At last he heard the squealing of wheels over wood, then a hand fumbling with a knob inside. The door parted halfway to reveal a skeletal shape tucked into a wheelchair with a blanket over his lap.

"Do you have my towels?" Hans Bechman asked.

"Yes," Blaine replied without hesitation.

"That's good. I ran out. I called yesterday. You didn't come." Puzzlement crossed his face. "I think it was yesterday. . . ."

The old scientist's words emerged still laced with a German accent. What little hair he still had hung in unkempt clumps. Blaine heard him muttering to himself in German as he slid back far enough for McCracken to enter with Wareagle just behind.

"Where do you want them?" Blaine asked. "The towels, I mean?"

"Kitchen . . . no—bathroom . . . no—kitchen."

Blaine turned back to Johnny. "Put Dr. Bechman's towels in the kitchen."

The old man's eyes flared to life at that. "My name. You used my name."

"Of course, Dr. Bechman."

"I don't hear it anymore. I don't hear it at all. Maybe my ears are going. I like hearing it." His eyes turned quizzical. "Do I know you?"

"No," McCracken replied flatly. "I'm new."

"Good. I don't like the ones I know. They don't talk to me. They don't call me by my name." His eyes glistened hopefully. "Will you talk to me?"

"I'd like that," Blaine told him.

CHAPTER 23

THE OLD MAN'S FACE SUDDENLY TOOK ON AN AGITATED EX-
pression.

"What time is it?"

"Almost two o'clock."

"What day?"

"Thursday."

"What year?"

"199—"

"Did you say *ninety*? It can't be. Surely it can't be. Tell me the truth now. Don't be like the others."

McCracken gazed at Wareagle, who had taken up a position by the window to watch for the possible approach of Holliday and his men.

"What if it were 1945?" Blaine asked the old man.

The creases of Bechman's face relaxed. "Then I'd have my work."

"What was your work, doctor?"

"I was a traitor to my country, you know. I could have given my discovery to them. We would have won the war. But, but . . . Wait, I know you now. You're the gestapo! You've come to take me away. I won't go, I tell you, I won't!"

Bechman's last words emerged in a shrill scream, and Blaine had to grasp the side of his wheelchair to keep him from rolling it away.

"I'm not the gestapo," McCracken told him calmly. "Listen to my voice. I'm American. The Americans saved you from the gestapo. We brought you to the United States and gave you a new life."

Bechman's face turned quizzical again. "What year did you say it was?"

"1990."

He shook his head. "What happened to the years? Where did they all go? There is a hole in my mind and the years keep slipping out. What can I do to plug the hole?" he uttered pleadingly. "Tell me what I can do!"

"You can remember."

"But where to start?"

"In 1945 when the Americans gave you a new life."

"Not a new life. No, just an extension of the old one. It was my own fault. I was scared. I wanted them to accept me. So I told them the secret I had hidden from the Nazis."

"What did you tell them?"

"About my experiments. Hitler's people never realized what I had happened upon. They wouldn't have understood it even if they had. Years ahead of its time, generations! It was brilliant. Brilliant, I tell you! But I didn't give it to them."

"You gave it to the Americans."

"Because I wanted no more wars, no more innocent people to die. The Americans could wield the weapon with judgment, with prudence. Yes, I gave it to them. All my research was completed. It was a simple matter of production, just a few additional tests from that point."

Blaine posed his next question calmly. "What exactly was produced?"

"When?"

"In 1945, Dr. Bechman. By the Americans."

The old man's features turned mad again. "How do you know my name? I don't know you. I'm sure I don't know you."

"I'm here to help you."

"Did you bring my towels?"

"Already put them away."

"Then why are you still here?"

"To listen to you. You like to talk, don't you, doctor? You like to speak of your past."

Bechman's expression grew dreamlike. "Yes, I suppose."

"What was the weapon you gave the Americans, Dr. Bechman?"

The old man's eyes focused suddenly again. "They didn't believe me at first you know. Thought I was crazy to insist such a thing could exist. But I knew it existed because I created it."

"In Germany. During those last months of the war."

"Yes! Yes! Hitler was obsessed with the United States, had been from the beginning. He hoped to delay their entry into the war long enough for the team I was part of to finish a weapon that could destroy them, wipe out their entire nation suddenly and swiftly."

"And your research was on the genetic level."

Bechman gazed at him condescendingly from his wheelchair. "Of course it was. Before anyone else even knew the terms, we were splitting cells, working with the DNA itself."

"You found something."

"Yes, but purely by accident, believe it or not. A chance coincidence arrived at from all our tinkering. We were working with viruses in pursuit of the ideal form of germ warfare. We wanted to alter the DNA of the virus so it would behave in a different way. But the altered DNA produced an enzyme which had properties that were terrifying, awesome in their implications."

"An enzyme?" Blaine asked, embarrassed for his lack of scientific knowledge.

"An enzyme is the biological catalyst for a reaction. We were working at the cellular level. All human life is based on cells dividing, reproducing, splitting. How? How?"

"I—"

"Glucose!" Bechman blared, a scientist again. "Sugar metabolism is the basis of life at the cellular level and thus life in general. Cells digest glucose at metabolic level to supply the most basic function of life. The process is called phosphorylation. Picture this now. Once introduced into the system through the virus, our enzyme penetrates and alters the DNA of the stem cells from which all other cells originate. The enzyme produces a more efficient pathway to metabolize sugar and produce life, the DNA of the stem cells altered to the point where they can no longer utilize their usual pathway. The cells immediately become dependent on this new pathway and can no longer metabolize without it. All because of our enzyme. *My* enzyme!''

McCracken found himself going cold, his limited scientific knowledge no longer insulating him from the impact of what he was hearing. ''You're saying whoever became exposed to your virus would become dependent on it to survive, wouldn't be able to live without being exposed further to it.''

''Precisely! One exposure was all it would take to produce total dependence. The process becomes irreversible after that. If exposure to more of the virus containing my enzyme is not maintained, life degenerates at its most basic level. All bodily functions cease because phosphorylation cannot occur within the stem cells.''

''The ultimate form of biological warfare,'' Blaine muttered, looking at Wareagle, starting to grasp what the gamma cannisters Bart Joyce had seen loaded onto the *Indianapolis* had contained. ''The virus invades the body and the host dies if he doesn't get more of the enzyme it contains.''

''A disease that breaks the spirit as well as the body, Blainey. Worse than death. The ultimate form of control as well.''

''You can see why I couldn't let Hitler have it,'' Bechman broke in. ''Imagine him able to destroy the military capacity of the United States while retaining its vast production capabilities and resources for *his own use*! Slavery is what it would have come down to.''

''But how would you contain it, doctor? Stop it from spreading beyond the borders of your enemy?''

''Many means were discussed. Aerosol release into the air was ruled out as too uncontrollable, as was the ethnic factor of infecting a specific food or finding a virus that attacks a single ethnicity. We settled on infecting a nation's water supply. The virus containing the enzyme would live in water for two or three days, programmed to survive for only that many generations. By then the cells of the victim would be dependent at the DNA level, and more of the enzyme would have to be introduced to avoid certain death. The effects would show up after only a few days. My estimates indicated that five hundred German agents could accomplish the entire task quite adequately. Germany or another attacking country could then issue its ultimatum: surrender or die.''

"Listen to what he's saying, Indian," McCracken urged Wareagle. "That's what Rasin has in his possession. That's what he's going to release into the Arab world."

"To deny them death is a worse fate than death itself, Blainey.''

"Right up Rasin's alley." And Blaine felt suddenly chilled. "But we had this enzyme in our possession and didn't use it. And then we sunk the *Indianapolis* because the cannisters containing it had to be buried forever. Why, doctor, why?''

Bechman looked confused. "I don't know what you mean.''

"Remember, you've got to remember!''

"Remember. . . . remember *what*?''

"It's 1945 again. You supervised the loading of dozens of cannisters marked with the Greek letter gamma on to the *Indianapolis*.''

"Yes, cannisters containing the virus. To be used against Japan to end the war." Bechman's eyes cleared as his mind regained its sharpness. "They called it the Gamma Option.''

Blaine felt even colder. "But there were atomic bombs on board the *Indianapolis* as well.''

"They formed the Beta Option, to be employed as a backup in the event something went wrong with Gamma. The Alpha Option was to take Japan by conventional attack. We were working down to the wire. The last tests on Gamma had not been completed when the *Indianapolis* left San Francisco. It was the perfect weapon, the ultimate weapon!''

"Victory without blood, Blainey," Wareagle commented. "But hardly without pain, a lingering agony that would persist for generations, for . . . ever.''

"But we didn't use it," Blaine said again. "Why didn't we use the Gamma Option, doctor? What did those final tests reveal? What made them change their minds?''

Bechman looked perplexed. "They changed their minds?''

"You must remember that!''

He didn't seem to. "I remember . . . my work being suspended. My papers, my samples, my equipment, all confiscated and impounded. They made me a prisoner. My assistant would have been made one too, if he hadn't escaped.''

''You had an assistant?''

The old man nodded. ''His name was Eisenstadt, Martin Eisenstadt.''

''Have you heard from him since, seen him?''

''Not in all these years . . . How many is it now? What year is this?''

''1990. Now look at me. What happened in those last days after the *Indianapolis* had set out from San Francisco?''

''Nothing . . .''

''Those last hours before it reached Tinian. What did you uncover?''

''Nothing!''

''The Americans didn't use the Gamma Option and then we sank the *Indianapolis* to insure that no trace of it would ever be found. Why, doctor, why? What was worth sacrificing a thousand men at sea for?''

Bechman smiled a mad smile. ''I escaped. Would you like me to tell you how? Would you like to hear how I escaped the Nazis while under watch at all times?''

''Sure, but I'd like to hear about the final hours the *Indianapolis* was at sea en route to Tinian first. I'd like to hear about the last work you did with your designer enzymes.''

''Yes.'' Bechman beamed. ''I've brought all my work with me. Let me help you put it into operation. We must be certain the world will never know another Nazi Germany in another time. I can insure that. My discovery can insure that. Why? You ask me why? I'll tell you. Listen and you'll understand. Listen and . . .''

Bechman droned on but Blaine shut him off. The old man was clearly exhausted. McCracken had pushed him too hard and now he was paying for it. It was conceivable that the last secrets of the Gamma Option were sealed forever, sunk with the *Indianapolis*. And while Rasin had managed to salvage the cannisters of Bechman's deadly virus, he had not salvaged those secrets. Possibly they didn't even exist. Maybe Bechman could recall no more because there was no more. Truman had simply changed his mind after weighing exactly what Gamma would mean for the future of the world. It made a chilling sort of sense.

"Yo, boys," a new voice came suddenly, "I think you've bothered the old guy enough for one day."

The voice was hoarse and raspy, like that of a man who'd smoked too many cigarettes in his time. McCracken and Wareagle spun together into the center of the room as if to search for it, knowing already it was being broadcast on some hidden speaker.

"Now I'd like you boys to know . . ." There was a slight laugh. ". . . Hey, don't this sound corny. . . . Anyway, we got you surrounded and I'd be much obliged if you would kindly raise your arms into the air where the camera can pick 'em up."

Blaine did just that as Wareagle glided toward one of the room's corners.

"Be a good idea if your rather large friend got 'em up too, boss." McCracken nodded the Indian's way. "Yup, that's better. Now just hold tight for a minute. . . ."

Actually it was considerably less than that when the door to Bechman's apartment burst open to allow six men armed with shotguns to charge through, half leveling their weapons at Blaine and the other half at Johnny. That remained the situation, frozen for upward of two minutes, before the sound of a Jeep squealing to a halt at the door could be heard. Boots clip-clopped in the apartment's direction, and from out of the sun stepped in a man decked out in black suit, black vest, and old-fashioned western tie. He had a heavy dark mustache and wavy hair hidden beneath a narrow-brimmed black cowboy hat. In his hands he held a double-barreled sawed-off shotgun, so much a part of him as to make it appear he may have slept with it nightly.

"Afternoon, boys," he greeted formally. "The name's Holliday, Doc Holliday."

"Don't tell me, let me guess," Blaine followed without missing a beat. "And your friends here are the Earp brothers, Bat Masterson, and Wild Bill Hickock."

Doc Holliday regarded him with a cold stare. "You boys be in a heap of trouble, I'd say."

"Gonna give us until sundown to ride out of town?"

"Nope."

"Settle this at dawn then?"

"Sorry."

"Then let's you and me go gun to gun at high noon." Then he added to Wareagle, "Whatever you do, darlin', don't forsake me."

Holliday showed his sawed-off a little higher. "Keep it up, friend. You're just makin' my day. Sorry I got to ruin yours by taking you and your injun friend over to my jail."

"Watch out, Doc. The rest of the boys are certain to bust us out. Have to get yourself a posse and everything, and I wouldn't want to trust my life to these here tenderfoots."

Doc Holliday fired a blast from one of his twin barrels that blew a huge chasm in the floor six inches before McCracken and showered him with splinters. Bechman looked on in amazement, waving his arms in protest.

"Was up to me, mister," Holliday continued, "I'd hang your ass right now, but I'm betting the United States government'll have its own plans for you and the big fella over there."

"For a minute there," Blaine said, "I thought we were in trouble."

"I know who you are," Holliday told him, lowering his still-smoking sawed-off gun as his deputies approached and fastened handcuffs around Blaine and Johnny's wrists. " 'Nam, right? The Phoenix Project?"

"You know, Doc, one thing I loved about that country was that they didn't discriminate over who could get in."

"I was in Eye-Corps. Bastards like you fucked us up good."

"For following orders?"

"Or your interpretation of them."

"I don't suppose if I say I'm sorry, you'll let me and the Indian go."

Doc Holliday stripped off his cowboy hat and mopped his brow with a sleeve. McCracken noticed his hair was as raven dark as his mustache.

"Out of my hands, pal. The line lookin' for you runs straight around the block."

* * *

The O.K. Corral's single jail cell was located in the back of the old-fashioned sheriff's office. There was a plastic toilet and sink and a pair of cots squeezed in across from each other. Holliday's deputies took the handcuffs off their prisoners, leaving with one guard posted outside the cell and another in view at the end of the corridor. Holliday was taking no chances, even rotated a shift regularly himself and spent it twirling the handlebars of his wide mustache.

"Not polite to wear your hat inside, Doc," Blaine taunted.

"Always wanted to have a fuck-up like you in my jail, McCrackenballs. Heard about England and France and all your other fucked-up exploits since you've been out. People like you give people like me a bad name."

"Yup, I know just what you mean. Here you are running herd over a bunch of old folks, giving them sponge baths and emptying their bedpans. Maybe call out an occasional bingo game on Sunday nights. You really have reached the top. Hell, I'd never want to give you a bad name."

Holliday came a little closer to the bars. "Know what I hope? That Washington misplaces the communique about you I sent and I get the privilege of watching you rot right here in my jail. . . ."

Holliday might have been about to go on when one of his deputies appeared with a note. The chief law-enforcement official of the O.K. Corral rose to take his leave and Blaine took a seat next to Johnny Wareagle on one of the cots.

"Is this what *our* retirement's gonna be like, Indian? Stashed away at a modified old-folks home under the watchful eye of a cardboard maniac?"

"We are already in the midst of our retirement, Blainey, and have been for several years now."

"Hasn't slowed us down much, though."

"My point exactly," Wareagle followed with the barest hint of a smile.

"Gonna come a time pretty soon when we'll have to figure ourselves a way out of here, Indian."

"The spirits have already revealed several."

"In one of your secretive moods, are you?"

"It feels like we belong here. For a time."

Holliday returned just then, looking red-faced and flustered. "Looks like I'm not gonna get my wish, McCrackenballs. Someone's en route from Washington now to pick you boys up."

"I knew I could rely on our blessed government to right this wrong."

"Not our government, pal. Your taxi driver hails from Israel."

It was six hours later, night having fallen in the Arizona sky, when Doc Holliday escorted a short but powerfully built man down the corridor leading to the single cell. The man's features were sharp and angular, his hair held in brown waves, and his eyes a strangely crystal shade of blue.

"Was this really necessary?" the man asked of Holliday.

"This is my town, pal."

"But they're my prisoners now, aren't they? Have your man take his leave."

Holliday gave the order but seemed inclined to stay himself until the short man thrust a powerful forearm in the office's direction.

"You, too, if you please."

"I don't."

"It wasn't a request. Just leave me the keys."

Holliday was steamed. "Pal, you go in there alone with those two and I hear screams, don't expect me to come running."

"If they wanted to kill me, there would be no screams."

"You know who I am," the Israeli said to McCracken after Holliday was gone. "I can tell by your eyes."

"Only one Israeli I know of would come here on his own. You're Isser, chief of Mossad."

The smaller man nodded. "Your government has been kind enough to place you in my custody. We've been looking for you for days."

"The ones at my home. Yours?"

Isser nodded again. "Ours. I imagine they ended up warning you off. It was a foolish undertaking, I suppose, but they were desperate, just as I am."

"You don't know the whole of it."

Isser's expression relaxed. "Precisely why I've exhausted considerable resources to track you down ever since you were identified in the Jaffa market."

"You want to know what made me work for the Arabs."

"With, not for. That much is already obvious."

"There's plenty more that isn't, Isser. We're running out of time and I can't think of a better man to talk to." Blaine thought briefly. "Unfortunately, there's something I have to do before we talk."

"What's that?"

"I have to die."

The bearded man watched them from the chair, head pressed high and tight against its back, arranged so his eyes could not leave the bed.

"Please," Tilly muttered, squirming so she was directly beneath Lace.

Their mouths met again as Lace's hand slid down Tilly's belly for her vagina, feeling the slit and slipping her fingers inside it. Tilly moaned. Lace was working the hand feverishly now, sliding and probing.

The bearded man bore silent witness to it all; silent because he was dead and had been for some hours now. Their failure in Boston had upset the women gravely. Failure was rare for them indeed, especially on the scale of Wednesday's debacle. Tilly and Lace took their passion from their killing, the ultimate intermixture of life and death. Neither saw anything cosmic in this; it was merely a means to extend pleasure beyond its momentary rush.

But there had been no pleasure after Blaine McCracken had first escaped and then turned the tables on them in Boston. The passion was stripped away and the women were left empty. The fact that he was by far the most competent adversary they had ever faced served only to heighten their expectations. The passion that would follow his killing would bring them to new levels of ecstasy. Yet the potential of that anticipated high made the low they experienced even greater in depth. Blaine McCracken would die at their hands. Soon. Very soon. But in the meantime, in the meantime . . .

It had taken forays into three bars for them to find a bearded man who looked enough like McCracken to serve as surrogate. Luring him to their hotel room had not been difficult. Barely inside the door, Lace had grasped his shoulders and, lowering her head, pressed her mouth against his.

Tilly slithered around to his rear.

Lace became more ardent, forced her tongue against his and felt his bristly McCracken beard scrape at her cheeks.

Tilly plucked up a length of twine and raised it for his head.

Lace pulled her mouth away in perfect rhythm with the smaller woman's looping of the twine over the man's head. She closed it around his throat and yanked out the slack, thrusting her leg against the back of his knees to pull him down to provide leverage. The bearded man whipped his hands wildly about, clawing for her—for anything—dying eyes locked on Lace.

Lace stood there smiling, letting Tilly have the kill.

At last he stopped flailing. His arms flapped to his side and twitched. A raspy gurgle pushed its way up his throat past the protruding tongue, all of it over faster than either of the women would have preferred.

They put him in the chair before the bed, and in the near dark of the room he could almost have passed for McCracken. Passion again. Pleasure again. Both, though, would be fleeting. With the return of light, the fantasy would die. The women could squirm in the dark with McCracken on their minds, but Mc-Cracken was still out there, the corpse in the chair a mere proxy.

We've got a chair waiting for you, Blaine McCracken, Lace thought, while beneath her Tilly arched her hips upward and screamed in ecstasy, the task of her fingers completed.

The bearded corpse looked on.

CHAPTER 24

"**A**T LAST WE HAVE A CHANCE TO SPEAK," GENERAL AMIR Hassani said.

Evira gazed out at him from her cell deep in the bowels of the royal palace. She had been taken there directly from the airport the previous morning, and had spent almost twenty-four hours with a cup of water as her only nourishment. The construction of the complex might have been relatively recent, but the Shah had been a man who liked to consider all eventualities. Hence the fully equipped prison hidden away in his grandest home.

"I have nothing to say to you."

"At least a comment about how surprised you are to see I'm still alive."

"Or how sorry."

Hassani waved a disparaging finger at her. "You disappoint me, Evira."

"I killed a double. But why would you need one?"

"You still haven't figured it out, have you?"

"Figured what out?"

"Telling you would eliminate the fun. I would have thought it would all be as obvious to you now as it would certainly have been to . . ." His eyes sharpened here. ". . . McCracken."

She came forward until she could smell the steel of the bars. "How do you know about McCracken?"

"No pointless denials. That is a good start."

"No start at all. His involvement in this couldn't possibly mean anything to you," Evira insisted, perplexed by the direction Hassani's interest was taking.

"Then you won't mind telling me what he knows."

"I have no idea."

His eyes scolded her. "Evira . . ."

"We haven't been in contact. I retained him to—"

"To what?"

"It doesn't matter to you."

"Doesn't matter to me that you coerced McCracken into finding Yosef Rasin for you and stopping him from employing a weapon that could destroy my world? Come now, give me more credit than that, please. You were helping me from the beginning. Why not help me some more?"

Evira felt numb. "You knew. How could you know?"

"It doesn't matter to you," the general shot back, using her own words against her.

"You're asking questions you already know the answers to."

"Then don't bother holding the rest back. Where can I find McCracken? What system of contact did you set up for him?"

"None," Evira insisted, trying to collect her thoughts while keeping her calm. How Hassani had learned of McCracken's involvement wasn't as pressing as why it seemed so important to him. If anything, as he had noted, the two men were allies in a twisted sort of way. Thanks to her.

"I am going to give you the benefit of the doubt, Evira. But only if you provide the answer to a question I'm sure you *do* know the answer to: where is McCracken's son stashed?"

Evira's response was to stare at Hassani in confused helplessness.

"You do know that, don't you?"

"Why is it important to you?"

"It is. That is all you need to know."

"The boy cannot possibly be of service to you."

"I'll be the judge of that."

"McCracken has nothing to do with you!"

Hassani grew still calmer. "I expected far more of you, Evira.

You have let me down. But I will give you one more chance to answer my questions."

"Then what? Torture? Drugs?"

He looked genuinely insulted. "A gentleman would never treat a lady so. However . . ."

With that, the general gazed back toward the staircase and signaled his guards. Seconds later a pair of them approached, dragging someone between them.

"I believe you know this boy," Hassani said.

Kourosh writhed and kicked between the guards dragging him along. His lips were bloody and the edges of his long auburn hair were wet with blood from a cut on his forehead.

"No!" Evira screamed.

The guards stopped just to the general's right. Evira's eyes met the boy's.

"Now you will tell me where I can find Blaine McCracken's son, won't you?"

"I . . ."

A nod from Hassani brought one of the guard's revolvers from its holster, barrel pressed solidly against Kourosh's head as the second guard held the boy in place.

"I will ask you again, and if you fail to answer, my man will pull the trigger."

"You . . . *animal!*"

"Where can I find Blaine McCracken's son?"

A thousand thoughts swam through Evira's head. The problem she faced was impossible, death for herself a better alternative than choosing.

"Kill me instead!" she begged.

"But then who would tell me what I want to know?"

"I can't! *I can't!*"

"How unfortunate," Hassani said, and nodded to the guard holding the gun.

The man pulled the trigger.

"Insurance," Blaine had replied to Isser's question of why the fabrication of his death was necessary prior to their leaving the O.K. Corral. "Before we parted in Jaffa, Evira assured me she could get my son away from Fett—and thus Rasin. But if she failed and he's still alive, his best bet to stay that way is if we put the word out that I'm dead."

"Because then Rasin would have no reason to kill him," Isser added.

Blaine nodded. "That pair of female killers who went after me in Boston were his from the beginning. He only let Evira reach me so I would lead him to her. And I almost did."

"Yes," Isser had recalled. "Ben-Neser in Jaffa. You saved his life."

"He saved mine first without realizing it."

In Washington they transferred from the small private jet into a larger one for the flight to Tel Aviv. Precautions insured no one saw Blaine at any point, so the fabricated tale of his death at the hands of Holliday and his deputies was left intact.

"Incredible," Isser commented when they were again off the ground. "This whole affair is incredible. This Gamma Option," he continued, putting it together for himself, "you claim it has as its basis the takeover of a country by exposing it to an enzyme contained in a virus the population becomes instantly addicted to?"

"For the sustenance of their very lives, yes. But takeover is a poor choice of words. We're talking about something infinitely more terrifying. Invasion without ever setting foot on foreign soil. Surrender without ever being faced with a conventional weapon. In a scant few days, an enemy country gets transformed into a massive prison camp, the whole of their population's DNA-altered and in need of more of Bechman's enzyme in order to survive."

"But with such technology available, why not just kill everyone in the enemy country instead?"

"To begin with you've got the Indian over there's theory," Blaine said, nodding at Wareagle, "that this is truly a fate worse than death for any proud nation. There's substance in that and practicality as well. To begin with, a poison potent enough to kill might show up by connection in the water supply early enough for the system to be shut down. And if you risked releasing the killer poison into the air, there'd be no way to control it. Think of it from the American viewpoint. Not only would Japan have been rendered impotent and our virtual industrial slave, but due warning would have been served on the Russians, as well. Hell, that's what dropping the bombs was all about anyway. Sounds tempting, doesn't it? In a twisted way, it might have solved all our problems.''

''Which is the very way Rasin sees it in terms of Israel. But how did he learn of Gamma's existence?''

''We can rule Bechman out, which leaves his assistant Eisenstadt. Others might have known about Gamma being out there, but only a scientist working closely with the project could furnish sufficient details and supply the expertise required to meet Rasin's needs.''

''And you're quite sure those needs have been met?''

''Everything points in that direction. Trouble is, Isser, we're forgetting that in spite of all this the Americans didn't use Gamma when they had the chance. I've got to figure that something was uncovered at the last minute, except Bechman couldn't recall anything of the kind.''

''And would Eisenstadt have known, as well?''

''Assume he didn't. Assume he handed Gamma over to Rasin unaware himself of the whole story.''

Isser wasn't convinced. ''We have no way of knowing there is any more to the story. Truman could simply have changed his mind.''

''It's possible, but in my mind the sinking of the *Indianapolis* indicates more was involved than that. The question is what, and Rasin has no better idea of the answer than we do. Hell, he doesn't even know the question.''

''So what do you suggest we do under the circumstances?''

''All we can do is take one step at a time. For now that means finding Eisenstadt and rounding up Rasin before he can unleash the Gamma Option forty-five years late.''

''That's two steps, my friend, not one.''

''Math was never my best subject. Besides, the third step's the most important one of all.''

''I'm listening.''

''We bury whatever's left of Gamma so deep that nobody will ever be able to dig it up again.''

* * *

During the last leg of the flight to Tel Aviv, Isser at last managed to drift off to sleep, leaving Blaine and Johnny Wareagle awake facing each other.

"You gotta make me a promise, Indian."

"If the spirits allow, Blainey."

"It's like this. We might walk the same path, but we do it with different steps. I've always relied on luck and God knows I've had plenty, while you, well, I don't know, I just think the odds of you getting out of this are better than me. Luck's gotta run out sometime, right?"

"There are those who don't believe in luck. There are those who call it fate instead, and fate is ruled by the spirits. It was what guided us through the hellfire and reunited us those few years ago when we at last relented to the truth of our souls."

"Then look at it this way, Indian. I've got a bad feeling; that's all. Maybe I'm hearing the words of your spirits at last and I don't like what they're saying. What matters is the boy, Johnny. If things don't work out, you've got to get him back. You've got to handle things just the way I would have."

"It will be done, Blainey."

"And if you're too late, if the boy is—"

"The balance will be preserved," Johnny Wareagle broke in assuredly. "Those who took the gift of the spirits will lose whatever they hold most precious."

"So long as it hurts, Indian. So long as it hurts."

Click . . .

The harmless strike of the pistol hammer sent a *whooossssh* of air through Evira. She could barely recover her breath.

"Oh, didn't I tell you?" Hassani taunted. "The revolver has six chambers, but only one has a bullet. Your odds are one in five now, decreasing all the time, Evira. Or should I say the boy's odds? If you just tell me where I can find McCracken's son, I promise to let the boy live. Simple as that."

"Why does it matter to you? Why does McCracken matter to you at all? He's helping you, goddamn it, you said so yourself!"

"It's you who does not see, Evira. You are missing the big picture. It's right before you and you're missing it."

Something struck her. "Somehow you and Rasin are working together. Why? *How?*"

Hassani almost laughed. "I'm waiting."

"Don't force me to make such a choice. You can't!"

"Life is full of choices. I've made my share, plenty of them painful. You too. Now both of us must make another. You first. Tell me where I can find McCracken's son or this boy dies."

She looked through the bars of her cell at Kourosh, who was so desperately trying to stay brave. Their eyes met and locked, his telling her so much.

It's okay. I understand. . . .

But it wasn't okay, not in any sense.

"Kill him and you'll get nothing from me," she spit at Hassani. "You know that."

"My dear lady, if you make me kill him, your punishment will be done. I would not dare kill you and put you out of your misery. Make your choice and live with it. McCracken's son or this boy. Choose!"

"I can't!"

"This is your last chance."

"No!"

Distressed, Hassani turned and nodded once again to the guard holding the pistol against Kourosh's head. Evira's face contorted in agony as he began to squeeze the trigger.

"General!" a voice called from the area of the stairs.

A quick hand signal from Hassani and the guard eased his pressure off the trigger.

"I have a message for you, General!" a guard announced as he made his way purposefully toward Hassani.

Reaching him, the guard handed over a piece of paper which the general read quickly, crumbling it in his hands with a smile when he was finished.

"It seems you have been spared the necessity of choosing," he announced to Evira. "Blaine McCracken was killed while following the trail of Rasin's weapon. I no longer require his son." Then he said to his guards, "Put this boy in the cell with her. Let them die together." He turned back toward Evira. "Now if you'll excuse me, I'm afraid my presence is required elsewhere. . . ."

* * *

The prime minister heard Isser's entire report without interruption while standing by his bay window. When the Mossad chief finished, the prime minister made no sound or move, just stood as if transfixed by the day as it began over Jerusalem.

"Rasin has this weapon. You're convinced of that?" he responded at last.

"McCracken's convinced. That's good enough for me, sir."

"So we are surrounded by madmen on all sides. One would destroy everything we are from the outside. Another would destroy everything we stand for from within. The lesser of two evils is what it comes down to, doesn't it?"

"I don't under—"

"Yes, you do, Isser. It was in your voice as you relayed the story to me. McCracken knew nothing of the immediacy of Hassani's plot or of his apparent possession of a superweapon of his own, did he?"

"I told him nothing."

"Then he has no reason to suspect."

Isser grasped the intent of the prime minister's words and returned to his feet. "Operation Firestorm is barely twenty-four hours away."

"And so is the first stage of Hassani's strike, and given what we know we can't trust Firestorm to prevent it, can we?" Isser remained silent. "Answer me, Isser."

"No, we can't."

"Then have your people put out the word. I want to meet Rasin. His terms. Anything."

The chief of Mossad just looked at him. "What have we become, sir?"

"We become what we have to, Isser. In the end we become whatever it takes to survive."

"Would you like me to repeat my terms again?" Yosef Rasin asked as the sun's warmth burned away in the afternoon sky.

"No," the prime minister replied to the younger man. "I believe I understand them."

Rasin leaned forward and dabbed the sweat from his bronzed face with a napkin. He smiled slightly and poured a glass of fresh orange juice from a glass pitcher before him. He had agreed to this meeting on the condition that it be held between only the two of them on his kibbutz in the Negev. Rasin liked the symbolism of that. Without asking, he refilled the old man's glass and then drained his own in a single gulp, leaving a pulpy residue behind from bottom to rim. Around him, the trees of the orange grove blew in the wind. To Rasin it sounded like the applause of an approving people. His people.

"But do you accept them?"

"Accept you as my minister of defense and my heir apparent? I'm not sure which fate is the worse for Israel."

The prime minister had expected a reaction of anger. What he got was a strangely closed smile.

"You have nothing to bargain with, Mr. Prime Minister. Your hand is folded before you. I hold all the cards."

"Not cards, Rasin, lives! Do you hear me? Lives!"

"You came to me. You came to beg me to unleash my weapon under your direction, with your charter."

"And I hate myself for it."

"It is done my way or not at all!"

"Madness! Listen to what you're saying!"

"I'm listening to you instead. Words of desperation, of futility, of failure. They are the same words I have heard for years, decades. We are an island surrounded by a vast sea of sharks. Instead of learning to control those sharks, you have allowed them to multiply and grow stronger until they are in a position to control our island as well as their sea. There is to be no compromise."

"Not compromise, merely redefinition," the prime minister implored. "Our major problem is Hassani, so all I'm urging is that you limit the initial release of Gamma to Iran. The rest of the nations will fall in line as soon as they see the results. We can prevent the use of his superweapon and thus the invasion will be stemmed."

"This invasion, yes. But what about the next and the one after? You, all of you, are so shortsighted. You accept a war every ten years so long as there is what you call peace in the interim. Releasing Gamma over a single country will make the others more militant, even more prone to the terror tactics that have torn us apart. Our enemy does not fear death, he cherishes it. All he requires is a reason to die, and your 'redefinition' would supply it. The moderates and radicals will join forces. We will accomplish ourselves what Hassani himself would have been hard-pressed to do." He calmed himself. "So it must be all the nations where the murderers hide behind the guise of politicians and diplomats. It must be made clear that any threat to destroy us means they destroy themselves and their only chance for the continued survival we allow them."

"You're forgetting the *Indianapolis*," Isser grasped. "The Americans sunk it to hide Gamma forever. They must have had their reasons, and now you're going to release it in spite of that."

"A risk I'm willing to take, just like you, as your presence here today indicates, Mr. Prime Minister. Our entire way of life has been at risk since our very inception. Only this time we are in a position to control our own destiny and destroy the Arab radicals who would otherwise destroy us."

"And if they still continue their fight after you open your cannisters, what then, Rasin? Do you let half a country die for every hundred of us they kill? A whole country for every thousand?"

"If necessary, yes. Absolutely."

"You're playing God, Rasin."

"As someone clearly must, as you have failed in your wisdom to dare. My terms are nonnegotiable. *All* my terms, including where and how my appointment to the cabinet will be announced to the country as Independence Day dawns."

"As insurance, no doubt."

"Precisely. Insurance against you changing you mind once I've done your dirty work for you. Rest easy, Mr. Prime Minister. I won't need you long. The people will rally to me. They will embrace what I represent. I speak for the masses who are sick of living in fear, of living amidst the constant threat of death."

"Better to live in hell, Rasin?"

"Better to live period."

CHAPTER 25

"**I**T'S ABOUT FUCKING TIME," MCCRACKEN SAID TO WAR-eagle when he heard the sound of a key being turned.

When they had arrived in Israel over twelve hours before, they were driven by Isser to a cluster of apartments in the Bayet-Gan section of Jerusalem that in actuality formed a Mossad safehouse. Blaine and Wareagle were stowed in a windowless basement apartment with a promise that Isser would return as soon as he sorted things out with the prime minister. They had begun to worry after six hours. After twelve had passed, the unseen Saturday morning sun was rising and the worry had evolved into a certainty that something had gone wrong.

Now at last they stood before the door. It swung open to reveal a stoop-shouldered, wizened old man.

"What's the matter?" Isaac asked, noting their surprise. "You were expecting maybe Moses?"

"No," McCracken answered. "Just the prime minister. Or the head of Mossad, at the very least."

The old man waved a knobby hand before him. "Ach, you don't exist to them anymore. Neither do we."

"We?"

"I'm one of four. There'll be plenty of time to tell you about it on the drive. Come," the old man beckoned, "we'd better get

239

going before your guards think twice about the story I gave them.''

"Sounds like we're getting sprung from jail again, Johnny,'' Blaine said to Wareagle. "Where to this time?'' he asked the old man.

"To play some checkers and maybe save the world.''

Isaac settled himself uneasily behind the driver's seat of the five-year-old Mercedes. He had parked hastily and the result was that the tires on the car's passenger side straddled the curb down the street from the beige stone apartment house they had just emerged from. Each motion brought a slight grimace of pain to his features.

"I'll drive, if you want,'' Blaine offered.

Isaac waved him off. "Don't worry, once I get going I'm fine. Besides, you don't know where we're headed.'' He squinted his eyes for the ignition as he probed the keys forward. His hand was trembling and the keys jangled together. "Just let me get my glasses on. . . .'' When he had done so, he peered back at Blaine. "There, much better. You, I know. But I don't know your friend,'' he added, gazing at Wareagle in the backseat.

"He's just my tour guide. He was showing me around Jerusalem when we took a wrong turn.''

"You would have been in that house a long time if I hadn't shown up.''

"I was beginning to get that feeling. But it still doesn't tell me who you are.''

"What's the difference? A little this, a little that, but mostly,'' he said with a proud thrust of his finger upward, "a soldier. Since maybe before you were born, Mr. Blaine McCracken.'' With that, Isaac screeched the Mercedes into traffic against the protesting horn of the car right behind him.

"*Haganah!* You were *Haganah*!''

"Not were, Mr. Blaine McCracken, am. The names change but the symbols remain the same.''

"And your name . . .''

"Isaac, as of late. Symbolic again. I've been reborn, you see. All of us have.''

"Plural once more."

"Because I'm not in this alone." Isaac swerved the car suddenly to stay on his side of the road as they banked round a curve. He narrowly missed sideswiping a car parked on McCracken's side of the narrow Jerusalem street and hunched forward behind the wheel. "And we've all been cut off, just like you."

"Cut off from what?"

"Truth," Wareagle said suddenly before the old man had a chance to respond.

Isaac gazed back at him and the Mercedes drifted once more across the center line to a chorus of horns.

"Very astute, Mr. Big Man."

"Just obvious."

"You mind explaining it to me?" Blaine demanded.

"Now pay attention," Isaac told him as he joined the chorus of honking horns caused by the frustrations of an eternal Jerusalem traffic jam that spared not even the sabbath. "The young men in this country are *meshuge*. We tried to teach them what we knew, help them learn from our mistakes, but no, they've got better things to do. Still, we never stop watching, advising. We watched this Hassani plenty. Dangerous man. Stood for all the wrong things. We knew where the path he was on would take him. It was inevitable. So that gives us an idea. You listening?"

"Just keep on with it . . . and drive. Traffic's moving again."

A new symphony of horns behind them punctuated McCracken's impatient suggestion. Isaac eased the car forward. "Stop distracting me, all right? Where was I? Oh yes. Hassani had to be stopped before he could bring the radicals of the Arab world together. We came up with a plan called Operation Firestorm. It's complicated, but let me summarize it for you this way. We sent several hundred Israeli agents into Tehran to organize the discontented masses and students into a counterrevolutionary force prepared to strike at a predetermined time. Every phase was thought out, every detail accounted for."

"A classic strategem."

"Especially in the case of Iran. Hassani took over a nation

bankrupt in spirit as well as pocketbook. But instead of rebuilding from the bottom up, he chose to do so from the top down, wooing the wealthy and ignoring the poor. The voice of the poor grew louder, but Hassani's revamped Revolutionary Guard has been able to quell all the disturbances thus far. But with Firestorm, barricades were to be erected throughout the city of Tehran, fires started everywhere as a sign to the people to rise against Hassani and his oppressive, backward regime.''

"Toppling him before he could accomplish his goal of unifying the militant Arab world," Blaine completed. "All well and good until you figure Hassani's got the power to quell this revolution as well."

"Don't worry. We thought of that. At the height of the fighting and confusion, fifteen American Comanche helicopters from Israel were to join the fighting on the rebels' side."

"You mean *Apache*. Built by McDonnell Douglas. Maybe the finest attack helicopter in the world."

"You figure. To me it's all steel and bullets," Isaac said, steering the big car farther into the Jerusalem traffic. "The Apaches would strike at the positions of the Revolutionary Guard to keep them at bay long enough for the new revolution to take hold and spread beyond the guards' ability to control it. The manpower's there, believe me, and so is the desire. Everything was set, confirmed. And then complications sprang up."

"Don't they always?"

"Not like this. One after the other, I tell you," Isaac continued, with his hands digging into the leather of the steering wheel. "It started with a woman who calls herself Evira. . . ."

"*What?*"

"Yes, we know of your connection to her. Just listen. We got word she was headed to Tehran to kill Hassani. One of our people was part of the counterrevolutionary cell that had agreed to help her."

"So she was going to do your work for you."

"No! Think, Mr. Blaine McCracken! Hassani was the symbol we needed to destroy with Firestorm. The people had to have something to rise against. Allowing him to be killed would have ruined everything. The revolutionary cells would have splintered and gone their own way. Anarchy would have resulted and the military would have taken over again. Firestorm would've died before it even got started. We did what we had to do.''

"You killed her?" Blaine screeched angrily.

"We tried, yes, but failed. Of what happened to her in the days after we do not know, only that she is now a prisoner in the basement of the royal palace. What's important is what brought her to Tehran in the first place."

"The same thing that brought you there. The desire to stop a madman from unifying a bunch of madmen against Israel."

"But we didn't know about the imminent invasion plans or about Hassani's insistence that he had some secret weapon to render Israel defenseless against his attack."

"Neither did she. Neither did I, damn it!"

Now it was Isaac's turn to look puzzled. "That doesn't make sense."

"Maybe it does. Don't tell me, let me guess. Somehow the Israeli government learned the specifics of Hassani's plan."

"The existence and timing of it anyway, yes. But how did you know?"

"Just a lucky guess."

"Not so lucky." Isaac sighed. "See, Hassani plans to meet next with his people on our Independence Day to provide details of his secret weapon and its employment. From what we can gather, the actual invasion will occur several days later, after his weapon has somehow paralyzed us. Our problem is that Independence Day also marked the start of Firestorm, which is very likely too late to stop Hassani from making use of his weapon. Our cells are not in communication with one another so moving the timetable up was not an option. The government said fine. They didn't need us anymore anyway, because they had found something better."

McCracken didn't grasp the old man's meaning until he saw his eyes. "My God, they're going to use Rasin's weapon! And I gave it to them. Told them what it was, how it worked. No wonder they had to turn the Indian and me into prisoners. We were the only ones who knew."

"Not quite the only ones."

"The damn fools! They didn't listen to me! The Americans had the weapon and didn't use it. Something happened at the last minute in 1945. Something changed, and they're going into this without realizing what it was."

"But there's someone else who does, isn't there?"

"Yes, a scientist named—"

"Martin Eisenstadt," Isaac finished. "We found him."

"We got lucky," the old man continued. "We arrived just as Rasin's people were carting him off toward an obvious fate after your work in America rendered him a liability. We had some younger people with us. It ended pleasantly. Not only is Eisenstadt alive, he's also willing to talk. We've got him stashed."

They drove through the Arab towns of Azaria and Abudise well into Seadaya, where the Judean Desert began to dominate the landscape. Isaac pulled the Mercedes off the road after a few more miles and they all transferred into a jeep that was waiting for them. Three miles of desert followed before they came to a valley housing a large Bedouin encampment. The Bedouins' nomadic tendencies were now restrained by the government, which restricted them to settlements. Despite this government ruling, though, the Bedouins retained many features of their old lifestyle. McCracken could see the makeshift tents and tin houses in which they slept on simple blankets over the dirt. Goats and sheep were penned up together on one side of the compound, and chickens walked freely about on the other. Mules and horses drank from a huge trough and a rooster crowed incessantly.

Getting out of the jeep, Blaine felt he was stepping back in time to a life unchanged for centuries. The Bedouins were a people who respected strength. They had chosen to settle in Israel. The country accepted them and encouraged their men to join the army, where a number excelled as trackers.

The settlement leader, an old man in white robes and *keffiya*, greeted Isaac with a hug. Isaac spoke to him in Arabic and the man laughed, then pointed to the largest of the tin houses, which was his home. His eyes fell on McCracken and Wareagle, and

Isaac offered some words of explanation. The man nodded approvingly and spoke softly to Isaac.

"He says you and the large one are the kind of men who are welcome in his village anytime," the old *Haganah* fighter related.

"Tell him many thanks."

En route to the tin house where Eisenstadt was waiting for them, Blaine passed a number of women washing clothes by hand in large bowls. Children sneaked peeks at them from hiding places behind adults. The only hint of modernity was a pair of tractors Isaac had presented the settlement as a gift some months ago, perhaps sensing he might need the favor returned soon after.

"No one will ever look for us here," he explained as they reached the tin house.

"Sure," Blaine answered. "Can't think of any place where I'd rather spend the rest of my life."

They passed through the blanket that formed the door to the leader's tin house. There, seated in one of four decrepit chairs around a small table, was Bechman's assistant Dr. Martin Eisenstadt. His features were creased and uncertain. He looked younger than the seventy years he must have been and would have looked better still if not for the pallor of fear that encompassed him. A trio of Isaac's cohorts had taken the other chairs, the one directly across from Eisenstadt staring forlornly at a checkerboard that had been set up between them. The pieces looked virtually untouched.

"He wasn't in the mood to play," a gaunt old man reported, and left his seat, signaling the others to do the same.

"I've been to see Hans Bechman, Dr. Eisenstadt," Blaine opened, taking the now-vacant seat across from Eisenstadt and feeling its exposed springs reach up to pinch him. "I know about the Gamma Option. I know the Americans sunk the *Indianapolis* to keep it a secret, and I know you gave it to Yosef Rasin in spite of that."

Eisenstadt's fearful eyes gazed his way. His shoulders trembled. "It was the noble thing to do. I *had* to do it to make up for all the errors of my past. Would you like to hear my story, hear about how I, a Jew, survived in Nazi Germany? By renouncing my heritage, by turning against my own people. I survived, but it was a life of hell. You know why? Because I felt no guilt. I was just so glad to be alive.'' He stopped for a deep breath. ''But then the opportunity came to escape to America. I seized it and the guilt came with me. The war ended. I was faced with my treachery, my deceit. I should have gone to the gas chamber. Any fate would have been better than the one I sentenced myself to.''

''You came to Israel.''

''For salvation, for peace. I became a citizen, a trusted member of the community. But it wasn't nearly good enough. The guilt, always the guilt!''

''And that brought you to Rasin.''

''I thought God had blessed me with a second chance. Here was my race again facing eventual extinction at the hands of a more numerous enemy. Rasin saw the future just as I did, with Israel perishing to an avalanche of Arab forces, both from the inside and out. A year from now or a decade. It didn't matter. It was inevitable. I went to him. I sought Rasin out!''

Eisenstadt's eyes were flaming now, the obsession of his guilt driving him once more. ''Did I not possess the means that could render Israel safe forever? If used, the Gamma Option would make it so she would never again have to fear an attack over her borders. She would no longer be dependent on the United States standing up for her.'' He looked deeply at McCracken. ''I knew where the *Indianapolis* went down. I knew she still held Gamma within her. And with Gamma the Jewish state would have the security and safety it deserved at last, even if . . .''

''If what, doctor?''

Eisenstadt sat there trembling.

''Finish it, doctor. What went wrong with Gamma forty-five years ago? What made the Americans pull back from their plans of releasing it in Japan? Why did they sink the *Indy*?''

''He could have been wrong.''

''Who?''

''Bechman.''

''Wrong about what?''

''It was an isolated mutation. We never had time to double-check the findings. . . .''

"Wrong about *what*? What findings are you talking about?"

Eisenstadt's eyes became less certain. "In the last stages of our research, Bechman discovered that Gamma mutates once entrenched in the host's system. Bechman told you of the virus's induction through a nation's water supply?"

"Yes, he did."

"Infection could be contained that way, because only those who drank the water would become dependent on the enzyme. But after so many generations of gestation within the host, the virus could become airborne. Spread from host to host through the air, not just limited to those exposed to it from drinking infected water."

"My God, the whole world could become infected."

"More than could—would eventually. But Bechman was wrong, I tell you!"

"What if he was right?"

"He wasn't!"

"If he was?" Blaine demanded.

Eisenstadt's stare was blank. "The mutated form of the Gamma virus carried a more virulent version of the designer enzyme Bechman had created. Instead of creating a new pathway for the stem cells to metabolize sugar, it destroyed the pathway altogether."

"Life itself destroyed at the most basic level. Everywhere! A killing machine!"

"No!" the scientist screeched.

But Blaine wasn't finished. "No one would be immune. You're describing the end of civilization!"

"Listen to me! Bechman went to the government *before* we could be sure. His findings made them abandon their own plan. They were forced to make sure all reserves of Gamma were lost forever. His claims could turn them into murderers of their own people."

Eisenstadt stopped to catch his breath, which gave McCracken time to compile what the scientist had said. With the possibility of worldwide infection looming, the Truman administration had opted for Beta in the eleventh hour and had then decided it could not risk having the reserves of Gamma coming back to shore. The truth could not be allowed to leak out and fall into the hands of those who might use it against the government and the country as the cold war dawned. The cannisters had to be buried forever, forgotten forever, along with the lives of more than a thousand crew members if necessary. But now Gamma was back, about to be let loose on an unsuspecting world forty-five years after the fact.

That thought enraged McCracken. He reached across the table and grasped Eisenstadt by the lapels. "You knew all this and you still gave Gamma to Rasin. You knew the chance you were taking and you didn't even warn him. You didn't warn him, did you?"

"Y-Y-Yes, I did."

McCracken eased up on the pressure.

"H-H-He didn't care. So long as Israel survived, that was all that mattered. The notion even appealed to him: the Jewish race becoming the last bastion of civilization."

"But with the mutation Israel will be destroyed too."

"No," Eisenstadt said softly. "We took . . . precautions."

"What are you saying?"

"I'll tell you because I want you to stop Rasin now. He went back on his word to me. He would have killed me, would have—"

"Talk! What precautions?"

"A vaccine to be released into the air over Israel that will protect against the possibility of any Israeli infection whatsoever, whether the virus mutates or not."

"Released *how*?"

"From dozens of points scattered strategically all over the country. Released a few hours before dawn so it will reach all our borders and then be killed by the sun's ultraviolet rays at dawn before it can stretch to any of the Arab countries, especially over water. We will be insulated!" Eisenstadt ranted.

"What about Rasin?"

"A part of it, a great part. He will release the largest allotment of the vaccine himself."

"From where?" Blaine demanded.

Eisenstadt's eyes fell on McCracken's watch. "It may already be too late."

"Where? Just tell me where!"

The scientist regarded him quite calmly with a smile born in the depths of a mind lost in the guilt-ridden shadows of the past.

"Where else?" Eisenstadt responded with terrifying matter-of-factness. "Masada."

PART FIVE

Independence Day

Masada: Saturday, May 13; noon

CHAPTER 26

THE MOUNTAIN PLATEAU OF MASADA RISES OMINOUSLY ABOVE the desolation that surrounds it. Standing on the border between the Judean Desert and the Dead Sea Valley, it is 1,400 feet from ground level to a rock-strewn summit that covers five acres. On the summit are reconstructed buildings dating back over two thousand years. The past lives and breathes on the desert wind that swirls the dust.

Israel's past.

More than any other single symbol, Masada typifies the plight of the Jewish people through history. It was built originally as a royal sanctuary and fortress by King Herod, but it entered history over a half century after his death. Jewish Zealots who had revolted against Rome fled to Masada and held it for three years, the final one against continued onslaught from the entire Tenth Roman Legion. Outnumbered by more than ten to one, the Zealots outlasted the legion until the Romans constructed a ramp up one of the mountain's sides and seemed on the verge of crashing through the fortress walls. Unable to accept either moral or physical enslavement, the Zealots denied the Romans their victory by taking their own lives. The Romans found nine-hundred-seventy corpses waiting for them inside the walls it had taken three years to penetrate.

Today the flow of natives and tourists to Masada is constant. So too is the army's tradition of ending the training of soldiers with a charge up the serpentine Snake Path that winds from the mountain's base to its buffeted summit.

The vast majority of visitors, though, opt for the faster and less tiring route offered by the cable cars that run up the mountain's eastern side. The pair of vehicles work in perfect tandem, carrying visitors up and down throughout the day.

The twenty-five men who packed into the cable car at the base station on this Saturday had arrived just minutes before on a tour bus. They were dressed in baggy, comfortable clothing well suited for the heat, and many had camera bags slung from their shoulders. No words were exchanged during the five minute trek upward. The khaki-clad tour-group leader emerged first on the unloading platform and approached a young soldier leaning complacently against a steel rail.

"You will evacuate these premises immediately," Yosef Rasin ordered him.

The soldier stiffened. "Excuse me?"

"You heard what I said. There are three more of your number atop the mountain as we speak. By now they have been approached by my men, as you have."

"*Your* men?"

With that the soldier's eyes scrutinized the two dozen men who had just made the trip up in the cable car. Those that he could see all had their hands tucked in their clothes or camera bags, intentions obvious, weapons a grasp away. Then he gazed at the long, winding line of patrons waiting to take the cable car down, disturbed by the sudden halt in its movement.

"Are we being taken hostage?" he asked.

"No, you fool. I want all of you off this mountain! You and the other soldiers will supervise the process but my men will oversee everything. We do not wish to make an issue out of this. Believe me, shedding Israeli blood is not our intention."

"I . . . don't understand."

"We are not terrorists, we are patriots. At the base of the mountain more of us are waiting to be taken up. There is equipment they will transport upward with each shift. Is that clear?"

"Yes."

"You will make no move to intercede. We are not enemies. It might not seem so now, but we are on the same side."

The soldier looked at Yosef Rasin more closely. "I know you. I'm sure I do. . . ."

"When you are away from the mountain," the fanatic continued, "you will tell the Israeli people to look to Masada. You will tell them that the ultimate step to insure the freedom of our people and our nation is about to be taken. A new meaning will be brought to Independence Day when it dawns tomorrow. Do you understand what I am saying?"

"I . . . think so."

"Be sure of it. You are blessed, young man, blessed to be the messenger of a holy mission. Go about your business now. Let us keep the people lined up beyond us calm."

The soldier's eyes widened suddenly. "I *do* know you. You're—"

"I'm nobody, young man. But tomorrow will change that."

"It's done," Isser reported to the prime minister, lowering the phone back to its hook. "He's taken Masada, as planned."

"What have you told the army?"

"To set up a perimeter but not to interfere in any way. The area must be sealed so Rasin can work his black magic undisturbed on that rock."

"You sound disturbed."

"He brought an army with him, Mr. Prime Minister, upward of sixty men. That was not part of the deal you made."

"But it doesn't surprise me. It's a warning to us, another of his symbols. The scene will look much better tomorrow when the television stations arrive at dawn for the announcement of his appointment as minister of defense." The old man paused. "Unless McCracken has something to say about it."

"We've confirmed it was Isaac who sprang him and the Indian from our safe house in Jerusalem. We're not trying to track him down. If he wants to walk away from this now, he can."

"But you know he won't, don't you, Isser?"

"You're probably right, and that's as good a reason for maintaining a military presence around Masada as any. If McCracken so much as shows his face near the mountain, he'll be shot on sight."

* * *

It was just after twelve-thirty when Isaac at last gained confirmation of the worst from a government contact.

"Eisenstadt was right," he reported. "Rasin and over fifty of his soldiers took Masada just after noon."

"And the army's supporting him, of course," McCracken concluded.

"They've cordoned off the entire area around Arad. Nobody gets in. The whole Negev's been closed down. The mountain belongs to Rasin and there's nothing we can do to change that."

A stiff wind rattled the walls of the Bedouin tribe leader's tin house. Outside a rooster crowed incessantly.

McCracken turned his gaze on Wareagle, who had spread out a map of Masada over an ancient crate. "What do you think, Indian, can we succeed in less than a day where ten-thousand Romans failed in three years?"

Wareagle looked up at him. "The army's presence has less to do with our problem than the fortress itself, Blainey. Slipping past the soldiers might be possible, but that would leave us with only these two routes of approach to Rasin." With that, Johnny traced a massive finger, first up the serpentine Snake Path which wound up the eastern side of the mountain, and then traced the path the Romans had left up the western slope with the ramp they had used to gain entry at last to the fortress. "Both paths are easily defensible with far less manpower and weapons than Rasin has by all accounts brought with him."

"Especially when he's got just the two of us and four Haganah fighters to contend with. No offense, Isaac."

"Give me a gun. Give all of us guns. We can still shoot."

"For that you need a target first, and right now we can't even get close to it. Okay, Indian, so ground approach is out. That would seem to leave us exclusively with air."

Wareagle frowned in response to that suggestion. "The Israelis know you, Blainey, and they know you will try anything. They will be watching the skies. We'll never get close."

"How about a low-altitude drop?"

"Again, it might get us by the Israelis fortifying the mountain base, but unless we could come up with a way to disguise our parachutes, we would be exposed to Rasin's troops the entire way down."

"We need cover then."

"Where cover plainly doesn't exist."

"Goddamn it!" Blaine roared. "We'll climb the rock face if that's what it takes to get up there. But we're going to stop Rasin, do you hear me?"

"I hear you, Blainey, but your words fail to consider the realities of the limitations before us. We have looked to the obvious. Now the time has come to look deeper."

"We're deep now, Indian. Over our heads, as I make it." Blaine stopped suddenly, obviously struck by something. "Okay, Indian, make believe you've got access to all the tech hardware in the world. Everything considered, could you find a way to get us on top of that rock?"

Wareagle turned his attention back to the map. At last he looked up and nodded emotionlessly.

"Yes, but it would take men as well as machines."

"But there *is* a way?"

"A means without any guarantees. The spirits provide alternatives, not certainties."

"That's good enough for me, Indian."

"Fudo-san," Hiroshi said. "I can hardly hear you."

"We've got a strange connection, Hiroshi. I'm talking to you from a Bedouin camp in the Judean Desert. Blame the bad reception on a radio signal traveling via land-line patch-through."

"And that is where your trail has led you?"

"Among other places, yes." McCracken paused. "Did you mean what you told me in Japan? Would you really do *anything* to right the wrong of your aiding Rasin?"

"I have violated my honor, *Fudo-san.* In days past that would be grounds for taking my own life."

"There's a way to regain your honor far more worthwhile than that."

"Anything, *Fudo-san.* If it is within my power, it will be done. Just name it."

"It's a long list, Hiroshi. Better grab yourself a pad. . . ."

* * *

When he was finished and the connection broken, Blaine acknowledged Johnny Wareagle's slight smile and Isaac's flabbergasted expression.

"Can this really be done?" the old man asked, incredulously.

"Hiroshi can pull it off. The only thing that might stop him—and us—is time."

"A foe we will have difficulty staring down," Wareagle reminded them.

McCracken checked his watch. "It's one o'clock now. Hiroshi says he can be here with the equipment within ten hours. We'll be cutting it close but we'll have time. We can't stop Rasin and the others from releasing their allotments of vaccine. But if we grab him on Masada, he won't be able to unleash Gamma on the world on Independence Day."

"And just how do you think he plans on doing that anyway?" Isaac wondered.

"If I'm right, the key is Tehran. Can you get a message to your people in the city?"

"I was about to contact our team leader. He can't reach the individual cells directly, but there's a signal he can employ meaning abort."

"No! You can't abort. Do you hear me? Firestorm is more important now than ever!"

Isaac looked totally confused. "Maybe you forget that the government was supplying the Apaches, and without them Firestorm has no chance of succeeding."

"We'll worry about them later. For now you've just got to trust me. Operation Firestorm *must* go on as planned."

"Then why did you ask if I could get a message into the city?"

Blaine looked him in the eyes as he spoke. "You know where Evira is. I want her rescued. Send the word."

"The risk! The danger!"

"It's like this, Isaac. Without her, I might never be able to find my son. If she dies, he probably dies too. Sound simple? Let me put it another way. If I can't save the kid, I might just help Rasin empty his cannisters filled with the Gamma virus." And then he added to Wareagle, "I just can't see the fucking point anymore."

"But you see something the rest of us as of yet cannot, Blainey."

"My eyes may be playing tricks on me, Indian. Let's hope to hell they are."

"Is there anything else?"

"No," Yosef Rasin replied to the leather-clad Lace, "I believe you have everything covered."

"Not quite," returned the tall woman with the hard-muscled body. Her eyes turned toward the base of the mountain, where motion was visible amidst the floodlights the army had set up for itself. "But our friends down there are sure to cover anything we may have missed."

"You still believe McCracken is alive?"

"I don't believe he could have been killed as easily as your reports indicate."

"So if he comes . . ."

Lace smiled and her neck muscles tensed. "Let him."

And then she took her leave to rejoin Tilly in a sweep of the fortified positions she had arranged on Masada before night had fallen. Rasin had elected to concentrate his base on Masada's northern front, just above the remains of Herod's palace. Much of the large bathhouse, terraces, and labyrinth of storehouses had undergone extensive reconstruction and regained a measure of their original fortification. The remainder of structures on Masada were scattered across its rock-littered vastness. Rasin had expected the posting of their forces to begin at the guardhouse two hundred yards from the northern edge. But, fearing an attack, Lace had elected to disperse a number of guards along the entire perimeter so security could be maintained from all directions. If an attack came, they would know about it well in advance.

All the lights atop the mountain had been turned on, casting ancient Masada in an eerie, modern glow. Rasin was amazed by it. He could almost see to the ends of the mountaintop from his perch on the bathhouse roof. He had been wise to listen to Lace, wiser still to bring with him his personal commando force composed of outcasts like himself—a carefully chosen group of men tossed out of the military for brutality to Arabs. In short, a band of cutthroats. He did not fear an attack from McCracken as much as one from the government should it change its mind. His men were there as a deterrent against that. There was no way even the army's most elite units could succeed in any assault on him. No way at all. Several of his commandos were armed with anti-aircraft weapons, for if an attack were to come, it would be from the sky.

Rasin breathed deeply and drank in the dry air. The power he had long sought, the power it had been his destiny to achieve, was now within his reach, thanks to Gamma. He checked his watch. Just five hours until he would fire his portion of the vaccine into the air. Around the same time a dozen others, placed strategically across Israel, would release their allotments to be swept by the wind across the small nation to render her safe from the imminent release of the Gamma virus. Since exposure to the ultraviolet rays of the sun would kill the vaccine organism instantly, the key was to time its release so it might spread as close to Israeli borders as possible by sunrise. It wasn't an exact science, but it was close enough. Besides, fate was on his side.

He had outmaneuvered them brilliantly, of course; he had outmaneuvered everyone. If they ever suspected the lengths he had gone through to assure the success of his plan, if they ever realized the charade he had enacted for the world . . . Oh well, no sense in pondering over that. The charade was rapidly drawing to its conclusion.

The wind blew over the Dead Sea, smelling vital and alive to him. Perhaps even it would live again with the coming of the morning. Perhaps Moses had not performed the last miracle at all.

What Rasin was about to do proved that much at least.

"Well, old friend, can we pull it off?"

Hiroshi's attention was so entrenched in Wareagle's map of Masada spread over the crates in the tin Bedouin house that he barely heard McCracken's question. Without speaking, he moved to a rip in the house's metal that served as a window. In the desert land just beyond the camp, bathed in the spill of flood-lights powered by portable generators, Hiroshi watched two dozen of his finest men assembling and preparing the incredible stores of equipment they had transported from Japan. A jet transport had managed the flight in eight hours, landing in a private field in Egypt where a pair of commandeered Israeli Sikorsky troop-carrying helicopters were waiting. The equipment was transferred and the flight to the Bedouin village negotiated without incident, arriving just after midnight.

"It can be done, *Fudo-san*," Hiroshi replied finally without turning back. "The idea is brilliant, but . . ."

"Yes?"

"The elaborateness of it confuses me. A strafing run aimed at obliterating the stronghold would seem a far more logical strategy."

"Too random," McCracken explained. "If Rasin dies or makes it off Masada in all the confusion, we lose our chance of getting the Gamma cannisters back. That's priority one."

"I understand, *Fudo-san*, but the fact remains we're going to be dropping into heavily fortified positions with little or no cover behind us."

Blaine looked at Wareagle. "Leave that to the Indian. I'm more concerned with how we're going to stop the soldiers at the base of the mountain from calling in the cavalry once they realize what's going on."

"Leave that to me," Hiroshi said.

The flat desert plain beyond the Bedouin camp lay bathed in a darkness broken only here and there by the floodlights. The only sound breaking the still cool of the night was that of the Sikorsky armored troop carriers warming their engines as the moment of takeoff approached. Hiroshi was kneeling, hands on knees, facing his troop of samurai warriors who knelt before him in a straight line. All had dressed in black tops and black baggy skirtlike bottoms called *hakama*. Though most would be outfitted with modern automatic weapons, their focus now was rooted on the sheathed swords lying before them. On Hiroshi's cue, they grasped the ancient weapons and pushed them through their belts, the collective motion eerie in its singular calm. McCracken stood nearby, reviewing once more the details of Johnny Wareagle's plan.

"You can call me a *schlemiel*," Isaac said, suddenly by his side, "but I thought you said dropping out of the sky was suicide."

"I said parachuting down was suicide. This is different."

Isaac humphed. "It's still the sky."

"And you?"

"I'm leaving now to pay Isser a visit. He won't be able to dismiss me after what Eisenstadt told us. We don't want you to succeed at Masada only to be killed by the real army."

"The thought had crossed my mind, but you'll have to reach him first."

Isaac winked. "I got my ways. It's just like checkers and now it's our move. The enemy might have more pieces, but we're the ones doing the jumping. Have a nice flight."

"Shalom, you old devil."

The Sikorsky helicopters streaked through the night sky at a routine altitude, making no effort to disguise themselves from either radar or visual contact.

"Two minutes to showtime, Indian," McCracken said to Wareagle in the cockpit, the floodlit expanse of Masada growing as they drew closer. "Time to join the others in the back."

Wareagle took a deep breath and Blaine noted the slightest smile force its way onto his features. "The hellfire, Blainey. Once again we join it."

"You sound almost glad."

"No, nor am I sad. I have learned that all exists to provide scale. The hellfire lends definition to who we are and were. The spirits are closest in times like these. They rise into the chaos, but to feel them you too must enter it. Never are their words clearer. Never do I feel closer to my ancestors."

"Just so long as you don't pick tonight to join them, Indian."

Major Ben Shamsi, commander in charge of the security force deployed around Masada, lifted the walkie-talkie to his ear.

"I read you, Corporal."

"Sir, I have a pair of troop carriers approaching from the south."

Just then Shamsi's ears picked up the familiar *wop-wop-wop* of two Sikorskys and he could see the flashing lights marking their path through the night.

"Lieutenant," he called to the man behind him, "are we expecting reinforcements?"

"Not that I'm aware of, sir."

The troop carriers dipped out of sight from the officers' viewing angle at the mountain base station on the eastern side of Masada.

"Raise them on the radio," Shamsi ordered. "Let's find out what—"

"Sir!" came the frantic voice of the corporal based on the southern edge. "One of the troop carriers has released objects over Masada!"

"Objects?"

"Bats, sir, they look like huge bats!"

The guard Lace had posted on the southern wall of Masada had actually raised his hand to wave at the lead Sikorsky passing overhead when he saw the black figures plunge out and soar instantly over him. He ducked out of instinct the way one does from a swooping bird. The guard was still fumbling for his walkie-talkie when the first *poof!* sounded from the northern flank of Masada. When he turned back, the entire sky seemed filled with the black shapes spilling out from the guts of the Sikorskys.

The motorized hang gliders had been the centerpiece of Wareagle's plan from the beginning. They were the only vehicles both quick and maneuverable enough to permit approach to Masada from above. Hiroshi had happened upon this lot by intercepting a shipment originally bound for Delta Force at Fort Bragg. But since he steadfastly refused to deal with the only market for them—terrorists—they had remained in his warehouse until now.

The gliders were truly a magnificent creation, far more technologically advanced than those used by Palestinian terrorists in raids over the Israeli border with Lebanon. Their black wingspan was barely six feet, and the weight of the small motor that propelled them was easily dispersed across the middle. Maneuverability was permitted in all directions, as well as rapid drops and climbs.

In the last moments before the initial drop, McCracken considered the strategy they were employing and how it had been arrived at. He and Wareagle had assumed from the start that Rasin would have lookouts posted all over Masada, not just to the north where his forces were concentrated. This ruled out making their way over by glider from a nearby ridge and necessitated an air drop from the Sikorskys.

"My greatest concern is the lights," Hiroshi had warned from the outset. "The problem is double-edged. If we shoot them out, my warriors will have nothing to guide their landing. If we leave them as is, we'll make inviting targets in the sky."

"What about dropping gas ahead of our approach?"

"More problems." Hiroshi shrugged. "First we must consider the possibility that Rasin's troops will have gas masks, and even if they don't, gas might work against us by supplying camouflage for our enemy and, again, obscuring our landing zones."

"The air holds our greatest strategic advantage and also our greatest vulnerability," Wareagle added.

"Grenades," Blaine said suddenly.

Wareagle grasped his intent immediately. "Two waves, Blainey?"

"Separated by twenty seconds, at most. Say six in the first wave. It'll be their job to scatter Rasin's troops and take out the guards at the highest positions. Picture it. By the time they're finished, Rasin's men will be running every which way, easy pickings for the larger second wave. Once they're sufficiently scattered, we land here and here," McCracken explained, pointing to the storehouses on the eastern fringe and the open expanse in the plateau's center.

Wareagle was nodding. "The first wave can drop smoke when they pass the exposed center."

"I like it, Indian. Create a wall of smoke the second wave appears out of. It's perfect."

"Not perfect, Blainey, but as close as we can come."

Hiroshi and his five warriors most skilled with the motorized gliders would make up the first wave. Twenty seconds later McCracken and Wareagle would lead the twelve samurai in their trailing helicopter down in the second. The remaining seven from Hiroshi's Sikorsky would spill out to form the rear of McCracken's attack phalanx on the northern front of Masada where Rasin's forces were concentrated.

"After you, Indian," he said to Wareagle as the southern edge of Masada appeared below and a wall of thick gray rose across the center of the fortress.

And together they plunged into the cool air, with another of Hiroshi's lead team's grenade blasts reaching them as hard rumbles in the night.

The first explosion brought Yosef Rasin from the hot room of Masada's bathhouse, where he had been making the final preparations to launch his vaccine into the air. His plan was to fire the cannisters by specially constructed mortar from the bathhouse roof, and he was going through the arduous task of removing them from their heavily sealed packing when the initial grenade blasts stung him. He emerged into the open to be blinded and deafened at the same time by a grenade that was all light and sound. A pair of soldiers crumpled to the ground and Rasin staggered back against the ancient ruins, holding his ears.

Lace leaped down to his side as rubble from more grenade blasts showered down upon them.

"It's McCracken!" she screamed above the chaos.

Rasin was in no position to argue, eyes clearing in time to see the huge black shapes swooping down from the sky and dropping grenades to scatter his troops.

He grabbed hold of Lace's steellike arm. "You've got to hold them off! You've got to buy me time! The shells! I've got to fire the shells!"

"Not from here!" she screamed, pulling him away from the next blast. And then she seemed to realize something, easing back into the dust-smoked fray. "The lights! I've got to get to the lights!" She swung back to Rasin. "Get back into the hot room. Wait there."

"Wait for wh—"

"You'll see. You'll know. Just do it!"

And Rasin obeyed as a fleet of the black-winged monstrosities crashed through the wall of gray smoke deployed a hundred yards away in the center of the mountaintop.

CHAPTER 27

"**S**AY AGAIN, PLEASE!" THE VOICE INSTRUCTED FROM JE-
rusalem.

"I said," Major Shamsi repeated from the base of Masada,
"that Rasin's forces are coming under attack on the mountain!"

"Did you say 'attack'?"

"Yes! For the third time, yes!"

There was a brief pause. "Major, be advised that a detachment is en route. You are not to engage. Is that clear?"

"Mister, I couldn't get up that rock if I wanted to."

"You fool!" Isser raged, storming into the operations center.
"You crazy fool!"

Isaac was standing by the window smoking a cigar, his with-
ered frame lost in the confines of his baggy overcoat. A pair of
soldiers looked on with rifles at the ready. Isaac had located
Isser at a Mossad command post in the guise of a luxurious
house in the Rehavia neighborhood of Jerusalem within sight of
the Knesset building.

"Temper, temper," he said to the Mossad chief, waving a
chastising finger. "To think that friends should speak to each
other in such a tone. . . ."

"You could have walked away. I set it up so you could. But
now you leave me no choice. You force the issue."

"That's the idea, old friend."

267

"What are you saying? Did McCracken put you up to this? Where is he?"

"As of this moment, starting to clean up the mess you have made of our world."

"Make sense!"

Isaac puffed away on his cigar. "I am. You're just not listening. But now you're going to. You joined forces with Rasin, and now it's time you learned just what you've become a party to."

"I don't have to listen to this!"

"Yes, you do. It's for your own good, you see," Isaac told him, and opened his overcoat to reveal a dozen sticks of dynamite taped to his chest. Before the soldiers could respond, his cigar was a touch away from the instantaneous fusing. "Now why don't you have a seat, Mr. head of Mossad? I've got a story to tell you. . . ."

McCracken and Wareagle passed through the gray cloud side-by-side in the air, amazed at how easily the motorized gliders handled. The ten-horsepower motor hung directly over their heads, attached to a shaft extending the glider's length. At the shaft's end a propellor spun soundlessly. Speed was controlled by manipulation of a single handgrip, much like that of a motorcycle, on the right side of the frame the fliers were attached to by a harness.

Below the chaos wrought by Hiroshi's initial six-man attack wave was already obvious to them. Rasin's troops were scattering for cover, positions of stronghold abandoned, all semblance of organization gone. The airborne samurai coming in now knew exactly what their role was from this point on.

Suddenly Wareagle swooped down, firing his M-16 on full automatic. In the narrow area lit by one of the floodlights, Blaine could see a gunman struggling to regain position on the blasted-out top of the guard tower that looked over the entire northern quadrant of Masada. The Indian's fire blasted the rocks briefly before locking onto the enemy. Blaine dipped his wings to drop next to Wareagle.

"That's clearing the way, Indian."

"The hellfire beckons, Blainey."

Around them the remaining eighteen samurai had broken into

a wide spread. Twelve were already firing toward positions where Rasin's soldiers were deployed. The key was to keep the enemy splintered, keep him on the run. That way the vastly superior numbers came to no advantage at all. Meanwhile, at the first available opportunity, the remaining six samurai, armed with swords as well as rifles, would land and start the process of securing ground control from the south northward. At the same time Hiroshi's team of six would close from the upper terrace of Herod's palace across to the south. The dozen gun-wielding warriors under Blaine and Johnny's lead would join the rest on the ground as soon as they had done as much damage as possible from above.

Blaine nodded at Johnny and the two of them darted through the air at divergent angles. McCracken had used conventional hang gliders on numerous occasions, but the feeling of this was totally different. He supposed it was as close as a man could ever come to flying, so effortless were the controls required to swerve and swirl through the air.

Down below in a high-walled section of the vast storehouses nearest the eastern wall, he caught sight of a small cluster of Rasin's men struggling to get an M-60 properly mounted. Blaine kicked his legs up to dip into a dive and roared down at a forty-five degree angle with machine gun blasting, curling into a rise just as he passed over the neutralized target area. Manipulations with his legs controlled the maneuvers effortlessly.

In the sky around him, the rest of the flying complement swirled and crisscrossed through the air. Sometimes the extended glider wings of one nearly grazed another, but the samurai flew with an instinctive sense of distance acquired by men who had trained often and long together. For them the sense of battle was no different; only the locale and rules had changed. Blaine watched Johnny Wareagle actually twirl himself upside down to quicken his escape after diving into a strafing run with his M-16. McCracken kicked his knees up to drop fast and provide the Indian cover, then eased himself parallel to the ruins with machine gun aimed straight down. He fired in short, controlled bursts at areas of motion, and saw Johnny flash him the okay sign as he soared back upward already snapping a fresh double clip home.

A stray bullet pierced Blaine's wing and he drove his glider into a rise to regroup. From that position farther over Masada the picture was akin to an ant farm constructed under glass. Rasin's men were responding with true professionalism by ducking for cover into any of the labyrinth of ruins. They concentrated mostly in the area of the vast storehouse remains of the northeastern flank where they could form a new stronghold. A number of enemy combatants toted heavy machine guns and RPGs with them, just the kind of firepower Blaine had been most frightened they would encounter. The samurai continued to soar over the ruins, but the angle was no longer to their advantage and Rasin's forces had regrouped sufficiently to fire up at them when they passed.

"Hiroshi, can you read me?" McCracken said into his wireless communicator.

"Loud and clear, *Fudo-san*."

"We've got them pinned in the storehouses for the most part. I'm going down to look for Rasin. I'll land between the inner wall and synagogue off from the northern palace lookout."

"My men and I are already down. Be careful. Something bothers me about their number. I counted only forty in our initial passes."

McCracken felt the familiar twinge of uneasiness creep through him, called up by the fact that Isaac's intelligence indicated upward of sixty troops had accompanied Rasin to Masada. "You hear that, Indian?" he asked, soaring low to drop into his landing.

"Troublesome, Blainey. We'd be best to stay alert."

Blaine hit the ground running, still in motion when he pulled himself from the harness and tore the glider off his back. In the process he was careful not to disturb the small earpiece and microphone rising from the rolled collar of his black turtleneck. He crouched low and charged into the remains of the synagogue overlooking the ramp path that had ultimately allowed the Romans to breech the fortress. The sound of rocks crunching beneath his boots seemed as loud as screams in the night to him, helpless as he was to silence his heavy footsteps. Pinning himself against one of the inside walls, he set about readying his weapons.

Above him, a complement of Hiroshi's samurai under War-eagle's leadership continued to wage the battle from the sky. They focused on the storehouse area where most of Rasin's troops were concentrated, swooping in any direction additional fire came from. In a sense the strategy the motorized gliders allowed was a microcosm of war itself: they provided air supe-riority to better allow ground based troops to surround the enemy and attack from a position of strength. The clincher, of course, was that a primary weapon of attack here would be the sword in addition to the gun. In such narrow, serpentine confines, with much of the battle certain to be waged in exceptionally close quarters, it was a more practical and versatile weapon when wielded by experts. The six men in Blaine's attack group were already closing from the south, Hiroshi's party from the north.

Machine gun fire continued to split the night, the blend of ancient and modern weapons bizarre enough to be almost lu-dicrous. But the plan all along had been to reduce this to a hand-to-hand battle where Hiroshi's samurai would have the un-doubted advantage even against Rasin's superior number of commandos. Blaine concentrated on the task of finding Rasin. As he eased back out through the synagogue entrance, though, the lights all over Masada died and the mountaintop was plunged into total darkness.

"Come in, Hiroshi!"

"I read you, *Fudo-san*."

"There's someone up here who's good, *sensei*. They chose the same response I would have. And we must expect whoever it is to do more."

"We must get the lights back on!"

"I'm going to call the Sikorskys down. Have them turn on their floods."

"They'll be sitting ducks!"

"Not if they stay on the move. Besides, what choice do we have? We'll have to rely on your people to keep them from solidifying positions to fire their RPGs from. Where are you?"

"Outer wall of the bathhouse. My men are all within sight. Were," Hiroshi corrected.

"Give me thirty seconds to turn the lights back on. Then we'll finish the bastards once and for all. You get that too, Indian? Johnny?''

McCracken waited, his only sight that of the khaki-colored rock wall an arm's distance away.

There was no reply from Wareagle.

''Come on!'' Lace ordered, almost dragging Rasin as they rushed along beside a courtyard wall. They came to an open stretch by the building that had been the officers' family quarters two thousand years before. The area was full of gray smoke the invaders had left in their wake.

''Where are we—''

Rasin stopped his question when Lace released her grip on him and drew a heavy scimitar from her belt. To use a gun now would be to risk exposure. If it came to battle, it would be with the sword. In her free arm she toted the heavy mortar Rasin needed to fire his containers of vaccine, held presently in a bag over his shoulder. But where could they fire from? Where was Lace taking him?

''You'll see,'' she whispered, responding to his unfinished question of seconds before.

They could hear the whirl of the motorized gliders soaring above them and then, louder, the *wop-wop-wop* of the Sikorskys that were speeding back onto the scene.

''I should have thought of that!'' Lace lamented. ''I should have!''

''Thought of what?'' an exasperated Rasin asked.

''Hurry!'' was her only reply.

They were running now through the uneven, rocky terrain, Lace doing her best to support Rasin. He felt the small cannisters that made up his ration of the vaccine clacking together in the knapsack strung over his arm. He had totally lost his bearings in the dark. He had walked Masada a thousand times since his youth, certain that in a past life he had died here among the Zealots, perhaps as the leader Eliezer himself. Only this time the cause would come to a far more fruitful end. The blackness deepened, and Rasin knew Lace had led him close to the southern wall; he was quite sure of it when the hovering Sikorskys switched on their lights, turning Masada ablaze. Lace had stopped, and now he followed her gaze forward and down.

They had reached the vast water cistern in the southwest corner of the fortress. The helicopter's stray light was sufficient for him to see into the cistern's vast depth. He realized Lace had led him to the perfect place from which to release his allotment of the vaccine.

But there was something else. Coming up from the depths to meet Lace was Tilly with nearly twenty of his soldiers behind her.

"We move," Lace told her, and then she led the rush off in a chorus of crunching stones, leaving Rasin to the task before him.

Major Shamsi saw the huge troop-carrying choppers hovering over Masada to return light to a scene that had been plunged in darkness. Confusion continued to rush through him. Those were Israeli aircraft all right, but did that mean they were Israeli soldiers waging war on Yosef Rasin's forces atop Masada? And if so, why wasn't he informed? He grabbed for the radio yet again.

"Base, this is Major Shamsi. Come in. Over."

"We read you, Major," returned the voice he had heard over nine minutes before.

"All hell's breaking loose here. Where are those troops?"

"They're en route, Major. Your orders are to keep the area secure."

"Secure? Secure from what? We need a drop on top of the mountain, do you hear me? There's a situation—Wait . . . Who is this? Identify yourself."

Static.

"Put Commander Herzel on now!"

More static.

"Damn!" Shamsi screamed to himself, tossing the useless mike down.

They'd been had!

He located his second-in-command nearby and pulled him aside.

"Take a jeep and get to a phone. Call base. Tell them what's going on here. Do you hear me?"

The lieutenant looked confused. "But, sir, the radio, you—"

"Our frequency's been jammed! No one besides us has any idea of what's happening here!"

The troops Lace had held back had left a number of battery-powered lanterns behind in the cavernous water cistern, and Rasin arranged them in a semicircle around him to aid his final preparations. The cistern was located deep within the bowels of the mountain itself, accessible only by a steep flight of stone steps. As for firing the shells, there was a window high within the cistern's south wall through which rain water had entered. That same window would now serve as the perfect exit route for his vaccine-loaded mortar shells.

Rasin checked the sights again. Mortars had been his specialty in the army, and that had been the very reason why he had opted for this means of release in the first place. Of course, firing them from the roof of the bathhouse was considerably different than angling the shots through a window-sized portal. Unhappy with the trajectory as presented, he had no choice but to prop up the mortar's base precariously with a rock and his crumpled knapsack to achieve the angle of fire needed to pass through the opening.

Rasin worked fast, blessing the brilliance of Lace for holding a third of his troops back here in expectation of just this sort of eventuality. He now believed she was right about McCracken. No one else could have devised such a plan, and only Lace's being present to anticipate it had saved his operation from ruin. But there was anticipation required on his part as well. His problems were still many and complicated. The mortar fire from the cistern would undoubtedly bring McCracken in his direction. Even if he managed to launch all twelve shells of the vaccine, what good would it do if he fell into the American's grasp? His plan extended far beyond this night, beyond this place. He had to be able to escape.

Satisfied at last with the position of the mortar, Rasin moved back toward the explosives Lace had left for him at the foot of the stone steps.

* * *

The fresh lights of the Sikorskys allowed the battle to resume on the northern face of Masada, with Hiroshi's warriors seizing even more of an advantage. In centuries past the labyrinth-like maze of storehouses had served as an enormous system for the stockpiling of many years' supplies of weapons, food, and other essentials for life. It seemed fitting to McCracken that Rasin's troops had chosen this maze of passages and rooms to make their last stand.

By now virtually all of Hiroshi's samurai would be moving to enclose them and make the battle hand-to-hand. Gunfire continued to rage, but Blaine could tell by the cadence that it was wild and desperate. Screams periodically punctured the night as another of Rasin's army of cutthroats fell to the silent approach and deadly swords of the samurai.

Blaine continued moving about. Rasin himself would stay beyond the battle, working frantically to fire his vaccine somehow into the air. Blaine had already searched the entire confines of the bathhouse and various ruins along the north and northwestern fronts. Coming up empty, he found himself gazing down from the northern palace lookout station at the three tiers of Herod's palace. The uppermost tier stood at the summit, with the middle terrace some sixty-five-feet below and the lowest forty feet beneath that. The view from all, especially the lowest, was clear and spectacular.

The perfect setting for Rasin to work his black magic.

Blaine rushed to the winding, modern, man-made stairway that snaked down the mountain to the various terraces. The bottom terrace was his target, and in that moment he was certain Rasin would be there.

Hiroshi slid through the ancient corridors of the storehouse, gliding so as not to disturb the rocks that might give away his approach. He held his cherished *katana* high overhead. It had been handed down through his family line for generations, fashioned in the Koto period of Japan, known for the greatest swords in history. Twenty-nine-and-a-half-inches of promised death, silent as it was sure.

One of Rasin's guards spun out toward him from an opening leading to a storeroom. Hiroshi brought the flat edge of his sword down on his rifle barrel, the bullets blasting errantly as he whipped the edge back up against the man's throat. The man slammed up against a rock wall, gurgling blood, and Hiroshi mercifully finished him with a thrust through his heart. The man slumped. The old *sensei* continued on.

His years meant nothing now. His ancestors had fought on battlegrounds not much different from this, sometimes in their own service and sometimes that of a lord. The rest of his warriors came from similar traditions, and they moved as he did through the storehouse maze. There were sporadic bursts of gunfire, followed almost always by screams from the gun's wielder as the samurai sent another to his death. Hiroshi continued on, licking the sweat from his lips and smelling the rusty scent of blood on the air. The battle refreshed and recharged him. He had been gone from the life of his ancestors for too long. This was where he belonged.

Something made Hiroshi stop still in his tracks. His ears caught a crunching sound, like that of horses carrying men on the attack. He rushed to the low point of the wall and peered outward into the dusty spill of light made by the Sikorskys' floods.

Soldiers! Fifteen, maybe twenty rushing across the empty plain northward toward the storehouses. Where had they come from? The situation was about to change markedly. Hiroshi could see in his mind his men being mowed down as these reinforcements swooped unexpectedly into the area to the rear of his men. He had feared just such a development as this.

"Blaine," he called into his communicator. His back pressed against the nearest wall, he broke the rule of radio silence they had set for themselves. "Blaine, come in! Where are you?"

"Down on the northern terrace. What's wrong?"

"Twenty of Rasin's soldiers are charging from the south. We missed them."

"Because somebody made us miss them, the same somebody who killed the lights. Goddamn it. . . ." McCracken put his lips closer to the microphone in order to whisper. "Johnny, can you hear me? Come on, Indian, I need you."

"I'm here, Blainey."

McCracken was about to ask where when he was interrupted by the abrupt and continuous fire of automatic rifles.

The sole source of the fire was Johnny Wareagle. He held in each hand an automatic rifle loaded with double clips, and was blasting away at the newly revealed troops. The news of the missing complement of soldiers had bothered Johnny from the moment he first heard it. He knew from the start they had to be hiding, and he was heading toward the scattered buildings to the south when he saw the troops led by a huge woman in black.

Immediately Wareagle darted back into the darkness, skirting the spill of the choppers' floodlights. The ravaged guard tower rose before him and he charged up its steps to the highest point on Masada. A trio of soldiers had lost their lives trying to defend it at the battle's outset, and Johnny added one of their Galil machine guns to his own M-16. Crouching low until the last, he waited for the sound of rocks crunching to tell him the troops were close enough.

McCracken's call had come seconds before and left Johnny no time to explain. He simply rose in the darkness, unknown and unseen, and began firing away at the charge against the northern strongholds of the fortress.

He felt no kick of the rifles as he fired, nor did he hear the screams of the men he was killing. Their bodies dropped in waves between the officers' family quarters and the stone quarry. It was several seconds before the return fire started, and by then the first of his clips was exhausted. Wareagle plunged downward to await the siege.

"No!" Lace screamed to the eight men who had survived the barrage. "Leave him! Follow me!"

Her eyes searched frantically for Tilly, finding her with a relieved smile propped behind a built-up storage hold in the ground. She rushed over and touched the smaller woman's hair gratefully, then raised her scimitar overhead to lead what remained of the soldiers toward the battle in the storehouses.

She wanted to believe the gunman on the guard tower was McCracken. Not only had the person riddled their numbers, he had also denied them position on Masada's most strategic point, from which the invaders could be cut down at will. That was his style, after all. But her feelings told her otherwise. This was someone else, equally dangerous to be sure. She would still have to find McCracken.

Hiroshi was ready when the fresh wave of Rasin's soldiers reached the storehouses. Wareagle's fire from the guard tower had bought him time as well as reducing the enemy's number and alerting his men to their presence.

One of them leaped atop the jagged wall the old warrior had crouched behind. As soon as the man began to fire controlled bursts toward areas his samurai were rushing from, Hiroshi rose and, wielding his sword in a great arc, sliced through the man's legs below the knees, toppling him over. Another soldier lunged rifle-first toward the wall, but Hiroshi extended his sword, and the man impaled himself on the blade.

A burst fired reflexively from the dead man's gun caught the old *sensei* in the side and spun him. Hot pain flooded his midsection, and Hiroshi felt the spill of warm blood. The wound wasn't mortal, but the blood loss would weaken him and make him a burden to his men. He had never lost grip on his sword's hilt. With an effort he yanked it free of the dead man's midsection and moved back down the corridor, using the wall for support.

"Hiroshi, what's going on?" came McCracken's desperate call.

"All under control, *Fudo-san*. Not to worry."

This was spoken into a chorus of screams and machine gun fire as the remainder of Rasin's men engaged Hiroshi's samurai as best they could. The sudden influx of enemy troops had moved several of his men to switch from swords back to rifles. Some of them were being killed and this pained him, but they were dying the death of warriors, a most honorable passing that defined the very essence of their lives.

Hiroshi moaned into the microphone.

"You're hurt!" McCracken cried. "Jesus Christ, where are you? Stay where you are!"

"Not to worry, *Fudo-san*. I can walk. That's all I need for now."

"I'm on the way. Just hold on," Blaine answered sensing the *sensei*'s wounds were more serious than he would let on.

"Yes," Hiroshi said, turning just in time to see a figure in black leather surge toward him.

He spun, leading with the sword. But his wounded side slowed his reaction, and even as his *katana* lashed out at the black figure he felt the strangely shaped blade he was powerless to block slice down at him. In the end he tried desperately to rotate his sword back to deflect the blow, but again his side betrayed him and his legs crumbled even before the scimitar sliced on a diagonal through his collar bone all the way to his heart. A bright flash of light followed and Hiroshi heard his ancestors calling as he spilled over.

Before Lace could move off, the muted voice of Blaine McCracken reached her ear, coming from the corpse's wireless transmitter which had spilled from his head when he fell.

"I'm almost to the upper terrace, Hiroshi. Be with you before you know it."

Lace smiled and sped off in that direction.

McCracken cursed himself as he rushed up the last of the steps that would bring him back to the upper terrace of Herod's palace and then into the battle. The straight abutment of the northern palace had seemed the perfect place for Rasin to launch his vaccine into the air over Israel. Placing himself in the fanatic's mind, he was sure of it. His mistake had been to forget that someone else was directing Rasin's strategems up here for him, someone who would never have permitted such an obvious move. Damn! He had committed the cardinal flaw, that of underestimating his enemy.

If that was his first mistake, his second was to dwell on it and to let his fear for the life of Hiroshi blot out his normal alertness. He sped heedlessly up the final steps onto the semicircular terrace that looked down over the remainder of the mountain. A sudden burst of automatic gunfire clanged off the steel support rail. His hand was stung and he was reaching for his Uzi when another spray sliced through the darkness and banged against the gun, ricocheting madly and stripping it from his grasp.

McCracken reeled sideways and grasped for the railing as the tracing fire searched for his shape in the blackness. His hands found the rail but, still numb, they slid off. His last measure of balance was lost and he pitched over the side of Masada to the dark abyss at the bottom.

CHAPTER 28

FEELING HIMSELF AIRBORNE, BLAINE HAD FLAILED DESPER-
ately for a hold as he began to drop, but he brushed the steel
rail with his fingers and that was all. Arms extended, he slid for
a brief time straight down the rock-face side before his legs
slowed his pace and then caught on a narrow ridge extending
out from the mountain. He gathered his breath and checked his
extremities. Miraculously nothing was broken. His hands and
arms were scraped but functional. His thick pants had been torn
and he could feel blood from the lacerations trickling down his
legs. No broken bones, though, nothing to stop him from going
on.

He inspected the area in the darkness around him. He had
gone over the rail on the side of the northern terrace, leaving a
straight drop of nearly a hundred yards if his perch gave way.
His eyes probed above him in search of handholds in the rock
face to take him back up. He could conceivably manage it, but
the time it would take would be prohibitively long.

He then looked downward and spotted beneath him the set of
steps winding from one terrace level to another. He could not
hope to drop onto it, but he could ease himself down, a difficult
and dangerous task but one requiring far less time. At once he
began to lower his legs over the ridge that had saved him, shifting his weight to make him top-heavy as his hands replaced his
legs on the ridge. He found a foothold firm enough for one foot

but not two, and eased his bulk onto it as he began to dangle his left leg in search of another makeshift step. As he was feeling around blindly, his right foot slipped and he came close to falling again. Only his firm grip on the rocks prevented a disaster, and he hung there in space briefly to recover his bearings.

Somehow that flirt with disaster seemed to charge him. Inside, Blaine knew he was going to make it; he could almost see the rocky face with his legs and feet. He found a twisted rhythm, body never balanced the same way twice. When his feet at last grazed the safety rail bordering the steps, it seemed as if only a few seconds had passed instead of several minutes. He touched down, possessed by a strange calm that swallowed all the hurt and wounds.

But the trail of a mortar shell speeding through the air high over Masada stripped the calm away and Blaine threw himself into a rush back up the stairs.

From the base of the mountain, Major Shamsi contemplated the direction of the shells. He had seen battle often enough to know mortar fire when he saw it, but this shell had been fired apparently at nothing. The battle raging atop Masada already defied explanation. This just confused matters more.

Shamsi continued to gaze upward toward the sky, but it was his ears that snapped alert next, picking up a familiar pulsating sound approaching from the west. He turned to see the flashing lights of a quartet of helicopter gunships slicing toward Masada like buzzards over a corpse.

"It's about time," Shamsi said to himself. "About fucking time."

Isser had issued the call-up five minutes into Isaac's story, before he had even heard the tape containing the claims of Eisenstadt. They were airborne inside of twelve minutes and covered the distance to Masada in ten.

"Say something," the head of Mossad said to the old man who was seated uneasily next to him in the rear seat of the cockpit.

"Like what?"

"Like telling me what fools we were to have joined forces with Rasin."

"I hate repeating myself. Help McCracken catch Rasin on Masada and I might just forgive you."

They were gazing at the Sikorskys hovering over Masada with floodlights blazing when a mortar shell flashed by the windshield, causing both men to shrink back instinctively with the certainty it was headed for them. Isser grabbed his handset.

"Ready drop displacement," he told the commandos scattered through the four gunships. "Prepare to secure the area. We're going down."

Rasin could only follow the path of his fired shells briefly before angle and distance stole them from him. He had six more to fire, another three minutes work at most. In spite of the attack spearheaded by McCracken, he was on the verge of assuring the successful completion of the first stage of his plan.

But he felt no elation, for there was the second stage to consider. And to effect that he would have to make it safely off this rock to freedom. There would have to be a way. Fate had gotten him this far. Fate had blessed him first with his own resolve, then with Eisenstadt, and at last with the Gamma cannisters salvaged off the *Indianapolis*. Yes, all this was happening because it was meant to. His was a holy mission, a blessed one.

Masada had indeed been the perfect choice for the setting from which Israel would at last achieve true independence. And yet if he died here as the Zealots had, then all would be for naught. Rasin started to worry until once again the strange feeling of calm reassurance surged through him.

He wasn't going to die. He wasn't going to be captured.

He was going to finish the first stage of the plan here on Masada and then move on to the next to achieve his destiny. Fired by that thought, Rasin reached for the first of the final six shells.

Three more shells had been fired before McCracken reached the plain of Masada once more. He stumbled briefly, suddenly dizzy, and had to lean against one of the ancient walls to steady himself. He still had a grenade, an Uzi he was able to pick up on the way, and a pistol. Enough. Plenty. But there was Hiroshi to consider as well, wounded somewhere and in need of help.

"Come in, Hiroshi. Sorry it took so long. Where are you? . . . Do you read me, Hiroshi? Come in."

There was no response, and another mortar blast pierced the air as the helicopter gunships sprinted through the air above him. If Hiroshi's plan to jam the Israeli soldiers' communications had failed, reinforcements would have reached here significantly sooner, which meant the gunships had come courtesy of Isaac's visit to the Mossad. But that did not insure the occupants of the choppers would be friendly. Blaine eased himself forward and waited for the next mortar shell to pin down where they were being fired from, his key to finding Rasin.

When it came, he was ready. He sprinted forward, with the last of the battle between Hiroshi's warriors and Rasin's soldiers still raging. The fact that gunfire sounded only weakly and sporadically was evidence that the tide of the battle had turned toward the samurai. All that remained was for McCracken to do his part.

He sped between the last wall of the storehouses and the higher one of a courtyard housing public toilet facilities. From there he darted past the quarry and into the open where the next mortar blast froze him in his tracks.

The water cistern! It was coming from the water cistern!

Blaine had started forward again when the rocks at his feet were kicked up by a burst from a machine gun. He hit the ground hard and rolled, bullets tracing him as he fired token return volleys in a wide spray. He didn't have the gunman pinned down and was starting to plan how to accomplish that when the figure of Johnny Wareagle rushed into the open, firing toward the area of a water station forty yards to the left.

"Go, Blainey! I'll keep him occupied!"

McCracken didn't argue, just rose and sped off again with Johnny's rifle continuing to spit fire. When the hammer clicked on an empty cylinder, he discarded the rifle and drew the massive killing knife from the sheath on his belt. He stood there holding it menacingly high so the gunman would know that rifle or not, he wasn't giving an inch. The arriving gunships dipped lower, kicking up huge clouds of ancient dust and rocks that Wareagle had to squint his eyes to see through.

"This is the Israeli army!" a voice hailed over a PA from within one of the choppers. *"Throw down your weapons and stand with your hands in the air."*

The warning completed, doors opened on all four of the helicopters to allow dozens of slick ropes to drop out and Israeli commandos to slide down toward ground level with guns at the ready. But by now their presence was superfluous. Those remaining to acknowledge them were a dozen of Hiroshi's warriors who had survived and their twenty prisoners who were being herded forward even then. Wareagle heard a rustle and turned back toward the water station.

He saw the huge figure in black leather quite clearly, saw her as she stooped to lift up and support the gunman grazed by one of Johnny's bullets. With the weight of the body taxing it, the figure in black could do nothing but gaze at the huge Indian with the large knife extending by his side.

Gaze and smile.

Then in the next instant the light from the Sikorskys wavered as they shifted to free landing space for the gunships, and by the time the area was lit again the two figures had disappeared.

Yosef Rasin had heard the choppers and the warning that had come from one of them and knew his stand on Masada was finished. The army, and thus the government, must have turned against him. He had been double-crossed!

But what had changed the government's mind? What had turned their reluctant sanction of his plan into sudden disavowal? McCracken again no doubt, and the old men who had turned out to be real thorns in his side, too. And yet they of all people should have supported what he was trying to do. Traitors! They were all traitors! He alone could set Israel on the proper course now. One more shell to fire and then he would flee the cistern and find a way off this rock before the army could find him.

Rasin reached out and dropped the final shell down the barrel.

The shell blasted outward when Blaine was ten yards from the start of the steps that led down into the water cistern. Holding the Uzi tight before him, he glided the rest of the way, not wanting to alert Rasin to his presence.

"Hold it right there!"

The call sounded from his rear and McCracken knew instantly it had come from an Israeli soldier. The sudden grinding sound of additional footsteps stopping against the rock surface told him the speaker had been joined by two others. He turned slowly, hands and Uzi in the air.

"Where's your commander?"

"Drop your weapon!"

"Call your commander here now. Is it Isser? Call Isser!"

"Drop your—"

The speaker's command was cut off when the figure of Johnny Wareagle crashed into him, spreading his arms to take down the two others as well. Blaine didn't wait to see the rest. He rushed the final stretch to the entrance of the water cistern and was halfway down the stairs in the pitch blackness when he heard Rasin's voice.

"I've been expecting you."

McCracken stopped, searched for the voice's point of origin. "Rasin?"

"You shouldn't have come down here, but since you have why not come all the way down?"

McCracken stopped at the bottom step. The pungent scent of mortar fire singed his nostrils. There was something wrong here, wrong with the scenario, wrong with where Rasin's voice was coming from.

"I can't see you."

"You'd like to, wouldn't you? You think you've won."

"Plenty of people died here tonight. Nobody wins."

"Israel can, now that I've released my vaccine. Israel can win at last."

"Only if hundreds of millions more die. That doesn't count."

"You've spoken to Eisenstadt."

"Give yourself up."

"Sorry."

McCracken finally pinned Rasin down to the far wall directly opposite him. But his voice had a strange echo, as if he were speaking down from a point *on* the wall.

Blaine realized what was happening in time to start his sprint back up the steep stone steps. Maybe Rasin didn't hear or see him. Maybe he just had to say one last thing.

"Good-bye, Blaine McCracken."

The explosion came as he cleared the final step and lunged headlong through the air to carry himself as far as he could from the cistern. The stairs crumbled instantly and the entire ancient structure trembled, as fragments of the walls cracked and splintered in the last instant before the cistern collapsed upon itself, leaving Blaine to gaze back at the rubble.

"He climbed out, I'm telling you," Blaine insisted to Isser while Isaac looked on. "He must have had a rope ladder or something extended from one of the portals."

"He hasn't left this rock, that's for sure. We'll find him."

"I want him when you do," Blaine said bitterly, thinking of the news Wareagle had brought him about Hiroshi. "There's a score to settle now."

"We'll settle it later."

McCracken looked up with frigid eyes. "Just find him, Isser. I figure you might be able to handle that much. But you've got to take him alive. Otherwise we don't find out where he stashed the cannisters of Gamma gas and we might be facing this whole scenario again real soon."

"I'd rather not think about that."

"You'd better."

Blaine had barely finished the warning when one of the gunships fired up its engine, propeller and rotor blades springing to life.

"I didn't authorize anyone to leave," Isser said in puzzlement. "What the hell is . . ."

McCracken was already running, charging toward the chopper which was nearly ready for takeoff. He knew in that instant the huge woman in black leather would be at the controls, knew she would have disabled the other gunships to prevent pursuit as well.

A group of soldiers reached the readying chopper ahead of him and were blasted back by machine-gun fire coming from just inside the door. Blaine approached on an angle that kept him from the gunman's sight, and was almost there when the chopper lifted off suddenly. At the last moment he leaped to grab hold of the chopper's landing pod as it rose, but his hand slipped off the steel. He plunged back down to the dust of Masada with the gunship shrinking into the blackness of the night.

CHAPTER 29

Evira LAY ON THE FLOOR IN HER CELL IN THE PALACE BASE-
ment. Time had lost all meaning to her; she slept, she woke.
There was little else to do. Kourosh lay against her, using her
shoulder as a pillow. Occasionally in his sleep, the urchin would
whimper and grab for her. Evira was more than happy to hug
and soothe him, her own desperation eased in the process.

How long had it been since Hassani had finished with them,
since the reports of McCracken's death? At least one day, perhaps two or more. Evira didn't know why they were being left
alive, unless it was to let them starve slowly to death. In all the
hours they had been there, no one had come with food or water.
She had long gone beyond being hungry, even thirsty. Her
strength had depleted, and with it her resolve. Hassani had won,
Rasin too. McCracken was dead and she was here. How ideal-
istic she had been to believe the two of them were capable of
defeating the plans of two madmen on their own.

By her side, Kourosh whimpered again, long hair matted to
his forehead by the sweat caused by the unremitting heat of the
air about them. This boy had become her burden. Watching him
die would be her punishment for how she had involved Blaine
McCracken. The gods worked in strange ways, but always with
method and purpose. She knew another day without food or
water would bring severe pains and cramps to the boy. Such an
awful way to die, feeling yourself wasting away. She had re-

solved that before her own strength ebbed too far she would end
the urchin's pain by killing him. It would be the last act of her
suddenly feeble life and the hardest to fulfill.

Evira felt herself nodding off again and hoped for a long,
dream-filled sleep this time. She wrapped her arm around the
boy and held him close to her. Her eyes slid closed.

A sound from somewhere jarred her. How long had she been
out, if at all? A dream, it must have been a dream that reached
her in the state between consciousness and sleep.

No, the sound came again, that of metal being worked; a
scratching, grating sound. Her ears tried to focus in, eyes useless
in the near-total darkness of the basement prison.

Suddenly there was a loud echo of metal being forced aside.
A wide beam of light darted haphazardly across the far wall.
Men were entering through some secret passageway or tunnel. She remembered Kourosh describing it to her. But who
were they? Why had they come?

The single beam became four. The beams were joined by
voices exchanged in a whisper, someone giving instructions, a
search underway.

They were looking for her!

Over here, Evira tried to say, but her mouth was too dry to
push the words out. She forced up some saliva and cleared the
refuse from her throat.

"Over here," she managed hoarsely. "Over here."

Instantly a pair of the flashlights turned in the direction of her
cell.

"Yakov, we've found her!" a voice followed in an excited
whisper.

"Alive?"

The light found her, blinded her, and she shrank back to
shield her eyes.

"Yes. Quite."

A third flashlight joined the first two. Evira struggled to gaze
past the beams at the men who held them.

"Can you hear me?" came the voice of the one called Yakov.

"Yes."

"I'm going to blow the lock on your cell. Back up as far as
you can in the corner."

She did as she was told and dragged Kourosh along with her. The boy started to stir, barely awake.

"It's okay," she soothed. "We're being rescued."

She held him close to her as a fizzle came, followed by a flash, and a *poof*! One of the men kicked at the cell door and it reeled inward to allow the group to enter.

"How long since you've had anything to eat or drink?" Yakov asked her.

"Two days, I think. Maybe three."

"Then that's our first priority," he said, helping her to her feet, while another of the men supported the urchin. "I assume the boy is with you."

"He is. Who are you? What brought you here?"

"A long story. For now I've got a message from Blaine Mc-Cracken. He says you should have stayed an old hag in Jaffa."

"What?" Isser blared at McCracken's assertion of the final piece in the mad plan of Yosef Rasin. "That's *insane*!"

"Of course it is," Blaine told him. "It's Rasin."

"But if what you say is true . . . "

"Then everything makes sense. Everything becomes clear."

"How could he have pulled it off, though? Think of the logistics."

"Forget logic. It doesn't matter anymore; it never did. We've got to think like him if we're still going to have a chance to win."

They were seated in Isser's office in the squat, innocuous complex of buildings outside Tel Aviv near the Hebrew Country Club that formed the permanent headquarters of Mossad.

"You know, Isser," Isaac started, "I think he's got a point."

"It's crazy," the head of Mossad persisted. "And you want me to risk everything based on this . . . hunch."

"Not a hunch and not everything. Just me and Operation Firestorm. I go into Tehran and get Rasin. All you do is let Firestorm proceed as planned."

"Including the Apaches, of course."

"More than ever, since one of them's gonna serve as my taxi in." He turned back toward Isaac. "So when's show time?"

The old man turned an empty gaze out the window where the first signs of light were still an hour or so away.

"Dawn," was all he said.

The Shah's secret tunnel ran nearly half a mile and ended beneath a street beyond the square that fronted the royal palace.

"You're Israeli," Evira said as they made their way forward with flashlights slicing through the darkness.

"Born and raised." Yakov laughed, taking his turn at carrying Kourosh.

Evira recalled her suspicions brought on by the comic books purchased in Israel. "But what are you doing here?"

"We're here to start a revolution. Several hundred of us were planted over a year ago amidst the young, the poor, and the students to organize their discontent into rebellion—and to supply them with the means to fight."

"Weapons . . ."

"No revolution is complete without them."

"An *Israeli*-inspired revolution?"

"Supported would be a better choice of words. It is the people's will. We are merely helping them exercise it."

" 'We.' Mossad?"

"Let's say we're an independent group working with their sanction. Easier to disavow involvement that way. Less likely to have leaks with an operation required to take place over such a long period of time."

"Jews working with Iranians. Incredible . . ."

"Not really. People working against oppressive, murderous regimes is never incredible. You must agree. You came here to kill Hassani yourself."

Evira stopped suddenly, and Yakov's men bringing up the rear nearly collided with her. "How did you know—"

"Because an order was sent by the mission controllers to insure you failed. With Hassani dead, the people would have lost their symbol to rise against. There would be no Firestorm."

"No *what*?"

"Code name of this operation."

"Then it was your people who betrayed that cell in Naziabad."

"Regretfully," Yakov acknowledged softly. "This boy, he saved your life?"

Evira nodded. "And to return the favor I'm going to get him out of this country. With your help, of course." *Thanks to Blaine McCracken,* she almost added but didn't. The fact that he had somehow arranged this rescue could only mean that he had fulfilled his end of the mission. Whatever happiness she might have felt over that, though, was tempered by the failure she had experienced at her end. But maybe it wasn't too late. . . .

"You'll have to be patient. The hour of Firestorm is upon us."

"When?"

The other end of the tunnel appeared as a grating in the ground that allowed the first light of the morning to cast a checkerboard pattern downward.

"Dawn."

"You up for another run, Indian?"

Wareagle's gaze was noncommittal. "How strange it seems that we spend so much of our lives trying to reconcile ourselves to the hellfire that forged our spirits. And yet each time it beckons we return to it without pause."

"You once told me the hellfire wasn't a place, it was a feeling."

"It is even more than that, Blainey. Our manitous are cleansed by the hellfire. It recharges us, gives us our worth. We lapse from it too long and we become the things we feared it would make us."

"Kind of like a fix, an addiction."

"More like an impulse to breathe. We cannot stop ourselves even if we try."

"This is no time to stop trying," Blaine said, gritting his teeth. "Someone's going to answer for killing Hiroshi, and I've got to get my son back."

"Dropping ourselves into a revolution might pose a difficult setting to accomplish either. The palace is our target, but even the spirits cannot lead us into it through the chaos and the crowds. We're going to need something more this time, Blainey."

"Precisely why a little present's going to be waiting for us on the aircraft carrier *Kennedy* when we land to pick up the Apaches."

The small group climbed out of the tunnel into the street with the first of the light and the first of the chaos. Already people were taking to the streets, haphazardly, with no real sense of purpose yet, as if some word had reached them and they were waiting for further instruction. Evira had been a party to such scenarios before. But the fervor she sensed in the morning air here was almost palpable in its commitment. The Israelis had done their job well.

"It is happening," said an Iranian student leader named Rashid who had been waiting for them at the escape hatch. "It is truly happening."

"And this is only Niavarin," Yakov reminded them. Then he added to Evira, "The uprising will be focused in Tehran proper, spreading outward from there."

"A good strategy, if Hassani's Revolutionary Guard doesn't stop you in your tracks."

"We're not totally alone here," he told her. "Fifteen Apache helicopter gunships will strafe the strongest of enemy positions, starting at the estimated height of the battle three hours from now."

"And in the meantime?"

"The streets will be barricaded to slow the soldiers down, buildings will be burned to bring the people out. Those who have lived in fear and oppression for more than a decade will welcome the chance to rise up and be heard. I have been in this city for a year now. Believe me, I know."

"Where do we go from here?"

"The starting point for our revolution: Talegahani Street, also known as Takht-e Jamshid."

"The American Embassy . . ."

"Fitting, don't you think?"

During the thirty-minute drive across the city, Kourosh and Evira were able to gulp a restorative meal of bread, cheese, and water. The driver of the car maneuvered skillfully down side

THE GAMMA OPTION 295

streets to avoid the throngs already beginning to spill out with screams of defiance. The Revolutionary Guards were restrained and fearful, unsure of the proper response to make. Clearly, they knew something was brewing. Reinforcements had undoubtedly been called in, but with the streets barricaded and, judging by the smoke spreading in the sky, some already burning, passage would not come easily.

"This is as far as we can go," Yakov announced when they reached an intersection that was barricaded in all directions. The barricades were constructed of wood, furniture, cinderblocks, abandoned cars, dumpsters, and garbage cans wedged firmly into place. An exultant mass of people was standing atop the heaps, shouting and waving their rifles.

"Soviet Kalashnikovs, American M-16s, and Israeli Galils," Evira noted. "Impressive."

"We got them everything we could lay our hands on."

"Revolution!" a freshly revived Kourosh yelled jubilantly as they exited the car, thrusting a tight fist into the air. "Kill the bastards! Kill them all!"

His long hair danced in the wind, small face taut in its resolve. His feelings mirrored those of a nation frustrated by watching a reconstruction effort that had left the people worse off than ever before. The frustration was rampant now, set to brew by the Israeli plants but boiling over on its own.

"What about McCracken?" Evira asked of Yakov as they shouldered their way through the masses, which grew thicker the closer they got to the former American Embassy. "Did he say anything else, anything about Yosef Rasin?"

"All I know is that he arranged for your rescue."

"Is he coming? Is he here?"

"I know nothing more than what I've told you."

Evira realized she had lost track of Kourosh and almost panicked. She located the boy rallying with a group of children his own age holding clubs and mallets as weapons. He was cheering them on and might have been all set to join them when Evira arrived to pull him back to her side. She marvelled at the restorative effects a bit of food and water had had on both Kourosh and herself. Of course, the fervor and excitement they were in the midst of deserved a measure of the blame, too.

"It's wonderful!" The boy beamed. "Isn't is wonderful?"

She wanted to tell him that war was many things, but it was never wonderful. Innocent people were unquestionably going to die there today. The Israeli plot had as its primary aim the toppling of Hassani from power. The loss of Iranian life to accomplish that end was simply a means, accepted and condoned. The people, the masses Kourosh was cheering for, were mere pawns, sacrifices to a greater end.

These thoughts turned Evira cold. Was it no different for her rallying of the Arabs of Israel, urging them to organize and work toward a greater voice in the government? Yes, her means were nonviolent, but people had similarly been hurt working toward a higher cause they could not wholly grasp. She was using them, just as the Israelis were using the Iranians, to fulfill her own ends and goals.

They continued forcing their way through the swelling mass, more people joining it by the second. The plan would be for those in the street to smother the Revolutionary Guard as best they could by neutralizing the guards' superior weaponry and keeping them from the strategically placed barricades for as long as possible. It was a numbers game, one of bodies as well as bullets, and success depended on the people wearing the guard down and outlasting it until the Apaches arrived. At that point the powerful attack ships would strafe positions of Revolutionary Guard strongholds in the hope of opening a clear path for the masses to their ultimate target: The royal palace in Niavarin. To be overrun, ransacked, destroyed.

A red-faced man struggling for breath spotted Yakov and approached. Evira recognized his features as Israeli as well.

"The guardsmen are taking control at the embassy area," he reported grimly.

"Already? How?"

"They responded quicker and better than we anticipated."

"Perhaps they knew, were warned."

"They didn't hesitate. They fired their guns into the crowds without a single warning. It was awful. The people fled in all directions, stampeding over the bodies left behind. I'm just ahead of them."

"The word will spread, then," Iranian student leader Rashid said. "Others will scatter and run when their own deaths confront them."

"All right," Yakov conceded. "Give Hassani round one. What do you hear of Shah Reza Boulevard?"

"The barricade is forty feet high at the head of the square. The people are chanting and are ready to burn buildings as soon as the guardsmen show themselves."

"We'll make our stand there, then. A different start for the revolution, maybe even an improvement."

They were changing direction now, fighting to make their way through the frenzied masses blocking the route to Shah Reza Boulevard. Evira grabbed Kourosh by the arm and held him tight, his eyes still gleaming at the sights around him.

"Come," Yakov beckoned her. "We can get to the boulevard quicker this way. It's only a few blocks from Talegahani Street."

And the Revolutionary Guard, Evira thought.

In McCracken's mind the Apache was without question the finest attack helicopter ever built, the latest generation AH-64A model's maneuverability matched only by its power. In appearance it was a species all to itself, sleek and narrow down the body with no bit of wasted space. It had a top speed of over one-hundred-eighty miles per hour and could maintain a five-hundred-mile flying range with the new fuel it was burning. The Apache's armaments included dual sets of four Hellfire missiles and nineteen aerial rockets suspended beneath each wing and a 30-millimeter chain gun mounted on the underside.

Blaine figured the chain gun would be the most crucial weapon at the start, followed by the Folding-Fin Aerial Rockets once Revolutionary Guard strongholds were effectively pinned down. Commands to fire both these and the superpowerful Hellfire missiles were channeled directly by the copilot-gunner through a TADS (Target Acquisition and Designation Sight) directly into the fire-control computer. The margin of error was almost non-existent as a result. From a defensive standpoint, the Apache's armored shell could tolerate rocket hits that would fell any other helicopter gunship and was virtually undetectable to incoming infrared missiles.

The only real problem facing them was fuel consumption. To circumvent part of this, the plan was to use the aircraft carrier *Kennedy*, on its patrol in the Persian Gulf, as the operation's staging ground. And even then one midair refueling would be required to reach Tehran and a second needed to return to the carrier upon the mission's completion. The jet carrying Blaine and Johnny Wareagle landed first on the *Kennedy*'s deck, which had been cleared of everything but the Apaches.

"This way, gentlemen," a barrel-chested soldier with an unlit cigar stuck in his mouth said after they had climbed down. He had to raise his voice to be heard over the idling jet engine. "I'm Gunnery Sergeant Tom Beeks. Got the equipment you requested all ready."

He led them through a hatch and then down a short corridor into a conference room deserted except for the materials laid out on the table.

"To begin with," the sergeant started, reaching down for a thick black bodysuit with the bulk of a catcher's chest protector and the look of long underwear, "this is a Kevlar bodysuit. Armors you from chest to ankles with added reinforcement in vital areas. It can stop ordinary and hollow point bullets of virtually any caliber. But the drawback is it's very hot and uncomfortable and the most you can wear it is a half hour before you literally bake alive."

"An eternity," Wareagle noted to McCracken.

Blaine accepted one of the suits from Beeks and ran his hands through it. "What about the firepower I asked for, Gunny? To take the palace we're gonna need something special."

"That was a tough one. Had to use my mind a little, but fortunately these babies just came in." He pulled back a dark plastic cover to reveal a pair of long weapons dominated by a thick cylinder with slots for six separate barrels on its end.

Blaine's eyes bulged. "Vulcan 20-millimeter miniguns. What'd you do, pull these off your antiaircraft stations? Not exactly light issue, Gunny."

"Lighter than you think, sir. These were designed to cut response time and fire differential. Teflon coated with extra-thin titanium construction. They're not really made to be hand-held, but when you described what you might be facing, I figured we'd better improvise." He pointed to the cylinder's multi-barreled front. "Fires 1,000 rounds per minute, but if you try that you'll end up with a melted casing. Short, controlled bursts are your safest bet, no more than five seconds in duration with a half second in between."

"I can handle that. How do the rounds get fed?"

"Through the pack worn on your back."

"Weight?"

"The ammo about sixty pounds and the gun assembly about seventy, down from over twice that."

Blaine didn't look convinced. "Which makes the Vulcans fine for firing straight ahead, but as soon as we try to maneuver them sideways the force of the cylinder rotation will kick either up or down."

"I considered that too, sir," the gunnery sergeant said as he lifted a leather strap with hooks on either end from the table. "One end of this fastens into a belt you'll be wearing. The other attaches to the Vulcan to take up all the slack. Gun might want to kick, but it won't be going anywhere." Beeks noted Blaine's approving stare. "Ever fire a minigun before?"

"Only from choppers."

"It's pretty simple," Beeks said, and moved closer. "Just lock the main cylinder home and turn it until you hear a click." The sergeant did just that and showed Blaine how to position his hands to repeat the motion. "Safety's here. Click it off and you're ready to go. Rotation of chambers assures no pause in ammo expulsion. Perfect for urban encounters with unfriendly masses."

"I should say so."

"Only thing that ain't perfect is what a 20-millimeter shell does to man at this velocity. Gonna make a hell of a mess by the time you're finished."

"Gotta make one to clean another up, Gunny," Blaine returned. The ready horn sounded on the *Kennedy*'s deck. "Come on, Indian, we've got a plane to catch."

"The Apaches took off from the *Kennedy* ten minutes ago," Isser reported to the prime minister.

"You didn't come here just to tell me that," the old man said knowingly.

Isser didn't hesitate. "If McCracken's hunch is right, we stand to lose even if he succeeds in Tehran. Never mind the problems Rasin can cause us if McCracken brings him back. The fact is we cooperated with him. In the end we sanctioned his madness, and that reality can destroy us as surely as Gamma."

"And McCracken?"

"McCracken knows. McCracken knows *everything*." The Mossad chief took a deep breath. "We cannot allow him to leave Tehran alive."

CHAPTER 30

THE CROWD WAS CHEERING LOUDLY WHEN THE SMALL PARTY led by Yakov finally reached Shah Reza Boulevard. It wasn't hard for Evira to pin down what the cheering was all about: at every corner, the street signs originally put up by Khomeini's Revolutionary Council were being replaced by crudely painted signs that returned the boulevard to its former name during the time of the Shah.

Those on the street not watching the small ceremonies taking place had their attention fixed on the completion of the massive barricade at the head of the boulevard. Nothing had been spared. It measured over three stories high and was sixty feet deep, stretching from the south side of the boulevard to the north, running from building to building to totally seal that end of the street. The construction was hardly thought out, the piled elements mundane, but the structure was awe-inspiring. The people rallied and packed toward it like bees to their hive, renewing and recharging their enthusiasm at its mere sight. The piles of wood and steel were stacked upon lower layers of cars both new and old. Where any holes appeared down low, cinderblocks were being jammed into place. The higher it grew, the lighter the debris composing it became, heap piled atop heap until the sky seemed a reach away. It looked invincible, but Evira knew this to be a fantasy that the first bomb would shatter.

301

A pair of Iranian jets streaked through the air above, causing only a temporary lightening in the enthusiastic, fervid cheers.

"Just a show of force," Yakov said.

"They would never bomb Tehran," Rashid agreed.

"Pride?" Evira wondered.

"No," the Iranian student leader told her. "Practicality. They have no bombs for their jets. They'll keep buzzing us, though, try to scare the people off."

They continued to make their way toward the huge barricade. The going got tougher the closer they got, the true fanatics of the uprising unwilling to yield their cherished spots. Rashid and Kaveh had taken the lead now, ordering the crowds aside in Iranian, knowing just the proper phrasing to use. The two other Iranian students in their party brought up the rear, effectively boxing Yakov, Evira, and Kourosh amidst them to keep them safe from the crowd.

"We're not natives," Yakov told her. "That could cause problems if we're spotted."

"I am a native!" Kourosh claimed staunchly, as if hurt.

"You don't look it, boy. Too western. Today, appearances are everything."

"I'd join them if I had a gun!"

"If we're successful here today, you'll never have to hold a gun. Not ever," Yakov assured him, which drew an angry stare from Evira, who knew his feelings for the Iranian people extended only as far as the need of Israel to make use of them.

"I want a gun," the urchin persisted, the demand too insistent to carry even a hint of cuteness with it.

"If things go poorly, we'll need every hand we can get," Rashid said, turning back toward them. "Let's all pray they don't."

They reached the barricade moments later. Rashid signaled those on watch and a car forming a moveable gate was driven aside to let them enter. The impetus of the swelling throng forced more in after them, and these were not so politely turned back and the car was driven back into place to seal the barricade once more.

Evira gazed around her and marvelled at what she saw. The

confines of the barricade made for a stark contrast with the cha-
otic rabble they had just left on the far side. Weapons and ammunition were laid out neatly on planks laid over crates and
cinderblocks. Posts had been set up for both food and the attending of wounded. There was a communications center in the
form of a table lined with radios and walkie-talkies, linking the
Israeli-led rebel leaders with every major sphere of the revolution as it progressed through the city.

The barricade had been built with its back to the very head
of the boulevard where it jutted off into narrow, easily blocked-
off side streets. The effect was that of enclosing those within on
all sides. Evira felt claustrophobic from it all and only slightly
reassured by the numerous gunmen posted atop the barricades
facing every direction. Still, she had to admit they were formi-
dably armed, what with the grenade launchers, RPGs, bazookas, heavy machine guns, and even several hand-held surface-to-
air missiles to use against possible attacks from aircraft. Yes,
the Israelis had thought of everything, but without the prompt
arrival of the Apaches to lend air support it might not be enough.

"It goes well, Rashid!" another student leader she had not
met said to the one who had escorted them here. The two young
men embraced.

"The word was bad from the embassy," Rashid returned.
"Have you heard anything since?"

"Who has had time to talk? There was the barricade to finish."

Yakov was already making his way over to the communications station. He looked nervous. The Apaches would be over-
due in a scant fifteen minutes, and as of yet there had been no
word from them. Evira followed him, close enough when she
stopped to hear his side of the conversation into one of the radios
he picked up.

"What do you mean?" he demanded into the receiver. "How
did they get through? . . . *That* many? Oh God . . . No, it's too
late. . . . Yes, we can still do it. Just stay where you are and
keep me updated." He lowered the receiver to the table.

"Bad news?" Evira asked lamely.

Yakov's eyes were glassy. "Hassani's forces responded in far
greater numbers than we expected, quicker as well. There are

between five and ten thousand in the streets already and more coming. Talegahani Street is totally theirs. They're heading this way.''

''You must have a plan, a contingency,'' she said, watching Kourosh helping to put the finishing touches on the barricade that would be under siege in a matter of minutes.

''Yes. The Apaches, damn it! The Apaches!''

''No word from them?''

''None at all.''

Evira and Yakov looked at one another, both afraid to speak the obvious, that the Apaches weren't coming and they had been abandoned.

''We've got to do *something*!'' Evira insisted.

''Yes,'' Yakov acknowledged, and raised a walkie-talkie that connected him to the members of his team scattered among the Iranian masses down Shah Reza Boulevard. ''This is Yakov. Commence the burning.''

The Apaches looked like huge june bugs floating lazily beneath the sun, all black and steel. Over ninety minutes before, the Persian Gulf had given way to Iranian landfall, but Mc-Cracken was resting no easier. He gazed nervously at his watch.

''We haven't made up enough time,'' he said to Johnny Wareagle. ''I figure an hour late minimum, Indian, maybe closer to an hour and a half.''

''The battle will still be there when we arrive, Blainey.''

''You sound pretty certain.''

''Isn't it always?''

The fires spread quickly down Shah Reza Boulevard, chaos growing out of chaos as the frenzied masses grabbed flaming objects and flung them through plate-glass store windows. Smoke rose in a shroud over the center of Tehran as if to cordon it off from the rest of the city and the world. The flames had the pronounced effect of further fueling the mass's rage. Whereas before many had been running without purpose, chanting with hands in the air, now no set of hands was without some sort of weapon. Yakov and his Operation Firestorm team had given out approximately 2,000 firearms beyond the barricades, but it was impossible to tell how many of those possessing them were concentrated here. Reports from other areas of the city indicated heavy exchanges of fire with Hassani's Revolutionary Guard, the latter emerging victorious at every turn. Their casualties were high, but for now the guards seemed not to care, fighting with a passion and heart Yakov and the students had never expected. When Firestorm had been conceived, some had gone as far as to suggest that the guards would actually join the side of the masses. Now nothing could have been further from the truth.

Evira found Yakov searching the sky hopelessly for the Apaches he now believed were not coming.

"They'll be here," she insisted.

"You don't understand. They haven't called and we can't raise them on the established frequency. That means the rules have changed."

"Only because whoever's leading the mission would never break radio silence and alert the Iranians to his approach."

"That wasn't the plan."

"Things may have changed," Evira said, clinging to the hope that McCracken was coming on the Apaches, though clearly she had no reason to. "They'll be here," she persisted. "We've just got to hold out."

"We're going to try," Yakov told her.

In the next instant he had summoned the student leaders to his side. His orders were simple: they were to take to the barricade with their various units and prepare to make their stand here and now. The young Iranians' faces grew red with excitement and fury. Their time had come, and they rushed off to gather their people. The word spread. There were screams of joy, of glee.

How naive, Evira thought to herself. *How foolish . . .*

Wooden crates were pried open and additional weapons distributed and ammo readied amidst the hooting. Evira hung back from it all. She had seen this scene before. Different countries, different causes, but always the same result: futility.

Armed now, the Iranians charged by her to their positions within and atop the huge barricade. She had lost sight of Kourosh again in all the excitement and feared he had wandered off into the streets to be swept away by the masses and lost forever.

Her heart had begun to thud when she caught sight of him arguing up a storm with a man issuing rifles who had refused to give him one. Evira hurried over and dragged him away.

"I want to fight!" he protested. "I want to shoot the bastards!"

"You want to die?" she demanded, words coming with her thoughts. "You've seen what it's like. Is that what you want?"

"I'll kill them first!"

"Not all. You can never get them all," she said, still holding him back.

"I'm not a coward! I want to fight!"

"It won't come to that," she said, trying to sound confident, eyes on the sky as if to make the Apaches appear. "It won't."

But she knew the sureness had left her voice.

Yakov grimly accepted the reports from his spotters scattered throughout Tehran.

"They are using heavy armaments!"

"The barricades are falling!"

"The people are running away!"

"The Revolutionary Guard is massing toward Shah Reza Boulevard!"

The final report was superfluous. Climbing to the top of the barricade, Yakov could see the first of the dark-clad Revolutionary Guardsmen pass onto the smoke-filled street before him. These first waves were set upon by the masses and crushed beneath the fury of fists and sticks. The screams of the anguished and frustrated became even more frenzied. The crowd tasted blood and wanted more.

In reprisal, the next blood spilled was their own. The initial barrages of fire that came from the second wave of guardsmen reached Yakov as soft thuds to his ears. In the huge congregated swell, men and women began to crumble and lurch backward, chests opened and heads spewed bone and brains. The smoke obscured much of the view, but Yakov saw enough. The enraged masses would hold out as long as their ammo and resolve held up, which was only as long as the truth of their plight's hopelessness could remain hidden from them.

More guardsmen charged onto the boulevard from the intersecting side streets. Yakov didn't have to pick up a radio to know that his was now or would very soon be the last standing barricade in the city. He had more than two hundred men to defend it, but the endless waves of Hassani's troops would wear them down, outlast them and blow them to hell in the end. He climbed down from the barricade and found Evira waiting for him.

"I think you and the boy should get out."

"To where?" she came back. "You think anywhere in the city is safe?"

"You're resourceful and he knows the city."

They both looked toward Kourosh, who had given up hoping for a gun and was busy distributing extra ammunition to his more fortunate countrymen who'd been blessed with one.

"What kind of world is it we make for our children, Israeli?" she asked Yakov.

"It was made by our fathers," he returned. "Made in a shape we are helpless to alter. The madmen come and go, always the same causes, the same rhetoric."

"Lies. To themselves, to all, and in the end the people pay."

Boom! Boom! Boom!

The explosions sounding in quick succession seemed to shake the barricade. Yakov nimbly vaulted back to a perch where he could peer out through a break in the structure. The sight sickened him. The Revolutionary Guard was firing rockets and grenades into clusters of the Iranian people still massed before the barricade. Screams raged, the high-pitched wails of women and children rising above the others as the entire city bled with agony. Yakov could not help but tremble as a fresh wave of Hassani's troops fired indiscriminate bursts of machine gun fire into the wounded and dying to silence them. The drab gray-black of the Revolutionary Guard uniform was now the dominant color in the street, blending with the smoke. As the guards launched their attack on the barricade, their charging numbers stepped heedlessly upon the freshly slaughtered bodies that littered the asphalt.

Yakov leaped back down.

"Prepare to fire!" he shouted into cupped hands, and the word was passed through the length of the barricade, thanks in large measure to Kourosh, who ran up and down the lines repeating it in his boyish squeal.

"Prepare to fire!"

The fifteen Apaches zeroed in on Tehran like locusts making for a wheat field. They had sped over Iranian territory much too low to be picked up by radar, and, as expected, the uprising in the capital city had opened the back door for them. Even the midair refueling had left them undetected and, more importantly, had resulted in only a minimal delay.

The pilots and gunners had drilled over and over again to meet the strange conditions of this mission. They were to restrict their targets solely to concentrated positions of Revolutionary Guardsmen and avoid civilian casualties at all costs. Thanks to the TADS system, if selective strikes were ordered, a soldier could be hit by chain gun fire with a civilian standing a yard from him spared. The whole strategy was based on intensifying the chaos and riddling the guards' numbers long enough to give the masses the edge they needed. Their numbers were sufficient to overrun the troops if the troops were divided and cut off from each other. And no machine of war could have been more perfect for that task than the mighty Apache.

"Christ," the pilot of the lead Apache reported to McCracken after checking his radar and noticing the smoky area now coming clearly in view, "the center of the city's lit up like the goddamn Fourth of July. This is gonna get awful hot, sir."

"You get to like the heat after a while."

The plan was for this Apache to break off from the convoy at the earliest possible time and make tracks for the royal palace so Blaine might fulfill his part in the mission. He and Johnny had just donned their Kevlar body armor suits and were already sweating heavily in them.

"How long?" McCracken asked the pilot.

"Three minutes to the battle zone and eight to the royal palace."

Blaine turned to Wareagle. "Well, Indian, it's back to the hellfire."

* * *

The masses in Shah Reza Boulevard began a full-fledged retreat, slowed by the huge and sickening collection of bodies littering the streets. Many were the corpses of soldiers, but far more belonged to the people. The guardsmen continued their steady advance on the barricade, their fire unrestrained and wild. Anything that moved was shot. Meanwhile, the initial bursts and volleys fired from the barricade met with great success. Soldiers seemed to be taken wholly by surprise, hordes of them dropping in their tracks as more rushed forward.

Evira watched it for a time and could barely keep down the contents of her stomach. She had never seen such carnage, and could liken it only to a feeding frenzy by sharks.

A woman holding a child by the hand was shot in the back. The child leaned over her and was shot twice.

Teenagers hurling stones were cut down en masse by soldiers, who were then caught in a hail of 50-caliber machine gun fire coming from the top of the barricade.

"You'd better take this," Yakov called to her, tossing an M-16 her way. "They'll be on us in seconds."

Kourosh saw the rifle in her hands and rushed over with a trio of spare clips.

"So we fight on the same side, Israeli," Evira said to Yakov.

"You can still get out," he returned.

"Help is coming."

He shook her off, and her statement this time was not followed by a hopeful sweep of the air with her eyes.

The boulevard before them was empty now of all but the bodies and charging guardsmen, close enough for the enemy to use their own grenades and bazookas.

"Down!" Evira screamed, and lunged from the position she had taken amidst the barricade to tackle Kourosh to safety before the first bursts made impact.

The impregnable barricade blew inward in several areas like a dam springing leaks. More heavy fire resounded against it with deadly thuds while waves of Hassani's troops charged forward. They rushed into the unbroken fury of the bullets pouring out from cracks in the huge pile of debris, willing to sacrifice themselves if the next wave could get closer.

Yakov's strategy here had been brilliant, for he had made sure to hold back firing of their heaviest arms until it was certain that the soldiers had passed the point of no return. He ran up and down the beleaguered barricade encouraging the defenders and shouting orders to commence with their small artillery fire. Almost immediately, Shah Reza Boulevard exploded in huge chunks as bodies were blown apart, more corpses added to the mounting pile. The firing from both sides was nonstop, its appetite insatiable. The battle became one of position versus numbers, and there was no doubt numbers were going to win out as the screams multiplied from all levels of the barricade. The dead plunged off; the wounded did their best to climb down. All those who could hold guns continued to do so.

Those within the barricade were making a truly remarkable stand. But the waves of Revolutionary Guardsmen were endless, blurring out the asphalt now. And suddenly the familiar sound of helicopters split the morning air.

"The Apaches!" Evira sang out from her perch near Yakov on a platform a third of the way up the barricade.

"No," he returned flatly, gazing ahead. "Look."

"Oh God," she muttered. "Oh God . . ."

"I got blips dead ahead," the lead Apache pilot told McCracken.

"You got a reading?"

"Look like Iranian gunships to me. The old Hueys from Nam we sold them."

"Shoot 'em out of the fuckin' sky, son."

"Not in range yet, Dad."

"Then get us there! Fast!"

Yakov was among the first wave of those within and on the barricade who fell to the barrage blistered down from the Huey gunship as it swept overhead. A few atop the debris turned upward and bravely fired on it, only to be sliced apart by the machine gunners spewing bullets out both sides. Evira managed to find cover during the first pass and slid back outward as a second gunship came in for its attack run.

"Not yet, you bastards!" she raged. "Not yet!"

A surface-to-air rocket launcher lay just before her. She

grabbed for it, strapped it round her shoulder, and climbed to the first platform of the barricade. The second gunship was coming fast as the first swung back around and made tracks in its wake. Orange began to spit from the machine gun bores of the now lead Huey as it crossed over the head of the barricade. Evira had time only to steady herself and raise the launcher to her shoulder before the chopper's fire pinpointed her. She fired without time to properly aim, fired up and to the right in the desperate hope the heat-seeking missile would launch close enough to lock on. There was a *whomp!* and the Huey's tail exploded, pitching it into a swirling dive.

But there was no time to celebrate. The second Huey roared overhead and she had no second rocket to fire its way. She saw a launcher on the platform to her left and leaped for it just as the orange flashes tore into her. She felt a series of kicks to her ribs and chest and then she was falling, tumbling, still searching for something to grab onto.

Evira felt no pain and maintained firm hold on her vision long enough to record the impossible sight of the second Huey being blown out of the sky as it hovered directly over the barricade. She tried to turn toward what she knew must be the Apaches, but her head wouldn't move and neither could the rest of her.

"Got him, sir!" The pilot beamed exuberantly after his Hellfire missile impacted squarely in the Huey's side.

"There's more where that came from."

"Can't wait to meet them."

"Just step on the gas," Blaine said, reaching for his binoculars with the barricade a mere ten seconds away.

The barricade was a shambles tumbling over upon itself. Well over a hundred dead and dying lay piled in heaps, some crawling back to their posts with weapons in hand and trails of blood left behind them. Those the battle had thus far spared clung to whatever positions they could forge out of the remnants of their fallen fortress, firing upon the onrushing soldiers until their bullets ran out or a stray shot found them.

Kourosh had been trembling in shock behind a fallen section of the barricade when Evira had tumbled. He screamed her name and rushed to her side as the smoke and bullets surged by him.

Blood had splashed on the rags he wore for clothes, and its
coppery scent was thick in his nostrils even before he reached
Evira. Whether she was alive or dead he could not tell. He only
knew that she was bleeding very badly. He spoke her name
softly and stroked her hair, then wailed again.

The resistance within the barricade was breaking down due
to the loss of leadership and manpower. The next wave of soldiers was closing, coming fast through the smoke. Catching a
glimpse of them, Kourosh grabbed the closest rifle he could find
and burst through a jagged hole in the crumbling barricade before him.

Blaine tore the binoculars from his neck, not believing what
they had shown him as the Apache had passed over the remnants
of the barricade.

"Circle back," he ordered the pilot. "The Indian and I are
making an unscheduled stop here."

"Say again, sir."

"You heard me."

"I have no orders to—"

"I don't give a shit, son. You do what I say or I'll drop you
into that corpse field and drive this thing myself."

"What about the others?"

"Order ten of them to proceed with Operation Firestorm as
planned. Have three or four others cut off the far end of this
street from the rest of the world. You maneuver around above
us and use your chain gun to help cut down anything in uniform."

"Whatever you say, sir. But it's your funeral," the pilot
warned, bringing the agile Apache around.

"Save your flowers." He turned to Wareagle while he
strapped the Vulcan minigun over his shoulder and attached its
harness to his gunbelt. The Kevlar bodysuit he'd just donned
was already baking him, the sweat clammy on his flesh. "Let's
call ourselves a taxi, Indian."

The buffer between the waves of Revolutionary Guardsmen
and the barricade was shrinking rapidly to nothing. There were

simply too few defenders left to do the job adequately, and many of those that remained lacked the strength to fire, or even reload.

Blood rushed down Yakov's face from his spill off the barricade. He had managed to climb back up to a fortified position, firing out with a mere pistol. Two shells were left when a single bullet split his skull and killed him. Of the Iranian leaders, only Rashid remained, untouched in his roving position, still giving orders up and down the lines to fewer and fewer fighters.

Kourosh hadn't fired his rifle when he emerged from the barricade. Unexpected terror had kept him still and hunched, and for a few moments that saved his life. Then a band of soldiers spotted his quivering form, saw the gun in his hands, and prepared to fire. The boy cringed and closed his eyes to the certainty of his own death. Instead of gunfire, though, he heard a powerful metallic clanging and felt himself being shoved backward against the remnants of the barricade.

McCracken and Wareagle had slid down from the specially adapted lead Apache on a pair of drop lines just seconds before, under cover from the attack ship's 30-millimeter chain gun. Blaine had glimpsed the fallen Evira through his binoculars and clung to the hope she was still alive. She was his only chance of ever seeing Matthew again, and he found that well worth facing off against a thousand soldiers charging headlong up the street.

He and Johnny allotted only one hand to guide their slide down, the other already steadying their Vulcans to assure they wouldn't be cut down upon landing by the soldiers nearest. Blaine's landing placed him between a boy wielding a gun almost as big as he was and a group of charging guardsmen. He was able to shove the boy backward behind the shield formed by his body without missing a beat on the Vulcan. It felt surprisingly light and maneuverable, and after a few seconds he forgot about the weight altogether.

McCracken had never known such a battle, such a feeling. Virtually none of the onrushing swarm of guardsmen had noticed his drop. From a distance it had been camouflaged by the black smoke and soot filling the air. The soldiers must have thought the Apache was one of theirs until it opened fire on them. Furthermore, their attention was too focused on the remnants of the barricade and its defenders to notice anything else. They charged forward in an unstoppable wave. He and Johnny had landed within ten yards of one another and were firing in the controlled bursts Gunny Tom Beeks had advised. Bodies didn't just fall in the paths blazed by the Vulcans' 20-millimeter shells and the 30-millimeter rounds coming from the Apache; they rocketed backward, limbs blown off or huge cavities left where chests had been. Death came fast enough to leave the guardsmen without even an expression of shock or pain, just an open, glazed stare as body piled atop body.

The Vulcans continued to clang metallically, hell on the ears, with the large shells speeding from their six rotating barrels. As Blaine and Johnny swept the area before them, wave after wave of dark-clad soldiers fell to their onslaught. Those trying to circle for better position were cut down by the Apache's gunner hovering above, who made all those not directly in the Vulcans' line of fire his targets.

Nonetheless, Blaine and Johnny's assault would have been finished hundreds of rounds before if not for the Kevlar. Mc-Cracken felt a fourth bullet and then a fifth smack his bodysuit, yet with the extra balance weight supplied by the minigun, he barely gave any ground. Three of the Apaches, meanwhile, had launched an all-out attack on the large concentration of guardsmen further down the boulevard. The result, just as he had hoped, was to splinter Hassani's marauding troops and catch those who remained in a crossfire between the attack ships on one side and the Vulcans and the lingering Apache on the other.

The miniguns continued to spit their metallic fire. The ceaseless intensity of the battle was the only thing that saved Mc-Cracken from being sickened by the incredible bloodshed before him. He had seen battle a hundred times before, but never anything like this. The bodies were two, even three deep in spots, and the smell of blood and death raked his mind. The stifling heat inside his body armor proved a worthy distraction, seeming to grow hotter with each bullet the Kevlar stopped.

He no longer felt the Vulcan as it pulsed in his hand, the heat generated by its rotating cylinder blowing back into his face. The reduced pounding to his back told him well over half his ammo was exhausted, more than five-hundred rounds, and who knew how many kills to count for that. He continued to fire for a time after there was no real target left, the barricade behind him secured again by the surviving troops. At last Wareagle came to his side and pried his finger away from the trigger. The multi-barreled cylinder spun to a halt. All of the Apaches but the one hovering above them had roared to their assigned runs throughout the city. Johnny rotated his eyes and the Vulcan with deadly awareness, as Blaine turned and followed the boy whose life he had just saved through one of the many breaks in the barricade's structure. The boy made straight for Evira who was lying wounded on the street.

Her eyes were open but dim.

"Better late than never," she managed when her eyes found McCracken.

"You blackmailed the right guy."

She coughed painfully and writhed back toward unconsciousness. Blaine looked to Wareagle, who by then was kneeling by her side.

"Indian?"

"Deep wounds, Blainey, but no vital organs touched. She'll live if medical attention is prompt."

"What are you doing here?" Evira asked, as if suddenly realizing his presence.

"I came to rescue a damsel in distress, of course."

"There's . . . more."

"Okay, I've got an appointment beyond the barricades at the royal palace," Blaine relented. "Which I happen to be late for."

"Hassani?"

"Long story. The Indian's calling our taxi down to get you the hell out of here." He glanced at the boy. "I assume the pup here goes along for the ride."

Evira nodded and found strength to reach up and grasp Blaine at the elbow. Her stare was intense through all her pain, as she fought to remain conscious.

"Why did you come?" she demanded.

"You up to hearing it now?"

Another nod. "Tell me."

Blaine obliged and Evira felt the shock of his revelation numb her along with the pain as the Apache lowered overhead with a stretcher dangling from its underside.

"What can you tell me about the rest of the city?" Blaine asked the Apache pilot while the gunner who doubled as a paramedic tended to Evira.

"Thanks to the Apaches, most of it's a fucking fire zone," he reported. "We've cut the soldiers off from their strongholds and splintered them. As planned. The people are everywhere. Looks like the revolution's working."

"And the palace?"

"The Revolutionary Guard has pulled back to make a last stand there. Best estimates say they can hold it for an hour, ninety minutes at the outside." The pilot paused. "Gonna be tough for the two of you to get inside."

"You just get us there and we'll worry about the rest."

CHAPTER 31

JOHNNY AND BLAINE MOVED TO THE BACK OF THE APACHE where they stripped off the stifling body armor that had saved their lives. McCracken resisted the temptation to count the impressions made by what surely would have been mortal wounds and simply discarded the suit atop the Vulcan miniguns in the corner. What he was just starting to consider was the fact that he and Wareagle had gone the limit with equipment that had been meant to get them into the palace. Without the Vulcans and Kevlar body armor, gaining access was going to be difficult indeed.

"There's a tunnel," a drugged Evira rasped after overhearing discussion of their dilemma.

"What tunnel?" Blaine asked as he moved back toward her.

But her eyes closed and unconsciousness claimed her before she could answer.

"Well, I guess that pretty much determines we take a more direct route, Indian. 'Less, of course, your spirits or somebody else can fill us in on this tunnel."

"How about me?" the boy Kourosh said from the corner.

With the Apache pilot acting on Kourosh's instructions, Blaine quickly transferred some of the supplies from his canvas duffel into a shoulder bag. Gazing out, McCracken could see the work accomplished by the rest of the Apaches. They had divided the

317

city into grids and had proceeded to strafe the major pockets of
guard positions. Most were roaming at present, flying low to
the street to rely more on their chain guns and Folding-Fin Aerial Rockets. The Hellfire missiles were used only sporadically
now that the guardsmen had dispersed into smaller groups and
seemed most concerned with finding cover rather than retaliat-
ing. Besides the regiment standing steadfastly round the royal
palace, no stronghold remained. The people were winning.

Blaine's Apache streaked through the smoke-choked sky. At
last the palace came into view and he found himself blessing his
luck that the masses surging into the area had not yet overrun
it, for this would have rendered the rest of his plan impossible.
The pilot's estimates were probably off, though. It was doubtful
the palace guard would be able to hold their lines for the hour
he had estimated.

The Apache hovered over the side street Kourosh had indicated and once again the drop lines were lowered. McCracken
almost had to have the copilot restrain the boy to keep him from
following, making him think of Matthew. Evira had started to
mention something about his whereabouts but Blaine had cut
her off. He didn't want to hear a thing about Matthew until his
mission was completed. If he survived the raid on the palace,
his reward would be the boy's location. If he didn't, Johnny
Wareagle would take over.

"Meet us on the roof in forty minutes," was Blaine's final
instruction to the pilot.

"I'll be there."

McCracken and Wareagle had both opted for Uzis this time,
weapons they hoped they wouldn't need, thanks to their covert
entry into the palace. The street they dropped into was strangely
deserted, a kind of temporary oasis in the desert of battle they
were a part of. It was a small street with enough buildings to
hide their drop from all who might have been following the
Apache's path. McCracken made sure his shoulder sack and its
contents were securely in place and then rushed toward the tunnel entrance's position as Kourosh had described it.

The wails and screams of the approaching masses were growing louder by the second and he had begun to fear they might

storm the street before the two of them could climb down. But they located the entrance easily and Johnny lifted the grating up and placed it back into position as soon as they were both safely inside. The Indian joined Blaine at the foot of the ladder and together they started down the tunnel, flashlights illuminating their way toward the royal palace and General Amir Hassani.

"How are we to get out of here?" the Syrian delegate demanded of Hassani, moving from the library window that showed the last complement of guardsmen preparing to make their stand against the onrushing masses.

"There is a way prepared," Hassani replied calmly. "I assure you."

"It is difficult to accept the assurances of a man whose government is toppling," shot out the delegate from Libya.

"Revolution is good for the soul at the proper intervals," Hassani told the seven of them. "It cleanses a nation's system and reveals the traitors in our ranks."

"But you're *losing*!" the man from Jordan blared. "Your 'people' will be upon us in no time."

"The losing is a mere illusion, easily corrected in barely any time at all. Besides, what does it matter? What do any of our countries or movements matter individually so long as we must all live in fear of a small and brutal neighbor? It will all change after tomorrow. You'll see. That's why you are here."

"You should have provided the details of your secret weapon before," the delegate from the PLO chastised. "Instead you called us here at the risk of our own lives, knowing full well your nation was crumbling."

"We've been through this before," Hassani returned. "It is all behind us while this, my friends, is what lies ahead."

Hassani moved to the table that had been set up in the center of the circle the seven men formed. Placed atop it were seven identical leather cases. The general opened one of them to allow his delegates to see the ten eight-ounce glass vials contained inside. A few shifted about to better their views. Others just sat there stupefied.

"You mean *this* is your secret weapon?" one of them blurted incredulously.

Hassani smiled like a teacher in front of his class. "Not quite. Two days from now I will release a deadly virus over Israel— the ultimate creation of chemical warfare. *That* is the secret weapon I've held back for this long." He pointed toward the table. "You see, a leak within our ranks might have allowed Israel to come up with a version of this: a vaccine that will render your people immune from the virus once it is released into the air. Within each of these cases are your allotments of that vaccine. Make sure the contents of these vials are dropped into the various water-treatment facilities of your respective countries and within twenty-four hours, ninety percent of your populations will be protected from what will destroy Israel in a similar period."

"What of the other ten?"

"Sacrifices to a much higher cause. Consider those who the vaccine does not reach to be casualties of a war we alone can win now."

"And what if we become casualties ourselves before leaving the confines of your . . . country?" the representative from Saudi Arabia demanded.

"You won't. The escape route is all prepared. You have nothing to fear." Before the Saudi could protest he added, "You have provided your subordinates with contact arrangements as I outlined in the event you do not return. If it becomes necessary to utilize them, additional vials will be made available from backup points."

Hassani waited to see if there was further protest. When none arose, he continued.

"Now, we have already gone over the precise details and agenda. If there are no questions, the . . ."

". . . *time has come for you to take your leave in pursuit of our destiny. My troops will buy you the time you need. I will summon your escort to take you to the escape tunnel. . . .*"

There was more, but McCracken focused all his attention on opening the latch for the electronic dumbwaiter that had allowed him to reach the second floor library unnoticed. He had found the controls for it in the kitchen, along with the convenient button marked "Library." Isser had informed him of the meetings that had taken place there over the last few weeks and Blaine knew that's where Hassani would choose to play his final card. Wareagle had chosen a more direct route through the palace itself, the two of them serving as insurance for one another. One of them had to reach Hassani. The madness had to be stopped here and now, buried in the rubble of the royal palace.

Hidden in the dumbwaiter, McCracken began to make out the voices as he rose toward the library. He couldn't capture the context of the heated conversation, though, until the dumbwaiter slid to a halt before its slot in the wall. None of it surprised him. The whole scenario was almost as he expected it would be. He managed to get the latch freed and went to work on the slot in the wall. He pried his fingers about to find the handhold needed to slide it open to the library beyond. He had decided to wait until the delegates had gone before making his move. The proper finish for this was just him and Hassani.

"From the escape tunnel," the voice of the general droned on, *"escorts will be waiting for you in the street. They are disguised as beggars and will lead you safely to the airstrip. Clothes for you to blend with the chaos are waiting in the basement. Go with Allah, my friends. Go forth to achieve our destiny."*

In the dumbwaiter, McCracken heard feet shuffling, farewells exchanged, and then the heavy door being opened and closed. A single pair of feet, belonging surely to Hassani, padded across the lavish carpet toward what McCracken guessed would be the window where he could survey the last stand made by the Revolutionary Guard. The time had come.

The dumbwaiter opened into the room's large alcove, dominated by books that provided further cover. Blaine slid the freed wall cover up and could see nothing before him other than dark, jammed-full bookcases running from wall to wall, with narrow aisles between and down the middle of them. The alcove was perhaps forty feet square, the bookcases taking up virtually all of that.

With the quick silence of a big jungle cat, McCracken slid out to the floor, kneeling with his pistol in hand since the cumbersome Uzi had been left behind in the basement. He glided forward, using the matched Oriental runners to hide his footsteps. He could tell exactly where the window was from the way

the rays of sunshine streamed through. And there was a shadow,
Hassani's shadow.

He reached the edge of the forwardmost bookshelf and spun
round it in combat position ready to fire.

"Don't move!" he screamed.

And found himself facing off against a black marble bust of
the Ayahtollah Khomeini that had been placed to cast just the
shadow it had. Before he could turn, another voice echoed
through the huge library hall.

"Drop your gun, Mr. McCracken," Hassani ordered.

Blaine obliged and then drew his hands into the air.

"Now turn around. Slowly. And keep your feet spread as
well."

Again McCracken obeyed and found himself standing fifteen
feet from General Amir Hassani who was holding a submachine
gun.

"You have been quite a nuisance, Mr. McCracken, I must
say."

"We meet at last, General," Blaine returned icily. "Or should
I say we meet again . . . Yosef Rasin."

The uniformed figure's reaction was shock first and then
hearty laughter. His free hand edged to his face and tugged a
good portion of his beard away to reveal a much tighter growth
and lighter shade of hair beneath it. A few more pulls and pinches
on the theatrical makeup and the face shown was unmistakably
that of Yosef Rasin.

"My regrets that you were not named minister of defense,"
Blaine taunted.

"I suppose I have you to blame for that, Mr. McCracken.
But don't fret. There'll be plenty of other ceremonies I'll be
attending before long."

"Funerals, Rasin, all of them your doing."

"Hardly. I'm going to be a hero. The people of Israel will
rally to me once the truth of what I've done becomes obvious."

"Millions of deaths?"

"Perhaps."

"You'll be likened to Hitler, not Moses."

Rasin stood there and tried very hard to show no emotion.

McCracken had to keep the madman distracted any way he could. While the two had been talking he had begun stealthily to close the distance between them. He'd already made up one yard, and with one more covered he'd almost be within lunging distance. If he could only keep the exchange going a little longer . . .

"Lace," Rasin called toward the door.

The double doors parted and the biggest woman McCracken had ever seen entered. A half foot over six feet at least. She was decked out in black leather beneath a pale face and stubbly blond hairdo.

"You!" Blaine exclaimed, recognizing her from Boston and Masada, realizing in that same instant this was the woman who had killed John Neville, Henri Dejourner, and Hiroshi, and kidnapped Matthew.

Lace's reaction to him was to stand to the rear and right of Rasin and fold her arms. A variety of weapons worn through her belt clanged together for an instant after she stopped moving. Blaine recognized one of them as a scimitar.

Hiroshi had been killed by just such a blade.

"You bitch," McCracken muttered under his breath.

The huge woman grinned at him.

"There were two of you, weren't there?" Blaine spit at her. "What's the matter, the other one getting it from someone else on the side?"

Lace's smile grew taut. The leather jacket worn over her midsection was tight enough to reveal long, hard bands of muscle bred from years of bodybuilding. Rasin might be a slouch, but this woman was anything but. McCracken was going to have to rethink his strategy, especially since the bruises inflicted by bullets pounding the Kevlar body armor at the barricade promised to steal some of his strength and quickness.

Go ahead, make your move, Lace's eyes told him, but Blaine fought to keep his hate for her down. Improperly channeled, hate could make you respond the wrong way at the wrong time. Stick to the subject, he urged himself, stick to the subject!

"How'd you do it, Rasin?" he asked. "How'd you pull off the greatest hoax in history since Elvis got himself embalmed just to fool his fans?"

"It was quite simple, really. The real Hassani contacted my

people in search of asylum in the closing days of the lost war effort. Figured he might as well sample the good life now that his country was falling, and my hatred for Arabs had him thinking he had plenty to trade in return.''

''And he did, didn't he? Far more than he ever suspected.''

''He told me everything I needed to know to take his place. Days, weeks of interrogation. Early on, the plot was just a fantasy, but the more I listened the more I started to believe with the proper preparations it could work. The military coup in the wake of Khomeini's death became an incredible stroke of fortune. When the Revolutionary Guard called to Hassani to return from exile, it was I who appeared.'' His face glowed with triumph. ''Imagine having Hassani contact me barely a month after Eisenstadt came to me about Gamma.''

''You saw the connection immediately, of course,'' Blaine said, but his eyes lingered on Lace, who was still standing there, huge and menacing.

''Certainly. Gamma was indeed a tremendous find, but to accomplish my true goal of leading the next generation of Israel, I needed a rationale to employ it.''

''You wanted to be a hero, so you worked up a means to make yourself one.''

''If you choose to put it that way, yes. Hassani and I were the same height and build. A professional makeup artist did the rest. Once I went into self-imposed exile four months ago, the impersonation was simple. Before then, and often even since, a double was utilized. The woman who drew you into this killed him.'' He laughed again. ''I might say she was quite shocked when I apprehended her at the airport on the verge of her escape. She didn't recognize me. I didn't realize how effective my disguise truly was until I interrogated her.''

''But it all worked out, didn't it? You had the militants of the Arab world eating out of your hand and begging for seconds. Must've been a hell of an acting job.''

''It was passion, McCracken, something a man like you should appreciate even if no one else can. I loathed them all so much. They could see the fire in my eyes and mistook it—I made them mistake it—for passion for 'their' cause. I've lived most of my life coming to terms with who these people are, what makes them tick. Their entire lives are fueled by dreams of destruction. Life to them *is* death. They have no appreciation for simple pleasures and absolutely no desire ever to live in peace. Believe me when I tell you that. There will never be a negotiated settlement, and if there is they would subvert and destroy it. Barbarianism has been their way of life, of death, for five thousand years. That won't change.''

''So the unified 'invasion' ends up helping you on two fronts. First it provides the reason for the Israeli government to embrace you and your weapon. And second it gives you the means to get Gamma released in all the countries at the same time through those vials you gave your 'delegates.' '' Blaine took a deep breath before continuing. ''You who claim to cherish life so much, how could you go through with this knowing what Bechman's findings showed and what stopped the Americans from utilizing Gamma when they had the opportunity?''

''Go through with it?'' Rasin asked, quite shocked. ''My dear, Mr. McCracken, that is precisely what I'm hoping for.''

''The end of humanity?''

''Hardly. Other countries, countries we choose, can be provided with the vaccine too . . . if they are willing to pay a premium, of course.''

''This isn't about running Israel, it's about running the world.''

''*Israel* will be running the world, with me as its leader,'' Rasin qualified. ''And don't we have—''

Rasin stopped when Lace turned suddenly toward the door.

''There's someone in the corridor coming this way,'' she told him.

''Tilly perhaps, coming back from escorting our friends to the tunnel.''

''No. Someone . . . bigger.''

''Check it out.'' When she seemed reluctant to leave he added, ''I'll finish with Mr. McCracken myself.''

Johnny Wareagle had lost count of how many guards he had encountered en route to the voices. It hadn't been necessary to kill any of them, although considering the fate that awaited them once the enraged masses beyond brought their fight within these walls, that fate might have been more merciful by comparison.

He had discarded the Uzis early into his stalk because of the noise they made clacking against each other on his back, but he was hardly weaponless. He had broken off the business end of a thick broom on the second floor, which left him with a shaft handle formed of olive wood nearly five feet long and a weighty inch in diameter. Not the finest staff he had ever wielded, but it would more than do and already had.

Rounding the hallway on the third floor, Wareagle could hear the voices clearly. One of them was McCracken's, and one was unfamiliar. Beyond the sound of the voices, however, Wareagle sensed an evil presence both cold and ominous, as deadly as any he had ever felt before. He grasped the staff tighter and continued on.

"And assuming Bechman was right in his conclusions and your . . . plan works as you hope," McCracken probed, "what then?"

"Civilization rebuilds, virtually from scratch, with proper guidance this time. So long the object of scorn, persecution, and holocaust, the Jew will be in a position to control all. A world without Arabs, Nazis, and with no one to replace them."

"Not quite," McCracken followed, his meaning obvious. "I'll give you credit for this much, Rasin. I've met up with a lot of madmen in my time, but your aims seem more genuine than any of the others. A shame they won't be realized."

"Don't be childish. Even you cannot change the inevitable now." Yet the expression on Blaine's face indicated assurance and determination. Rasin was suddenly unnerved. "The clothes you're wearing, I know those clothes. . . ."

"These? Happened to pick them up at the end of a certain tunnel the Indian and I used to get in here. Figured they had been left there for a number of Arab gentlemen to aid in their escape from the area."

"No! You're bluffing!"

Blaine showed the miniature detonator he had pulled from his pocket thirty seconds before. "I figure they'll be well into the tunnel by now. Don't worry, I was sure to place my plastic explosives at key structural stress points. Assure an even and fair collapse that way.''

''You can't press it! *You can't!*''

''Drop your gun, Rasin.''

''No! . . . Lace, stop him!''

The leather-clad woman giant lunged back through the double doors at the same time Blaine turned toward them. The gun he had been forced to discard was only a yard away. He dropped for it as she whirled a chain from her belt in his direction.

It can't be on target. She had no time to aim. . . .

Blaine looked away from the blur, hand going for the pistol. The ease of reaching it surprised him, for he didn't realize that Lace's intended target was his other hand, the one holding the detonator. He felt the gnarled edges of the link dig into his wrist, powerless to maintain his grasp of the detonator against the pain. It flew outward, and Blaine felt his wrist explode in fiery agony as he was yanked away. He had the pistol briefly, but the vicious thrust of Lace's motion stripped it from him.

Stunned, McCracken awaited certain death as he watched Rasin bring the machine gun up to fire. Suddenly a second huge shape charged through the open double doors. Johnny Wareagle's staff preceded him and smacked hard into Rasin's ribs, which caused his first burst of fire to stitch a jagged design in the far wall.

Instantly Lace released her grip on the chain digging into McCracken and sped inside the second strike, which Wareagle had aimed for her. The miss carried Johnny sufficiently off balance for the huge woman to pound a shoulder into him with force sufficient to propel both of them through the door into the corridor.

Blaine saw Rasin staggering, machine gun dangling from the shoulder strap supporting it. He knew the madman was struggling to right it on him again and just as fast made the decision to go for the detonator and not the pistol. He couldn't take a chance that the Arab delegates carrying the Gamma vials would make it out of the tunnel while he and Rasin were fighting. He dove headlong and slid off the carpet onto an exposed portion of the hardwood floor to where the detonator had come to a rest. His outstretched hand just managed to find the red button when

Rasin's desperate burst coughed fragments of wood everywhere around him. He was rolling to avoid the next burst when the floor in the hall began to shake, the tunnel underlying the royal palace caving in on itself under the force of the blasts. The explosion blew out a number of windows in the library, turning the glass into flying shards that fell over a prostrate McCracken and then slid harmlessly to the floor.

"Ahhhhhhhhhhhhhhhhhh!"

Rasin's scream barely preceded the *rat-tat-tat* of his machine gun fire aimed at the downed figure of McCracken. But Blaine was already in motion away from it, rolling over the shattered glass that had coated him toward the cover promised by the long shelves of books.

Wareagle still felt the battle was his to win. In close, the advantage of his staff was negated, but there was strength to consider at this proximity, and the woman's was no match for his. Strangely, the thought that he was battling a woman never crossed his mind. His feelings revealed to him a spirit as black on the inside as her leather garb was on the outside.

Johnny felt his back smash up against the wall and drove his knee hard into the rippling muscles of the woman's abdomen. The move drove her from him and started to double her over; the Indian's next intention was to dip behind and loop the staff round her throat to crush it.

He saw the scimitar sweep up at him only after he had committed himself to the move. A heavy sword with a sharply angled edge, it could be wielded accurately only by the strongest of warriors. He managed to backpedal at the last moment, sliding enough to the side to allow him to block the sword with his staff. The heavy blade dug into the wood but couldn't cut all the way through.

Lace was quick to pull it free and send the scimitar at him a second time in roundhouse fashion. But Wareagle anticipated the move perfectly and countered by darting to the innermost point of the strike. This allowed him to accept the blow at its weakest with the lower end of the staff while he crashed its upper end downward against the woman's face.

Lace wailed in agony, her cheekbone shattered. Wareagle

went for the finish, a thrust to the throat while she was dazed.
But Lace managed to duck under the move and used a sweep
kick to take out Johnny's left knee. He went down, maintaining
the presence of mind to keep his grip on the staff, so when she
charged at him, snarling, wielding the scimitar in a downward
blow, he was ready.

He jammed the staff up to meet the blow and felt his elbows
lock tight an instant before the clash came. This time the wood
split on impact, leaving Johnny with a segment in either hand.
Lace wasted no time and swung the scimitar round again.

If he had tried to regain his feet, death would have been the
inevitable result. But Johnny did the last thing expected of him
by remaining on his knees and actually closing *into* the blow
while he jammed the more jagged piece of the staff hard against
the woman's blade-wielding wrist.

Lace screamed again, the sound still piercing Johnny's ears
when he slid behind her and lashed the hard wood into her
kidney through the padding of her leather jacket. Impact separated him from the more brittle portions of the staff, and he
succeeded in smashing the woman's already-damaged face
straight into the wall. She spun around with the left side of her
mouth curling up from the bulging swell of her broken cheek.
Her leather pants were tight enough to let Johnny see the rippling
tension in her leg muscles as she came forward, stalking him,
clip-clopping on her boots and waving the scimitar through the
air.

It was instantly clear to Wareagle that those high-heeled boots
were anything but ideal for rapid motions, and he seized this for
his next strategy. She came at him when he expected her to—as
he was climbing back to his feet. She came at him with the left
side of her face swollen twice the size of her right.

Johnny stopped rising, went down all the way to the floor,
and swept the staff half he still held back at her as she passed.
The blow broke the heel off her right boot. But Lace didn't
realize it until she planted to steady her next swing. With her
heel gone, her leg buckled. She went down and Wareagle spun
over her, brandishing the jagged staff half aloft, making ready
to plunge it into her.

The second shape lunged atop him from behind just as he

started his motion. A scream punctured his ears and he felt himself going down, the weight of another, smaller woman enough to strip his precarious balance away. He struggled to pry her off while before him Lace had risen to her knees, almost to her feet, scimitar in hand, readying to come for him.

"I'll kill you, McCracken! I'll kill you!" Rasin raged, and Blaine felt the machine gun fire skid close to him as he sped between the first and second book-lined aisles.

The bullets followed him as far as the end of the row when he rounded the shelves and pressed himself against the books in the next aisle. Instantly, more rapid fire spit books from their places around him, pages torn from bindings and set to flutter free. McCracken went down but kept moving, propelling himself on his elbows. Another burst fired just over him showered Blaine with more book fragments. Rasin spun round one end of the book-lined aisle just when Blaine climbed back to his feet at the other. Again he was moving amidst the books, varying his path and target while Rasin's bullets splintered the shelf into fragments and scattered classics everywhere.

McCracken heard Rasin jam a fresh clip home an instant before another burst covered him with books jetting out under the bullets' force. He pinned down Rasin's position and steadied himself. He had to put some distance between the fanatic and himself and he had to do it fast, if he hoped to emerge from this alive.

Blaine crept to the end of the aisle and pinned his shoulders up against the wood. Total camouflage this way. Rasin wouldn't see a thing when he swung into the last aisle before the wall, and by then it would be too late.

Now!

McCracken swung hard to the right and bolted for the third aisle down. With Rasin's gunfire struggling to right itself, he gathered momentum and slammed his right shoulder into the shelf of books directly before him. That shelf toppled into the next under the force of the collision, creating a domino effect that sent books and wood crashing backward. McCracken thought he heard a scream as Rasin was buried by the debris, and then there was nothing.

* * *

With the smaller woman still yanking on his throat while holding on to his shoulders, and the big one fighting to regain her feet, Johnny Wareagle seized the only move left to him. He jammed the jagged edge of the staff piece he still held back toward where he judged the smaller one's throat to be. He closed his eyes for an instant and pictured it perfectly. The sharp wood parted the soft flesh and cartilage beneath the small woman's Adam's apple and sprayed him with blood. Her hands flailed from their grasp to stem the flow of the life pouring from her. It still took all his strength to toss her writhing body from him.

By then, though, the huge woman had regained her feet with a scream of incredible rage born of watching her lover die. In the flash of an instant, he found the scimitar rising in her hand and then dipping into a straight downward motion as she lunged for him. Johnny started his arm upward into the strike, no choice but to sacrifice a limb and hope he could fight down the shock long enough to win.

He felt the calm resignation flow through him a blink before a trio of deafening roars split his already-seared eardrums. Directly over him, Lace spasmed in her tracks, eyes bulging. She was still trying to force the scimitar down at him weakly when a fourth shot rocked her head forward. Blood exploded from her mouth as fragments of skull and brains coated the ceiling and walls.

She fell straight over, legs thrashing in death, at Johnny's feet to reveal Blaine McCracken kneeling in a combat crouch a dozen feet away with smoking pistol still clutched in his hand.

"Nice for me to be able to save your life for a change, Indian," he said, rising.

McCracken lowered an arm to help Wareagle up, but his eyes stayed on Lace and the three scarlet holes stitched down her back.

"That was for Hiroshi, you bitch."

After digging Rasin's unconscious body out from the rubble of the broken shelves and fallen books, they climbed to the palace's top floor and reached the roof through a skylight. Wareagle held Rasin while Blaine waved frantically for the hovering

Apache to sweep down and pick them up. Around the outer wall of the royal palace, the Iranian masses had taken the battle to the last stronghold of Guardsmen. Blaine heard the gunshots, the screams, the wails of both fervor and pain, and found himself looking away. This portion of the palace roof was flat, and with no wind to impede him the Apache pilot was able to bring his ship to a point where his landing pods were only a yard from touchdown.

"Lower!" Blaine ordered upward, as he started to push Rasin's unconscious frame ahead of him into the attack ship.

He never heard the gunshot, felt only the thud of impact as Rasin's body smacked against him, the back of the fanatic's head blown totally away. The kill shot was much too precise to be random, the mark of a top grade sharpshooter.

"You bastards," Blaine muttered, turning away from the Apache. *"You fucking bastards!"*

Wareagle grasped Blaine at the shoulders and shoved him upward.

"Now, Blainey! We must go now!"

The corpse of Yosef Rasin slid from his grasp and McCracken finished the climb into the Apache on his own.

"Hell of a shot for an Iranian," the pilot noted somberly, lifting the Apache upward.

"It wasn't an Iranian."

"Huh?"

"Just take us up, son, and blow the shit out of this place."

"The . . . palace?"

"Unless my eyes deceive me."

His gaze turned toward the first of the masses who were starting to clear the outer wall. "But the people . . ."

"Keep wasting time and you just may have to kill them. Fire your missiles now and they'll get the idea."

The pilot shrugged. "You're the boss."

"Then we agree on something anyway," Blaine said, and leaned back against the Apache's bulkhead, indifferent to the rest of what transpired.

It took all eight of the Hellfires fired in the space of twenty seconds to reduce the royal palace to flame-soaked rubble and

It took all eight of the Hellfires fired in the space of twenty seconds to reduce the royal palace to flame-soaked rubble and leave whatever remained of Gamma to smolder within the debris.

"This is Shooter," the report came from the marksman on the roof of the building two-hundred-fifty yards from the royal palace.

"What is your report, Shooter?" asked the voice that would relay the message back to Israel.

"Rasin won't be coming home. Dispatch complete."

"What about McCracken?"

"Sorry. No could do."

"I didn't copy that," the voice of the contact came back.

"No could do," Colonel Yuri Ben-Neser repeated into the microphone held in his single hand. His punishment had been exile to Tehran as part of Operation Firestorm, a sniper once more. "McCracken saved my life in Jaffa Square ten days ago. I owed him one."

EPILOGUE

"IT'S ALL YOU NEED. BELIEVE ME."

McCracken inspected the piece of paper Evira had handed him from her hospital bed. "Just an address in Paris. This is where I'm supposed to find my son?"

"You'll find the answers."

Blaine eyed her quizzically. "There's something you're not telling me. I'll accept that, but God help you if it's something I won't like when I get there."

Evira smiled in spite of herself. "After all this you still sound like my enemy."

"Friends and enemies are transitory for the most part. I've learned to accept that, too, over the years. I saved your life in Tehran, but you can be damn well sure the life of my son was the only reason."

Her gaze was distant. "I couldn't understand what you were feeling, the strength of the obsession."

"Spoken in the past tense because something's changed you. That Iranian urchin we brought with us from the barricade no doubt."

"You took care of him once we reached Israel?"

"He's in a state-supported children's home . . . waiting for you to get well enough to pick him up."

Evira's face almost brightened. "It's strange, but at first I thought it was gratitude. After all, he did save my life. Then I saw it was something much more. He needed me, and realizing that made me need him.''

''Ah, so now we come to the crux of the issue. You and I live in a world where we can't get close, can't reach out, can't touch. So when those moments come when we're forced to, when we're *allowed* to, we prove ourselves to be as inept in the normal world as normal people would be in ours. It makes us vulnerable, not to others so much as ourselves.''

''Difference is you're at least free to make a choice while I— Well, the Israelis you saw outside my door aren't doctors.''

''You'll be freed as soon as you're well enough.''

''What?''

''Governments have this thing about embarrassment—Americans, Israelis, even the Soviets. They fear it more than anything. They may have killed Rasin, but they missed their chance at me, which means I'm the only one who can expose the truth of how close the Israeli government came to bringing about the world's untimely end. Only I have no plans to as long as my terms are met.''

''My . . . freedom?''

''Among other things. Did promise them that your underground and commando days were over, though.''

''Because you knew I'd seen enough. . . .''

''Not really. I just knew you didn't have the stomach for it. I could tell by the questions you asked me when we first met, the way you reacted to my responses. I wasn't what you expected, and it was easier emulating a fantasy.''

Evira grimaced. ''I learned that in Tehran.''

''For sure. You'll make a great politician. You care too much about causes to keep operating out of flea markets.''

''And you don't?''

''Nope. My thing is people. To me every single individual life is as precious as a homeland for your people or peace for the Middle East in general.''

Evira looked at him like an old, trusted friend. ''You've made my decision easy. I suppose I owe you an even greater debt now than I did before. 'Evira' is finished. No more shadows, no more crevices, no more . . . flea markets. I'm taking my fight public, into a different arena.''

"Beware, my lady. The rules are different, too. Less bullets. More lies."

"Not more. Just increasingly difficult to separate from the truth." She hesitated. "And what about you?"

"That depends on Paris."

Johnny Wareagle made no move to leave the car after Blaine had pulled into the no-parking zone in front of the Paris hotel Evira had sent him to.

"Worried about us getting towed, Indian?"

"You won't need me in there, Blainey."

"Why is it everyone knows more about what I'm going to find upstairs than I do?"

"The patterns are there for all of us to see; they have been from the beginning."

"What am I going to find in that room, Indian?"

"Truth."

" A popular word lately . . ."

"A journey must come to its own end. We can choose our path, and with luck find another after it has ended. Without luck we become immobile, afraid to go back because we know what's there. Unable to go forward because our way is blocked."

"Like me these past few months?"

"Perhaps. The key is to seek out that next road, Blainey, and accept the transition it offers from the last."

McCracken left the car wordlessly and entered the hotel. In the elevator out of habit he touched his gun, despite sensing he would not need it. His heart was pounding when he reached the door in question and found it already partway open. His guard up again, he lunged through it into a combat stance that was already half-hearted before his eyes found the single figure seated by the window.

"Bonjour, mon ami," said Henri Dejourner.

Blaine didn't lower the pistol, not right away.

"Do I need this or not, Henri?"

"That will be up to you to decide."

"You bastard! You set me up!"

The Frenchman shrugged. "Regrettable, but necessary."

McCracken looked at him with a strange calm. "Then the boy . . ."

"Not your son. Lauren's yes, but not yours. I created the fiction out of reasonable fact."

"To make me work for the Arabs, because you already *were* working for them."

"Not for—with. The difference is crucial, *mon ami*. Their concerns, Evira's specifically, mirrored my own. You were the only one who could help us."

"It was your idea, goddamn it!" Blaine exclaimed.

"Both of ours. We needed you, had to have you."

"And when I refused to listen to the messenger boys you sent, you cooked this up." He shook his head. "You violated principles, Henri, and that makes you a rat."

The Frenchman shook his head deliberately. "No, *mon ami*, principles were only a part of it; practicality was a far greater part. We needed the McCracken of a decade ago, a year ago. Not the McCracken I found on that island off Portland, Maine. The fabrication of a son was meant to assure your services, *oui*, but it was also meant to insure we were getting a man who would stop at nothing, who would accept nothing, until the affair was satisfactorily brought to a conclusion."

"Is that how you would explain it to John Neville, or doesn't his life matter either? No, don't bother answering. I can't stand any more of your bullshit. You broke every unwritten rule in the book and I ought to kill you just for that."

Much to Blaine's surprise, the Frenchman reared back his head and laughed. "I see my plot has accomplished exactly what it was supposed to. Tell me you don't feel better standing there now. Tell me that gun in your hand does not feel different than it did when I came to you on the island. Tell me a flame you may have thought extinguished forever has not been rekindled."

Blaine lowered the pistol. "Fuck you, Henri."

"He's not your son, *mon ami*. He is nothing to you. It is over."

"You know it's not like that. You know, damn it!"

The Frenchman rose with a knowing gleam in his eye. "You're involved, *mon ami*, with the boy and his life. You told him

simply you were a friend, mentioned nothing of what you per-
ceived to be the truth, and on that basis your relationship with
him was founded.''

''Get to the point.''

''He is my niece Lauren's son, and she is dead, making him
an orphan. That much is true. So what has changed? Plenty in
your eyes, yes, but nothing in the boy's. Everything is perspective. I wanted to meet you like this to be sure at least this one
point was presented to you.''

Blaine found himself wanting to be angry but not succeeding.
''You're still a rat, Henri.''

''But it was your needs that led you to take the cheese, *mon
ami*.''

''You knew,'' Blaine said to Johnny from behind the wheel
of the car.

''The spirits provided indications I could not ignore, Blainey.''

''You know the worst thing, Indian? I knew too. From the
first time I saw the boy, I felt he wasn't my son. But I wouldn't
face up to it because I wanted him to be. Make sense?''

''As much as anything. More than much.''

''I wanted him to be my son because that would have been
my escape, my convenient out. An excuse, a rationale to let
myself change, to *make* myself change.''

''But doing all you have done to save the boy made you realize
you did not want to change, that you were only happy within
the hellfire that is both place and feeling.''

''Not happy, so much as able to succeed. I tried to turn my
back, to walk away, to withdraw—I really did. God, how much
I'd love to be able to live alone in the woods like you.''

''And has that helped my withdrawal from the hellfire, Blainey?''

''No, because I keep drawing you back in.''

''You come because you must. I go with you because I must.
Where is the distinction? We both do what we have to. Only the
origins we emerge from are different, and in themselves those
origins are meaningless. It is the destinations that matter, and
ours are the same.''

Blaine looked at him reflectively. "We've been fighting the same war for twenty years, Indian. What kind of destination is that? The names and places keep changing, but I'll be damned if they don't seem interchangeable after awhile."

"Because the journey is what matters. Moving is living. Motion is life. One cannot exist without the other."

"I wanted that boy to be my son, Indian."

"A passenger on the journey, Blainey, regardless of label."

"Yeah, I get the point."

Blaine arrived at the Reading School in the twilight between afternoon and night. The teacher who had replaced John Neville as housemaster directed him to a small pitch in the school's rear where a number of boarders were kicking a soccer ball leisurely about before dinner. He approached without hesitation, his step purposeful and sure, but his thudding heart betraying the fear within.

Fear of acceptance.

Fear of truth.

The boy had been involved in this because of him. One way or another that made it his responsibility to do . . . something. So much to be said, so many explanations called for. Where to start?

"You didn't tell me that."

"Got to save some stuff for later."

"And what about what you did in the Phoenix Project?"

"Also later."

Their first meeting weighing heavily on his mind, he'd composed a dozen speeches en route there, and dismissed them all. None came even close to expressing what he felt, what he really wanted to say. His thoughts swam wildly as he approached the boys clad in sweat suits kicking the muddied ball about in the falling shadow of dusk. He couldn't see Matthew and wondered if the housemaster might have been mistaken.

The boy turned and seemed to rush for him in the same motion. Blaine saw the smile beaming, thought perhaps it might have been the greatest sight ever, knew then that he didn't need the words ready because they would come on their own.

The boy lunged the last of the way with long hair flapping in the breeze and threw his arms around Blaine, head buried against his chest. McCracken returned the grasp as tight as it came to him, and the embrace lingered for a time before he eased the boy away gently at the shoulders.

"It's later." Blaine smiled.

About the Author

Jon Land is the author of THE DOOMSDAY SPIRAL, THE LUCIFER DIRECTIVE, VORTEX, LABYRINTH, THE OMEGA COMMAND, THE COUNCIL OF TEN, THE ALPHA DECEPTION, and THE EIGHTH TRUMPET. He is thirty-two years old and lives in Providence, Rhode Island, where he is currently at work on a new novel.

JON LAND

presents the
most complex,
action-filled
thrillers